REVIEWERS' PRAISE: (I

"Highly entertainin

penned a fascinating account that helps to illustrate the point that every life touches a dozen others in completely different ways. If 'who done its' are the kind of book you crave, then this is one to pick up. You won't be able to put it down until you're done! And when the reader finishes reading, the ending is completely unexpected. A true delight!"

-Theresa Norman,
Denise's Pieces Book Reviews (Mystery/Suspense)
www.denisemclark.com

"I never figured out the truth behind Kizzy's murder, and I like to consider myself very good at solving 'who-dunnit' mysteries. The truth is shocking! Real talent shows within these pages or I would not have bothered posting a review about it."

-Detra Fitch, Huntress Reviews,
www.huntressreviews.com/efict.htm

"Ms. Laure writes with an honest poignancy. Only a person who understands loss and guilt can portray it so truly. I read *Evolution* with sincere interest and sympathy. The experience is well worth the time and effort."

-Jeanette Cottrall, Ebook Reviews Weekly,
http://www.ebook-reviews.net
(Ms. Cottrell is the author of *There's No Such Thing*)

" . . . the story is complex and satisfactory. There are twists waiting in every chapter, and the story is a quick, easy read. . . . will appeal to many mystery fans."

-Tracy Farnsworth,
The Romance Readers Connection (Mysterious Corner)

Books coming soon from this author:

The Bunkhouse

Alana–Evolution of a Woman
(The sequel to *Evolution of a Sad Woman*)

Watch for excerpts from these books at
www.a-bookstore.com

Evolution of a Sad Woman

The Story of Kizzy

By

GALE LAURE

Evolution of a Sad Woman, The Story of Kizzy, is a complete work of fiction of the author's imagination. The characters, events and occurrences in the locations have been invented by the author, andany resemblance to any actual person, living or dead, or event or occurrence, are purely coincidental. Storyline concerning the ethics of any cities, departments of government or the morals of these cities' inhabitants or their officials or any religion or religious leaders are strictly fictional.

Order this book online at www.trafford.com/07-0936
or email orders@trafford.com

Edited by Prof. Nick Lewis & Barbara Landry

Cover Design by Gale Laure

Photography by Polly Vee

Most Trafford titles are also available at major online book retailers.

Note for Librarians: A cataloguing record for this book is available from Library and Archives Canada at www.collectionscanada.ca/amicus/index-e.html

***Warning: This book contains language, violence and sexual situations which may not be suitable for all readers.**

Printed in Victoria, BC, Canada.

ISBN: 978-1-4251-2730-5

www.trafford.com

North America & international
toll-free: 1 888 232 4444 (USA & Canada)
phone: 250 383 6864 ♦ fax: 250 383 6804 ♦ email: info@trafford.com

The United Kingdom & Europe
phone: +44 (0)1865 722 113 ♦ local rate: 0845 230 9601
facsimile: +44 (0)1865 722 868 ♦ email: info.uk@trafford.com

10 9 8 7 6 5 4 3 2

DEDICATIONS:

This book is dedicated to my sister, K. B., who gave me the confidence to write this story by recognizing my gift to imagine and tell a story. God Bless You!

Thank you for the wonderful inspiration! I Love You!
This book is written in memory of my grandfather, Archie L.N., who showed me my first hummingbird. I miss your special love.

I dedicate this book to the everlasting memory of all the victims of 9/11. May God's blessings and love be bestowed on their families and friends.

Soli Deo Gloria

Acknowledgments:

I graciously thank the following people for consulting on the subject matter in this book:

Nancy Hugon Mikeska, attorney and former Director of the Criminal Justice Division for the State of Texas, consulted providing detailed information about law issues.

Sergeant Lanny Moriarty (now Judge) consulted providing information about police procedure and crime scene detective procedures.

Officer Arnold provided information on the homicide division.

Cecelia Wilkenfeld, a Texas attorney for the defense, consulted providing detailed legal information.

Jane Asber, a staff member of the Sacred Heart Catholic Church, consulted on matters of Catholicism.

I graciously thank the following special people in my life:

Pat McMillian, my forever friend, who supported me and would not let me give up on my dream.

William, my wonderful husband, who used his love for me to help me reach my dream!

PROLOGUE

Death is our final trip, our final adventure. For some, death is more of an adventure than for others. If someone is prepared for death, it may be more welcomed. However, if the death is *murder*, who can be prepared for such a tragedy?

Death is the unknown. The death of a loved one is never an easy thing to abide for anyone. Yet, if murder causes the death suddenly and unexpectedly, it takes on new, unbearable tones. If the murder is excessively brutal, a stirring of forgotten feelings, memories and necessities occurs, and it becomes an obsession which needs relief. An unforgettable picture is left, and it troubles the soul, the mind and the heart of everyone touched.

This story is about five different men who are strangers. They have one important thing in common. At different times in their lives, they have loved the same beautiful woman. Love is the most powerful sentiment in the world. Love can make you happier, sadder, madder and more distraught than any other emotion. It is the strongest feeling and evokes many other affections and expressions. This special woman, who develops before your eyes from childhood into adult womanhood, evokes these feelings and more in these men. In many ways, she is the same woman to them all. Yet, to each she is so very different. She is their dream, their nightmare and their reality. She is a woman who has brought to each man agony and happiness, but most of all wonderment. This woman is the biggest influence on each man's life in the past and in the present. Little do these men know, but she even influences each of their futures.

Each man holds her in a different place sincerely in his heart. To each man she has been the representation of something different, but special. At the same time, she has possessed a compelling power over each man. This power has held their souls and hearts hostage to her memory and to the need of her. Ultimately, as hard as this is, these men must open their hearts and their minds to one another.

In this way her death, or murder, becomes an intolerable event in their lives which they must resolve. Each man holds a detail about this wonderful, mysterious woman. Each detail is separate and different, and must be shared, investigated and resolved.

The South is the setting for this murder. It is a large bustling city with sultry Southern style and charm This place, the heat, the humidity, and the wrenching passion of the fiendish murder investigation are what the men must endure. They cannot change the past. Though they must come to terms with their pasts before they can move forward into their futures.

Resolving power to this crime of murder may be held in their minds and their memories. The power of resolution may even be held tightly in their hands.

However, most of all,

the *power is deep in their hearts . . .*

CHAPTER I
The Saturday Night Murder -1996

1

Kizzy lies nude on her bed as she listens to the music. Briefly, her mind reviews the upsetting visitors of this day. She has tried her best to phone him. He never answered. Quickly, she erases the thoughts from her mind. She tries to relax her twitching body. The music is soft, soothing, the kind that would make you want to sleep. Yet, she cannot unwind enough to sleep. She is significantly nervous. The least small sound makes her jump.

Outside, she hears the clicking of light hot humid rain, not the soothing kind that cools the earth, as it beats upon the window glass. An occasional crack of lightning typical for a summer in Houston, Texas, startles her, jolting her nerves even more.

The pills will take effect at any time. She looks slowly around the room. As she takes the last sip of wine from the glass and rolls it around inside her mouth, she savors the taste, in retrospect to her first glass of wine.

2

On her sixteenth birthday, William had taken her to the most wonderful, expensive restaurant in town. He had been her sweet "Unkie Wills". He had looked so handsome sitting across from her at dinner. His blue eyes had seemed to shine. His smile had been so gentle and never showed his teeth—only his lips. Yet his lustrous blue eyes had smiled gently with his lips. He had ordered the wine and insisted on another wine glass for Kizzy because they smudged hers. Because of his fanaticism about cleanliness, the glass had been replaced. Wine had been poured in William's glass for him to sample. In detail, Kizzy had watched him as he slowly sipped the wine and rolled it around inside his mouth. Then, he had exclaimed, "Um, wonderful!"

Wine had been poured in Kizzy's glass. She had sipped the wine and tried to imitate William's actions by rolling the wine around in her mouth. Pungent and bitter are how it tasted. Kizzy had exclaimed, swallowing with a distasteful frown upon her face, "This is awful!" This memory brings a smile to her lips. Those had been such happy times for her.

3

All these years later, she loves the pungent taste. She collects the clock from the floor and places it on the bedside table. The clock says ten forty-five p.m. While sighing, Kizzy welcomes the feeling of rest as it overwhelms her body. Filled with lightheadedness, nausea and weakness, she knows the pills are the reason for these feelings. Maybe she should not have taken so many. Yet she knows she needs the pills. She wants to fall sound asleep. She lies in the bed, barely able to see the ceiling from the dim lamplight beside her bed. Briefly, she observes the empty wine glass sitting on the bedside table, tasting the wine as she runs her tongue around the inside cheeks of her mouth. How she loves the pungent taste of wine.

When she lies on her back, tears run from her eyes, down to her ears and into the back of her hair. Yet she is not crying. She will not sob. Therefore, from where are these tears coming? Her nose is stuffy from the increased mucous caused by the tears. She tries to breathe through her nose, which is not possible. Gently, she parts her full lips to breathe and sucks in the air. She is not sad because she is finally in control.

Kizzy jumps as the CD player in the living room clicks off indicating the music is over. Only the sound of the rain pervades the air. As she looks around the room again, she listens to hear the silence. She is waiting for the pills to take effect, hoping they will establish unconsciousness. The pills are taking forever. Maybe the hot bubble bath will help. In the bathroom, she has the tub drawn and ready. Barely, she can sniff the vanilla candle as it perfumes the bathroom, the wonderful soothing smell overflowing into the bedroom through the open bathroom door. Briefly, the smell reminds her of a bowl of vanilla ice cream. She tries to take a deep breath of the scent, but cannot.

Suddenly, she hears the rattle of a doorknob turning, coming from the living room. Someone has entered her apartment through the locked door. As she musters the energy she has left, she stands beside the bed with terror filling her very being. Her legs are shaking. As she staggers and sways, she stiffens her legs, standing still. Her vision is becoming blurry. With overwhelming weakness, her paramount instinct is to call for help. Except for the intruder, she knows she is in the apartment alone. She wants to scream and talk this intruder out of doing this. Maybe she could stop this from happening. She tries, but she does not have the strength to call out. Her body is limp from the pills. Trepidation pervades her rapidly beating heart. Her heart flutters, making her even more lightheaded and dizzy. She tries to walk, to run, to move—something! She is frozen and cannot move. The telephone is in the living room. Kizzy has always meant to have an extension phone installed in the bedroom. Whom would she call? Why is she thinking about this now? She cannot run to the phone in the living room. The intruder is in the living room. The pills have made her too weak. Besides, she knows the intruder will stop her before she can get to the telephone. She knows this intruder has come to kill her. She tries to speak, hoping to plead to stop this, but cannot utter a word. She looks toward the open bedroom door, her heart throbbing with the anticipation of the intruder's entrance.

She can barely see him as he enters. She is afraid, really deep down afraid. Death has not seemed frightening, earlier, but now the actuality of death is terrifying to her. She tries to speak and cannot. She cannot form the words on her lips or in her throat. Clenched tightly shut, she cannot separate her teeth. The pills have left her defenseless. He towers over her. Kizzy's green, emerald eyes stare upward, deeply, into his large, dark eyes. His eyes are cold, vacant. For a moment there is another sound. Kizzy moves her eyes focusing to look slightly around him. Behind him stands a woman. With her blurred vision, Kizzy cannot identify her. She does not seem familiar. Kizzy looks back in his eyes, trying to communicate with him through her eyes. He does not try to understand. Horror fills her eyes. He stares stolidly, looming over her, looking down in her eyes. She wants to run, but she knows she has nowhere to run.

While he grabs her with one mighty arm, clenching her arm tightly beneath his large, gloved hand, he leans close to her, whispering, "I'm sorry." In his large dark eyes, she can see the dread. With a deep grunt, he plunges the knife, with all his mighty force, deeply into her upper abdomen. Desperately, Kizzy's shaking hand clutches onto his gloved hand. Beneath their two hands, the knife pushes deeply into her flesh. She can feel the blade against her rib bone. By pushing toward him on his hand with her hand, she tries to inhibit the knife from plunging deeper. However, she is too weak to fight, and he is too strong for her to overcome. Beneath her hand, she can feel the handle of the knife under his hand. The pain is sharp, tearing, burning. Too late to stop death, a painful frown covers her face. She whimpers softly, but she cannot cry out or even speak. With tightly clenched teeth, she breathes rapidly from the desolation, sucking the air through her parted lips. Electricity from her silent suffering permeates the air, charging it with her pain. Looking deeper in her eyes, he twists the knife inside her, tearing and ripping her insides. The sharp pain travels straight through into her back. The misery intensifies, spreading throughout her back from her neck to her buttocks. At first, she leans against him, using him to support her as she stands beside the bed. Her legs feel weaker. He stands against her strongly, not objecting, supporting her weight. Then, she collapses back upon the bed, lying on her back. She can barely see him in the dim lamplight. He stands over her holding the knife in his hand. Kizzy's blood exudes from the knife onto the floor. Kizzy can feel the blood draining from her body. She can feel herself lying in her own blood. Through her stuffed nose, she can smell the strange freshness of her own blood. She feels colder. Her eyes can barely see the ceiling above her bed through her truly blurred sight. She can feel the tears once again run from her eyes onto her cheeks and into her hair. Her breathing is shallow and rapid, as she fights to keep the breath inside her. She feels tired, weaker and weaker. She cannot move at all. He continues to stand over her, staring down at her. It becomes even harder to breathe, soon impossible. Gasping desperately for air as though to cheat death, she holds on to the last moment of life. She does *not* want to die. Kizzy *wants* to *live*. Her life starts flashing before her eyes. Memories flood across her mind like the fast flicker of a movie projector. Briefly, she clears her mind of the memories. She clinches the sheets between her fingers and palms. Wetness from her own blood causes the sheets to stick to her hands. Opening her eyes widely, she tries to clear her blurred vision, grasping at the last sight of him—the last sight of her life. The killer does not move. He stares down at her, silently and shows limited remorse or emotion. Holding the knife in his gloved hand, it still drips with blood. He watches the increasing redness of the sheets and the wideness of her green eyes. Kizzy takes her last breath, a deep breath. With her green eyes wide open and her teeth still tightly clenched, she dies. Kizzy goes toward the light.

He lays the knife on the sheet beside her statuesque nude body. He grabs her body by the legs and pulls it off the bed onto the floor, face down. He stands over Kizzy, pausing briefly and admits that even in death, she is beautiful. Yes, she is so genuinely tantalizing. Enjoyably, he sucks in a deep breath of Kizzy's fresh blood. He looks down at her drained body. He has forgotten about the woman standing quietly behind him. After opening the small pouch around his neck, he places the bloody knife inside.

From the pouch,

he pulls out a large meat cleaver.

CHAPTER II
The Murder Scene, Sunday

1

As she jerks the rain jacket sleeve back, Alice looks at her watch which says seven thirty a.m.. Drizzling rain drips off the visor of the police hat feeling more like steam than rain. She hates the rain because it reminds her of the day her father was buried. Dampness on the sidewalk makes it slippery. She sees Pete as he arrives on the scene. While walking, they start speaking.

Alice articulates in her Texas drawl, "Yo, Pete."

"Hi, Alice. What's up?" Pete yawns. Her abrupt telephone call has awakened him from a sound slumber.

"Pete, one of the residents reported a foul stink coming from a top floor penthouse apartment. We went in, me and Jeb, and secured the area. A DOA is in the bedroom, or at least that's what Jeb said. It was dark, so we just left it like you and Evan like. We didn't touch anything."

"Are you sure about the death?"

Alice responds, "Yeah, it's a DOA all right. The strong blood smell verifies the death. Wait'll ya see. The place is registered to a Ms. Keziah Theriot."

Pete stops in his tracks. Instantaneously, the blood leaves Pete's face and pallor replaces it. Even his balding head looks ashen. Thin strands of black hair combed back across the top of his head look striking compared with the paleness of the skin below it.

"Not a good way to start the week, huh? Are ya okay, Pete? You look kinda funny."

"Yeah, I'm okay. Your phone call just woke me up. Where is Evan? Did you call him?" In his usual nervous routine, Pete rubs his hand across the top of his head as the two officers resume walking.

"No, Pete, he didn't answer his cellular. I tried several times. I called his regular phone number, but he never answered. All I got wuz the machine and that stupid recording."

"Hey, no problem. It's best that you called me first on this one. Let's not let Evan know until I've reviewed the scene." Alice agrees.

Pete, a homicide detective with law enforcement, goes to the penthouse floor with Alice. Several other officers are in the hall just outside the elevator door awaiting instructions. Pete usually worked with his partner, Evan Picard. However, Pete has decided to take this case on his own tonight because uniformed officers were present for back up. Usually, uniformed officers discover a murder, secure the area, and then call the detectives such as Evan and Pete. Evan and Pete, a different kind of detective team and notably competent in their jobs, are given plenty of room to surmise on homicides. Their decision is to review the scene untouched by uniformed officers as soon as possible, allowing them to get a feel for the case from the beginning. By following Pete and Evan's rule, no one removes or changes anything from the murder site before they arrive. Uniformed officers do not touch any of the evidence. Discovery and the fetid rankness of the gruesome murder have alerted the uniformed officers to phone Pete, the senior officer of the detectives' duo. The minute Alice and Pete step off the elevator, they are overcome with the same malodorous smell. Alice's eyes start to water.

"I don't know what Jeb found in that bedroom, but he had to leave and go home, Pete. All he said wuz that he was sure she was dead."

"Oh, whew, I know this smell. It's blood and flesh!" Pete says, putting his handkerchief over his face. "You did *perfect* calling me first, Alice."

"Wait'll ya get inside. No sounds were comin' from inside the place before we entered," Alice inputs. By the use of a pass key, they enter the apartment through a closed and locked door. Alice mentions aloud that there was no forced entry through the door. Much stronger now, the foulness inundates the two officers. The apartment is in shambles as though someone were searching for something.

"You two officers didn't touch anything, right," Pete asks.

"Nope. We did just like y'all ordered, Pete."

Fine works of art removed from the walls have their backs slashed. Someone has overturned the coffee table. Even the trash can is emptied onto the floor and left overturned.

In the kitchen they find the same disorder. "Look at this, Pete. They got blood heavy in the sink."

"Yes, I can see, Alice."

"Look at this! Smears are on the light switch and on the counter next to the sink, but the blood smears don't show any fingerprints."

"Don't touch it, Alice."

The two officers enter the bedroom, the focal point for the odor. Only a small lamp on a bedside table illuminates the room dimly. Pete canvasses the room covering his face with his handkerchief. Slowly, they walk around the room, noticing details and evidence. Another lamp is broken and laying on the floor by the dresser. Pete's foot pushes against something. "What the hell!"

"What'd you say, Pete?"

"You got a flashlight? I can't see. Shine it over here."

Alice shines the flashlight over at Pete's feet. Next to Pete's foot is a bloody human arm. "Dear, God!" Alice declares.

"Damn, an arm! *Don't move, Alice.*"

"I'm not moving."

Pete yells to the uniformed officers in the hall. "Hey! *Hey!* One of you bring me a flashlight!" A uniformed officer enters with a large flashlight in hand.

"*Stop!* Hand it to Alice right there at the door! Don't come in here! We found a body part on the floor, and there may be more." Pete's voice changes to a low whisper. "I hate this."

Alice tosses the flashlight over to Pete. "That smell! No wonder it's worse in here!" she exclaims.

As they stand perfectly still, Pete and Alice shine their flashlights around the room. Blood is spattered on the walls and drapes and soaked in the carpet. Alice's flashlight gets dimmer and fades into blackness. She beats her hand against it. "The battery has gone dead," Alice informs Pete. "Over there! Stop, Pete! By the dresser, what's that?"

"Yeah! Yeah." Pete says. He spotlights his beam against the bottom of the dresser.

"No, Pete! Not on the bottom! On top of the dresser by the mirror!"

Pete shines the beam upward. "Oh, geeeeez, *a leg*! Shit! Blood is smeared over the mirror!"

"Why would somebody do this? It must've been a sicko, Pete."

Pete mumbles an inaudible obscene phrase to himself. While searching, Pete shines the beam of his flashlight toward the bed.

Alice gasps and says, "Aw, shit! Pete, it's the *torso!* Beside the bed—on the floor—*where's her face*?"

Pete, shining his flashlight beam, walks over to the bed and kneels beside the torso. Alice joins him, moving cautiously across the room. Alice feels weak. Here they find the bruised, battered torso of a woman in her late thirties. Slowly, Pete turns her over.

"Should ya do that, Pete? Isn't that disturbing evidence?" Alice takes a deep breath, holds Pete's flashlight beam on the body and mumbles to herself that she is not feeling so well

Pete ignores her and continues with the task of turning the torso over. He is not prepared for what he finds. Her eyes are open—noticeably wide open—staring outward. Her white skin makes the large green eyes alarming—a site that startles the two officers. Pete frowns at the sight and jolts backward away from the DOA, "Ahhhhh—*Damn!*" In consternation, he stalls and spouts abominations.

"Oh!" Alice drops the flashlight as she becomes ill and runs to the bathroom, gagging. "I feel—Ugh–!"

One of the other officers in the hall hears Alice and comes inside the bedroom to continue helping Pete. Pete stands with his legs far apart as though to brace, rubbing his hand across his balding head nervously and staring at the green eyes. Pete irritably spouts, "Get the *hell* out of *here*! I didn't tell you to bring your nosy ass in here! *I'll take care of this!*"

While lifting the flashlight, he recognizes the DOA as Kizzy. The DOA, or what is present of the body—the torso and head—is rigid. Pete, regaining his composure, examines the torso. Rigor mortis has set in. A deep stab wound is in the upper right abdomen. Blood fills the back of her hair stiffening it. Someone has blackened her right eye, and her upper left lip is swollen, cut and bloody. He mutters, "Damn! Why did they do this to her? Why?" Various bruises are covering her nude body. As he walks guardedly around the room with his flashlight, he finds her other leg in an open doorway leading to the closet. Her other arm is found under the edge of the bed on the opposite side from her torso. Someone has searched the bedroom. An almost empty wine glass is on the table beside the bed. Pete bags it as evidence. The room is in shambles, and someone has ransacked the closet. Even the drawers are removed and emptied from the dresser. Fine works of art, removed from the walls lie with the backs slashed open, as though someone was searching for something. Sheets on the bed and on the floor beside the bed are saturated with blood. The stench of the blood and open, rotting flesh fills the air.

"Pete, I'm sorry I had to run out on ya! I was feeling lousy for a minute there!" Alice remarks as she returns to the bedroom. "No wonder poor Jeb had to leave sick. He didn't even warn anybody about any of this."

"I can take care of everything in here, Alice."

"Okay, well I'm here to back ya up."

"I don't need backup, Alice. All that's in here is a *DOA!* I can handle it. *Go on out!*"

Alice does not withdraw from the apartment as instructed by Pete. She loiters just outside the bedroom door. Pete can see her out of the corner of his eye, which irritates him. After searching his pocket for his cellular phone, Pete realizes he has left it downstairs in the car. His hands are shaking. After exclaiming an obscenity, Pete gives instructions to Alice. "Alice, go call the coroner from the telephone in the living room. Can you handle that order?"

"Yes, of course I can. What's with you?"

Pete ignores her question. "Tell the coroner I've identified the deceased as Keziah Theriot, the resident at this apartment. Oh, and don't disturb any prints that might be on the phone. I left my cellular downstairs."

"Can't we send one of the uniforms to go down to your car and get the cell phone?"

Pete sighs in disgust. "No! *Damn it!* I instructed you to—just go do what I told you to, Alice!"

Alice shrugs, vacates the bedroom and goes to the living room as instructed by Pete.

Pete examines the bedroom for more evidence, and goes in the bathroom. Here, he finds an opulent, oversized bathtub full of water and melted bubbles. On the ledge beside the tub is a small, perfumed, burnt candle. The candle holder is still warm to the touch. Towels are emptied from the cabinets, and even the toilet tissue has been removed from the roller. Pete mumbles to himself. "Wow! Somebody sure was looking for something!".

Alice overhears his mumbling on her way to the living room to make the phone call to the coroner. "What did ya say?" Alice asks.

"Nothing!"

Alice enters the living room. The telephone is sitting on the floor beside a small sofa table. No one has overturned or even disturbed this table, leaving it neat and orderly, unlike every other table or cabinet in the room. The phone receiver is off the hook, but the alerting recording is not playing. Alice listens with the receiver against her ear, trying not to smudge any possible prints on the phone. No dial tone is present. The phone is dead. She notices someone has unplugged the phone. She plugs the wire on the phone in the wall outlet for proper operation, again trying not to disturb prints. On the small table, neatly placed, is a lady's purse, a key on a shiny key ring and a security card key just like the one the security man gave the officers to operate the elevator. Alice surveys the room in detail. In the entire room, the table is the only thing in order. Alice yells at Pete in the other room. "Hey, Pete! You should see this one little table in here that's neat as my Granny's cupboard! Weird, huh?"

Pete grunts and makes note of it in his notebook. Again trying not to disturb prints, Alice with caution checks the answering machine for messages while on the phone with the coroner. None are there. Positively, no messages are on the tape, not even old ones. As though they had been erased, the tape is blank. Alice thinks this is unusual. She checks the redial button on the telephone. No number appears for redial. She checks the memory numbers on the phone, finding them blank. She turns the phone over and looks beneath the cover. One of the batteries used for backup in case of electrical failure has been removed. She yells loudly. "Pete, there's no tape in the machine, no redial numbers and one of the batteries has been removed from this telephone. What do ya think?"

"Is the other battery still there?"

"Yeah!"

"That's strange to remove just one battery. They go dead at the same time and you usually remove them both for replacement. You know, by removing the one battery and unplugging the phone, the phone will lose its memory, destroying any numbers in the redial or memory."

"I bet the perp removed that one battery on purpose" Alice alleges.

"Yeah." Pete shakes his head in an appeasing manner. On the floor beside the small table where the purse and keys are neatly placed, Alice finds a small gold ink pen. Gingerly, to not disturb fingerprints, she lifts the pen and notices the letters "T.U." are engraved on the side. She bags the pen to dust for prints.

"I found a gold pen, Pete!"

"So?"

"Well, maybe it belonged to the perp," she answers.

"Did you find a note, too, Alice?" Pete vocalizes sarcastically.

"A note?"

"Never mind."

Pete and Alice look around the apartment for a while, bagging several items of evidence. When they enter the kitchen, after placing the knives in sets, they conclude that none of the knives or sharp kitchen utensils are missing, or at least it does not look as though any are missing. They had thought maybe one of the kitchen knives was the murder weapon. Pete makes a note to have the knives checked for blood traces. The kitchen drawers and shelves are in great disarray. Even the trash can has been overturned, scattering the garbage on the floor. On the floor beside the overturned trash can is a fresh, half-eaten sandwich.

"Do you think he stopped to eat a sandwich?" Alice asks.

"I don't know, Alice. You ask too many questions."

Back in the living room, Alice says concluding, "The perp must've been looking for somethin'. Look at all this expensive stuff the perp left behind!" Even though the back of the expensive art has been slashed open, the art is still in perfect condition.

Pete responds again angrily at Alice. "You don't know what the hell you are talking about, Alice. I'm the detective here! Stop irritating me!"

"Geez, Pete, ya don't have to be a detective to see there's a lot of expensive stuff in this place!" Alice answers, finding Pete's attitude rude and contentious, a behavior foreign for Pete. After finishing in the apartment, Pete and Alice withdraw. Alice looks down at the carpet in the hall outside the apartment. "Look, Pete. No bloody footprints are in this hall. How did the perp keep that much blood from getting on his shoes?"

"I don't know, Alice. Maybe he covered his shoes somehow. Again with the questions . . ." Pete announces flippantly. Pete and Alice advance out to the street, after instructing the other officers to seal the apartment and area. Pete commands the officers that no one will have access to the crime scene except him after the coroner and crime lab finish. Adamant about this order, he stresses it over and over to the other officers, among them Alice, almost to the point of an obsession. Alice and Pete ride down the elevator together. Pete still looks pale.

"Say Pete, why do ya suppose the place was such a mess? I mean I'd think it was a robbery gone awry, but robbers don't usually dismember." Peculiarly quiet, Pete ignores her. He seems to have something weighing heavily on his mind. Alice finds this strange for Pete. She has worked with Evan and Pete on countless cases earlier. He is usually talkative, mentioning in detail his thoughts on found evidence at the murder scene.

Abruptly, he exclaims, pointing his finger in her face cantankerously, "I told you, I'm handling this case. Is that too *damn tough* for you to understand? That's how it's going to be! You got it?"

"Dang! Yeah, okay, Pete. Don't get excited."

Pete and Alice leave the building. Pete walks over to his car. While walking to his car, a voice comes from the crowd of reporters. "Hey, Pete, it's me! Over here, Pete! Petie Boy, what-cha got?" the voice asks in a strong abrasive vernacular. The voice is coming from Bettey. Pete ignores the voice. Bettey pushes the wet wisps of her straight, dark brown hair back under the edge of her rain jacket hood.

Pete looks and sees the voice is Bettey's. "Not, now, Bettey. I'm not in the mood! *Get out of my face!*"

"Gee, Pete! What's your problem?" Bettey yells.

Pete, ignoring her, wipes the drizzling rain from the top of his forehead. He retrieves something from his car, then walks to the pay phone booth on the corner.

Alice walks over to the reporters. Inquisitively, Bettey and Alice watch Pete. Bettey squints for a good view through the drizzle. They stand together, neither saying a word. Alice wonders why Pete is walking across the street in the rain to a pay phone. The department supplies a cellular phone for Pete's use. Pete is in the booth for quite some time. Alice peers down at her watch. When he turns sideways, Alice notices his cellular phone is in his hand. Alice walks away from the reporters to get a closer view of Pete at the pay phone booth. Pete walks back over to her.

"Who'd ya call, Pete?" Alice asks.

After a silence, Pete looks straight at Alice and brushes his wet strands of hair across his bald head with his hand. His face is red. "Uh—uh—um. Yeah, okay. I called Evan. I got hold of him. You see he knew the deceased very well," Pete acknowledges, fumbling for the words. Alice then perceives why Pete is handling this case alone—to spare Evan. Because Pete recognizes the deceased, he, too, must have known her. The relationship between Pete and Evan is much like a father and son relationship. He is protecting Evan, taking the emotional distress for Evan. Alice feels bad for Pete. When someone you know dies, especially so brutally, it is hard. She understands Pete's erratic behavior.

After pushing by reporters including Bettey, Pete returns to the hall leading to the apartment. Preoccupied, as he paces nervously, he stands around the hall with the other officers. Pete jingles the change in his pocket and chews on his lower lip.

2

Down on the street, Bettey is not happy about how Pete is treating her. Bettey Russell is a reporter for the *Houston Register* newspaper. Very good at her job, she frequently works closely with the police. Always, she keeps everything confidential, unless the police tell her that she can write her story. She finds this method to be much more persuasive than harassing an officer and printing information that could damage a case. As crass as she is, Bettye has a somewhat selective moral code, but a moral code all the same. As Evan and Pete's friend, she likes the men. Usually, Pete is cooperative with Bettey, but his actions this time are not within the normal realm of his behavior. What is different about this case? Bettey wonders what is going on.

In the hot Houston drizzle, Alice waits at the front of the building with the other officers. Her police hat is giving her a headache. With her dark, curly hair contained under it, the hat is too tight. She removes her hat, shaking her dark, shoulder-length curly hair free. The drizzle falls on the curls, plastering down the ones around her face. Alice sees a frustrated Bettey and motions to her. She likes Bettey a lot. Then, she motions for the officer to allow Bettey to come over to her. Bettey is happy that someone has finally acknowledged her. Bettey walks over to Alice. "Say, what's going on with Pete, Alice?" Bettey probes.

"Well, it's a really brutal murder. Pete knows the deceased. It's really hard on him. Try to cut him some slack, Bettey."

"How does he know her, Alice?"

"I can't give ya any details right now. That's all I can give ya."

"Is the deceased Keziah Theriot?"

"Yeah. That's her name. It's a really bloody mess up there."

"How was she killed?" Bettey asks, scribbling on a pad.

"I can't give ya any more details, Bettey." Bettey thanks her and moves behind the police line.

In the drizzling rain, Alice stands on the street. She can hear the noise of the reporters and other officers around her, but is oblivious to the sound. Alice finds it hard forgetting the poor, dismembered woman upstairs and difficult to wipe from her thoughts that gruesome sight. Alice is no rookie; she has seen countless murders. However, this one was exceptionally bloody, especially brutal. Why were this poor lady's arms and legs removed? Who could do such an atrocious thing? Maybe she identified with the deceased because she looked only slightly older than Alice. Alice has seen corpses before this, but the look on that poor lady's face is not one of surprise, but of acceptance. She had accepted the death. Yet, from the wideness of her eyes, she had been grasping for the last ounce of life. Her green eyes were sending a haunting impression deep into Alice's thoughts.

Alice looks upward to the crime scene apartment windows and shudders at the thought and the memory of the DOA there. People could pass this spot and never know the macabre deed that has just happened upstairs. Alice wonders about the strange look of acceptance on the victim's face and in her eyes. Why was this woman not afraid? She should have been terrified. Someone was brutally murdering her! She was dying. Even though Alice is not officially on the case, she plans to follow the investigation closely unofficially. Detective work fascinates Alice. With aspirations to be a detective herself and no women detectives in the department at this time, Alice will make sure that she is the next detective. Then, she will become the best detective in the department!

3

Pete talks to the coroner. The coroner places the time of death between eleven o'clock p.m. and midnight. Pete thinks of Kizzy and recollects the times he has seen that rapturous creature. Kizzy looked like a bewitching portrait that you see hanging on a museum wall. She was too beautiful to be real! She moved as a graceful, svelte cat. Pete was feeling sick over her death, finding the brutal, bloody slaying painful. How could someone dismember her in such a deplorable way? A crime of passion is what this must have been. Pete knows his feelings are nothing compared to what Evan is enduring. His feelings are nothing compared to what Evan is going to feel for a long, long time. Evan is such a good man. Pete loves him as if he is his son. Evan is a good detective, too. Pete knows Evan is going to pursue this case doggedly. This great calamity should not have happened. Kizzy should not have died. She was such an exceptional woman. With so limited beauty in this world, why had Kizzy's beauty been taken away? He truly had liked Kizzy. Kizzy was a special woman—strong, friendly, sweet—and easy to like. Pete knows this is going to be an arduous case. Difficult? No, this is going to be a distressing, painful mess! Pete tries to regain self-control, dreading the time when Evan arrives on the scene. Pete knows he is right in the middle of this thing! He feels sick for Evan, for Kizzy and for himself.

CHAPTER III

EVAN

1

Evan streaks down the road in his police car. His siren breaks the morning air with its wailing. The windshield wipers swish back and forth across the drizzle. At times, when not enough drizzle is present, the wipers noisily scrape across the glass. Nonetheless, Evan is incognizant of the sound. He had forgotten to recharge his cellular phone and had turned his regular phone off and let the machine answer. Anger fills him for pulling such a moronic stunt. He had been exceedingly tired last night. So many cases were transpiring lately, and so much paperwork. Evan was stressed out! Upon waking, Evan had listened to the messages on his machine. Alice had left a message notifying him of a murder case. As soon as Evan received the message, he had plugged in his cellular phone for recharge and started to dress. She had not left the name of the deceased, only an address of the murder scene. Immediately, Pete had called Evan on his regular phone, giving him the bad news. The lump in his throat is choking him, this brave policeman. He cannot believe this is Kiz. Oh, dear God! What if Kizzy tried to call him last night and could not reach him? No messages were on his answering machine from her. Still, maybe she tried to phone him for help, got the machine, and just hung up! *Damn!* Oh, no! Please, do not let this DOA be her! Not her, but a mistake! Deep inside, he knows this is Kizzy because Pete recognizes her.

Pete had met her when Evan had been attending the academy. Pete had visited the academy and had given an exemplary speech that impressed Evan. Pete is an exceptional cop for whom Evan has much respect and admiration. Throughout his career, he has been an important model for Evan. Evan was so proud when he became Pete's partner—like a dream come true. Forthwith, he and Evan had become friends.

Evan prays that Pete has to be wrong! The words keep blaring in his head. Evan can feel the pressure in his temples intensifying. He cannot bear the idea that this is her. She was the love of his life. No! *Damn*! She *is* the love of his life. That fact would never change! No other woman ever compared to Kiz.

Somehow he finishes dressing and finds himself in his vehicle. His vehicle runs through the red light. Another car almost hits Evan's car. The squealing of the tires breaks the morning air, almost silencing Evan's siren. He bellows profanities at the driver.

Evan pulls in front of the high-rise, top-dollar condo building. He knew she was still in Houston, but had no idea where. He had passed this building often. If only he had known she was inside. He had tried to find her so many times. Evan wipes the perspiration from his face with his hand, flicks it into the air and gains composure. While flashing his badge, he walks hurriedly inside. He can hear Bettey ranting and raving at him from the crowd of reporters that the officers are holding back behind a line. Evan does not even turn to look at her, or stop for her this time. He takes the elevator to the penthouse apartment, which seems to take forever. Only one other apartment is on the same floor with Kizzy's. Police are guarding the hall. Immediately, Evan sees Pete.

Pete walks toward Evan gripping his arm. "Wait Evan. You don't want to go in there. Blood is everywhere! It's awful, Ev."

Evan can smell the foulness of blood. He knows the rankness in a familiar way. "*Son of a bitch!* Let go of me, Pete. You know I have to go in there. Nobody's going to stop me, *damn it!*" Evan pulls away from Pete.

Pete knows that seeing her will be catastrophic for Evan and will devastate him. Pete knows how much Evan had cherished, and still to this day, loves Kizzy. He steps in front of Evan to hinder his passing. "Evan, *I* can tell you it's Kizzy. Don't go in, man. Don't put yourself through that. The smell of bloody stench is everywhere. Some son of a bitch cut her damn arms and legs off."

Driving his fist in the wall of the hall near the apartment door, Evan cries out loudly a lurid expletive. Adversity and agony flood his body. He leans against the wall angry and helpless.

"Evan, you can do nothing for her. Man, remember her alive. Remember those phenomenal green eyes. Leave it at that!"

Evan does not toss a coin from cupped hand to cupped hand in his usual manner. Evan sighs, leans his back against the wall and puts his hand to his forehead. "*Damn! Shit!* I don't know if I can stand this, Pete. This may be more than I can bear! I know she wasn't with me. But, at least I knew she was out there alive, somewhere! Now, she's gone. I always hoped she'd come back to me someday. Now, that hope is gone! Now, she never can come back to me no matter how long I wait!" Evan takes a deep breath. "Her green eyes will haunt me forever. Did they *get* the sorry son of a bitch that did this?"

"No, we have no leads yet, Ev."

"Damn, Pete! *Shit!*"

"Wait, Evan. We'll get him! I've called in the lab to comb the apartment. The coroner is here. The place was ransacked, probably robbed."

"Robbers don't usually cut the arms and legs off! Man, you know that!"

"No, but you know they've been getting more violent lately. People will do anything for a buck these days, Evan. Hell, they will kill you for a pair of shoes!"

"Pete, was she dead before they hacked her? Shit! I have to know whether she went through that damn pain."

"No way of knowing, but we'll get the autopsy to determine all that."

Evan freezes in horror as the gurney pulls out in the hall near him. The top sheet, covered in blood, covers Kizzy's body and head. The gurney rolls by and Evan gawks. Pete holds on to Evan's arms tightly. The pressure in Evan's temples is absent, replaced by his heart pounding loudly and persistently throughout his head. He feels as though his head will burst into a million pieces. Evan pulls away from Pete, leans against the wall facing it, pressing his forehead against it. He pounds his clenched fists in the wall above his head and yells out in heartache, "God! Please, God, no! Not her! Please, don't let this be happening!" Disorganized profanities flow from Evan's tormented mouth, pleading for consolation.

Pete walks over putting his hand gently on Evan's shoulder trying to comfort him. Pete has tears in his eyes. He can almost feel Evan's malaise and suffering. "Hold on, Ev. Don't let it get the best of you, son."

Evan turns around, leaning his back against the wall. "Damn, Pete, how could somebody destroy something as beautiful as she was?"

"I don't know, Ev. It's as though beautiful women attract weirdos these days. Remember that Lafferty case?" Evan feels weakness filling his body. His face suddenly grows pale. His lips and fingers feel tingly.

"Hey, Ev, you don't look too good. You okay? Listen, take the rest of the day off. I'll okay it with the Captain."

Evan knows he is not all right. He will never be all right again. She is gone! Evan does not say a word, but nods his head yes at Pete. He does not feel like talking. He takes the elevator down to the street. The smell of blood fills the elevator and Evan's nostrils, even after the gurney has already gone down. Evan knows this is *her* blood. As he leans against the wall of the elevator, he looks up. Oblivious to the brightness of the reflective lighting of the elevator, he cannot focus his thoughts on anything except this horrible event. He feels physically and mentally ill. He knows he will never hear her voice, inhale the freshness of her hair or skin, feel the warmth of her in his arms. The lump in his throat feels as though it will choke him. He arrives outside just in time to watch as the ambulance drives away down the wet street. He stands there until the ambulance is out of sight, feeling the dampness of the drizzle upon his face, head and neck, but not caring. Not bothering to wipe the drizzle away as it drips from his nose and from his eyelashes into his eyes, he can feel the life draining from him. She was his life. Just standing there in the rain, he stares at nothing, and sees nothing.

"Hey, Evan, what the *hell* is going on up there? Alice gave me just the basics. Come on, what can ya tell me?" Bettey yells from a crowd of reporters, as she pushes and shoves the people pushing against her. Bettey's voice is loud and drastically distinctive. She outcries obscenities at the other reporters pushing her. Bettey, a tough lady, always perseveres against intruders. Evan ignores her. "Hey, come on Evan! Give me the shit! Get me by these officers! Let me in!" Bettey tries again.

Evan continues to ignore her. A uniformed officer grabs his arm suddenly, pulling him back to reality and back to the wet street. Evan comes out of his trance glancing at the officer briefly, but looking right through him as though he is purposely ignoring the officer. The way Evan is feeling, he does not care whether the officer is speaking to him. At this time, voices seem to be slowed, distorted and distant. He can still smell the bloody odor. He rubs his nose, but cannot wipe the smell from his nostrils. After getting in his car, he starts driving. His mind wanders back in time to a date when Kizzy was alive.

2

He recollected the first time he had ever seen Kizzy when he had been five years old. His parents, going out for the evening, had called an agency to send over a sitter. His mother had explained the babysitter's name was Kizzy. Evan had thought this was a strange name. He remembered the first sight of her. She had stood in the front doorway to his home in Hollywood. The porch light had been at her back, creating a silhouette. As only a soft shadow, she had stepped forward in the light of the entryway. Her dark hair had framed her face and fallen softly on her shoulders with gentle curls at the ends, and bangs that rested softly against her forehead. Occasionally, she had pushed them from her eyes. Her dress had been flowered and feminine, draping against her body. Evan thought at first she must have been an angel. He had seen beautiful women such as Kizzy on television and in magazines, but she had been even more lovely than any of them, and she was real! She had been the most beautiful woman he had ever seen. When his parents were leaving, Kizzy stood at the door with him. Gently, she pulled him against her leg, rustling his hair with her hand. He remembered observing her, relishing the sight of her dazzling green eyes. She had tilted her head to one side and smiled gently down at him. Softly, she had put her palm against his cheek as he leaned against her. Kizzy had noticed a bruise under his eye. With her forefinger, she lightly touched his eye and asked, "What happened right here, little man?"

"Two boys at school held me while one guy hit me," Evan had answered meekly.

"Why did they do that to you?"

Evan had become infuriated, not at Kizzy but at the thought of the incident. "Because they're mean! Just plain mean! They're hoods. I hate hoods. Everybody at school hates them, Kizzy!"

"They sure must be lonely, Evan."

Evan, surprised at her comment, said, "What do you mean by that?"

"Well, if nobody likes them, they must not have any friends. That would make anyone lonely, and maybe even mean."

Evan had found a reassuring wisdom in Kizzy's response. Much calmer, he had replied, "Someday, I'm going to be a policeman. Then no more hoods will be around to hurt people. I'll make sure!" Kizzy had smiled at him.

"When I'm a policeman, Kizzy, I will keep you safe," Evan had said as he surveyed her. Kizzy had bent down, smiled and cuddled him in her arms gently. Evan had felt safe with her. She had been so wonderful.

The night had passed too quickly. She had read stories to him with such enthusiasm. Never before had Evan listened with such intensity. The stories had been old and familiar, but the way she had read them made them brand-new. The characters had seemed alive as she changed her voice to suit each character. They had run through the house together playing a crazy game of tag that she had created. Whenever he had caught her, they would tumble to the floor, together, with her tickling him and her laughing aloud with him. The entire night, Evan had *not been able* to take his eyes off her. She had become his best friend that night. They had laughed and cuddled. She had made him love being alive. As it came time to tuck him in to bed, she gently kissed his mouth and tussled the hair on his head with her hand. Kizzy had started to leave the room. Evan remembered what he had felt deep in his heart at that moment—a feeling he had never had before in his entire life. It had hurt, but had felt wonderful. Evan recalled beckoning to her. "Kizzy, I love you," he had said with a serious tone, meaning it with his entire, tiny, young heart.

"I love you too, you little rug rat," she had responded playfully smiling.

Evan had raised himself in the bed to protest her taking his comment so lightly. He had looked directly in her entrancing green eyes. "No. I *really love you*," Evan had repeated sternly. Kizzy had smiled, turned off the light and walked from the room. Evan had lay down under the covers. He had known he would convince her that his love was genuine. Evan had planned to grow up and marry Kizzy. They would play tag and read books all day long. He would be a policeman and keep her safe always. Finally, Evan had drifted off to sleep. He had dreamed of Kizzy. They had been romping and playing. He had been so happy.

The next morning he had awakened in a wonderful mood. He had rushed down the stairs only to find Kizzy gone. His heart had sunk. Many times after that day, at Evan's insistence, his parents had used the same agency, requesting Kizzy each time. Evan had always waited with anticipation, his small heart pounding in his chest. She had never come. His disappointment had escalated. He had pressured his mother to question the agency about Kizzy's location, but found out little. All they had been told was that she had moved to Houston, Texas, from Hollywood. Evan had written down "Houston, Texas" on his tablet. Someday he would visit Houston and find her.

3

The years passed and Evan grew into a young man. He dated many young girls from his school, but not one of them ever compared to Kizzy. The young girls made him feel awkward and stupid as he never knew what to say. He had never forgotten Kizzy. Her beguiling, green eyes haunted his dreams. Her caress filled his thoughts, and her amiable smile touched his heart. He thought of her constantly and could still hear her giggle echoing hauntingly through his mind. He knew what he had felt for her was true love. Sometimes he felt he could close his eyes and imagine her nuzzling his cheek. His heart had pounded rapidly. He always opened his eyes, breathless, but did not find Kizzy there.

Two days before his eighteenth birthday, his football team had gone to Houston, Texas. His school had won a free weekend for the team to go to the Astrodome. The Pittsburgh Steelers and Oilers were playing. The game was on Monday night; however, the team arrived in Houston on Saturday. The Oilers had agreed to meet some of the boys on Sunday at the hotel in which his team had been staying. His coaches were almost as excited about meeting the professional players as the students. With the hoopla, Evan felt the coaches would not miss him. Evan knew this was his chance to find Kizzy. When he arrived, he began to search the Houston telephone directory in his room. The directory lists a page of "Theriots". In Hollywood it had been an unusual name. Here it seemed to be common-place. Three "K. Theriots" had been present. Evan began to call each number. His hands had been shaking; his fingers pushed the buttons on the phone with great anticipation. He called the first two, which were not Kizzy. The last number listing had no address beside it, only the phone number. He heard a voice on an answering machine—it was Kizzy. Just the sound of her voice made his heart beat faster. He laid back on the bed listening to her melodious voice. He had forgotten the way the sound of her voice made him feel. After leaving a message for her to call and hoping she would, he lay in his bed, thinking and waiting. What if she did not remember him? His hands were shaking and cold. What if she would not call because she remembered him as a child? Evan walked over to the dresser, looked at his image in the mirror and thought. He was not a child.

He was a man.

The time seemed to creep by slowly. Finally, the phone rang, and it was Kizzy. Her voice was the sweetest music to his ears. She only spoke to him for a short time. "Hi, sweetie."

"Hi, Kizzy. Do you remember me?"

" I do, Evan. Listen, do you want to meet?"

"Yeah!" he answered eagerly.

"A coffee shop is just around the corner. I'll meet you there in an hour. Do you think you can find it?"

"Don't you worry! I will be there!"

"Bye, sweetie." Kizzy hung up. Evan's hands turned cold and clammy, and he began to shake again. He began to think. This might be the only chance he would get with her. He could not lose this chance. Combing his black, curly hair back, he changed his shirt, and splashed a gallon of cologne on his neck, face and hands. He tucked in his shirt in his pants with much difficulty, because he was so nervous. Evan raced around the corner on foot to the coffee shop. While sitting in the booth, waiting, an hour passed. Then, an hour and a half passed, and he was starting to lose hope.

"Hey, good lookin'! Buy a girl a cup of coffee, huh?"

Evan knew the voice. From the booth where he was sitting, he looked and saw Kizzy. Her eyes were more enticing than he had recalled. Full of voluptuous, womanly charisma from her head to her toe, she looked more tantalizing than his memory had recalled. The light pink dress she was wearing clung against her body. Her cleavage tastefully showed from the low neckline of the dress. Her sterling skin was as soft as smooth velvet. As she slipped in the booth next to him, the dress slightly opened, exposing her curvaceous smooth thigh and the lace at the top of her hose.

Evan's heart raced. "I was afraid you wouldn't recognize me," he said nervously.

"Why wouldn't I? You were the cutest little boy I ever saw. I could never forget you, Evan. You were very special to me. Look at you! You're a handsome man."

Evan watched the words as they had formed on her beautiful, full deep pink lips. Her lips were soft and moist. Evan smiled and blushed. Kizzy tilted her head to one side and laughed her special childlike giggle. She found a guileless pleasure in his blush. Evan looked around the room. Every man in the place, no matter what age, was watching Kizzy. Each man seemed to be caressing her ever so gently with his eyes. Evan felt important. She was the most beautiful woman in the room, and she was with him.

"So, how old are you, Evan?"

Evan lied slightly. "I'm eighteen."

"Do you play sports?" Kizzy said between sips of coffee.

"Yeah. My football team is here. We won the free trip and game tickets to see the Oilers' game."

"Tell me what position you play," she said gently wiping her lips on the napkin.

"I play tight end. What about you? What have you been doing, Kizzy?"

"Oh, a little modeling, some commercials. I've done a little of this and a little of that." Then, oddly she changed the subject. "You know, they have great hamburgers here. If we had time, we could get one with lots of onions. Mmm."

"Well, if you want a hamburger, hey. I'm in no hurry, Kizzy. Order one." Evan pulled money from his pocket.

"No, we don't have time. I'll get one maybe another time," Kizzy said as she looked around the restaurant nervously.

The conversation continued. Evan had never felt comfortable talking with the opposite sex. However, with Kizzy, it was so easy. The words poured from his mouth, and the thoughts from his mind. With years to reminisce upon, they drank several cups of coffee during their conversation. Evan loved watching Kizzy drink coffee. The way she pursed her lips and gently sipped the coffee was beautiful and special. She held her little finger out away from the cup handle as she sipped.

As though it came from nowhere, Kizzy placed her hand in Evan's. She looked deep in his blue eyes and said, "Do you still love me, Evan?"

Evan did not hesitate. "I love you as much today as I did all those years ago. I have never stopped loving you. I couldn't, even though I tried. Kizzy, I don't want to try." She leaned even closer to Evan. Evan inhaled the perfume surrounding her beauty.

She looked him over in detail, scanning every inch of his body slowly and gently with her eyes. "Evan, you are all grown up. You're a beautiful young man. Let's go somewhere else." She clenched his hand tightly in hers gently piercing his hand with her fingernails. Evan was proud that she had thought of him as a "man." He was not sure what she had in mind, but he would have gone to hell with Kizzy. In reply, he shyly nodded.

They left the coffee shop and walked slowly, talking all the way. "So, how are your parents, Evan? They were such pleasant people."

"They are fine. Dad has retired. Mom is still involved with her church work."

"Is your Mom still as lovely as ever?"

"Yeah, but not as lovely as you. No one could be more beautiful than you!" Evan took Kizzy's hand in his. Childishly, she giggled at his response.

After passing a man smoking a cigar, Kizzy stopped on the sidewalk with her eyes watering. She began sneezing. Evan smiled remembering her sneezes when his Dad had smoked all those years ago. She always sneezed three times in quick succession. "Oh, I hate smoking. It drives me wild!" Kizzy said as they continued walking.

In no time at all, Evan found himself in a luxurious, brand-new hotel room with Kizzy. Lost in her, he did not recollect entering. He had lost all time and space as he talked to Kizzy.

"Evan, I am going to slip into something a little bit more comfortable. You wait right here. Make yourself at home," Kizzy said as she lifted the bag she had been carrying the entire evening. Evan paced nervously while she was out of the room. He felt afraid without her presence. His mind raced. He had one worried thought at this, the gravest moment of his life. What if he did not do this right?

Kizzy came out in a beautiful light pink negligee that was sheer and soft, just like her. Not cheap or ugly, but lovely, it was an expectation a man has of his new bride's attire on their honeymoon. Evan just stood there, frozen or mesmerized, he was not sure which. Kizzy came over and sat across from Evan on the bed. She reached out and gently took his hand in hers, pulling him down to sit on the bed.

"You have grown into a very beautiful young man, Evan. I always knew you would grow up to be a handsome man. Special little boys grow up to be special men." She leaned forward and had gently kissed Evan on his lips. He trembled. She smiled sweetly. Evan kept his eyes wide open, wanting to remember every moment with her. He wanted to memorialize the sight of her.

"Please, move even closer next to me on the bed, Evan."

Heart pounding and eyes watering, Evan did as he was told. "Kizzy, uh—I have, I mean—I haven't ever, well you know. I—uh— "

She pressed her fingertips gently across his lips, not letting him speak and said, "Sh-sh-sh." She kissed him, sweetly and gently. Somehow, he forgot what he had been trying to tell her. With her hands, she gently touched his cheek and neck. Her kisses were many, but each was patient and soft. They took his breath away. They were better than he had ever dreamed possible. Evan felt more love that night than he believed imaginable. Still, he kept his eyes open, wanting to take in every vision of her. He wanted to memorize the feelings, the sights, everything about that night. This was his life long dream at long last coming true! His heart ached for her. Kizzy was gentle. She did not speak a word. She did not let him speak a word and guided him, knowing all the moves. They made love all night. Kizzy was patient and supportive. As he held her in his arms, he felt more like a man than any other time in his life. Evan, from sheer exhaustion, was unable to keep his eyes open any longer. He fell asleep peacefully. The most irresistible woman in the world was in his arms, and he felt loved.

He awoke the next morning to find Kizzy gone. Anxiety filled his body. No one at the hotel desk knew where she had gone. Again, she had disappeared without even a word. After returning to his hotel, he tried several times to telephone her, but always heard the machine. He begged her in the messages he left, to call him. She never returned his calls. He begged the operator for her address with no success. No choice was left for Evan.

Evan left Houston with his football team and returned home. After a couple of years in college, he embarked on police work as a profession. It was another dream of his, just as loving Kizzy. The thought of helping people made him feel important and gave him purpose.

4

Evan returns his thoughts to the present. Somehow he has made it back to his apartment. Not remembering his journey there, he goes inside. This is the apartment he and Kizzy had shared for a short time while he was attending the police academy. He sits in his chair, thinking of the day when he found her again in Houston.

5

It had been raining that day. He was on his way to the academy and had stopped at a restaurant for lunch. He had just finished his burrito, when he noticed all the men turning and gazing at something or someone who had just arrived. A rapturous woman with damp hair clinging to her face had entered. Dressed in a rain soaked all-weather coat, she carried a leaking umbrella. Evan looked closer. It was Kizzy. She sat at a table, wiping the wetness from her face with her hands. Evan motioned to the waitress and readily placed an order to be sent to Kizzy's table. Just out of her view behind some plants, he sat, watching her. As she dug through her purse, he could see she looked tired. The waitress arrived at Kizzy's table. "Here, honey."

"What's this? I didn't order yet," Kizzy said.

"It's a hamburger with extra onions. The guy over there ordered it for you." The waitress pointed over to Evan. He peeked out from behind the plants.

Kizzy looked pleasingly surprised. "Evan! Evan, get over here, you stinker," Kizzy said smiling. Evan picked up his soda and joined her. She ate every bite of the hamburger, with the juice dripping from her hands. Mustard smears on her mouth only endeared her to Evan.

"I'm on my way to the police academy, Kizzy."

"Oh, that's great, Evan. You've really done well for yourself. Listen, I've really got to go. Thanks a lot for the hamburger. I enjoyed seeing you again."

Evan clutched and held tightly onto her hand, deciding not to let her get away. "No, *damn it!* You are not going to leave me this time, Kizzy! Have you forgotten all the love I have felt for you all these years?"

"No, but it's better if you forget it, Evan," she pleaded. Straightaway, she walked outside the restaurant.

Evan followed her, pursuing her relentlessly. "I won't forget it, ever! I love you, Kizzy, as much today as in the past. Hell, maybe even more! I won't let you go! I want you to move in with me, baby!"

"Hey, you're moving a little fast, Evan. I have a place of my own."

Evan seized Kizzy and pulled her close as they stood together in the rain. He kissed her deeply on the lips. Not even her strong onion breath deterred him. Kizzy responded to his kiss with a deep sigh.

"I don't care whether you own fifteen places! You're going to be with me. I love you, Kizzy. Don't you love me?"

"Of course, I love you with all my heart. But there are things . . . ." She hesitated to go on.

"I promise you, Kizzy. It'll be all right. Whatever it is, we can get by it together!" Evan kissed her again, deeper. Evan felt her melting in his arms.

Kizzy sighed. "Oh, okay, Evan. I would enjoy waking up with you next to me. But, not today—I have to finish some things. Then I'll move in with you."

"Promise me, Kizzy!" Evan said, desperately holding her.

"I promise," she said, gazing deeply in his blue eyes.

Evan without hesitation scribbled his address down on a piece of paper. He put it in Kizzy's hand and closed his hand around hers. He looked deeply into her green eyes. Kizzy did not blink.

"I'll be waiting, Kizzy," he said. She smiled and walked away in the rain.

A week later, Kizzy had moved in with Evan into this apartment.

6

Evan's telephone rings, returning him to the present. The machine picks up. He can hear the voice, "Shit! I hate freakin' machines. Evan, it's Bettey. Please, pick up if you're there. I need to talk to ya. Okay. Call me later. Ya know the number. Shit!"

Evan hears the dial tone as the phone disconnects. Slowly, he surveys the room. His thoughts start to run amuck. Kizzy's ghostlike image stands in front of him, dripping wet with only a towel around her. Evan closes his eyes. He sucks in the fragrance of her wet hair and delights in the perfume of the damp towel surrounding her. The smells seem so close, as though they are right here—as though this is real. When he reopens his eyes, the image is gone. His mind wanders back to the memory of Kizzy.

7

Kizzy was sitting at the dresser mirror, wearing only a towel. She was combing her wet hair back away from her face. She removed the towel, and knowing Evan was watching, ran it gently across her face. She wiped the towel seductively down between her breasts. The entire time she was performing this ritual, she stared intensely in the mirror in Evan's eyes. Hypnotized, Evan had been staring back, never blinking, seeing every motion she had performed without breaking the lock between their eyes. While sitting, she put her foot upon the dresser. She ran the towel up her legs gently drying the drops of water away.

8

While taking a deep sigh, Evan aches with nostalgia. His pulse is rapid, even now after all these years. Her beauty and sensuality haunt his very thoughts. Evan wipes the perspiration from his face. These thoughts stir the yearning of her in the deepest recesses of his body. Here, now, his heart throbs for her just as the first time he had made love to her in his youth. Evan recalls the nights he had held her.

9

She had awakened sobbing. He had held her saying, "It was only a bad dream. I'm here, baby. Nothing is going to hurt you, ever."

She had held him as tightly as she could, crying, "Everyone leaves me! Everyone! Someday you'll leave me, too! Evan, hold me!"

"I'll never leave you, Kizzy! Never!" Yet, no matter how much Evan had reassured her, the dreams always had returned.

10

Evan remembered the day he returned to the apartment to find Kizzy gone. All she left was a note. Evan has kept this note throughout the years. Occasionally, he would read the words slowly to savor the last thought of her. He retrieves the note from his bedroom and sits in the dimly lit living room to read. At first, he just runs his fingers gently across the paper of the folded note. Evan envisions that once her gentle fingers had touched this paper. He puts it softly against his nose. Faintly, he can sniff her perfume on the paper. As he opens the note gently, he hopes to preserve the emotional value of the note.

Don't look for me. If you find me, I will just leave you again. Forget me. We can never be happy together. It would hurt too much. I will never forget you. Thank you for the beautiful time you gave to me. I'll never forget it. Hold life in the palm of your hand at all times. Never let it get away from you because you can never get it back!

Kiz

Closing his eyes, Evan runs his fingers across the lip marks, Kizzy's insignia, the kiss, on the paper. If he uses his imagination, he can almost feel her lips under his fingertips. He opens his eyes and folds the note, gently. When she left him, he had not looked for her. He knew Kizzy. She would have only left him again if he had found her. Later, he had tried to find her, just to know where she was living. She had left a message on his machine saying only that she was fine, she was living in Houston, and she did not want him to continue to look for her. Her words were irate, cold and bitter. She did not want to be with him anymore, ever. She made that clear. Evan had never understood that last written note from Kizzy. Maybe she felt she could not be happy with him because he was a cop and she would worry about him getting killed. Still, that did not make sense. She was so happy and proud of his "cop" status. The note never made sense. They never fought. They only loved each other. What went wrong? He had kept his word. He had never left her. If things had only been different. If she had stayed with him, she might be alive today. Damn, why did she leave? *Why?*

Evan puts his head in his hands and swallows hard. The lump is larger than ever. He sits in the solitude of his apartment. He is no cop here. He is only a man with a broken heart. He has not had agonizing feelings like this since she left him. Today, she has left him again. This time, she can never come back. Evan's entire body aches.

11

Pete spends much time writing his reports. The facts go over and over in his head about Kizzy's slaying. He looks over the bagged evidence. The gold pen is shiny and extraordinarily expensive. Who in the world is "T.U.?" No fingerprints are on the pen, not even Kizzy's. Who owned this pen? Why was it left at Kizzy's apartment? The clues had a million questions attached. Pete gets an idea. He reviews the hundreds of paroled burglars in the Houston area. He knows it will be a slow process, but this is important. He cross references the burglary M.O. with the vicious assaults. He feels he has some possibilities.

12

The phone interrupts Evan as he lies in his bed trying to sleep. He observes the clock which shows the time as seven o'clock in the morning. Pete is telephoning.

"Evan, I got good news. We've rounded up the usual parolee cons with the burglary M.O.. Come on down to the station. I've got about ten. I'll let you be around for the questioning."

"Great, Pete. I'll be right there." Evan, exhilarated about this ray of hope in his doubtful mind, dresses posthaste. He goes through a drive-thru at a fast food restaurant ordering a large cup of coffee. He is hoping this will give him some much needed energy, feeling drained from the insomnia of last night.

Evan hurries inside the station, gulping down his last swallow of coffee. He is wrong. The coffee gives no energy, just a caffeine buzz. As he goes over and pours another cup of coffee, he looks around for Pete. He sees Alice. "Hey, Alice."

"Gee, Ev, ya look awful!"

"Yeah, yeah. Where's Pete?"

"Are ya kiddin'? He's been questioning those suspects for that lady's homicide. You know, the lady y'all knew."

"Damn it! What is wrong with him? He called me down here to be in on the questioning, and he starts without me!"

"Really? That's weird, huh? Pete's almost finished. He's on the last one now, Evan. Ya better hurry!"

"Where is he?" Evan wonders why Pete has started the interrogations without him.

"Evan, he's got the suspects sitting in interrogation room number four. You know, the biggest room. He's in room number two."

"What the hell is wrong with him? He starts without me after calling me, and getting me down here so early! Oh, well. Thanks anyway, Alice."

Evan passes room number four. The door is open so he looks inside seeing the suspects sitting. What he sees surprises Evan, as this is an odd group. This is a shock for Evan. Pete's action is abnormally strange. One man has an arm missing. Another man is in a wheelchair. The others include two old men too old to even hear, a pregnant woman, a young blind man with a Seeing Eye dog and a cane, and a tiny, skinny fragile man who appears anorectic and paces nervously. Evan wonders what in the world is going through Pete's brain. *These* are suspects? Evan enters room number two through the closed door without knocking.

In the small, warm room, Pete is leaning across the table staring in the man's face that he is interrogating. This suspect, as the others, takes Evan by astonishment. He is a young man, but he appears half dead with sickness. He is pale, thin, and frail looking and gasps to just get enough air to breathe.

"Hey, Ev. Come on in. I was anxious to get started. This guy doesn't have an alibi for the night of the murder. He picks up garbage for the city. He just happens to be on the same route as the deceased's apartment. Very coincidental, don't you think?"

Evan asks after sitting in one of the chairs, "Mister, what is your name?"

"John Westerlin."

Evan takes over the questioning at this point. "So you work for the city?"

"Yes, sir," John answers.

Pete yells at the suspect, "Tell him exactly *where* you pick up garbage, Westerlin!"

John, upset by Pete's yelling, tries to speak and gasps for air. John is nervous, only having a record of being arrested once for burglary. The caper had in actuality been his friend's idea. He had only gone along for the ride and had no idea how much trouble would happen just by waiting in the car. He knew stealing was wrong, but he had been so hungry. By going to prison, he had paid society for his crime dearly. He did not know his friend during the burglary had fatally stabbed a man inside the store.

"Yeah, my route includes that nice apartment building where all those rich people live. But I didn't know that lady. I looked at that picture he showed me. Honest, I ain't never even seen her! Y'all got the wrong guy!"

Evan beseeches, "You don't have an alibi for the night of her death?"

"No, I'm—"

Before John can answer Evan's question, Pete interrupts. "Yeah. Right. Nobody can vouch for him. He claims he was home alone, but I bet you were over trying to rob her apartment. Weren't you? You're as nasty as the garbage you pick up! Like you said, 'all those rich people live there'. What happened that night? Did she catch you? I bet you had been watching the place for months until you figured out the way to get inside past those security devices. That's right, isn't it? You killed her without any thought for her life! You probably enjoyed *watching her die*!" Evan does not recognize this side of Pete. Pete is grasping desperately at straws and duplicitous suspects.

John, the desperate and panicky suspect, speaks slowly because he is frantic and trying harder and harder to breathe. "I swear I didn't kill that lady. I was home, sick! Yeah, I was alone. But I'm too sick to kill anybody. I swear!"

Evan asks, "What do you mean you are too sick? What is wrong with you?"

"I have lung cancer. I had surgery about a month ago. They're now saying I have it in other places in my body. I'm dying myself. I couldn't kill that lady. Y'all, please, don't do this to me." John is a pitiful sight. He pleads with the officers. "I can give you the name of my doctor. He'll tell ya I'm too sick to kill nobody!"

Evan does not think John has the strength to kill Kizzy. It would take someone with great strength to use that cleaver to dismember her. Evan takes Pete aside.

"Pete, there is no way in hell that this man could kill Kizzy. He's not physically strong enough. Look at him, Pete."

Pete looks over at poor John. Maybe for the first time, Pete sees the frail, sick, weak man. "Yeah, I guess you're right. He does look pretty pitiful doesn't he? Okay, John, you can go, but leave the name of your doctor with the officer outside. I plan to call him about your illness." John vacates the room.

Before Evan can withdraw from the room, desperate Pete turns anxiously. His face is flushed. To not lose Evan, he quickly speaks loudly and insistently. "*Listen, Evan.* Some more out there might be good suspects. I've talked to them already. I thought this guy, John, was our best bet, but maybe one of the others might be the perp."

"Pete, are you serious? Did you see that bunch? Not one of those people are physically strong enough, let alone physically capable of dismembering Kizzy. Look at them! I'm not wasting my time on questioning them. That's just wasting time while the real son of a bitch gets away!"

"Okay, Ev. I'll interrogate them again. Maybe if one of them is not the perp, they might know who is. You go on home. You look really tired. Try to get some sleep if you can. I know it's tough, buddy. I'll let you know, if I get anything when I question them again. I'll call you at home."

"Yeah, right, Pete," Evan says doubtfully. Disappointed in Pete's suspects, he leaves the room. He knows Pete is a better cop than this. What is going on with him? How can he not look at these people and see their physical disabilities? Besides, Evan is not sure that Kizzy's murder is a botched burglary. Something is not right here. Something is missing. Evan wonders what they are missing.

Evan goes home and starts thinking. He feels exhausted, but cannot rest. Restlessness travels up and down his spine as his mind pursues thoughts. Pete is not his usual efficient self. What is wrong with him? You would think he would want to find the perp because he knew Kizzy. He lies briefly on the bed; he moves to the chair; he leans against the windowsill and peruses the streets of Houston. Then, Evan comprehends what is happening with Pete. Pete liked Kizzy, too, and they were good friends. Pete is not thinking straight. Her slaying is affecting him, too. Evan feels incompetent and selfish. He was so involved with his own suffering that he has not seen the pain Pete is feeling. After all, Pete is only human. He is trying so hard to cover this for Evan. Evan feels lousy about the doubts he has been having about Pete. Pete is hurting, too.

13

During the next week, Evan spends time at the station going over Pete's reports with a fine-toothed comb; the evidence, anything and everything about Kizzy's death. He tries to brainstorm with Pete on the case; but, Pete is extremely uncooperative, seeming not to want Evan's help. Evan knows Pete is just trying to protect him from the heartache of this case.

One day when Evan is leaving the station tired and frustrated, a reporter approaches him. "Hey, Detective Picard. My name is Ed Masterson. I'm with—"

Before he can finish his statement, Evan interrupts saying, "I know who you are. You work for that rag, *Scandal.* I don't want anything to do with reporters such as you!"

"Come on. I just have a few little questions about the Keziah Theriot murder case." Before Evan can decline, a pushy Ed continues to speak. "Is it true she had ties to organized crime?"

Galled by this question, he thinks while the man hammers away at him with rude questions and accusations. How dare this man ask questions about Kizzy! What gives him the right? He starts walking toward the car to escape the insolent, persistent reporter.

Ed follows him hammering away with the questions. "Is it true that she had several lesbian lovers, including the wife of an organized crime kingpin?"

This comment infuriates Evan who knows Kizzy to be heterosexual. "I don't want to talk to you! Get the *hell* out of my face, you lowest kind of *damn trash*!" Evan roars in hate.

Not giving up, Ed pushes Evan against a car in the parking lot. He grabs Evan, tearing the front pocket on his brand-new shirt. "Just give me an answer," Ed yells. Ed is determined to do his job. No one, including this cop, is going to stop him. This is all it takes to drive Evan into a frenzy. His emotions are running high. Evan seizes Ed, shoving him hard against the car hood. Evan clinches his hand into a fist wanting desperately to hit the pushy, rude man.

Pete, walking out to his car in the parking lot, witnesses the fight. Pete comes running over to Evan, grabbing Evan's fist, stopping it in midair. "Hold it, Ev. Man, what is going on here?"

Evan broadcasts, trying to calm his emotions at this point, "This trash will not leave me alone. He grabbed and tore my shirt. He wants to know about Kizzy. He's with that crappy rag, *Scandal*."

"Oh, is that what *you* called her? Kizzy? Gee, ya must have known her pretty well yourself, huh cop? Ooo, she has ties to organized crime and the police department. That'll make great coverage in my paper!" the reporter states disparagingly, hoping to provoke Evan into giving him more information.

"What is your name?" Pete asks the reporter in a repressed tone of voice.

"Ed Masterson. I just wanted info on the Keziah Theriot murder. This cop," he alleges, pointing accusingly at Evan, "gets all excited and starts threatening me. I'm just trying to do my job, just as y'all do your jobs. I ought to sue him for assaulting me. You saw it. You could be my witness, huh?"

Pete's manner is polite, but stern, not liking this reporter any more than Evan does. "Mr. Masterson, you don't want me to be your witness. From what I saw, you accosted Detective Picard first. If you don't leave immediately, I'll charge you with assaulting a police officer!"

Ed murmurs and swears viciously under his breath saying, "I should have known you cops stick together!" Ed walks scoffingly away. Pete walks Evan to his car hoping to calm him.

"I wanted to kill that son of a bitch, Pete. He was saying terrible lies about Kizzy."

"What kind of lies?"

"That she was participating in lesbianism and—"

"Lesbianism? Are you kidding? Kizzy was the most heterosexual person I've ever known!" Pete yells, laughing at the absurdity of the statement.

"That's not all, Pete. He said the woman was the wife of an organized crime kingpin! Maybe this woman is the one with the initials 'T.U.' on that gold ink pen. You know there was that time— "

At hearing Evan's comment, Pete stops laughing. Seriously, he says interrupting Evan, "Don't let trash such as that get to you, Evan. You can't believe what people such as him say. He's not worth it!" Evan shakes his head in agreement. He enters his car and leaves Pete standing in the parking lot.

Evan thinks recurrently about the things that the reporter has said to him. They cannot be true. He knew Kizzy overly well. She would not be in stuff such as that! Evan knows the trash that *Scandal* writes in its pages. He has seen the newspaper at the grocery store checkout. He has also seen many people buy and believe the lies, just because they were in print. Some people believe, if something is written down, that something is fact. How wrong they are! He shakes the reporter and what he said from his thoughts. He will not let this affect him.

14

At home one evening Evan receives the notice from a downtown law firm that mentions him as a beneficiary in Kizzy's will. He can hardly believe this is happening. The reading of the will is this next Monday. Kizzy was only in her late thirties, so if she wrote a will she must have sensed she was in danger. This will seem a long time to wait to find out whether any clues are in the will. Evan considers talking to Pete about getting a warrant to review the will in advance as it has not been probated. Yet, maybe waiting would be better, to see who shows up for the reading, and watch their responses.

Evan knows that probably no clues are in the will, but he has to have hope. With perseverance, Evan knows he will search for her killer. No one, or nothing will *stop him!*

CHAPTER IV

William

1

William rides in the cab through the rain, listening to the windshield wipers swish. He is in Houston, Texas, a place he has never before visited. He hopes he will never visit it again, at least not for the reason he is here this time. The love of his life has died. He cannot understand how this has happened. She was young, and oh, so picturesque. She should have been coming to upstate New York to his funeral. God only knows he is getting up there, sixty his next birthday. William coughs a wheezy cough laboring for breath. The Houston humidity is killing him. This must be the hottest place on earth. He peers out the side window, remembering the first time he saw Kizzy.

2

Only four years old, she was running in a field, wearing a white lacy dress with tiny pink embroidered flowers and a satiny pink ribbon in her light brown hair. What a beautiful child his eyes beheld. Her long silky curls bounced with each step she took. The wind faintly blew the curly bangs away from her forehead. Her light brown hair fell down her back curling meekly on the ends. The large bangs across her forehead kept getting caught in her beautiful long lashes as she talked. She brushed the bangs aside with her hand, squinting her green eyes to pull the lashes from her hair. She tilted her tiny head to one side as she smiled. The dimples and rosiness in her cheeks paled with that angelic wide smile. She was tiny, petite and delicately feminine with an amazing inquisitiveness. With unending questions, she sought knowledge about everything. A vivacious child, she loved and trusted everyone. Her naivete was refreshing and winsome. With an uncanny resemblance to her mother, an exceptionally enrapturing woman, they even named her Keziah, an old family name, after her mother. "Kitten Kizzy" was her nickname. Her father, Alan, or Al as they had named him, and William had been in the armed forces together. Once Al had saved William's life during an accident at the base. An explosion had left William unconscious. Al had risked his own life, entering the burning building and carrying William out on his back. William had never forgotten that he owed Al his life.

Kizzy possessed the cutest high shrill laugh or giggle. Unmistakably hers alone, her laugh and quick sneezes had been unique. Her little sneezes came in groups of three and were always followed by an "Uh-oh" from her. Then she would giggle. She had loved having a "milk moustache." Kizzy would drink her milk as sloppily as possible so that it would make a large one on her upper lip. She had said it made her feel so beautiful. She would throw up one shoulder and look down her nose with this huge "milk moustache" above her upper lip. Putting her hands on her hips, she would walk around with a prissy walk snubbing the rest of the world, so dramatically. William doted on her as though she were his own child. He attended her birthday parties and school programs. He was so proud of her accomplishments. She had been a smart little girl. She had been so special to him, which made loving her easy. Often, she sat in his lap and pinched his cheeks in her tiny hands. She would get infinitely close to his face and say, "What kitten do you love the best, Unkie Wills? Tell me quickly!" He could still hear her voice as though she were standing right beside him.

3

William, back in the present, takes a deep breath and clears the tears from his eyes using his handkerchief. He wipes his nose, looks down at his watch and sees it is ten o'clock a.m.. He removes his suit jacket, feeling as though he is melting underneath it, and loosens his tie. William is accustomed to New York weather and lower humidity, not the weather in Houston. The weather in Houston is so different. "Hey driver, move it along will you. My appointment is for ten thirty, and please lower that air conditioning. The heat is stifling back here!" William divulges in his polite, but stern attorney voice. The driver shakes his head in a patronizing way and lowers the air conditioning. William's mind wanders again to an antiquated place in time.

4

He remembered when Kizzy's mother died of pneumonia. Kizzy was about twelve. She cried the biggest tears. Her tiny face and the front of her dress were saturated with the wetness from the tears. "Why did my mommy leave me, Unkie Wills?"

William answered, his heart breaking at her question, "She did not leave you, honey. She will always be with you, Kizzy."

"But she can't hug me anymore. I miss her hugs. I want her here to hug me like before! So, you're wrong! She has left me!" William hugged her, trying to gladden this tearful little girl.

Kizzy adulated the people in her life so sincerely. He had never seen anyone that could cry such large tears, pooling in her large green eyes, soaking her eyelashes. As she lay in his arms crying aloud, he felt his heart breaking.

Everything about Kizzy was performed grandly. She laughed hard and cried hard, and she even became angrier than anyone he had ever known.

Once when another child had purposely broken the head of her doll, she screamed with anger and hit the other little girl hard. Kizzy outcried loudly, "She is a murderer! She hurt my poor baby!" William tried to explain that hitting the little girl had been wrong, but Kizzy insisted the little girl had killed her doll and must pay. Her poignancy spilled over into everything she lived in her life.

Because raising her alone after his wife's death was profound for Al, William tried to help as much as he could. Together they had given her birthday parties. She would find the gifts, unwrap them, and after enjoying them for a minute, rewrap them. Then, she pretended she had never seen them before opening them. Al and William knew she did this, but they never let her know that they knew her little secret.

William tried to help by retrieving Kizzy after school, taking her shopping, chaperoning slumber parties, making school lunches for her, sitting with her when she was ill, attending school programs, and meeting teachers at the school open house. Every minute spent with her and her little friends he relished. Everyone loved Kizzy. Her teachers found her delightful because she was a smart little girl. With an insatiable appetite for knowledge, Kizzy was every teacher's dream.

Al became ill when Kizzy turned about fourteen with incurable cancer. He was in and out of the hospital for a year before he died, suffering terribly. Kizzy had tried so hard to be brave. Watching him suffer had been grueling for her. She had taken care of her father in such a gentle way when he had been home between hospital stays. She had loved him so much. He was all that Kizzy had left in this world. Kizzy had been destroyed when he died. Devastated, she cried constantly. Then, depression replaced her devastation. William had tried to soothe her.

"Why does everyone I love leave me, Unkie Wills?" she had asked William one day.

"Well, don't you love me, Kizzy?"

"Of course, I do, Unkie."

"Well, I haven't left you, have I?"

"No, not yet, but you will. Just as my mommy and dad did. You'll leave me. Then, I'll truly be alone."

In her short life, this young girl had suffered so much loss. During this time, nightmares started. Kizzy would awaken screaming and sobbing uncontrollably. She would say, "They've left me! I'm alone! What can I do? I am *all alone!*" William had held her until she dozed back asleep. The dreams had never given her peace. She had at least one a month.

In his will, Al had given William custody of Kizzy. William was frightened to death. After all, what did a bachelor know about raising a fifteen-year-old girl? Still, Kizzy had no other living relatives, so William had been forced to take her. Besides, he remembered he owed Al his life. He did love little Kizzy. Kizzy's angst seemed to lessen when she learned she would be living with William. He tried hard to replace her parents.

She so loved for William to brush her hair. William said as he brushed, "Brushing your hair is crucial, Kizzy. The brushing removes the dust from the hair between shampoos."

"So that makes it cleaner, Unkie Wills?" she asked, cocking her head to one side and smiling so beautifully.

"Your hair is soft and silky," William said, letting the strands run through his fingers. Glancing around her bedroom, William said, "Please, give this room some cleaning attention. This room is mussed and cluttered, Kizzy!" Dirty, empty glasses, plates and utensils and clothes had been spread over the floor. Neatness was not easy for Kizzy.

"It's no mess! It's just a little scattered. I like it this way. It shows someone lives here! Me!" Kizzy said, making light of William's request. Kizzy's disarray had driven William nearly insane. He had insisted on cleanliness and order. In disgust, he shook his head and left her room.

5

In an amazingly short amount of time, he learned that Kizzy had developed into an enrapturing, young woman. The beauty of a woman had replaced her childlike beauty. She had developed the curves, bumps and bulges a young woman needed to attract the opposite sex. She had fallen in love with an older boy named Tom Hastings. He was "Mr. Popularity" on campus. He was a senior, star football quarterback and all-around athlete. Tom came from an old family that had lived in the same neighborhood with William for years. He even knew Tom's grandparents. Tom and Kizzy were the most popular couple at school. Everyone thought they were the perfect couple. She stood so tiny next to the overwhelming muscular size of Tom.

One day while traveling through town on his way home from the office, William saw Tom. William, stopped at a long traffic light, saw Tom standing outside the local hamburger place that he and Kizzy frequented. However, this time he was without Kizzy. Attractive young girls surrounded Tom. They were touching and hugging him. With much enjoyment, he was reciprocating the motions. William rolled down his window. "Hey Tom! Where is Kizzy?"

Tom, surprised to see William, yelled impertinently at William from where he stood, without even the decency of approaching William's automobile window. "I don't know. I guess she's still at school. Aren't you the parent? Shouldn't you be keeping up with her?" Tom's laughter mocked William.

William was so enraged at Tom's reply that he wanted to hit him. However, the light changed to green, and the cars behind William began to honk. William continued home where Kizzy was waiting for him. He tried to talk to her about the upsetting incident.

"Kizzy, I saw Tom at the hamburger place. He was surrounded by girls."

Surprisingly, Kizzy smiled. "Everyone loves my Tom. He is so lovable. Isn't it wonderful! I am so lucky to have him as my boyfriend."

William was aghast by her acceptance of Tom's behavior. "I think what he was doing is called flirting, Kizzy. Doesn't that bother you?"

"Of course not. Tom just is kind of flirty. He does not mean anything by it, Unkie Wills."

"Nonetheless, he spoke to me so rudely when I questioned him about—"

Before William had finished, Kizzy had interrupted angrily. "I can't believe you were questioning him! He hates people questioning him. How rude of *you!* I have to phone him and apologize! I'll be in my room! You stay away from Tom!" Kizzy stormed upstairs. Frustrated by the situation, William sat in his chair.

Kizzy went everywhere with Tom, which daunted William. Tom was a pompous young man who just luckily came from a good family. He had future aspirations which William was afraid did not include Kizzy. William was afraid not even Kizzy and her beauty would keep Tom from reaching those aspirations. He feared Kizzy would be hurt. William had tried to protect her all that he could. However, Kizzy had a mind of her own. She was stubborn and independent about most things. She would not listen to William's warnings, and she idolized Tom. She had developed a dire, hungry urgency for Tom. Much as everything she had done, or ever did in her life, Kizzy jumped in over her head. With every fiber of her being, she treasured Tom. When he was around, Kizzy never took her eyes off him.

William had not recognized how much of a woman Kizzy had become until the night of the school prom. She had shopped for weeks before the prom to find just the right outfit. She had refused to let William go along on the shopping trips, or to allow him a preview of the dress. Kizzy loved giving surprises to other people. She always took such an innocent, but wicked joy in it. The night of the prom, she took forever getting ready. Surprisingly, Tom arrived on time. Dressed in a classic black tuxedo, he was a strikingly handsome young man. He had a very tall and muscular physique, brown curly hair, big brown eyes and dimpled cheeks when he smiled, shyly. With a face of rugged appeal, he was a rare mixture of shyness and narcissism.

Suddenly, Kizzy came walking down the stairs. She was a vision from a dream. William's eyes could not believe the entrancing, voluptuous woman he saw before him. Smoothly and gracefully, with the eloquence of a scintillating woman, she moved. She wore a tight-fitting, strapless gown made of dark green satin with sheer material covering. With bare shoulders, the dark green seemed to accentuate the color of her eyes making them even greener, more radiant and erotically appealing. Her hair had turned darker like her mothers. On that special night, it fell gently against her bare shoulders. William saw the way Kizzy and Tom's eyes met and locked together. They were entirely involved with only each other, as though no one else was in the room except the two of them. William noticed the way Tom looked at her. He ogled. Decisively, it was the stare of a man looking, and *wanting, a titillating woman!* Her beauty hypnotized Tom. Kizzy looked so seriously at Tom. William saw the deep love radiating from her stunning green eyes, feeling fear striking throughout his body. Kizzy's and Tom's eyes locked together for a long time, neither of them moved nor blinked. Gently, Tom took her hand and placed the wrist corsage on her arm. Never unlocking their eyes, they left the house arm in arm.

William remembered dozing off that night sitting in his chair. He knew he had dreamed of Kizzy, but he did not remember the dream. However when he awoke, sweat was dripping from his face. His heart was racing and his breathing quick and deep. Worry filled his soul as he looked down at his watch and saw it was late. He wondered why they had been so late.

Many thoughts raced through William's mind that night. Where were they? What were they doing? She had been his little girl.

Kizzy came home later than usual that night. William was waiting in his usual chair for her. She was on a peaceful high as she walked in the room.

"Where have you been, Kizzy?" he asked.

"On the most wonderful night of my life!" she said, twirling around in a circle with a huge smile covering her face.

"No, Kizzy, I mean—"

Kizzy interrupted him. "The prom was just wonderful! I am so happy, Unkie Wills! Tom is so wonderful. I love him more than anything in this world! He is the most handsome man in the whole wide world! Oh, but you're awfully handsome, too, Unkie Wills!"

"Thanks, honey, but what I am trying to say is—" Again, Kizzy did not allow William to finish.

"Well, I'm really tired," she said, yawning. "I'm going to shout out my window upstairs how much I love Tom and how much he loves me. Then I am going to turn in. I need my beauty sleep for my handsome Tom. Good night!" Kizzy ran upstairs. William heard her shouting from the upstairs window so the entire town would know.

"Tom Hastings loves me! Kizzy loves Tom, forever! We're going to get married and live together always!"

Several days later, William tried to talk to Kizzy. Again, she did not let him speak. Kizzy planned to marry Tom after he finished college, and she high school. The dreams poured from her heart. She smiled gently with a wonderful peace that William had never seen on Kizzy. William tried to slow her. However, no one could have slowed or dampened Kizzy's enormous enthusiasm, which seemed to grow with each word. William tried his best to warn her, that a lot can happen in four years. These thoughts were Kizzy's dreams. Her dreams, much as everything else in her life, had become bigger than life to her. She refused to listen to William's warnings in any way. She begged him with tears in her eyes, to not even think that these dreams would not come true. They must! This dream was the most important thing in her entire life. Ceaselessly, she stressed this and would not listen to anything different. Then, she shrugged him off saying their love would just grow stronger and stormed upstairs. William's frustration grew. He knew this relationship would only lead to disaster. However, he was not able to stop this cataclysm from unfolding.

6

Two months later, Tom went away to a college in the West on a football scholarship. Kizzy spent the next month writing Tom letters. After the school year started, William suddenly noticed a big change in Kizzy. She became reclusive, not her usual outgoing, enthusiastic self. The rosy bloom in her cheeks began to wane. She spent her days waiting for the mail to arrive and Tom's letters. He noticed the letters were becoming fewer and fewer. Each time she waited and no letter arrived, he watched the disappointment and heartache grow in her face. After awhile, the letters ceased.

One day when he came home from the law firm early, William had found her in the living room sitting with the curtains drawn. The room was dark and quiet. She was alone and curled in the fetal position in his big chair. He turned on the lamp and looked at her. Kizzy's face was wet with tears. Her eyes were filled with the same big tears he had seen in her eyes as a child. William knew something terrible had happened. He had been almost afraid to find out what it was.

"Uncle Wills, I'm in big trouble. I don't know what to do. I'm so scared. Please, please help me. You are all I have left in this whole world. Tom doesn't write me anymore. I guess he has forgotten about me."

William took her in his arms and comforted her. Kizzy had seemed as a little girl again, needing him. "Whatever it is, honey, Uncle Wills will help you through it. You know that don't you, Kizzy? We can get through anything together, honey."

"Yeah, but it is so awful," she said, whimpering.

"Tell me, Kizzy."

"I think I am—I mean, I know I am—I can't say it!" she cried out.

"You can tell me anything, honey. Anything!" he said, reinforcing his love and devotion for her.

"I'm pregnant!" she shrieked out hysterically. William was shocked and overwhelmed by this terrible discovery. His first response was to beat Tom Hastings to a pulp. He drove his fist into the cushion of the couch. Kizzy jumped with dismay and cried harder, not expecting this action from William. Kizzy did not want him to tell Tom because this news might ruin his career. Tom had been igniting the college football field. Pro scouts had been looking at him already. Kizzy had followed him closely in the newspapers. Kizzy admitted to William that she still loved Tom with her entire heart. She made William promise never to tell Tom, so reluctantly, William gave his word. Kizzy knew once William had given his word, it would never be broken. She trusted William. She had said she would kill herself if he had told, and William believed her. Kizzy had always been impulsive and emotional. William and Kizzy had discussed giving the child up for adoption. Kizzy was petrified that somehow Tom would find out about her pregnancy. She was also terrified of the pain of giving birth. Abortions were illegal during this time, the 1960's. William began to ask questions of his friends. Being an attorney, he finally found a physician upstate that performed illegal abortions. Guilt for arranging this illegal act filled William's being. He battled inside between his conscience and his love and devotion to Kizzy. However, he had given Kizzy his word to help her resolve this. He would not go back on his word. William made the arrangements.

7

One weekend in early September as the weather began to cool, he drove Kizzy to a house out in the woods in upstate New York. The winds had been blowing hard that day.

Kizzy said, "Maybe these winds will blow away my troubles." She had never referred to the pregnancy as a baby, nor had she let him. Only two people were at the old house. Dirty and looking abandoned, the thought of her being in such a filthy place set the cleanliness fetish in William on an edge. William was forced to wait outside as the woman took Kizzy inside. William looked at the trees, flowers, anything he could to keep from thinking about what was going on inside that filthy house.

After only an hour and a half, but seeming like forever, the door opened. The woman had her arm around Kizzy. Kizzy, pale and looking downward, leaned against her. William asked if they were sure she was able to leave so soon. The man assured William she would be fine and just needed to rest until the anesthesia wore off. William handed the man an envelope with money inside. He quickly counted it and helped William put her in the back seat of the car. Kizzy lay on the seat limp, like her little rag doll, never saying a word. William began to drive. He had rented a house for several days not far from the old house—about a twenty-minute drive. Neither William nor Kizzy said any words. He heard her breathing and saw her as she lay on the seat in the rearview mirror. Some of her hair had been tossed, with some hanging down her back. Because she had faced the back of the seat, lying on her side, he could not see her face.

After they arrived at the house, he lifted her and carried her inside the cottage. She lay limp against him, looking down. After he put her to bed inside, he said, standing over her, "Someday Tom Hastings will pay for what he did to you. I promise!" Kizzy turned away from him. She slept the rest of the day and entire night. William read, checking on her periodically.

The next morning, William awakened to find Kizzy standing over him with a big smile on her face. She began talking rapidly, explaining how she wanted to stay a couple of days before going back to school.

When William asked how she was feeling, she exclaimed, spinning around with a big smile on her face, "What is to feel bad about in a beautiful place like this? I love it here, Uncle Wills."

William was happy to see the beautiful young woman back. William called the office and told them to cancel his appointments. He would not be in the office for several days.

The following few days were the most wonderful days of William's life. Kizzy ran through the wildflowers while he watched. He watched the sunlight shine through her hair, and through the delicate white dress she wore. Each sunbeam relished the curves of her divine body. He watched her as she sat and trickled the gentle sand of the fields through her bare toes. He watched her wade in the spring near the cottage as she held the bottom of her dress in her hands. The cloth draped across her beautiful, smooth legs. He watched her laugh as she splashed water on her face, her eyes looking like jade stones compared with the wet flesh of her face. Then tilting her head to one side, she splashed William with the water, giggling her special laugh the entire time. William began to realize that he had fallen in love with this timeless beauty. When he looked at her, he recognized in no way was she a child.

One evening Kizzy leaned against William as they stood out on the porch. The brightness of the starlight shone upon her skin. Her green eyes looked as if they were emeralds in the moonlight.

Her voice seemed different, more intense and exorbitantly sexy, "William, I can no longer call you Uncle. I love you. I love you so very much."

William kept telling himself that Kizzy was vulnerable. He tried desperately to quell what he was feeling, but found himself overcome by the moment. William had always been a man who never lost emotional dominion, or control of his thoughts, the people around him, or any situation, but when she had looked at him with those eyes, he could not stop. Shaking, he leaned forward. Their lips barely touched as he felt her breath against his face. He kissed Kizzy. He kissed her with great depth, but gently, trying to caress her soul the way she had touched his. It had been as though their souls had fused as one.

William increased his sabbatical from his office, not caring if he ever returned. He had searched his entire life to find a woman to love. He had never felt so much deep love inside him. William had lost constraint, for the first time in his life. He adored surrendering to his feelings. He did not care, at that moment, about anything or anybody except Kizzy. Each day his love grew stronger and stronger. He had not thought, only felt. However, they had not made love. He repressed that part of the relationship. He did not know whether she was ready for the physical side of their relationship. He would not take advantage of Kizzy's weakness at this point. He loved her too much for that. He worshiped everything about her. Everything about her was different, unique and so exorbitantly special. Her laughter, her voice, the thoughts running through her head, her abundant, endless energy, these things made Kizzy different from any other woman William had ever known.

The weeks flashed by as they reveled in every moment of their time together. William had been so blissful, and he believed he had made Kizzy happy.

8

The time to go home arrived. William was unable to take more time away from the office. Kizzy was quiet driving home. William thought she was disappointed at vacating their special Garden of Eden. After arriving home, in her usual way, Kizzy took her bags upstairs to her room, lay down on the bed and fell into a slumber. William looked in on her, gazing around her room. Every item in this room yelled "Kizzy". She had chosen the furniture, the fabric, and the decorations. They echoed her feelings, her tenderness, her special panache. Her bags stood in the corner, unpacked. From the dirty dishes on the night table to the clothes piled in the corner, this room was Kizzy. He looked at Kizzy asleep on the bed. He noticed the white bear she had cuddled in her arm, the lacy top of her canopy bed, the rag doll she had on the bedside shelf, and the stuffed dog laying on the bed beside her.

At that moment, reality hit him! She still was just a young girl! Where had the woman that he had loved at the cabin disappeared? William raced downstairs. The horror of the reality that he was in love with a girl crept inside him. He sat in his large overstuffed chair. His hands were shaking. *He* had lost control. He thought, how could I have let this happen? With sweat beaded on his face, he leaned forward, clasping his hands together against his forehead. Guilt flooded through him. He wondered, what am I going to do? She had been as a daughter to him, or a niece at the very least. He knew what had to be done! He had to stop these feelings and knew he could never make physical love to her. *Never* could it happen!

9

Kizzy threw her energy into school. She never mentioned Tom, the abortion, or the special days spent with William as though these things had ever happened. Kizzy slept in her own room, and William slept in his. The two of them returned to their previous uncle-niece relationship. Kizzy joined the drama club. She loved being on the stage. With Kizzy's ample energy and intensity, she became exceedingly good on the stage. Kizzy had always been a dramatic person. William believed it stemmed from the passionate side in her. He also believed it had been the practice with "milk moustaches." She received honorable mention in the local paper for her dramatic performances. The stage gave her the attention she so wanted and needed. It was all she thought about, talked about or dreamed about. At this time, she decided she might like to be a movie star, not an actress, but a movie star. Kizzy had so much ardor that an actress seemed boring to her, but bëing a movie star would be just her cup of tea!

William was incapable of believing it was time for her to graduate. She was eighteen years old. When he asked her what she wanted for a gift, she answered, "A new car or a trip to that great cabin we went to that time. Remember Uncle Wills? I loved it there! Yes, that's what I want even more than a car. But let's stay a long time this time."

William hesitated at hearing her response. He bought her the new car, a cute little sports car. Disappointment seemed to fill her eyes, when she had seen it.

He knew she had truly wanted to return to the cabin. Hesitant at first, with a cool head he thought it over. He was in control, so he made the arrangements.

10

The day after graduation, they drove together to the cabin. He had taken a month long hiatus from the office. She was so excited. Upon arriving, she eagerly ran through the fields. Kizzy picked a large bouquet of wildflowers to put on the table. They ate lunch together. The lunch was her favorite: hamburgers heaped with onion, chips and soda. Then she chased William around the cabin giggling, breathing her onion breath on him. Afterward they sat at the table finishing their soda while Kizzy questioned him about the names of every wildflower in the table bouquet. They sat on the porch that night watching the lightning bugs.

Later, during the night, William awakened to find Kizzy standing next to his bed. He was shocked and almost frightened. She looked at William seriously and said, "I want to be with you, please. I need to be with you. Don't send me away. You need to love me. I need to feel you touching me."

With a worrisome frown, William looked at her. "Kizzy, honey, please, don't do this. I can't let this happen," he begged.

"Why? Don't you love me? It's not as if you're my *real father*. This is only wrong if you were my real father. We're not any kind of blood relative. We're only kin on paper."

"Even so, I am *as* a father to you, Kizzy."

"No, you *were* like a father to me. Now, you are only a man to me. I need you, with all my heart. I'll beg if you want. If you don't love me, I might as well be dead. I lost one man I loved with my entire heart. Please, don't make me lose another man that I love with my entire heart!" she said, putting her hand against her heart.

"Kizzy, don't say that! Yes, I love you. You are my special kitten, remember?"

"Then hold me. Love me, not as your little Kitten Kizzy. Love me as Keziah, a woman who loves you so very much. Don't send me away. I couldn't stand it! Please." She pulled back the sheet and climbed in next to William. She snuggled against him and looked upward at William briefly. Their eyes seemed to fasten together. She was so tempting. Gently, he kissed her soft and moist lips. She fell asleep in his arms. William held her the entire night, but did not make love to her. He wanted to make love to her. He wanted her to love him just the way he yearned to love her. Powerless to slumber that night, he only watched her sleep in his arms, keeping constraint over his feelings. He did not give in to the manly love within him, even though it ached through every fiber of his being. She was so warm, smooth and soft laying in his arms. She had this natural sweet fragrance that radiated from her skin and hair. William felt relief as he saw daylight peeking through the curtains. The night had passed without him losing control. He felt relief, but not happiness.

However, Kizzy, filled with tenacity, did not abstain. As she pursued him, Kizzy weakened William. When Kizzy wanted something, nothing could stop her. She made it sound so right and logical. Chronically, to brainwash William, she echoed the words. He was only twenty years older than she, and they were not kin by blood, so why shouldn't they love each other? He had no logical argument. Maybe he was tired of arguing. Yet maybe he just wanted her with his entire heart.

The next evening while having dinner together, Kizzy came over and sat in his lap at the table. Poignantly, she looked in William's eyes with seriousness and said, "I want you. I want you at this moment, here, and won't wait anymore for you to love me. Please, please love me!" William knew Kizzy was a proud person. He knew it took a lot for her to say please. Almost in a drugged stupor, her charms intoxicated him. He was powerless to master himself any longer and wanted her as much as she wanted him. He kissed Kizzy, going deeper and deeper with each kiss to their souls. As he fell more in love with her with each kiss, his hands touched her hair, her face, her neck. He was helpless to stop. Before Kizzy, William had sex with many women. For the first time in his life, he was making love. She stirred feelings and sentiments in him that he had not thought were possible. Becoming lost in those resplendent green eyes, he never wanted to stop loving her, ever.

They had filled their days together with happiness and enjoyment. William found himself truly having fun. While using self-control taught to him by his father, he had restricted himself from having fun since his childhood. Now he and Kizzy were skinny dipping in the spring and sleeping next to each other every night. William would awaken in the night, just to make sure she was by his side. He was unable to believe this was happening to him. Feelings such as these could not be genuine, but must be dreamed. He would lie beside her and watch her sleep. Her hair would drape across her face and tickle her nose. She would coyly wipe it away and turn over. In his entire life, William knew he had never been in love like this.

Kizzy had a way of making you trust her with your soul. Once, he had seen a wild deer, a large buck with large horns, come close enough to Kizzy that she had petted it. She had been so gentle with that animal, and the wild animal had been so gentle with her. Even the wildest beast had been tamed by her innocence, beauty and love.

Maybe William was ineffective in *stopping* what was happening because he wanted her so badly. Kizzy possessed womanly allure no *man* had been able to *resist.* Not even William was in the possession of the strength to resist her. William had been familiar with many women in his day. He had been considered a lady's man. However, he had never been in love with a woman such as Kizzy. She took his breath away. Her energy in everything she did was the most arousing aphrodisiac to every inch of him. She made even the smallest task, like picking flowers, full of energy, excitement and beauty. He never wanted to let her go. He wanted to spend the rest of his life loving this vivacious electrifying woman!

11

Sadly, the month had to end, and William went back to work. After returning home, they were sleeping apart. Kizzy liked the independence of her own room. Things changed with Kizzy referring to him as William, instead of Uncle Wills. Many nights, Kizzy would slip beneath his covers next to him and they would make love. The feel of her soft, smooth, hot skin against William's chest, was weakening for him. She brought out unending fervor.

One day when William returned home, he found a note from Kizzy. In her note, she called him Uncle William. She explained she had gone away to Hollywood to become a movie star. She told him not to worry. She had borrowed money from his petty cash drawer, but had left an IOU. As soon as she was settled, she said she would write to him. She asked him to trust her and let her have this chance at fulfilling her dreams, demanding that he not follow her or make her return home. She said she would just run away again. William knew she meant it, so he did not try to find her. He knew she would only run away again. In frustration and agony, he destroyed the note. He knew the difference in their ages had taken her away from him. He knew that he had not replaced Tom Hastings in Kizzy's heart. William cried out so loud that the clouds moved from a fear that echoed throughout the heavens.

A few days later, William received another letter from Kizzy through the mail. She had arrived in Hollywood and had been staying with some young friends at the YWCA. For over a year, William received regular letters from Kizzy. They became the highlight to his life. Occasionally, he sent her money. She always sent back an IOU. Then, the letters became less frequent and stopped coming, altogether.

12

William became ill, suffering from emphysema. He sent Kizzy letters, but they were returned with no forwarding address.

William purchased the cabin in which he and Kizzy had found their special love. Even though she was gone, he would go to the cabin and sit with his thoughts of her. At least once a month, every month, he performed this ritual.

William had met and married a woman named Sylvia. For a couple of years they had been happy. Sylvia was a kind, astute woman. However, Sylvia was resentful of William's private time spent at the cabin.

One day Sylvia told him, "William, I do not blame you, but I know you don't love me. You love Kizzy, and you always will. I can't compete with her, and I am tired of trying. This house and that mysterious cabin are shrines to her." William knew Sylvia was right. Soon, their marriage ended sadly in divorce. William was alone. The sum of what he had left fully comprised the memories of Kizzy and their wonderful love.

13

William remembered the last words he had received from Kizzy, two years ago, on his fifty-eighth birthday. The beautiful card in the mailbox surprised him that day. He kept the simple card with a single flower on the front and carried it with him wherever he went.

14

Distracted from his reverie by the stifling heat of the taxi, William pulls out the frayed and wrinkled card. Worn from the times he had unfolded and folded it back over the years, he opens it with forbearance. Inside the card, Kizzy wrote:

William,

Sometimes the petals fall from the flower. Yet, it can remain beautiful. Happy Birthday!

All my love forever!
Kizzy

Kizzy sealed with her usual insignia, the kiss. William wonders what the inscription means and why she had written it. The postmark had been from Rio de Janeiro, but it had no return address. He has kept the card close to his heart. With great respect, William folds the card, placing it back inside his jacket pocket. The taxi cab pulls up in front of the attorney's office. William grabs his jacket. With handkerchief protecting his hand from the germs, he grips the door handle and opens the cab door. He pays the driver, giving a big tip, as he takes his one bag from the seat and stands outside the building. William looks upward at the skyscraper, a modern, almost solid glass building. He takes a deep breath, coughs, and thinks, damn this humidity! He wipes the perspiration from his forehead with a fresh handkerchief. He always carries several. Again using the handkerchief to protect his hand, he opens the door to the building and enters.

CHAPTER V

Tom Hastings

1

Tom had received a shocking and unexpected notice. Still, this thing is an incomprehensible shock. The notice listed him in Kizzy's will. He is taking the flight from Denver to Houston. The flight has cost him a fortune; in actuality, it put him to his limit on his credit card. He wonders how he is going to pay his hotel bill. In retrospect of the last time he saw Kizzy, he sits in the seat, gazing out at the billowy clouds.

2

About six years ago when in Houston for a game, he decided to stay awhile longer just to nose around the city. Because he had injured his knee in the last game, he was placed on medical furlough. Tom found the South immeasurably interesting with so many exceptionally tempting women. The women were a sweet mixture of beauty, brains, and sultry Southern persuasion that he had found only in Southern cities. Well, actually, he had been too hung over to make the flight back with the team. The irresistible women had been just an added incentive to stay and visit longer. He went down to the hotel lounge for a drink. He saw this breathtaking woman sitting at a table with a distinguished looking man, much older than she. His hair was thick and dark with slight gray on the temples, and his face was wrinkled giving away his older age. She was Southern essence with an unbelievable, sultry Southern look and the sparkling gleam of intelligence lurking behind those eyes. She had dark auburn hair and the most glamorous green eyes he had ever seen. Her hair was swept away from her face and pulled tightly back in a bun. With a sophistication and opulence, she exuded class.

Her long, expensive earrings lay softly against the side of her neck. The stones looked authentic. From time to time, methodically, seductively, she would put her forefinger nail against the right earring, touching and fondling it as it dangled. Occasionally without thinking, she moistened her full lips gently and slowly with her soft pink tongue. Her beige dress adhered to her body, accenting each divine curve, and many curves were present to accent. Tom was efficient in telling her curves had been genuine—a talent he had. He was always right. Tom never passed on a captivating woman. However, this woman was more than captivating. She was hypnotic. Tom was powerless to take his eyes off her, maybe because of her familiarity, or maybe just because she was so spellbinding. He slowly sipped one scotch after another, waiting patiently for the older man to depart, leaving her alone. The time crawled by as he waited for the man to vacate. At long last, she kissed the old guy on the cheek. He stood and left. Tom thought this could be his chance to make his move on her, but did not make his move. He was frozen as though in a spell. She pulled out a compact and began to slowly apply her lipstick. Tom watched each stroke of the lipstick against her lips. The color was soft and dignified, not adding too much hue to her lips, only accenting the beauty of her mouth. To watch this woman put on lipstick was almost a seduction. She saw him watching and smiled meekly, but seductively. Tom breathed harder and faster. For a moment, after finishing the application of the lipstick, she held the compact so that their eyes could meet in the mirror. Tom knew this was an intentional act on her part, but he had not cared. Her eyes were hypnotic, as if green stones held in front of his mind's eye, spinning, putting him in a trance or spell. Tom did not look away as it was a pleasurable spell. She walked over to Tom at the bar. She sat on the stool next to him and crossed her legs notably slow, watching him watch her legs. Tom was not able to take his eyes off her. He felt his stomach shivering, but was not chilled. She said, "Hi, Tom. Remember me?"

Her words dazed Tom. Nervously, he stroked his moustache. "No, honey, I don't. I don't think you're a woman a man could ever forget." Tom paused as his eyes scanned slowly over every inch of her.

Then, it happened. She laughed aloud, giggling his name with a childlike laugh that could only be Kizzy's. Tom was shocked.

"Kizzy? Kizzy, is it you?" She nodded and continued to giggle. The surprising, radiating newly found elegance from the little girl back home, astounded Tom. She had always been a beautiful young girl, but at this moment she was an *unbelievably* ravishing woman.

At first they sat together quietly just drinking. Kizzy smiled at him coyly, and Tom, shocked by the revelation of this ravishing woman, shook his head and smiled. Then the conversation began.

"Tom, I have really been following your career in the newspaper."

Tom blushed at her comment. "Yeah, I'm doing okay."

"Okay? You're doing great. It seems your dreams have come true for you. Haven't they?"

"Yeah. I guess they have. How about you, Kizzy?"

"Oh, me? I'm not doing anything so important."

"What are you doing? From the high-class, expensive clothes you're wearing, you must be doing something right, Kizzy."

"Well, I've been doing some modeling and some small bit parts. It pays the bills." Kizzy frowned and began her special way of sneezing.

Tom looked around and saw a man sitting behind them smoking a cigar. "You want to leave, Kizzy? I know how you and tobacco smoke get along."

With her eyes watering, Kizzy answered, "Oh, please." Kizzy and Tom walked together to the lobby. Comfortably, they sat together and talked.

The next two days they spent together. They went to the zoo and museum. While visiting the zoo, an incident made Kizzy laugh. They had been walking around the outside of the snake pit when they approached a man on a ladder. Kizzy ran under the ladder. "Come on, Tom!"

Tom insisted as he walked around the ladder, "I'll go around." As he reached the other side, Kizzy laughed and ran under the ladder to the other side.

"Damn it, Kiz. You know I don't like walking under ladders."

She laughed at him teasingly. "Scaredy cat! Tom, a big man like you and you're just a big ole scaredy cat!"

After some time, Tom coaxed her into coming through the ladder to his side. They walked together in the park. Tom was incredibly happy when he was with her, not even craving a drink. In some ways she had not changed at all. They talked about their old school days, old friends and memories of wonderful dates together. He remembered the wonderful way Kizzy made him feel all those years ago. She made him feel as if he was the most important person in the world. The only other person in the world whoever made him feel that special had been his mom. Because Tom was an only child, his mom had made sure the whole world revolved around him. His father had always been intoxicated, so his mother devoted her entire life to Tom.

One thing led to another, and soon, Tom and Kizzy found themselves making yielding and torrid love in his hotel. Tom had never realized what he had missed by leaving her. Tom fondled her pretty, dark auburn hair allowing it to fall slowly from his fingers. It was like spun silk thread, shimmering in the light. He found himself lost in her green eyes. He held her smoothness and softness tightly against his chest. Her tiny, womanly body had made her feel like a living doll in his arms.

After they finished making love, Kizzy began to speak. "I know you will leave me again, Tom, just as before." Before Tom could respond, she continued. "But it's okay. Loving you at this moment is all I need. You are all I want. You are all I have ever wanted."

He found it impossible to desert her again. Kizzy was wonderful in every way. In Kizzy, Tom had found the most imaginative, sensual lover that he had ever encountered in his entire life. However, it was not just the physical aspect of their relationship. Tom had not taken one drink the entire time they had been together. He had not even wanted a drink. She somehow filled a great compulsion inside him that he usually filled with alcohol. Her energy intrigued him. Tom's words to Kizzy poured from him so easily. Sharing his thoughts, dreams and ideas was easy for Tom with Kizzy, so natural. "Someday when I'm too old to play football anymore, Kizzy, I am going to be an NFL coach. I'm going to have the best Super Bowl team ever! Then, I'm going to have summer football clinics for little kids. What do you think?"

"I think it's great. So, you like little children? Well, remember, not all dreams come true, Tom. I know." Tom held her close because she seemed to need comforting. Then, they went out for dinner.

A few things about her were puzzling to him. She never allowed him to call her or take her home. She tried to explain that the mystery made it stimulating.

One day, Tom awakened to find her gone. He waited for days for her to call. He paced and drank, but Kizzy never returned. He checked with the bartender trying to find someone who knew where she lived. No one acknowledged ever knowing Kizzy. He searched through the phone book for her name or number. She was not listed. He desperately phoned the telephone information operator. The operator declined giving out her number, explaining that it was unlisted at her request. Tom had no choice.

She had melted into the mystery of oblivion.

3

Distraught, he returned to Denver for knee surgery. Several years later, he injured his knee permanently during a football game. He had been through several surgeries, but none of them helped. He had never seen or heard from Kizzy after that magical time in the hotel. Yet, the last six years, he had thoughts of her often—the way she had looked in the bar that night, the way she had smelled, the soft caress of her lips against his, the special magic that had been between them. It had been a magic he had never found again since Kizzy.

4

Tom rubs his cramped knee. With no place to stretch out his leg, he thinks they do not make plane seats for tall people. His thoughts return to the past. He remembers Kizzy, the young girl he left in New York those years ago. Tom remembers the first time he had kissed Kizzy.

5

She had been looking at him and smiling. She had been so tiny that she had to stand on the porch steps at William's. Tom had known she idolized him. He had loved that fact, making him feel important, as a man. Once he had entered college his time had become too scarce. He had stopped writing, not because he stopped caring, but because there just was not enough time. He had been dating many other girls, too. The girls at the college had been eager to be with Tom, the big successful football player. The last letter Tom had received from Kizzy had burned a painful hole in his memory.

Tom,
I love you so much. I miss you so much. I'm thinking of trying out for the school play. I have been practicing in front of my mirror. Uncle Wills has been wonderful, but he always is. He tries to keep me busy so I won't miss you so much. He took me shopping and bought me three brand-new outfits. They're my favorite color, green. Remember how you love me in green? We went out for hamburgers three times last week.

Yes, I had extra onions.

Love you always,

Kizzy

6

"Excuse me, sir," the stewardess says jolting Tom back to the present.

"Yeah, yeah."

"Can I get you something to drink?"

"Scotch on the rocks," Tom answers and grumbles. "I hope it's strong." The stewardess hands Tom the drink. Instead of sipping it, he gulps it down. As the liquor burns his throat, his eyes water. He thinks that maybe the scotch will kill the pain in his knee. Sighing, he shifts his body around in the uncomfortable airline seat and returns his thoughts to the past.

Tom recollects how the words of Kizzy's letter made him feel as he read it. William was always important to her. Tom hated that fact. Good ole William gave his time, an effort Tom had been unable to fulfill.

7

The memories of their youth together and Kizzy were wonderful. Once at the county fair while Kizzy visited the ladies' room and he waited outside, several wonderful young girls approached and were flirting with him. Tom did not refuse their attention. Kizzy left the restroom and angrily kept walking to get away from him. He followed her pleading, "Kizzy, you have to understand. All they do is make me feel important. I need that feeling, Kiz."

Kizzy turned to face him with a sympathetic look upon her face.

"I need that attention, babe. If I don't have it, I think I will die."

Kizzy reached out and hugged Tom. "It's okay, Tom. I understand. I guess after living with such a confident man as Uncle Wills, I forget other men have needs. He is so self-sufficient. Don't feel bad. I love you, Tom."

Tom hugged her back, but he felt animosity at her comment about William. Tom always thought she felt William was a better man than he.

Tom loved the football games where he knew that he could turn around and see Kizzy staring at him, cheering him on to victory. Tom remembered the movies and the nights parked in the woods. That most special, wonderful night, when they first consummated their relationship. She had lay against him holding him tightly and weeping the largest tears. He thought he had hurt her physically. She was quick to explain that her tears were filled with happiness. He knew her love was genuine, unconditional, precious and so pristine.

8

The plane hits an air pocket and jolts slightly, bringing Tom back to the present. Tom wipes the sweat from his forehead with his bare hand. The heat in this plane, or maybe the thoughts of Kizzy, still broach a sweat in him. Sometimes the air conditioning on these planes leaves a lot to desire. Reaching, he tries to adjust the air conditioning by turning the little vent knob. However, no more air is emitted. He wipes the sweat again from his forehead. He notices the woman beside him, holding a young child in her lap. The child appears as though she is a little girl. As his eyes gaze out the window at the clouds, his mind starts to wander back to Kizzy. The clouds look murky somehow as he recalls one day.

9

He had taken Kizzy shopping during the wonderful time that they had spent together in Houston. She adored shopping. For Kizzy, shopping was as breathing, a requirement. She would try on clothes for hours, even clothes she had no interest in buying. She was a saleslady's nightmare. One day, she bolted unexpectedly over to the baby department, wearing a hat with a price tag hanging off it. She became serious and somber, which was out of character for Kizzy. "Tom, look at the baby things. This little hat would match the one I am wearing. Maybe I should buy them. They're very nice. Don't you think?"

Before Tom was able to answer, she disappeared in the dressing room.

She dropped the baby hat on the floor. Tom noticed she had torn the sales tag from the little hat. Later, when she came out, he tried to question her strange behavior. "Why did you act like that with the little baby hat, Kizzy?"

In the way usual to Kizzy, she ignored him and answered, "I don't know what you are talking about." Before Tom was able to speak further, she said, "I'm starved. Let's go get a hamburger overflowing with onions. I'll go pay for these items." Tom never got an answer about her strange behavior. He figured she must have made excellent money modeling and acting because she bought tons of expensive clothes and paid cash.

10

Back in the present, Tom pulls up from his airline seat and goes staggering to the men's room. He washes his face with water, trying to cool off. He looks in the mirror, feels nauseous, but only dry heaves.

11

His memory takes him back to one morning in his hotel room when he looked in the mirror and saw Kizzy standing behind him. He could still remember her voice and her special words.

"Tom, you've always been so handsome and so big. I feel helpless in your arms, as though you could crush me with one big mighty, squeeze. I always loved that, almost as much as I loved you. You are so very special to me, Tom. You will always be the most special man to me!" She then gently turned him around. Tom, loving the statement, but feeling a little embarrassed at the compliment, looked down at her and clinched his lips, shyly. Kizzy tickled the hair on his moustache, laughing. Then she placed her little finger from each hand in each of his dimples. She searched his eyes with hers and said in a serious tone of voice aberrant for Kizzy, "I almost fell into those dimples and became lost forever. Sometimes I wish that I had with all my heart."

Without warning, she changed the mood, broke the embrace, and said whimsically with a false heavy Southern dialect, "You're a powerful man, Tom Hastings." Then, she ran away laughing playfully.

Tom ran after her and caught her on the bed. As he held her tightly in his arms, he said, "Tell me again that good shit about my good looks, babe!"

Kizzy smiled. "Let's see. Your brown eyes are captivating. Your muscles are overwhelming. Your lips are delicious. And those dimples—" Tom kissed her deeply at this point and never let her finish.

12

As he stands in the airplane lavatory, Tom observes the time on his watch. Tom gathers himself together and goes back to his seat. The stewardess brings him another drink as he has ordered. Is it his third, or is it his fourth? He cannot remember. Tom has been drinking a lot since he was forced to quit football. He has squandered the money he had made during his football career, wasting it on frivolous, foolish things. He has tried his hand at coaching, unsuccessfully. At this time, he is a broke, failure of a car salesman. Not even successful at selling cars, his manager is always pushing him to sell more. Lately, selling cars has been tougher than usual for him. Selling was never really easy, but standing on his bum knee throughout the day talking to people is painfully impossible. Tom has not reached the company-required quota in the last few months. He knows it is only a matter of time until they will fire him. What can he try next? He has sold insurance, managed a sporting goods store, worked in the city tax office, driven a beer delivery truck, and now sold cars. Nothing has been successful for him since football. Maybe football was more than a way to make a living. Football was his life. No, football *is* his life. He misses the game, the adoring cheers from the crowd, and oh yes, the money! Football was Tom's only way of life, but now only a memory.

For some reason, Tom is dreading the reading of the will. He can use the money, that is for sure! However, Tom hates the way he is getting this money.

The plane arrives at Houston Intercontinental Airport. Tom leaves the plane and enters the airport. After retrieving his luggage, he takes notice of his hands. They are shaking. He feels weak with his nerves on edge. He goes inside the airport bar for just one more drink, orders a scotch and views his watch. Running late, he gulps down the drink. As it goes down, it burns, making his eyes water. He takes a deep breath, and retrieves his luggage from beside the barstool.

Tom takes a cab to the office building of the attorney. As he stumbles from the cab, he knows his drinks are beginning to take their toll. The cab driver, noticing Tom's inebriation, helps him with his few pieces of luggage—deserting him and the luggage on the sidewalk outside the building. He only has enough money to pay the cab bill, but not give a tip. The cab drives away. Tom bends over to lift the luggage. His head is splitting with pain. Overwhelming him with misery, he pauses for a moment as the hurting in his head staggers him. He thinks that he sure could use another drink. No, he *needs* another drink desperately. His knee is paining him terribly. This bum knee is the only thing football has left him. He rubs his knee before lifting the luggage, sucking in the pain between his teeth.

After he enters the building, Tom stops at the water fountain in the lobby. He takes a pain pill the doctor has prescribed for his knee. He knows he needs surgery again on his knee, but he does not have the money to cover the medical bills. After pausing for a moment gazing at his reflected image in the glass covering the building directory, Tom touches his moustache, fondling the individual hairs. It is not a happy sight. His eyes are bloodshot, and he looks dreadful and feels loathsome. His ruby nose is exceedingly swollen. What would Kizzy say if she could see him? He tries, but he cannot hear her words in his head. The fact is that the truth is staring at him in the reflection. Seeing himself, fat, red faced, and tired looking, Tom knows he is a drunk, just as his father was. He finds no pride in the fact and almost feels sick at the sight. Tom rationalizes, maybe if he had never left Kizzy, their lives would have been different. Maybe she would be alive. Maybe he would look forward to living. Tom sighs, filled with repulsion. He refocuses his eyes and finds the attorney's name and suite number in the building directory. With luggage in hand, he enters the elevator, staggering

CHAPTER VI

Jimmy

1

In his taxi cab, Jimmy sits in Houston traffic, thinking how awesome it is being mentioned in Kizzy's will. He is ecstatic about the possibility of receiving money. He figures she owes him, but has never come across with any payments to Jimmy. Jimmy is not the polished sort of man. His childhood was spent on the slum-filled streets of Chicago, New York City, Houston, Dallas, Atlanta and Birmingham. No one has ever given him anything. Jimmy looks in the mirror. He is not so young anymore. Lines are beginning to show around his eyes. But, hey, he still turns the ladies' heads. He has radiant, dark blue eyes. He combs his dark hair back. The cleft in his chin always is a draw with the ladies. Jimmy still likes what he sees in the mirror staring back. With approval, he smiles. Jimmy straightens his shirt, clenching the cigarette butt between his lips. Damn, won't this light ever turn green? He does not have all day! Jimmy's mind wanders back through time.

2

Jimmy met Kizzy in a Los Angeles audition while making a shampoo commercial. She was supposed to be in a shower with suds on her hair. He remembered the way the suds dripped over her thick, dark eyelashes into her gorgeous green eyes. His job was to enter the shower and join her. You know, one of those "sex sells" commercials. Then, in the next scene, her hair would have been beautiful, and he would have sniffed and touched it. Anyway, they did their part, but the shampoo people said that Jimmy and Kizzy did not have enough chemistry on the screen. Boy, had they ever been blind! The commercial was canceled, at least as far as Kizzy and Jimmy were concerned. As he was leaving, Jimmy lit a cigarette and stood on the steps shaking his right leg as was his usual custom. He noticed Kizzy was sitting out on the steps of the building crying. Her large tears tugged at Jimmy's heart. The tears clustered her thick, dark, long eyelashes together. He was usually immune to women's tears, but not Kizzy's.

Jimmy, sucking on his cigarette, asked, "So what the hell is the matter with ya?"

"I'm just tired and hungry. Do you have to smoke that right here?"

"Yeah! Shit! If you don't like it, you move!" Jimmy answered rudely. "Damn broad!"

Kizzy began to sneeze three quick ones in a row. "Oh, what does it matter! I have no home. I got thrown out of my apartment today and don't know where I'm going to go!" she said, crying.

Jimmy stamped out his cigarette and sat on the step beside her. "Hey! Don't cry! It's Kizzy, ain't it?"

She nodded, but did not stop crying. Jimmy felt sorry for her, as he would a stray cat. He tried to change the subject to stop her from sobbing. "So how long ya been in town, Kizzy?"

"About three years," she whimpered between tears, "here in Hollywood. Your name is Jimmy, right?"

"Yeah. So are commercials the only thing you've done?"

"No, I've done some modeling—"

"That's no wonder," Jimmy said under his breath, turning his head away from her while speaking.

"What did you say? I'm sorry I didn't hear you."

"Nothin'. Go on. What else have ya done here?"

"I have also done some babysitting, waiting tables, acting, you know, bit parts and, of course, the commercials."

"Hey, look, Kizzy. I—I got a small apartment, not even large enough for your tits. You can crash with me a couple of days until ya get on your feet. Is this your shit?" Jimmy asked looking around at the bags sitting beside her on the steps.

"Yes," Kizzy said elated with happiness as she hugged Jimmy's neck. "Oh, you're wonderful, Jimmy!"

"Yeah, yeah, get your shit, Kizzy," Jimmy said pulling her tightly clasped arms from around his neck, not enjoying her blatant show of affection.

Kizzy was the typical "small town girl coming to Hollywood to be famous story". The story was typical across the city. Jimmy's apartment was just one small room with an even smaller bathroom. A small counter stood in one corner with a hot plate and a small refrigerator. Instantly, Kizzy moved in with only her few meager belongings. Jimmy was a good-looking weight lifter in those days. He was tall and lean and filled out his clothes. At first, it was only a friendly relationship, even though they slept in the same bed. Sometimes, she would cuddle against Jimmy in her sleep. He would awaken feverish and sweaty. He would look at her and try to push her away. However, with great unconscious persistence, she would cuddle against him again, without ever waking. Kizzy hated Jimmy's cigarette smoking. She had almost forbidden him to smoke in his own apartment. They had several arguments over his smoking habit. Their relationship had never been anything but friendship until this point in time.

One night, in her usual frolicsome mood, Kizzy said, "So Jimmy, are you gay?"

The thought appalled him. Jimmy had always thought of himself as an extremely masculine man, totally heterosexual. "Are ya screwy? I'm no *shittin' homo!* Look at me! Does this look like the body of a *homo?"* he screamed at Kizzy. To make his point, he threw her on the bed forcefully, denying explicitly any homosexual feelings. Deeply, he looked in Kizzy's splendid green eyes. To reinforce his heterosexuality, without thinking, he found himself kissing her. Kizzy, impassioned, profoundly returned his kiss. The kisses were deep, caressing his being. He had never felt a kiss like this one. Well, that was all it took! Emotion Jimmy had suppressed came tumbling forth, covering Kizzy with his passion. Incapable of looking away, he looked deeply into her green eyes. He touched her smooth, soft skin beneath his calloused hands. She held her breath and closed her eyes when he touched her. He crushed her gently beneath his muscular physique. They made love the entire night. Cries of passion from them rang throughout the apartment and perhaps throughout the building. Jimmy had made his point strongly. Kizzy never asked whether he was gay again.

Jimmy abstained from his cigarette smoking for Kizzy. She explained that she had an allergy to tobacco smoke. From that day forward, they slept together every night as lovers. He loved waking to find her next to him in the morning. He loved the way she would help him read the newspaper in the morning since he had very little formal education. Kizzy was patient and taught him a lot about reading. Because they were a couple in love, he even thought of proposing marriage to Kizzy. He wanted to spend his life with her. Jimmy found Kizzy the most arousing lover ever, generating a bodily excitement throughout the atmosphere. She had so much passion, abounding energy and imagination.

Many nights she awakened screaming from nightmares. Kizzy always insisted that Jimmy promise he would not leave her. Jimmy held her tightly in his arms and said, "I promise, doll. I'll never leave ya, ever. Doll, even the bad times with you are good. I ain't goin' nowhere!" In a short time, she fell asleep in his arms. Jimmy never knew what the nightmares were about.

Work had became scarce for Jimmy and Kizzy in the tinsel city. She was not happy when money was scarce. Not even enough money was available for food. She said angrily, "I'd kill for a hamburger overflowing with onions right now!" She was temperamental and paced like a cat in a cage.

"Yeah, I know. I'd love a shittin' cigarette, Kizzy," Jimmy spouted and continued swearing.

"You and your stupid cigarettes! Is that all you ever think about, Jimmy?" Just at that time, the electricity was disconnected. The room became dark, pitch black.

Jimmy was unable to see Kizzy. "Shit! Damn it, I can't see! Where are ya, Kizzy? I *hate* the shittin' dark."

"Over here, Jimmy. Don't be such a baby. The dark can't hurt you."

Jimmy found Kizzy in the dark. Shaking, he held on tightly to her.

"What is wrong with you, Jimmy? Why are you squeezing me so tight? Why are you so scared?" Kizzy asked.

Jimmy thought back in time to his childhood. "When I was about five, my mom married this guy who was involved with the mob. He was a mean son of a bitch! One night because I wouldn't eat the shittin' supper he thought I should, he locked me in a dark closet. He and my mom went out somewhere. They left me locked in that damn shittin' closet for two days and two nights. I don't know. I just ain't been able to take the dark since then."

"I'm sorry, Jimmy. You poor thing. That was an awful thing for that man to do. Your own mother left you alone locked in that closet!" Kizzy pulled Jimmy close to her, placing her arms around his head and laying it in her lap. She stroked his hair gently until he fell asleep.

The next day Jimmy sold some blood to get money to turn on the electricity. Kizzy tried to sell blood also, but her weight was too low.

3

One night while Jimmy and Kizzy stood outside a ritzy, exclusive restaurant trying to make valuable movie industry contacts, a man asked Kizzy whether she would sleep with him for money. Jimmy was so embittered that he punched the man without thinking. The thought of another man touching her made Jimmy sick. Before the police had arrived, Kizzy and he ran away. Kizzy found this exhilarating, giggling loudly the entire time they ran. Jimmy promised her while they ran, "Someday we'll be rich, doll. Just wait and see."

After that incident, Jimmy noticed something different about Kizzy. She never liked to wrestle around on the bed anymore. She became more serious and pondering. Their lovemaking also changed drastically. Kizzy somehow lost the tender passion she previously enjoyed. Her actions became robot-like, as though the feeling had left her soul and heart.

The nightmares came much more frequently. However, she was incapable of talking about them with Jimmy.

One week, Kizzy was gone for three days and nights straight. Jimmy searched everywhere for her without success. He was ready to go to the police, when she just appeared at home, acting as though she had never been gone. While watching her, Jimmy sat at the table tapping his fingers nervously, trying to gather the courage to question her.

"Will you stop that damn tapping, Jimmy? It drives me nuts!" she said, greatly irritated.

"So, where in the hell have you been, Kizzy?"

"What business is it of yours where I have been?"

"I've been shittin' worried, Kizzy. I thought something might've happened to ya!"

"You sound like an old man, Jimmy, worrying all the time! Lighten up, will you?"

"So why don't ya just answer my damn shittin' question, Kizzy?" Jimmy said finishing his comment with more obscene expletives.

"Shut up! Mind your own business! I don't need this third degree, Jimmy!" Such an outburst was an unexpected reply for Kizzy. Usually, she was a patient and loving soul. She told him angrily, "You don't own me. Nobody will ever own me! If you try, I will leave! Don't push me, Jimmy! Don't!"

Angry at her threat, Jimmy left the apartment and stayed at a friend's for a few days. Unable to eat or sleep, he discovered that the deep tenderness he had been feeling for Kizzy was considerably overwhelming. No matter how bitter he was, he was helpless when it came to avoiding her. He missed Kizzy terribly—her touch, her voice, everything about her. When he returned home to the apartment, he noticed Kizzy had not been there.

However, she returned home that night. Everything seemed to be fine. In his usual nervous way, Jimmy tapped his fingers on the table, staring at her and looking away when she returned the glance.

After some time, he mustered enough nerve to begin the conversation. "So, where have ya been all this time, Kiz?" Jimmy asked.

"Well, I've been to San Francisco."

"What for?" Jimmy pursued.

"I went to try out for an opening in a play up there. It was a waste of time. I didn't get the part." Usually, Kizzy was always depressed after losing a part, pouting for days, scoffing around the apartment mumbling to herself. However, she was not this time.

"So you don't seem upset, Kiz. How come?" Jimmy asked, puzzled by her behavior.

"Let's not talk about that, Jimmy," she said as she wrapped her arms around him, pulling him close.

Jimmy had missed her so much. The questions seemed trivial. Holding her at that moment and regaining the love that they had shared were the only important things to Jimmy. For Jimmy, making love to Kizzy suddenly made the questions he had been simmering in his brain look unimportant. During their lovemaking Jimmy whispered, "I love ya, Kizzy. If I have to share you with this secret side of ya, I will. I can't lose ya, doll. I love you far too much." Kizzy kissed him and fell asleep in his arms. He forgot the questions, accepting and respecting her privacy, independence and mystery. This was a part of Kizzy. Maybe it was a highly exciting part of her to Jimmy. Jimmy knew that if he loved her, he would have to live with this part of her, and so he had.

4

The horn honks loudly, bringing Jimmy back to the present. Startled, Jimmy looks in his rearview mirror and blurts out an obscenity at the honking driver behind him. He steps on the accelerator and speeds down the street. Gee, the humidity is high today. The air conditioner in his cab is not working right. He beats on it with his fist and bellows profanity. Cars ahead are stopped, just as he has made it to the freeway—wonderful Houston traffic! Oh great! Jimmy stops in line with the other vehicles. He rolls down his window and quickly rolls it back up when exhaust fumes from the old car in front pour inside the cab. Jimmy coughs and makes a lascivious gesture through the exhaust smoke to the driver. Jimmy sits in the traffic, sucking on a cigarette, thinking and drumming his fingers nervously on the steering wheel remembering the last day he saw Kizzy.

5

Jimmy and Kizzy had been living together almost two years. She had become independent, going and coming as she pleased. He had never been allowed to question her, or she threatened to leave him. Jimmy had known that having a part of her was better than having none of her. Jimmy had fallen deeper in love with her than he ever thought had been possible. Mad as it made him that he had been helpless in questioning her, losing her would have been devastating. Still, they had been fighting more and more.

One day, Jimmy asked Kizzy to go to their favorite spot, a pool hall. Jimmy had done a little hustling there from time to time for money. Kizzy usually loved to go. Jimmy remembered the conversation as if it were yesterday.

"What is wrong with you, Jimmy? I don't like going to trashy places like that!" she snapped.

"Well, your majesty, let me roll out your red carpet," he said playfully.

"Shut up!" she said, throwing a dirty glass at him that had been sitting on the bedside table.

"Okay, so how about cleaning up some around here? This place looks like a shitttin' pig pen. I'm tired of doin' all the cleaning myself, Kizzy!"

"You sound as if you are William! I don't need this, Jimmy!"

"Who in the hell is William?" Jimmy asked never hearing the name before.

"It doesn't matter! I'm not *'into'* cleaning. Okay, Jimmy?" she screamed, pointing her finger at him.

"So, what in the hell are ya 'into,' Kiz, tell me!" Jimmy yelled back at her following with additional obscenities.

"*Screw it!* I'm out of here! I warned you, Jimmy," she said with a piece of luggage in her hand. She began to throw clothes inside the luggage. Jimmy snatched the luggage from her and threw it across the room.

"No, Kizzy!" Jimmy yelled as he grabbed her holding her tight in his arms. Kizzy shrieked and beat her fists against him.

"Okay! Okay, doll. I'm sorry. I won't ask questions. I won't tie ya to me. I swear! Damn, don't leave me!"

Kizzy stopped hitting him and leaned her head against his chest. "I really do love you, Jimmy."

"I know, doll! I know," Jimmy said, holding her tightly.

"Please, don't leave me, Jimmy. I can't be alone!" she said.

Jimmy was distressed and puzzled by her words. *She* had been the one just packing to part company, *not him.* However, Jimmy did not question her.

"Leave you? Never! Never, Kizzy," he said, holding her.

From that point on, Kizzy never seemed to kid around anymore. She seemed irritable constantly. Jimmy missed their capricious frolicking, but loving her was all he needed.

One evening a couple of days later, while driving around with a friend, Jimmy made a startling discovery. When they drove by the same restaurant where Kizzy had been propositioned a couple of years ago, Jimmy's friend said, "Whoa, Jimmy! Look at that sensational looking blonde whore!" Jimmy glanced at her. His friend was right. She was luscious. She had the kind of look that takes a man's breath away. Jimmy, who looked closer, was astonished, seeing those majestic green eyes. It was his Kizzy. He almost wrecked the car because of his preoccupation at looking at her.

"*Shit! Damn it*, I know her!" Jimmy spouted loudly. He had almost not recognized her. She was wearing a revealing, flashy red dress and a long, curly blonde wig. Heavy makeup, including bright red lipstick, was covering her face. Kizzy usually wore tasteful, understated makeup, only enough to accent her natural beauty. Jimmy parked up the street, because his old car had not been the kind permitted to park around this classy restaurant. The two men walked to the entrance of the restaurant. Jimmy tried to go inside the restaurant, but the doorman stopped him.

"Man, how do you know her, Jimmy?" his friend questioned.

Jimmy remembered his agitated feelings at this point. "I know her very, very well! Just leave it at that! I ain't leavin' until I talk to her!" Jimmy and his friend waited outside. Jimmy stood there shaking his leg nervously.

About an hour later, she came out with a man. Jimmy approached and grabbed her arm, "Kizzy, what the hell are you doing with this shittin' guy?"

The man turned to Kizzy and asked her whether she knew Jimmy. Kizzy looked coldly at Jimmy and said, "I've never seen this man before in my life." She then laughed to humiliate Jimmy. Sickened and hurt, Jimmy released her arm. Kizzy climbed in a foreign luxury car with the man and drove away, never looking back.

Much later that night, she returned home, wearing the same dress, but absent the makeup and wig and carrying her shoes. Jimmy had been waiting for her, smoking, pacing, drumming his fingers on the table and shaking his right leg nervously. Kizzy began her usual three little sneezes, frowning from the cigarette smoke. "How many times do I have to ask you not to smoke in here, Jimmy? It drives me nuts."

Jimmy angrily snuffed out the cigarette in the sink and asked, "Was that *William* you were with, Kizzy?"

"What? Are you *crazy*? That wasn't William!"

"You looked like a cheap assed whore tonight, Kizzy! Is that what you are?" Jimmy asked. Kizzy ignored him and busied herself with packing her clothes.

Jimmy, who was intensely fuming, grabbed her arm and spun her around. Kizzy firmly pulled away. Jimmy slapped her knocking her onto the bed. With an icy cold stare, Kizzy unemotionally stood. Jimmy had never seen this look on Kizzy's face. Jimmy grabbed her and stroked her cheek gently. "Oh! I—I'm so sorry, doll. I've never hit a woman before. I shouldn't have hit ya! Forgive me, Kiz! Please, forgive me!" Jimmy pleaded holding her tightly. Then, he looked deeply into her eyes and kissed her passionately, hoping to spark the longing they had previously felt—a passion Jimmy was still feeling. Kizzy lay in his arms, limp, showing no passion, love or sentiment. After the kiss, Kizzy spit in his face with disgust. Jimmy released her and wiped the saliva from his face. He was unable to believe she had done this to him. The hurt was great, an emotional pain new to Jimmy and unfelt before now. He had never let anyone get close enough to hurt him. Kizzy had been different. Neither of them said a word. Jimmy was shocked because she was so cold and aloof. Kizzy hoisted her bags and left. Jimmy gazed out the window watching her as the starlight brilliance of the sullen raven sky swallowed her. He never saw her again.

After visiting a friend in Houston a couple of years later, Jimmy left Hollywood. He remembered Houston from his childhood. He did a little catalog modeling on the side in Houston. His friend helped him get the taxi cab job, so he stayed in Houston.

6

Jimmy's memories vacate him. Gazing at his own reflection in the rearview mirror, he swallows down the lump in his throat. He has forgotten how much she had meant to him at one time. No woman has ever spurred so much emotion—hate and love—from him. He feels weak, maybe from the heat, or maybe from the sentiment he is feeling. Jimmy did not see the article in the newspaper about her death. He is no big reader. After all, it had been Kizzy who had taught him to read the little that he could. Now, she is gone forever.

The traffic starts to move. Jimmy lights a cigarette and flips the radio knob in his usual impatient way, searching rapidly for a station, never satisfied with any tune playing. He hits an oldie station. A beautiful song by a popular male duo starts to play. The song is so familiar. Jimmy's thoughts once again return to Kizzy.

7

He remembers a night in the early period of their love when this song played on the apartment radio. Slowly, he danced with her in his arms. She sang the song softly, just loud enough for him to hear. Barefoot and dancing on her toes, she stretched herself taller upward toward him. She was wearing only a simple, loose-fitting blue dress, looking so innocent and sweet and smelling of fresh soap and shampoo. He felt so loved and needed that night. Such a beautiful memory is insufferable for Jimmy.

8

He pushes the memory back within his mind. Kizzy had hurt him unduly. By remembering this, he feels he is letting her hurt him over again. Jimmy knows he is not stupid. Only a stupid fool allows the same broad to hurt him twice in a lifetime.

Again, he searches through the stations trying to forget the emotion these thoughts of Kizzy have stirred within him. These are emotions he would rather forget. Jimmy does not like feeling emotion. During his childhood on the streets, he learned early that emotion is a sign of weakness. Jimmy hates feeling vulnerable and weak. He moves along slowly in the traffic. Later, he arrives at the building and parks his cab.

CHAPTER VII

C.D.

1

C.D. Casmiersky runs his fingers through his salt-and-pepper hair and straightens his rigid, white collar, thinking of Kizzy as he does. She used to tell him it was a waste for a man who looked as good as he did to be a priest. This thought brings a smile to his face. He knows she had meant it, but not in a disrespectful way. C.D. is a devoted Catholic priest. He recollects with thoughts of that special lady, Kizzy.

Kizzy had never shocked him, but she had always puzzled and surprised him. C.D. had always been a responsible Catholic who followed the rules. Yet, over and over again, he had broken the rules for Kizzy. She was not Catholic and had never promised to change her religion. Yet she had been compelled to confess things to him. C.D.'s intuition told him that she had been a lonely, desperate soul, fighting to survive. Somehow she had seemed to always touch him deeply within his heart in a way no one else was able. C.D. had known in his heart that our creator, God, had made a beautiful world, the flowers, trees, children, mountains. He believed in his heart that Kizzy had been one of God's masterpieces. He remembered his first sight of Kizzy.

2

His first appointment in the priesthood was in the Los Angeles area. He was in his early twenties, and so was Kizzy. At an apple stand, outside a fresh produce store, one of the few in the city, Kizzy arrived and purchased an apple. In a coy way, she watched C.D.. C.D. was unable to *not* notice her. Her hair was long, full, and hanging softly down her back. He noticed the loveliness of her mouth as she bit into the apple and said,

"Ummmm—good." C.D. could see the deepness of her exquisite dimples as she had expressively clenched her lips.

She then giggled and said, "What's up, Doc, I mean Father?" C.D. was at a loss for words. She crunched her teeth in her apple. The juice of the apple ran out unto her cheek and down her chin, and it dripped from her tiny hand. She seemed younger than he was in so many ways with such a trusting innocence about her. She abounded with energy, reminding C.D. of a flawless butterfly flitting here and there. The two of them began conversing, and she followed him back to the church. Filled with a million and one questions, she questioned Catholicism and the philosophy of life. Somehow they had gotten on the subject of helping street people. C.D. had not known how they had approached this subject, since Kizzy had been changing subjects at the drop of a hat. Her mind seemed to move quickly, much faster than his could ever move. C.D. told her of his soup kitchen and how they helped the hungry. They had been giving people food and a warm, safe place to sleep for the night. Kizzy was excited and wanted to help.

She loved helping people. She shared with them her energy and zest for life. She had this wonderful way of reaching even the most lost soul and giving it consolation and hope. This was a true gift of Kizzy's. Kizzy worked in the soup kitchen for many weeks. C.D. caught her several times partaking of the soup herself, but never approached her about the subject. He believed Kizzy to be hungry herself. Kizzy would scrape the scraps from the dishes and put them out for the stray dogs and cats. She had an intolerance to anything or anyone being hungry or needy. She had a heart the size of Texas. C.D. and Kizzy became incredibly close friends. Her childlike quality was refreshing at times, especially when caring for the street people. She was so gentle when gentleness was required, and funny and lighthearted when humor was needed. C.D. was thankful to God for making a creature so sublime in every way. Whenever he was feeling down and depressed for any reason, Kizzy would somehow lift his spirits. He wondered sometimes who the teacher was and who the student was in this relationship.

C.D. had a strong passion for photography. Kizzy made a beautiful subject. She loved the attention. He had taken pictures of her serving, eating, walking in the garden and just living. Capturing the light of her spirit behind those dazzling eyes on film was an obsession with C.D.

After a short time, Kizzy's visits became less frequent. After a while, she never came again to the soup kitchen or the church. C.D. missed her smiling face, her gentle words and the way a room would enlighten when she entered. He looked for her in every crowd on the streets, hoping to see her.

3

About six years later, C.D. surprisingly ran into Kizzy again in a different area after being placed at a church in downtown Houston, Texas. One Sunday while he had been performing mass, he noticed a beautiful, conspicuously sophisticated young woman in a pew in the back of the church. She was wearing a large-brimmed black hat with a black net that covered her beguiling, dignified face. She was wearing a conservative blue dress that clung tightly to her curves. Without meaning to, she brought the attention of the congregation to her. Her beauty was mysterious and fascinating. No one was immune to this woman's beauty from the youngest to the oldest of the congregation. After mass, he had hurried to the church rear to try and catch her before she had left the chapel. C.D. enjoyed welcoming visitors to his services. When he got closer to the strange beautiful visitor, he recognized her as Kizzy.

Ecstatically she said, "Oh, C.D., I am so happy to see you. You look great!" she said hugging him.

"Where did you go when you left so quickly, Kizzy?"

Evasively, Kizzy exclaimed laughing, "Oh, you know me! I'm here! I'm there! I'm everywhere! How do you like it here in Houston?" Kizzy asked, changing the subject.

"Well, the humidity is bad, but I've adjusted."

"Well, it's great seeing you, C.D. I really need to run." Before C.D. could say another word, she left the church hurriedly. C.D. realized that Kizzy had made sure no detailed questions had been allowed during the conversation. Everything had been kept a mystery. He had been exiled from questioning her reasons for relocating in Houston, or disappearing the way she had. When she left the building, C.D. noticed that one of the parishioners, Mr. Paoli, followed her.

4

Three months later during a colossal thunderstorm-filled night, C.D.

was in the chapel. The sky had been crackling with lightning and thunder. A young woman came in covered from head to toe, in a long blue cape drenched by the blowing rain outside. She knelt at the altar, shivering. Bowing her head and praying quietly, she seemed troubled. He noticed her folded hands shaking. C.D. walked over to her to offer words of tranquility or assistance. "My dear, can I be of some help to you?" He put his arm around her. With disheveled hair and makeup, the woman looked into his eyes. C.D. recognized the young woman as Kizzy. She did not speak a word.

"Kizzy! Come back with me to my office. We can talk there. You need to get out of this wet cape."

In the office, C.D. took the wet cape from around her. Her beautiful, black evening dress had been soaked and clung to her body. Her face was pale, and her right arm was covered with bruises in which someone had been grabbing her arm with great force. C.D. hung the cape over two chairs to dry. Her dampened hair stuck against her forehead.

Kizzy was wearing large, diamond earrings and a large diamond necklace. C.D. knew these must be extremely valuable. When she saw C.D. taking notice of them, she promptly removed them.

"C.D., take them. Use the money for the hungry and poor. I don't want these things! They make me sick!"

"Kizzy, are you sure? They look as though they are worth a lot of money."

She held the jewelry out to him in her shaking hands. "Yes. They're worth an awful lot of money. You'd be surprised, Father. They're yours. Take them!" She seemed bitter. C.D. poured her a small glass of wine hoping to stop her shaking. She asked him to join her, gulped down her wine, and poured herself another, and then, another. The paleness began to be replaced by the warm glow of the wine, or the usual impeccable glow of her skin.

C.D. placed his arm around her. "You look as though you need to talk. You know you can tell me anything, Kizzy."

"Some things are better not spoken about," she said, gulping down another swallow of the wine and pulling away from him.

"Kizzy, nothing can shock me if that's what you're fearing. Dear, I have heard everything in the confessional."

"No, no, not shock." She paused briefly and then continued. "Pain. Pain can kill too, you know, Father. It can kill your very soul!"

C.D. put his arms around her and hugged Kizzy tight. She fell in his arms, weeping as a child. Her entire body was shaking, maybe from the cold wet clothes, or maybe from the pain to which she had been referring. She wept long and hard until her body was tired from the effort, laying in his arms, limp and sighing. He felt helpless as a priest, and helpless as a man. He wanted desperately to help her, but he did not know the problem.

The earrings she had given C.D. were genuine diamonds and gold and markedly valuable. After selling them, he used the money to feed the hungry, as Kizzy asked.

Sporadically after that night, C.D. saw Kizzy at church. C.D. found himself lying to the other priests and parishioners about Kizzy being Catholic. He was unable to prevent her from the services or communion. He knew this was wrong, but he allowed it anyway, for her. She seemed to draw strength and solace from the services and a resolution from the communion. Yet the sins she confessed seemed reserved, as though she were not telling everything. It was as if she were unable to reveal the entire story. She only confessed lying and being selfish to C.D.

Once C.D. saw Kizzy in the park near the church. She did not see him watching her. She was giving an old man of the street who had been sleeping on a park bench a stack of money. C.D. wondered how and where she had gotten so much money.

C.D. noticed in church that one of the parish couples, the Paolis, had taken an interest in Kizzy. Kizzy seemed to enjoy them, and they liked her. C.D. was happy for them. The Paolis were older than Kizzy, but were not blessed with children. C.D. figured that she became as a daughter to them. A little unusual, they always stayed alone not mingling with the other parishioners. When they made friends with Kizzy, C.D. felt they would find friendship with one another.

One night, Kizzy phoned C.D. in the middle of the night. She was sobbing and out of control. She wanted him to come to see her without delay. C.D. went to the address she had given him, a chic penthouse suite in a plush downtown hotel. She met him at the door, hysterical. Large dark circles were under her eyes. C.D. noticed that she had not slept for days. "Kizzy, what is wrong? You look awful!"

"I can't sleep! It's the dreams. They won't leave me alone!" she said, nervously wringing her hands as she paced. She was shaking as if she were a scared child. Her brilliant green, emerald eyes were wild and filled with terror as she ranted on and on about the pain. "I can't take this pain anymore! I *can't!*" she screamed hysterically. "It *has* to stop, *please,*" she cried as though to beg him for some sort of relief. Crying hysterically she paced and rubbed the tops of her arms.

C.D. took her and held her in his arms hoping to calm her. He sat on the sofa with her head against him. He rocked her in his arms as though she were a child. She had been crying for awhile when she dozed off to sleep in his arms. Her limp body lay against him. He carried her to the bedroom and put her to bed. Just as he lay her down, he noticed what she was wearing. Her gown was black, sheer, clingy. She was wearing nothing underneath. The lace around the edges of the sheer fabric lay against her skin in such a sensuous, feminine way. Her womanly charms had shown through the fabric. C.D. began to cover her, saying successively in his mind, God give me strength to walk from this room.

Kizzy awakened. She desperately shoved the covers back away from her. "No, please. Don't leave me alone. I'm afraid. They'll hurt me again. I know they will!"

"Who'll hurt you, Kizzy? You must tell me. I can help you." No matter how he tried to appease her, or cover her, she clung to him.

"No, I can't tell you, don't ask, don't ask, don't ask . . ." she said, hysterically shaking her head.

C.D. sat on the bed next to her to comfort her. "Okay. Don't tell me. Calm down. I'll stay here with you. No one will hurt you. I'll be here. I'll not let them hurt you, Kizzy! I promise."

"Hold me, please, hold me. Hold me close and tight." C.D. lay down next to her and held her.

"No, tighter! *Tighter!*" Kizzy said pleading with him. Throughout the night, he lay beside her while she slept. During her sleep, she whimpered as a scared little girl, but it was explicitly a woman he was holding in his arms. He felt her body pressing against his. Each time he tried to release the tight hold and move away, she pulled him closer, cuddling against him. C.D. clenched his square jaws unable to sleep. He did not possess the strength to leave her.

At long last, morning came. C.D. saw the sunlight peeking around the edges of the drapes. Gently removing himself from the bed, he went in the living room area to use the telephone. He called down to room service for fresh coffee and toast, which was soon delivered. When he returned to the bedroom door, it had been closed. He heard movement inside and knocked.

"Come on in," she said, cheerfully from inside.

C.D. pushed the door open with his foot, holding the two cups of coffee in his hands. The drapes had been drawn, but the lamp on the dresser was on. Kizzy was standing at the dresser brushing her hair. She had removed her gown and was completely naked. C.D. tried not to look, but gawked without success. His hands which were holding the cups of coffee were shaking. The hot coffee began to slosh out onto his hands. Quickly, he placed the coffee down on the bedside table. His eyes stared at her. Mustering the control he had inside, he tried to look away. However, he could only pull his eyes off her briefly. Each time, his eyes returned to the beautiful woman that was standing before him. He wondered. What was happening inside him? What were these feelings that were pouring to the surface of his flesh? Deep inside, he had known she would not be dressed before he opened the door. Maybe, he had even hoped she would not be dressed. Why had he entered? He could have stayed out in the living room! He had not. He knew Kizzy.

"Kizzy, what are you *doing?* Are you *crazy?* I'm a *priest.*" C.D. blurted out angrily. He was seething that he was experiencing these uncontrollable feelings and furious at Kizzy for causing them.

Kizzy laughed coyly and childlike and said, "Yeah, but you're a man first. In case you can't tell, I am a *woman!*" She slowly ran her hands across her body as she spoke.

C.D. left the room as speedily as he had been capable of moving, closing the bedroom door behind him. His hand shook upon the knob. Hurriedly, he left the room, moving out into the hall. The pulse of his blood beat rapidly in his neck, leaving him with a sensation not felt before. He left the hotel. He should have run, but he did not. His legs were unable to move that quickly. Maybe a part of him had *wanted* to see her, caress her. God forbid, he had known he could never touch her! Why had he even been thinking that he could?

Out in the street, he noticed the sweat beaded upon the skin of his olive face. His hands were ice cold, and he rubbed them together. His face and body were burning with a rare fever. He felt as though he could not catch his breath. He had never gone through feelings such as this. As quickly as possible, he went to the church. Immediately, he went to the confessional, praying for God's forgiveness for what he had been thinking and feeling, sweating in misery the entire time. He did penance.

That was the last time he had ever seen Kizzy. A memory is left that still wells up a passion within him even today. He tried to reach her in the penthouse several times after that night, worrying that she would not be all right. However, Kizzy had hastily moved. No one knew where she had moved. It was as though she had suddenly disappeared off the face of the earth.

5

The present edges its way back into C.D.'s mind. Now, he is mentioned in her will, an impossibility to C.D. Gently, he closes his brown eyes and takes a deep, cleansing breath. He knows that the one person in the entire world who has ever tested his faith would now do so again. He does not know how, but he knows that she will. He knows only God will get him through this despicable ordeal. Someone has murdered her horribly. He feels the lump well up in his throat again. He wonders if what he has felt for Kizzy has only been sinful lust. He knows he will finally have to face the feelings he has buried deep inside for her. C.D. knows this will be hard, and he does not know if he is strong enough to face this test of his endurance. No, this will be a test of his faith. He knows he will have to depend on his faith and on God! God will help him through this ordeal. He needs God and His wisdom and His special strength. Without delay, he goes to the chapel, to the altar and starts to pray. The lump in his throat enlarges, choking him as he cries out loudly for strength from above. "Oh my God! Please do not forsake me! I *need you, desperately*, Father!" He has no strength on his own. Throwing himself upon the altar, he weeps alone. With a tired heaving, his chest lapses into a stillness.

CHAPTER VIII

Pete's Suspect

1

The phone rings early. Evan runs from the bathroom to answer it. He is just finishing his shower before leaving for the reading of the will at the attorney's. "Yeah?" Evan yells, irritated at being disturbed.

"Evan, it's me." Evan recognizes the voice as Pete's. "Listen, we picked up a guy last night. He was caught breaking in the building just across the street from Kizzy's apartment. I think this guy is our perp, Ev. Can you come by the station?" Pete declares, excited by this glimmer of hope.

"Yeah, I'll be right there!" Evan says as he hangs up the phone. He rushes around his apartment dressing. His thoughts are happy at perhaps finding the perp and livid at the thought of facing the person who hurt his Kizzy. Evan drives like a crazy man down to the station. Police officer, Jack, sits at the front desk. "Where's Pete, Jack?"

"He's in one of the interrogation rooms with Alice."

"Thanks, Jack." Evan rushes past the rooms gazing in the doors. He notices that the door to room number one is closed. With his hand on the knob, he takes a deep breath. This just might be the perp. Evan feels his soul stirring. This might be the man for whom they have been looking. Evan has a good intuition about this one. He opens the door and enters just as Alice is coming out. Alice whispers to Evan as she passes him. "This one's a tough cookie. Good luck, Ev,"

Pete notices Evan as he enters and nods his head. "Okay, Moore. Let's go over it again so Detective Picard can hear this impossible story," Pete sneers, trying to bring as much pressure as possible on the suspect. The suspect is a street-wise fellow who could handle any situation either physical or mental. Evan notices a tatoo of a snake on his forearm.

"I ain't really sure where I was the night of that broad's murder, but I think I was at Quick Willie's Pool Hall."

Conscientiously, Evan looks at the man and listens to every word painstakingly. Evan takes out a coin from his pocket. He tosses the coin from one cupped hand to another as he watches the man's hand gestures, attempting to learn if he is lying. The suspect is about six feet tall with a muscular build. Maybe Pete is right. Maybe Kizzy's murder was just a burglary gone awry.

Evan does not plan to let this guy get away with anything. He joins in and starts his questioning of the suspect. "Where is this pool hall, Mr. Moore? Your name is Mr. Moore isn't it?" Evan inquires, grasping the coin tightly between his thumb and fingers in his usual way. Tossing this coin helps Evan to think.

With a note of sarcasm in his voice, he answers, "Yeah, Armstrong Moore. My friends call me Army."

"Well, I'll call you Mr. Moore because I don't consider myself one of your friends." Evan thinks Alice is right. This guy is going to be a tough nut to crack. He does not get rattled. He keeps control. Evan continues questioning him as he resumes tossing the coin between his cupped hands. "Mr. Moore, you didn't answer where this pool hall is. Would you like to tell us, or is it some big secret?"

Army smirks, finding Evan's remark rudely funny. Evan knows this guy is a wise guy. He senses this man knows more than he is saying and is hiding something. Evan wants to know what.

"Nah. It ain't no secret. Hell, ya can look it up in the phone book. It's on Main Street. I don't know the address. Y'all look it up if it's so important to ya!"

"I know where it is, Evan. It's that damn sleazy place where we're always getting calls to go break up fights," Pete remarks, sitting in a chair near the table.

Evan and Pete notice the smirk on Army's face. Evan has this suspect pegged as an uncooperative street punk, but a punk with brains. Evan knows he is going to have to pry each little bit of information from this scum's lips. This guy's smile looks like the smile on a cat that has just swallowed a canary. He knows something he is not revealing.

"You were there all night, Mr. Moore?" Evan analyzes rubbing his coin between two fingers.

"I don't even know for sure whether I was there that night. I said, I *think* I was there. Don't even think about putting words in my mouth, cop. It won't work! Hell, I don't keep a diary ya know!"

"Okay, but you were caught burglarizing the building across the street from her apartment house." Evan, now feeling the tightening of his nerves, holds the coin tightly between his forefinger and thumb.

"Yeah, so?" Army says.

"Why should we believe that you were playing pool the night she was killed?" Pete asks.

"Hell, I didn't even know this broad! Why would I kill her? I don't do apartment jobs. I'm strictly a commercial kind of guy. There's less risk of running across a person at night in a business. I like low risk!"

"Pete, does this guy have a rap sheet?" Evan asks.

"Yeah, mostly a history of breaking, entering and burglary. He's been out of prison about three years without any incidents."

"Damn, I'm good, huh?" Army says laughingly and confidently, as he leans back in his chair, raising the front two legs off the floor. A disgusted Evan kicks the two front chair legs, almost causing Army to tip the chair over backwards. "*Shit, cop!* Take it easy, will ya?"

Pete smiles, neither disgusted nor flabbergasted by Evan's action. If Evan had not kicked his chair, Pete was thinking of performing the same act.

Evan places his coin in his pocket, goes to the door and steps outside. He calls Alice over for instructions.

"Alice, call Quick Willie's Pool Hall. It's somewhere on Main. Ask if anyone can vouch for this guy's alibi the night of the murder." Alice nods. Evan pours a cup of coffee. He sips the hot coffee almost burning his lips.

He steps back inside the interrogation room. Evidently, Pete has continued questioning Army about the night of the murder in Evan's absence.

Army says mocking Pete, "Let me tell ya one more time, cop. I'm sure the story won't change from the last time I told ya. Listen, maybe ya need to take notes. You seem to have a hard time remembering what I'm saying. Maybe it's because ya ain't so young anymore!" Pete is scarlet faced with anger. Army continues his mockery of Pete, staring Pete straight in the eyes. "I *think* I was playing pool. I'm a really good player, ya know. I usually stay there until at least one when they close." Army looks over toward Evan inhaling the fresh cup of coffee in his hand. "That coffee sure smells good. I sure could use a cup."

Evan opens the door and yells out at Alice who is on the phone. "Hey, Alice, bring me a cup of java for this guy, will you?" Alice nods.

After finishing on the phone, Alice retrieves the cup of coffee. She opens the door. "Evan, here is the coffee." Evan strives to take it from her hand, but she holds on to the coffee not releasing the cup. Alice stands with the door open. "Uh—Evan, let me speak to ya for a moment out here, please." Alice says motioning with her eyes.

Evan withdraws from the room with Alice. "What's up, Alice?"

"Well the manager of that pool hall clarifies Moore was there until about ten thirty."

"Ah-hah!"

"Not so quick, Evan. Moore was there until the manager called the police to come break up a fight. It seems Moore spent the *dang* night after eleven o'clock in police custody here at the lock up! He assaulted a police officer who tried to arrest him. The unit arrived just a little after ten thirty at the bar."

Evan's enthusiasm drains from his body. Once again, another tragic dead-end is what he is up against. "Damn, Alice. Why didn't Pete see that arrest on his rap sheet?"

Alice releases the coffee cup. "The officers left the paperwork with a rookie. It hadn't been entered in the computer yet. It was just a human error and wasn't Pete's fault. Sorry, Evan."

"This smart ass, wise guy hood knew this all along. He was taking us for a ride," Evan blurts out.

"Maybe he is. But listen, ya can't go in there and lose it with him, Evan. You've gotta keep some dang control," Alice says, trying to calm Evan's hostility.

"Oh, I'll keep control. Damn, I hate guys such as him."

"Listen. I had an older brother like 'im. I learned that the facade he wears as a tough guy only hides the vulnerability beneath. Sometimes, really nice men are underneath, Evan."

"This guy has a record! He's a loser!"

"Okay, he has a record. You're right. But don't lose it with 'im, Evan!"

Evan starts walking away from her. He takes a deep breath to calm himself and walks back inside the room. Army looks at him with a smirking little grin on his face. Evan hands Army the coffee.

"What's up, cop?" Army broadcasts mimicking Evan to make him feel foolish.

Evan knows that Army has known all along that he was here in lock up. Evan feels sick inside. "Pete, we can't hold him for Kizzy's murder. He was here in lock up the whole night starting at eleven o'clock."

"*What*? What the *hell* is going on around here! I checked his rap sheet, Evan!"

"Yeah, I know. A rookie made a mistake. It wasn't your fault. It was human error. But you got him on the burglary of that commercial building across the street from Kizzy's. You nail his ass good for that, Pete. Stick it to this smart ass punk!"

An angry Pete lunges at Army, grabbing him by the neck of his T-shirt. Army spills his coffee on the desk during the scuffle.

"You cheap little son of a bitch! You knew all along you were locked up here. You allowed us to interrogate you as if we were a couple of idiots! *Nobody* makes a fool out of *me!*" Pete says.

Evan grabs Pete trying to restrain him. "Let it go, Pete. He's not worth it." Pete's face is blood red as he looks at Evan and releases Army. Pete and Evan motion for the uniformed officer to take Army back to lock up.

Army yells as he leaves, "You *are* a couple of idiots. *Stupid* idiots!" Army laughs riotously as the officer drags him away.

2

Evan goes out to his car and starts the engine. After looking at his watch, he drives rapidly to the attorney's office. He is going to have to hurry if he plans to make it on time. Disappointment fills Evan's soul. He thought this guy was Kizzy's killer. His mind returns to the obvious. A burglar does not dismember the victim. He stabs, shoots and may even strangles but he does not dismember. A burglar only kills so that he can gain a safe exit with his stolen loot. A burglar would not risk taking the time to dismember her, with the chance of someone else catching him in the apartment. The dismemberment would take too much valuable exit time. No burglar just happens to be carrying a meat cleaver. This is just not logical. Something is wrong here. It cannot be a burglary gone awry, but something else.

Evan finds the office building of the attorney. He looks upward at the large glass building. Dreading this event, Evan takes a deep breath and goes inside.

CHAPTER IX

The Will, Monday,

(A Week After the Murder)

1

William enters the hall from the elevator. He finds the office of "Alexander & Webster, Attorneys At Law". He enters hesitantly, as this is not an event to which he looks forward. A lovely young woman shows him back to Mr. Alexander's office after offering him a cup of coffee and showing him a place to put his one piece of luggage. William declines the offered refreshment. William listens, finding the young lady's Southern dialect a pleasure to hear. The words are slower spoken and sensual. He has noticed the Southern Texas drawl from a couple of attractive ladies in the airport, also. The Southern women's charm in Houston might be the only pleasant part of this entire trip.

He enters the attorney's office. Mr. Alexander, a distinguished older gentleman, rises and shakes his hand in a friendly, welcoming way. William wipes his hands with his handkerchief. William researched Mr. Alexander before coming to Houston and is satisfied with the results, finding Mr. Alexander to have an excellent professional reputation as an attorney in the state of Texas. He always likes to know with whom he is dealing before he meets them. He supposes this "research habit" is a personal preference of professional legal etiquette. William sits, noticing several of the other men present, sitting around the room. No one is talking. William surmises that these men must be strangers to each other. One last man enters, in a big hurry, apologizing the entire time. He is a nice looking young man who introduces himself as Evan Picard to Mr. Alexander. He has clean cut, dark brown curly hair and attractive, lucent blue eyes. He is neatly dressed in a tie, sports jacket and dark trousers, looking classic. William, with a history of being a good judge of character, infers that he is trustworthy and confident.

Mr. Alexander, pleased at having everyone present, starts. "Well, now that we are present, I can persevere, gentlemen. Each of you is mentioned in this will. The decedent wrote this will in her own handwriting, personalizing it. Why she chose me to be the keeper of this, her last testament to her life, I have no idea. I did not know Ms. Theriot. This will was received last week by special carrier. She wrote a simple note telling me that it was her will that was in this envelope, and to please hold it in safe keeping. This is not something I usually do for people except my own established clients. However, she wrote in the note that she felt she could trust me. She also wrote that people she could trust were rare in her life. Something about those words touched my heart. Thus, I kept the will. Upon seeing her name in the newspaper, I phoned the police station and notified the beneficiaries, you gentlemen. After the reading, I will take proper legal action to probate the will and finish the filing in the courthouse." Mr. Alexander's secretary phones, interrupting him with a message. He explains that he must handle this problem and excuses himself from the room, leaving the five men, strangers, alone.

William looks around the room again at the other men. He notices the priest, the young man casually dressed in old blue jeans and a white T-shirt, the large, tall man with brown eyes and moustache who looks familiar, and Mr. Picard, the last man to enter. He wonders how these men with such different lifestyles and personalities were attached to Kizzy, an enigma he knows will resolve soon. William, not surprised the beneficiaries are men, knows Kizzy always had closer male friends than female.

Jimmy looks around at the others. He wonders what the hell Kizzy had to do with the priest. He never heard of Kizzy going to church, let alone being a Catholic. If he is Catholic! Well, he is not bad looking. Maybe she had a thing for priests at one time. Who knows? Jimmy would not be surprised if a bitch such as Kizzy had a sexual relationship with this priest. He smiles at the thought of Kizzy with a priest. What about the old man? He looks a little reserved for Kizzy's taste, so properly dressed in his suit and tie, with everything matching so neatly. Jimmy notices how he ridiculously keeps wiping his hands on his clean white handkerchief. Kizzy liked the wilder kind, fulfilling her huge sexual appetite. Jimmy knew about that appetite. The other two men, the young man named Picard and the big guy, he could see the attraction she might have for these two guys. They were good-looking dudes. For a moment, Jimmy feels a pang of jealousy. The Picard dude seemed a little reserved for Kizzy, also. In his little blue sports jacket and preppie pants, he is so cutely dressed. He is the flashy kind. He keeps tossing that coin, showing everyone he has money. In his opinion, these guys were not as nice looking as him. Jimmy smiles confidently with conceit at this thought, running his hands across his dark hair. He adjusts the tightness of the white T-shirt across his muscular chest. Confidently, he straightens himself in the chair and starts to tap his fingers on the desk where he is sitting. A dauntless grin spreads across his face.

Tom looks closely at William. He is a different man from the person he saw Kizzy with years ago in that bar. That guy was heavier. Tom does not remember the old guy with Kizzy too well. Maybe? This man does look familiar. Tom cannot place where he has seen him. He looks even closer noticing the steel colored blue eyes and gray hair. He watches as the man nervously wipes his hands on his handkerchief, repetitively. Suddenly the resemblance hits him! He smiles, thinking, I'll be damn! The old guy is William Newton, Kizzy's childhood guardian. Next he takes notice of the priest. He bets Kizzy was good friends with him. He has a kind face. Kizzy would have chosen someone such as him as a close friend and confidante. Tom feels this priest would have been good for Kizzy. His eyes look at the young man who introduced himself as Evan Picard and the man with dark hair in the blue jeans and T-shirt. Tom feels a little resentful at the thought of Kizzy being with either of these men. The guy in the T-shirt looks arrogant. Kizzy was too confident herself to like someone such as him. That Mr. Picard looks around closely at everyone. He keeps tossing that coin and searching each man in the room with his eyes suspiciously. What in the world could Kizzy see in this guy, all this distrust!

Evan looks suspiciously at the details of each of the men, studying them closely. Tossing his coin repeatedly, he wonders if maybe one of these men could be Kizzy's killer. What if the perp is sitting right here in this room? The priest is a farfetched choice, but who knows? Even priests have emotions. The big guy with the moustache sure does have the size and strength and could physically have dismembered her easily. He looks drunk, too. His clothes are nice but wrinkled, as though he slept in them. Maybe in a drunken state he killed her. This is a strong possibility, and it would not be the first homicide he had seen that was committed under the influence of alcohol or drugs. The old guy looks a little too reserved and intellectual. Except history proves that even the older and reserved types have a knack for murder. The reserve serves as their mask. Some of the most malevolent and successful killers throughout time had high intelligence. However, the most probable suspect is the ass hole punk in the blue jeans and T-shirt. What kind of an outfit is that to wear to an attorney's office? Evan wishes he would stop that annoying incessant tapping with his fingers. Something about him forecasts trouble, and maybe even killer. He has that dark hair, combed back. He looks as if he is a pretty boy street punk to Evan. Look at that! He has an earring in one ear. Evan is sure this ass hole punk believes he is God's gift to the world! Yes, Evan guesses, the hood is the one! With great satisfaction, he smiles at the fact of a new lead in Kizzy's case. Gentler, he continues tossing and fingering his coin.

Mr. Alexander enters the office apologizing the entire while for his necessary quick exit. Mr. Alexander clears his voice. He takes out the pages from the opened envelope lying on his desk and starts to read aloud to the men sitting.

"I, Keziah Elaine Theriot, am making this my last will and testament. It will be the last communication I have with this world, but it's not the last time you will hear from me. My life has not turned out the way I wanted. Perhaps I wanted too much from life. I have found it difficult to follow the rules. I have hurt myself and others because I couldn't follow the rules. Please, know each of you are here because, at some time in my life I have loved you very much. No, I still love you all. True love, such as I felt for you men, never dies. You were very special men, good, strong men—Evan Picard, Father C.D. Casmiersky, Thomas Hastings, Jimmy Smithson, and William Newton. I am leaving the money and everything I own to be controlled by the five of you equally and to be used for the care of my most prized possession which you must find. I can only give you a few clues. Please, take care of my possession if you have ever felt anything for me. This possession is the only good thing I have ever given to this rotten world in which the kind suffer and the evil are rich and comfortable. It is the only thing that makes me immortal. Only the five of you, together, can give and care for this precious possession. I will never forget any of you, EVER! God bless you all, you'll need it!

Keziah Elaine Theriot"

"Two lipstick lip prints are on this will as though she kissed it. A responsible notary notarized the will. I have verified that the notary witnessed the writing and signature of this document." Mr. Alexander sets the will down on his desk.

"The kiss was Kizzy's special insignia. She put it on everything that she penned herself," William says.

"That's right," says Evan in agreement. Tom and Jimmy also nod their heads in agreement.

Jimmy stands in impatience. "Get to the shittin' point. How much money did the damn *bitch* leave me?"

Evan outcries lunging toward Jimmy grabbing him by the neck as they fall to the floor. "You dumb *ass hole punk*!" They are beginning to fight when Tom seizes Evan and pulls him off Jimmy. Jimmy jumps to his feet and throws a punch into Evan's stomach. C.D. and William yank Jimmy pulling him away from Evan.

Jimmy yells at Evan, "You *sorry sack of shit! Nobody* puts their hands on me! I'll beat the son of a bitchin' bullshit outta yore cracked ass!"

"Please, sir, a priest is present," William declares. Jimmy calms his demeanor.

Mr. Alexander, stunned, says, "Will you two gentlemen please be seated so we can continue?"

Tom informs them, "Look, you two guys hold it in check, or I'll get in the middle of this! As you can see, I'm bigger than the two of you put together!"

"I apologize, Father. And, to the rest of you gentlemen," Evan says.

"Please, this mayhem has traumatized us! We must keep a myriad of poise and presence for Kizzy," William says. "We must be gentlemen."

Jimmy declares, "Yeah, okay, I think, but he keeps his hands off me! Or I'll kick his tin badged ass! Yeah, I can tell by lookin' at ya that you're a cop!" Evan starts to lunge at Jimmy again, being held back by Tom.

"Mr. Picard, please," Father C.D. pleads.

"Okay, but no more of that rude sh—crap about Kizzy!" Evan warns pointing his finger at Jimmy. "Sorry, Father." Jimmy pulls a cigarette from the pack in his T-shirt pocket. Mr. Alexander points politely to the "no smoking" sign, so Jimmy crams the cigarette back in the pack. Evan and Jimmy sit. Evan stares at Jimmy watching every finger tap on the desk.

Mr. Alexander continues to answer Jimmy's question. "Mr. Smithson, it is Mr. Smithson, isn't it?" Jimmy nods his head yes. "Mr. Smithson, a million-dollar life insurance policy pays in case of death, except suicide. Another million in cash and savings bank accounts is in her name. She had no checking account. She also had extremely expensive jewelry and furnishings in her penthouse according to the information I got from the police department. They should release these belongings once the police investigation is over."

Jimmy leaps to his feet saying, "I can't believe this shit! She leaves me a fortune with all kinds of strings attached. What the hell is this 'possession' shit she's talking about?"

"In actuality, I don't know, Mr. Smithson," Mr. Alexander answers.

Evan has been watching Jimmy throughout the reading. "Sit down and *shut up*, you little punk. I've had all of you I'm gonna put up with!" Evan blurts out losing his patience again with this strange, insolent young man, Jimmy. Evan thinks of Jimmy as a punky trouble maker. He knows the kind, dealing with them every day in his job. He knows his suspicions of Jimmy have been right on the money so far. Evan cannot believe Kizzy was ever involved with such a man. Jimmy sneers, walks over to the window and gazes out, jiggling his right leg nervously.

William sits forward on the edge of his chair, saying, "Mr. Alexander, do you know how Kizzy died?"

"Oh, I'm sorry. I thought you knew. She was murdered."

"Why would someone kill Kizzy?" Tom asks. Evan notices the genuine concern on his face and in his voice.

Tom continues, "She never hurt anyone. She loved people and never met a stranger. She made friends with everyone she met."

"I'm sorry, Mr. Hastings. I don't know the details. I know her body has not been buried, but is at the city morgue." The secretary disturbs Mr. Alexander again. After making excuses, he leaves the room to take care of other pressing business. The five men loiter around the office, nervously.

Evan takes advantage of the attorney's absence to interrogate the men present. "I'm a detective with the police department," Evan remarks showing his badge. Observantly, William looks at the badge.

"I have a few questions for you men. Can each of you tell me where you were the night of Kizzy's murder, June the sixteenth?" William takes out his pocket diary and starts to thumb through the pages.

"What day of the week was that?" Jimmy asks.

"Saturday," William reveals, looking at his diary.

Father C.D. answers first. "I was at my church in the confessional. We stay open until midnight, detective."

Tom offers the information without reservation. "I was at my dealership in Denver selling cars. We close at ten o'clock on Saturdays. After that, us guys usually go to a bar for a couple of drinks."

"What is the name of the dealership?" Evan asks as he jots down the information in his pocket notebook.

"Cally's Cars. The bar we usually go to is Larry's Bar and Grill." Tom volunteers without reserve.

William speaks next revealing his alibi. "I was at a business dinner party until around midnight in New York City with my partner and a client. Here is one of my business cards which has the phone number you can call for verification. My partner was with me and will be happy to corroborate my alibi."

Evan looks at Jimmy, drumming his fingers on the arm of the chair and jiggling his right leg, and waits for his alibi. "Well?"

"I was driving my cab, cop. If ya wanna know about the fare, call the cab company. They keep records of where we pick up fares and where we go with 'em! That's all I remember! What the sh—crap—"

"Please, sir, your language is appalling," William says. "Do you not see there is a priest present?"

Jimmy pauses and then answers, "Yeah—Okay. Sorry!"

William says, " Thank you, sir!"

"Yeah, okay," Jimmy says to correct his language. "Good! Good!"

Evan says, "I *will* call the cab company. I *will* check on everyone's alibi." However, he has noticed the truly genuine responses from the men. Even Jimmy's reply with his alibi is without fear, hesitation or reserve. Besides, Kizzy trusted these men, so they must be trustworthy. Evan decides to volunteer a few revolting facts of Kizzy's slaying hoping to spark a bit of guilt in one of the men, especially the ass hole punk, Jimmy, for whom he still holds doubt. "Kizzy was dismembered and died a horrible death. The lowest snake I know shouldn't die the way poor Kizzy did!"

Jimmy, standing with his back to Evan, turns around in amazement. The look on his face is one of surprise. "Are ya saying somebody cut her up? Are ya saying somebody tortured her?" Jimmy asks. Genuinely, his response is disgusted astonishment.

"Hey, I don't know whether the killer hacked her up before or after death," Evan responds. C.D. bows his head at overhearing this vile news and performs the sign of the cross. Evan can see the priest is truly moved.

"Shit!" Jimmy contorts as he sits in his chair shocked and pale faced. Then Jimmy looks over at Father C.D. "I'm sorry, Padre. I didn't mean no disrespect," Jimmy says with an afterthought about his disrespectful, obscene comment.

"Look, whoever did this, I plan to make pay, and pay dearly!" Evan blurts out angrily. Evan can see that none of these men are the perp. Their shock and pain look too genuine. Evan trusts the accuracy of his own instinct.

Mr. Alexander enters the room and notices the unnerved atmosphere within the room and among its inhabitants.

William speaks with an outburst deviant to his masterly deportment. "I want to view the body. Where is the morgue? Can you give me directions or an address?" Mr. Alexander starts to get the address when Evan agrees to show William the way, but explains he must make a phone call to make the proper arrangements. Mr. Alexander realizes that whatever transpired during his absence from this room has shaken these five men to their souls. Tom insists he is going to the morgue, also. Evan excuses himself, goes off alone and makes a call on the cellular phone. Evan calls the station and Alice answers. Evan seeks Pete, but he is out. Evan asks Alice to research the men's alibis. While being exact, he gives her names and information from his pocket notebook. Evan phones the morgue, makes the proper arrangements, finishes his call and joins the other men. William mentions that he also wants to see the place of Kizzy's death. The men exit to Evan's car. Evan grinds the starter trying to get the engine to turn over. He phones a wrecker from his cellular phone because it will not start. Jimmy says they can ride in his cab because he is off duty. William expresses some concern for the irritation of his emphysema by Jimmy's cigarette smoke. With some hesitation, Jimmy agrees not to smoke around William while mumbling atrocities under his breath about William and Kizzy being anti smokers. The four men enter Jimmy's cab.

Someone taps on the window. Jimmy rolls down his window.

"Got room for one more?" Father C.D. asks.

"Yeah, sure, get in the back, Padre," Jimmy answers tapping his fingers on the steering wheel. The priest climbs in the back with Tom and Evan as the cab pulls out. Evan looks back discreetly over his shoulder.

"Don't look around, but we've got a tail," Evan says, instructing the others.

"Damn! I can lose this son of a b—, uh—tail," Jimmy says, smiling.

"You notice I cleaned up my words, huh?"

Father C.D. asks nervously, "What should we do?"

"Wait Jimmy! Nothing, Father, we'll just let them follow us. We're fine. Don't worry about it."

"What kinda car is it, cop?" Jimmy asks.

"Uh—looks like an old, large model car with a trail of black smoke following it. I can't see the plate." Evan discloses still discreetly looking around as though he is talking to the others.

William beseeches, "Do you want one of us to try to see the license plate number?"

"No, don't look around!"

"Hold on! I got an idea!" Jimmy yells as he starts making different turns trying to lose the tail. Father C.D. starts to pray aloud, fearing for their lives with Jimmy behind the wheel. Jimmy enters an alley he knows does not have an exit. He spins the car around, facing the vehicle that has been following them.

Evan pulls out his gun and stands behind the opened back door. "Police! Get out of the car with your hands up very *very* slowly. Make *no* quick moves," Evan shouts.

An old man, slovenly dressed, gets out with his hands held high. He looks terrified and nervous. "Don't shoot me! Please, don't shoot me! I ain't doin' nothin' wrong!" he enunciates with a heavy Texas dialect.

"Why are you following us?" Evan continues still with his gun drawn and aimed at the old man.

"I wanna hep! That's all. I jest wanna hep."

"Help us do what?" Evan asks.

"Hep y'all find who kilt Miss Kizzy. I jest followed ya from that lawyer's office and seen your car, cop, the night y'all found her. I jest been following yore car. That's all! I ain't meanin' ya no harm. Jest put that li'l pea shooter away, cop."

While sensing the men are in no danger, Evan puts his gun away. The men walk toward the old man with Evan leading the way.

"How did you know Kizzy?" Evan inquires upon reaching the old man. Evan can see this old man is defenseless, poor, dirty, maybe even homeless. With teeth missing, he nervously grinds the few left, intermittently between words.

"Miss Kizzy hepped me. She gots me this here car and a place to sleep. She wuz a very nice lady. I wanna know who kilt her! I wanna hep y'all!"

"What is your name, sir?" Evan continues.

Jimmy standing, arms folded across his chest, hands under his armpits with a sickening look on his face, lets everyone present know he is fed up with this situation. With his legs far apart, nervously he shakes his right leg and sucks in on a cigarette he lit after exiting the cab. Jimmy whispers quietly to the other men, losing patience and thinking they are wasting their time talking with the old man, "Cop, why do we want to waste our time with this shittin' old guy? He's just an old bum! Man! He stinks! Look at 'im!"

William wants to say something to Jimmy. However, before he can speak, C.D. answers Jimmy. "Kizzy thought this man was worth some time. She spent her time and money on him!" Jimmy does not like C.D.'s reply, but cannot think of a proper way to respond to a priest. In frustration, Jimmy throws down his cigarette and stomps out the butt.

The poor old man, hearing the whispering responses from the men, decides to answer Evan's question. "My name is Fred. Please, let me hep y'all!"

Not wanting to be saddled on this case with still another civilian, Evan knows he has to answer this one tactfully and with kindness, especially because a priest is present. "Mr. Fred, I don't think you can do anything. This is a dangerous situation."

Fred, rejected by Evan's reply, remarks, "I ain't stupid ya know. I's been followin' ya, and ya didn't even see me, cop, right?"

Evan knows the old man is right because he had not noticed the tail. Evan knows and deduces he has been too traumatized to be observant. A mistake such as this can cost a cop his life. He will not let this happen again.

Fred says, not getting an oral acknowledgment from Evan, "Well, I'm gonna hep! I'll keep onna followin' y'all! You'll see! Ya can't get rid of me that easy! I'm like an old bulldog. I don't give up once I gits a mouthful! An—I gotta mouthful of this stuff!"

Tom says, "The old guy is harmless enough. Maybe he could just feed us information."

"What kind of information can an old bum give us? He's so eat up with the dumb ass, he'd get it backasswards," Jimmy says laughingly.

"You shut up, cabby! This is my damn decision to make," Evan says as the air once again intensifies between Evan and Jimmy.

"Oh come on guys! You're both being stupid!" Tom says.

William senses an urgency of his knowledge to resolve this situation. William asks Evan for a business card with his home phone number written on it. Evan gives it to William without questioning him, wondering what he has in mind. William walks over to Fred and gently puts his hand on Fred's shoulder. Fred finds William patient and respectful. Together they start walking back to Fred's car. William speaks loudly, purposely, wanting the others to overhear this conversation. "Mr. Fred, I think you can be of use to us. How about you keeping your ears open on the streets? You run across many people on the streets that might know something, right?"

"Yes sir, I does."

"Mr. Fred, if you hear anything, please call Detective Picard at the station or at home and give him the information. Here is his card." William puts the card in the old man's hand. Fred holds the card tightly and smiles.

"His home phone number is on it. We're trusting you to handle this branch of this investigation. Do you think you can handle that assignment?" William asks.

The two men have reached Fred's car by this point.

"Oh, yes sir. I can do thats, easy. Now it's gonna be all right. Mr. Fred will keep both his ears clean and open for any news 'bout Miss Kizzy." The old man looks back over his shoulder toward the other men and nods an approving nod. "I'll call ya, Mr. Cop. Ya can bet that—I'll call ya!" Fred articulates loudly to Evan. William shakes hands with the old man respectfully.

"You ain't never gonna hear from that old bum, cop," Jimmy divulges with a grin.

Fred enters his car and leaves a trail of exhaust smoke behind him and William coughing. William thoroughly wipes his hands with his handkerchief removing the noxious odor of Mr. Fred.

William, Jimmy, Evan, Tom and C.D. get back in the cab and continue their dreaded, but needed journey. The men talk on the way to the morgue.

"You handled that old man, Fred, nicely, William," C.D. says.

"Yeah, you're a quick thinker," Tom says.

"You know Kizzy must have genuinely cared about Fred," William says.

"Kizzy always cared about other people much more than she cared about herself," C.D. says.

"Yes. She would have been proud of the way *William* responded to Fred," Evan comments partly because he believes it and partly to irritate

Jimmy.

Jimmy leers at Evan's comment and then changes the subject. "Hey Tom, are you that former pro-football player, Tom Hastings?"

"Yes, I am that *former* pro-football player," Tom answers.

"Aw, man! I can't believe I am finally meeting you! You were great! Man, this is a privilege!" Jimmy says smiling.

"Jimmy, remember the important word is that I was a *'former'* pro-football player. Those days are long gone," Tom says.

Evan, surprised with the way Jimmy drove the cab to get away from the tail, refrains from complimenting him. Evan's cellular phone rings from his pocket. Discreetly, he takes the call. Alice has finished researching the information Evan gave to her about the new men he has met. Their alibis check out perfectly. He is specially interested in Jimmy's alibi. Jimmy was taking a dinner break on the other side of town from Kizzy's apartment with two other cab drivers from eleven p.m. until midnight the night of the murder. He picked up a fare at ten minutes after midnight just two blocks from the restaurant, and delivered the fare to the airport. Evan is not surprised. He thanks Alice for her help, feeling at ease with these men's involvement in this case. However, he does not let the other men know the topic of the phone conversation. William smiles, knowing that Evan has received corroboration of their alibis.

The men explain how each of them knew Kizzy. The way they are talking among strangers, giving personal details and expressing past feelings they each felt and are still feeling for her to this day, is strange. They do not reveal complete details or sentiments, keeping their private desires secretive. In regard to Kizzy, the men have two things in common. First, each man has loved her and still has feelings toward her. Second, each man expresses confusion in the mysteries of how and why she left each of them. Each man has a supposition or two of why she left, but no conclusive reasons—only this common thread in the Kizzy puzzle.

2

The visit to the morgue is not a pleasant one. Evan uses his police clout for approval for the men to view Kizzy's body. His phone call has only set the reason for the visit. What they face is abundantly revolting. Evan briefly breaks down having seen her body for the first time, but gains control in his usual way. Seeing her covered in bloody sheets on the gurney was one thing. However, to see her bruises, blood soaked hair, paleness and dismembered limbs tear him apart. Evan feels enormous anger. William loses his breath and collapses at the sight of Kizzy's battered body. Not even he can constrain his emotions upon seeing this sight. Weakness covers Tom's body. He becomes silent and does not move, staring into space for a short while. His body is aching with the need for a drink. He wants desperately to kill the fiendish agony of these feelings. Father C.D. falls on his knees beside the body and starts to pray profusely for her soul and his tranquility. This is a sight he has never seen.

Jimmy goes running from the room to the men's room. Hot feelings engulf him as he vomits violently. At the lavatory, he tries to cool the hot flush by splashing water on his face. This feeling scares Jimmy. He wonders, what in the hell is happening to me? He thinks that he has hated Kizzy throughout the years since and because she abandoned him and his love. Nevertheless, you do not feel hurt like this when someone you hate dies. Evan and Tom enter the men's room. Jimmy turns to them, his face wet and still considerably flushed. Suddenly, Jimmy leans against the lavatory and speaks to the men. "Are the old man and Padre okay?"

Evan answers, "Yeah, they're fine. No pretty sight, huh? How could somebody do that to her? She was so damn beautiful. It didn't even look like her anymore!" Evan knows for sure, without reluctance, that Jimmy did not kill Kizzy and neither did the others. Their pain and grief are too authentic.

"Look, cop, I wanna help ya catch the *shit slippery bastard* that did that to her!" Jimmy says with much insistence, leaning against the lavatory to support his weight.

"I don't think so," Evan declares. "Civilians getting in police business is dangerous and against police policy."

Jimmy responds to Evan's comment with his usual pigheaded attractiveness. He approaches Evan gaining hasty, willful strength. "Look, I got freakin' street contacts you could never imagine having, cop! Civilian? Hell, I ain't been a freakin' civilian since I was ten years old and began living on the *damn* streets of Chicago. You can let me help, or I can do it by myself. I don't give a slimy shit which one ya choose! Hell, maybe I'd work better alone anyway!" Jimmy boasts back to Evan while lighting a cigarette. "I sure as *hell* don't need your damn help!"

"Street contacts, huh?" Evan says with vast interest in what Jimmy is saying. Every policeman is interested in street contacts. Contacts from the street can lead a detective in a different path on a case. These contacts can save much valuable time, before the murder trail becomes cold. Jimmy wipes his wet face with a paper towel. Evan, pondering over Jimmy's statement with great detail, removes a coin from his pocket. While holding his hand waist high, he starts tossing the coin between his cupped hands in his usual way. He thinks maybe Jimmy might have contacts that he does not. Evan looks Jimmy over carefully. Jimmy is tough, streetwise. Evan is no fool. He can see Jimmy has been around, and he knows people on the streets. Yet this guy drives him nuts! Oh well, he thinks, I can tolerate him for just this little while for Kizzy.

"Okay, okay," Evan declares slowly trying to convince himself this is the proper decision to make. Evan gets uncommonly close to Jimmy's face, points his finger and speaks seriously and sternly. "Maybe you could be some help. We will work together, but I make the rules. *You* remember that *fact, clearly*! I'm taking a big chance letting you in on this case. This could cost me my badge. Damn! I must be crazy!" Evan holds out his hand to Jimmy. "Deal?" Reluctantly, these two very different men shake hands.

During the making of their agreement, they have not noticed that Tom is standing in the room, dazed and silent, but listening to their conversation. Tom promptly speaks, "Count me in, too. I must be in on this!"

Evan feels as if he is being crowded with unofficial, unprofessional assistants on the most important homicide case of his life. What he needs are more police investigators, not these civilian amateurs. "Hey, I don't know, football. What could you possibly do to help?"

Tom pauses to think for a few minutes, but not for long, gathering his thoughts quickly. Determined to persuade Evan, he quickly and convincingly states the facts. "I knew things about Kizzy neither of you knew. You forget she loved me first. I knew her before she ever came here."

"Well, that was a long time ago, Tom. I don't know what you could tell me about her today," Evan answers.

"I ran into her about five or six years ago. I may have pieces to this puzzle that neither of you has." Tom knows he is begging his case. He must convince Evan that he needs him to solve this murder.

"Well, it's none of my business, cop, but I like the damn guy. Shit, man, let him in!" Jimmy says and leaves the men's room to Tom and Evan for their argument. However, Evan follows Jimmy, trying to ignore Tom's begging argumentative statements.

Tom follows them, persistently pleading his case. "Come on, I need to do this for Kizzy. It's important to me. You know she would want me helping!"

"I know no such thing. You don't know what Kizzy would have wanted," Evan states.

"Listen. I walked out on Kizzy once when she needed me those years ago. She loved me then, and I knew it. I left her alone. I was wrong! Haven't you ever wanted to right a wrong?" Tom says. He continues, not giving Evan a chance to answer. "I know she is dead. This is the only way I can come close to making things right. Come on, give me the chance. Let me help you and Jimmy solve her murder."

William and C.D. overhear the men arguing. William, the oldest and perhaps wisest of the group, says, "Hey, wait just a minute here. Like it or not, we are all in this. Kizzy brought us together, and joined us. *She* joined us together. Remember, she left us a dilemma to solve, or have you guys forgotten that? We have to decipher what this 'possession' is that is referenced in her will. We have to ascertain where we can find it."

C.D. adds, "Mr. Newton is right. She trusted us, all of us, to solve this mystery regardless of how we feel about each other. We still loved her, right?"

"Yeah, sure, Padre," Jimmy answers in an abnormally polite, agreeable voice for Jimmy.

"Jimmy, please dispense with your cigarette," C.D. says. Jimmy smiles with disdain and throws the cigarette butt down on the hall carpet stomping it out.

Evan sees the point that C.D. and William are making. Evan understands Tom's feelings, sharing some of the same. He feels guilty about not being there to protect her. Sternly, Evan speaks to the men stating how they will handle this case. "Okay, men. Damn, I must be *crazy* for doing this!" He sighs and then continues. "We'll work together, but *I* am in charge, and the first man who forgets that fact is out! We'll do this *my* way, by the law. You have to give your word to follow my instructions to the letter. This isn't a game! Whoever killed Kizzy is still out there. This perp—"

"Perp?" C.D. asks.

"Yes, perpetrator, killer, could kill again. She left this mystery, perhaps to hide from that killer. Hell, maybe the perp killed her to get the mystery, whatever the hell it is. Do you, all of you, agree to follow my lead?" The four men nod their heads and shake hands, giving their word confirming the agreement.

William looks at the group. Evan is in charge, but even he is out of control at times. Without Evan knowing, William knows he will have to supervise this group and control them. William, who decides to guide these impulsive men somehow, someway, speaks using his convincing lawyer-toned voice. "I think we should solve the murder first. Then, we'll solve the quandary—mystery—Kizzy left us in the will. We will have to find her prize possession. Is everyone in agreement?" Everyone agrees.

As he looks at the men, Evan thinks that he has made a big mistake. How in the world will he lead an attorney, a priest, an ex-football player, and a wise guy to solve this murder? At least *he* will be leading and preventing them from being out there alone, getting in the way of the police investigation and the solution to this case. They could get killed!

Evan uses the telephone, telling the others that he is getting approval from his superiors to spend the night in Kizzy's home. While he has Alice on the phone, he has her check for police records on the men. He especially wants to know about Jimmy. Then, he talks to the Captain and gets approval to spend the night in Kizzy's home and the murder sight. Before he hangs up, Alice comes back on the line, giving a clean "thumbs up" to the other four guys. None of them have police records. He does not mention to the Captain that the other four men will be accompanying him to the apartment. He has to trust these men. Kizzy trusted them very much.

The five vastly incompatible men leave the morgue on the way to Kizzy's home, the murder site. While in the car, they start discussing the findings of her body. C.D. writes the details in a notebook that he brings along. Evan gives the details from the police reports from Pete, the coroner and the police forensics laboratory. "Her face had been bruised, as though someone had been hitting her. Her lip had been cut severely with dried blood on it. She was pregnant only a couple of weeks." Evan stops talking and looks in the passenger side rearview mirror. A black sport-utility vehicle is following them. He strains his eyes to get the license plate number. "Listen, don't anyone look around! We are being followed."

"Oh, dear Lord!" Father C.D. says. "Not again!"

"Can you see who is following us, Evan?" William solicits.

"No. It's a black S.U.V."

"S.U.V.?" C.D. asks.

"A sport-utility vehicle—listen. I want everyone to make sure their seat belt is fastened and hold on tight. Jimmy, I want you to lose this tail!" Evan announces.

Jimmy smiles delightfully at the request from Evan. "Y'all better hold on tight! I drive like a freakin' bat out of hell! Shit! Sorry, Padre. *Yee-hah*!" Jimmy, loving the adventure, increases the speed and starts turning randomly. After a time, he loses the sport-utility vehicle.

"Why do you think that car was ensuing—uh—following us?" William asks.

Evan discloses, "I don't know. But evidently someone is exceptionally interested in where we go and what we do. Maybe they're afraid we might find something."

"What's this 'sport-utility vehicle' shit? That sounds like a car advertisement. It was a damn four-wheel driver! It didn't have no license number, but it had a bright red bumper sticker that said—uh—'shit happens'," Jimmy says.

"Yes, you're right, but you shouldn't have been looking back, Jimmy! I told you not to!" Evan responds. "Thanks so much for announcing what it said."

"Don't get your shittin' panties stuck up your crack, cop! I didn't look back. I could see in the rearview mirror while I was driving!" Jimmy replies back at Evan. "Hey, I'm trying to clean up my language for the priest. I've been cutting out some of my words."

"Thank you, Jimmy," C.D. says interrupting to encourage Jimmy's respectful behavior. "Nevertheless, it would be pleasant if you could get in the habit of not using any lewd words. Now let's get back to the information we were reviewing. We've lost that car." C.D. hopes he has dispelled the anger in the air between Evan and Jimmy.

William reveals the date on Kizzy's will was two weeks prior to her slaying. William's action impresses Evan, because he did not notice that little bit of evidence. With the date seeming too coincidental, they agree she must have suspected she was going to die. Jimmy's fingers tap rapidly on the steering wheel.

After giving Jimmy a dirty look, Evan starts again with the details. "The perp had severed her arms and legs from her body, and from the cutting marks, a meat cleaver was used. The police have not really found much in the apartment. An expensive gold ink pen with the initials 'T.U.' engraved had traces of Kizzy's blood on it. Pete's report reveals blood was in the bedroom and in the kitchen, probably where the killer washed. The blood found was Kizzy's. In the bathroom, a bubble bath was drawn, as though she were preparing to bathe, and a small candle beside the tub that was burned."

Jimmy adds, "Kizzy loved long, soaking bubble baths."

Evan continues with the details. "Only a few fingerprints were found anywhere in the place, all Kizzy's. The other prints were purposely wiped clean. No murder weapon was found. A knife was used for her stab wound in the abdomen. Then the meat cleaver . . ." Evan stops speaking here briefly. Jimmy's irritating tapping on the steering wheel seems louder and harder to Evan. "Marks were in the carpeting beside Kizzy's bed. Probably this was the place the severing of her limbs took place."

C.D. turns away from the others to hide his repulsion, feeling nauseous. He tries to take deep breaths to dispel the nausea, wondering how a human being could do such a ghastly thing to another human being. What is happening to mankind?

Evan progresses with his explanation. "The knife that was used for the stab wound was a large knife with a serrated blade."

Jimmy, after thinking over Evan's evidence, says at this point, "Then the killer must've came with the intention of killing her and severing her limbs. A meat cleaver is not the usual weapon a killer just happens to be carrying in his pocket. Surely a burglar doesn't carry both a knife and meat cleaver."

"You are correct about that," William interjects in agreement.

Evan is happy that the men are thinking on the same pattern as he. Evan starts revealing further detailed information to the group. "Several kinky sex gadgets were in Kizzy's closet: a piece of rope, an electrical cattle prod, a gag, and a whip like device."

C.D. asks, "Were these horrible torture gadgets used by the deviate that killed her?"

"Unfortunately, a few of them had been used, probably two or three hours before she died. Several whip marks were on her back and legs," Evan discloses. The men, troubled that someone had tortured their beautiful Kizzy, cannot imagine the pain she must have withstood. After the revelation of these grisly facts, a hesitation is in everyone's speech to gain limited composure. The men think of Kizzy as a genteel, gentle, delicate young woman they hold in the great depths of their memories and hearts. Someone had hurt her severely. How in the world could someone torture a woman as beautiful and full of life as Kizzy? Over and over in each man's mind that question screams.

Evan continues giving details while C.D. takes notes. "Not one of the neighbors seemed to know Kizzy. Not one of the neighbors or the security guard saw or heard anything unusual the day or evening of the murder. The guard says she went out at about two o'clock p.m. on Friday in a hurry. She arrived home by cab at about nine o'clock p.m. He helped her carry many packages to her apartment, using his security card key for the elevator. Kizzy said she had left hers in the apartment. That was the last time he saw her. She was murdered sometime between ten forty-five p.m. and midnight on Saturday night. No one supposedly gained entry to her apartment except for her."

Tom asks, "Does she use the same card key to get in her apartment or just the elevator?"

"Just the elevator and the front door to the building," Evan answers.

William asks, "How did she get in the apartment? Did the security man let her in?"

"No, according to the report, Kizzy had her own key. Good eye for details, guys! I'm impressed," Evan responds, thinking maybe these men will be some help after all.

Evan continues to explain in great detail. "Someone had ransacked the place, but they could not tell if they had stolen anything. If they had stolen anything, it must have been worth a fortune, because many valuable art pieces and jewelry had been left," Evan says. "The only other entrance to the apartment is through the parking garage."

Jimmy says interrupting, "Ya know, I wonder where she got all that money she left to us in her will? Shit! A million in insurance and a million in money, that's no damn chump change!"

Suddenly, C.D. says, "I have always wondered where Kizzy got her money. Plenty of it existed. She also wore expensive clothing and jewelry."

Evan interjects in the conversation, "Hey, you want to know something else? Her apartment was paid for. She owned it and paid cash! Wait'll you see this place!"

3

The men arrive at the penthouse apartment building. Jimmy has a rough time finding a parking spot. He lets out a foul remark, excuses his behavior with C.D., lets the other men out and drives down the block to park. William looks upward at the tall glass building, overwhelmed with an eery foreboding. C.D. notices the textured, attractive red carpet leading from the curb to the door. Evan knocks on the glass door, flashes his badge to the security man and gains entry. The men, except for Jimmy, go inside. Behind a high, massive oak desk trimmed in shiny brass, the security man sits on a high, plush red velvet stool. The security man recognizes Evan from the morning of the murder investigation and greets the men. Jimmy beats on the door.

"He's with us, unfortunately. It's okay to let him in," Evan says. The security man opens the door, and Jimmy enters. A special security card key that must be used to enter the elevator is given to Evan. Jimmy takes it from Evan's hand, takes a close look at it and returns it to him. Evan explains to the others that after getting on the elevator, you have to insert it again and push the button for your desired floor. Evan goes through the ritual. The other men watch closely taking in every action. Kizzy's penthouse apartment is on the twenty-eighth floor, the top. After leaving the elevator, there is a small hall and only two doors. The doors are in close proximity of each other in the hall. Evan uses the apartment pass key that the security man has given to them and opens the door. The vile bloody smell has lessened a great deal, but still is traceable. When the door is opened, the rancid smell wreaks, lashing the men.

"Wow! The effluvium is disgustingly offensive in here," William says, covering his face with his handkerchief, not realizing the source of the odor.

"The awful smell is nothing now compared to the day they found her DOA," Evan responds and then continues. "It's the smell of blood." The men look at one another, moved by Evan's comment. After entering, the men accustom themselves to the rankness, until the smell is imperceptible after a while.

Jimmy expresses, "Damn, this place is like Fort Knox to get into. How in the hell did a killer get in here?"

Evan answers instantly, "Yeah, that's exactly what I'd like to know."

The men view the room, going over every detail in the furnishings. When Evan had explained to the others that Kizzy had furnished the apartment lavishly, he was making a great understatement. The carpet is so thick that their feet sink in it like soft, loose beach sand. Purposely positioned, providing just enough illumination, the light showcases the pieces of art work on the walls, some of which is still found sitting around on the floor.

Jimmy walks over to the couch and sits, running his hands across the texture. This couch is surely a piece of furniture Kizzy would have chosen—soft and silky much like her skin. He notices the neatness of the purse and keys on the table beside the sofa. Someone has destroyed everything else in the apartment in some way. Jimmy says, "Look, this joint is a shittin' mess, but look over on that little table. The purse and keys are on there really neat like!" This information is added in C.D.'s notebook. Evan did not remember seeing this in Pete's report. He planned to check on the detail later.

William walks over to a large oak cabinet covered with glass doors, gazing at his own reflection. His mind rambles back to the time when he and Kizzy had been at their special cottage. He remembered the way she had reacted when she had seen her own refection in the water of the lake. He could almost feel her standing behind him. In his imagination he could see her reflection beside his in the glass. His eyes refocus to the items in the cabinet. Behind the glass are elegant oriental and Aztec art pieces. Several of the pieces have been broken. William is no art critic, but they look expensive. William starts looking through the disarray of the room. He notices the backs are ripped from the paintings. Evidently, someone was looking for something small. He mentions this to C.D., who adds it to the clue notebook.

C.D. walks out onto the balcony and the muggy air. At the end of the patio is a glass greenhouse filled with plants and flowers. A few of the panes of glass are broken. The flowers are literally dug up, removing them from the soil. He redeems one of the petunia plants and remembers when he saw Kizzy in the chapel garden. She had been gently touching the petals of a few petunias that had been growing. C.D. recalled the smile that had been on her lips and the innocent look in her eye. How had that chaste, beautiful child come to this end?

Upon his entrance in the apartment, Evan goes straight to the kitchen. The blood has been cleaned but is still faint from the stain. Several dishes and utensils have been replaced in the cabinets. Others are still strewn around the floor, broken. He opens the cabinet. Pushed back in the cabinet is an unbroken crystal glass that brings about a special memory forgotten until this moment. As he holds the glass in his hand, his mind goes back in time.

Evan had been undercover. At a party for an organized crime leader, he ran into Kizzy in the kitchen. She was holding an empty glass in her hand—the same glass now in his hand. Her hair was bound in a bun framing her alluring face much as a picture frame frames a masterpiece. She looked picturesque dignified, like a special lady. Their eyes met briefly, but no word was expressed He was anguished she would blow his cover, but she did not. Evan's eye locked onto hers. After gazing in his eyes briefly with her magnificent, jewelec green eyes, she promptly left the room carrying the empty glass with her. Wher the police stormed the place to make the bust, Kizzy was not present. Evan dic not know when or how she left, or who had accompanied her to that party. He remembered the crystal glass had an arrow engraved on it.

In his hand is that same glass. Evan holds the glass in his hand gazing at i running his fingers across the smooth stem. Evan believes it is strange that she has kept the glass throughout the years. He will investigate the details of thi memory further. With great care, he places the glass in the cabinet, closes the door and jots the information in his little notebook, not wanting to share it witl the others until he has given this memory more thought.

Evan thinks of the information the rude reporter was asking him. Th reporter connected Kizzy with an organized crime woman. The "woman" ide was ludicrous, but the idea of organized crime was not so wrong. Evan' memory proves Kizzy had organized crime ties of some sort, but what kind Why did he not remember this sooner? Excessively overwrought by her deatl he had been in a fog—a heavy fog.

Tom glances in the kitchen, sees Evan covering this room and decides t enter the spare bedroom, the most sparsely furnished with just a simple bec dresser, and rocking chair. He opens the closet door. High on the closet shel sits a white teddy bear with a green ribbon around its neck. The back is rippe open, exposing its stuffing. A small amount is missing. Tom holds the bear a it looks familiar to him. Could it be the same bear he had won for Kizzy at th fair the year he graduated from high school? He cannot believe she has kept throughout the years. To rest his aching knee, he sits in the rocking chai briefly gazing at the bear and holding it in his lap. He remembers how happ and proud Kizzy had been to have that simple little bear. You would hav thought it had been worth a million bucks. She had promised Tom that sh would sleep with it every night. She had told her girlfriends at school about th prize. He had thought at the time that she had been just a foolish young girl. Now he realizes she had loved him with her entire young, naive heart. Tom feels bad about that fact. After putting the bear back where he found it, he limps from the room and goes in Kizzy's bedroom. He sees the outline of Kizzy's body on the floor beside the bed. The outlines of her other body parts are spread around the room. Tom gasps in air trying to gain composure at the horrible site as the harsh blood stench is reintroduced into his nostrils. The vision of her body flashes through his mind. Feeling weak and lightheaded, and to rest his aching knee, he sits on the bed, and it moves. The water ripples in the bed, a waterbed. Then, it comes to him. If the killer used a meat cleaver, why had the bed not burst or even punctured? Maybe the killer had known in advance the bed was a waterbed. He runs out to discuss his conclusion with the others. "Hey, Kizzy has a waterbed," Tom says.

"So?" Evan says making light of Tom's revelation.

"Well, why did he drag her off the bed to cut her up? The killer must have known it was a waterbed," Tom says.

Tom's observance impresses Evan. He is right. She had lain on the bed bleeding. Why had the perp dragged her off the bed to dismember her? If the perp would have used either the knife or the cleaver on her while she was on the bed, it would have punctured—an extremely interesting fact. C.D. and Evan make note of this information in their notebooks.

In desperation, the men start to search the apartment for more possible clues. Evan, feeling he should share the little he has with the others, explains about the organized crime party and agrees to research it further.

More clues must be in this apartment. These are the men who knew Kizzy better than anyone else alive. One of these men will know whether things irregular to Kizzy are present in this apartment.

C.D. finds Kizzy's jewelry box. The jewelry consists of genuine gold and silver pieces with diamond, ruby and emerald jewels. Why would a killer or thief leave jewelry of such value behind? He proclaims this loudly to the others. William notices no photographs are anywhere in the apartment. Kizzy loved photographs and collected pictures of everything, and none are to be found. Tom and C.D. agree with William's conclusion. Jimmy remembers Kizzy always had a diary. She loved to write down her little secrets. Evan remembers she also kept one when they were living together. Evan has forgotten about Kizzy's diary. How could he forget this? Evan explains that the police have not found a diary. Why? C.D.

starts to write down everything in his notebook, the evidence, the conclusions, the questions.

Jimmy is going through the desk when he accidently hits the answering machine button. Loudly the voice echoes through the apartment, "Hi, it's Kizzy." The men stop frozen in their tracks. "I can't come to the phone. I'm probably *real, real busy*. Soooo . . . leave me a sweet message. You know I'll call you back." The message ends with the sound of Kizzy's kiss.

C.D. sits. She still stirs sensations in him. They are feelings he should not be experiencing. He knows he has to resolve this, or he will never be free of the guilt; the guilt he feels because he loved her as a woman, and the guilt he feels because he never allowed himself to express that love to her. This day, it is too late!

The men go back to their searching. Within their senses, the smell of her blood has familiarized itself. Something wonderful has replaced it. Kizzy's scent fills the penthouse, her perfume and the natural bouquet of her skin and hair are on the clothes in her closet, the towels, the furniture, everywhere. The scent fills each man's nostrils, evoking strong sentiment and deep memories. Each man expects to turn around and see her standing there before them.

Evan notices the hair on her hairbrush and pulls out a strand. He runs his fingers across the hair, so smooth and silky, just as he remembers her hair.

"Why do ya suppose this joint is torn up so much?" Jimmy asks.

In a patronizing style, Evan answers, "Well, it's obvious to me someone was looking for something,"

"Whatever they were looking for, it must have been small," William says.

"Why do ya say that?" Jimmy asks.

"Jimmy, the backs of the pictures were cut. You cannot hide anything too large on the back of a picture," William conveys.

"Yeah, and they even tore up her spare bedroom. They even cut the back of a little stuffed bear I gave her when we were in school," Tom says. C.D. is writing quickly in his notebook.

The men search, remember, relive and feel throughout the night in Kizzy's home. Half the time they are detectives. The other half of the time, they are men.

Time passes quickly. In the early morning, they depart leaving behind a bit of their hearts. They decide to have Mr. Alexander have the belongings in the apartment appraised if the police give the approval. They know this is only the beginning of their search. Nonetheless, they are determined, each man in his own way, to put to rest Kizzy's soul and their own hearts.

Upon leaving the apartment building, the security man gives Evan mail that has arrived in Kizzy's box. Evan takes it along with him in the cab. He glances through the mail as Jimmy drives finding chiefly junk mail. Suddenly, he sees a windowed envelope that looks as if someone has enclosed a check. Gently, not to disturb the contents, he opens the envelope. A check made out to Kizzy for fifteen thousand dollars from a company called Fun Coin is inside. The address on the check is in southeast Houston.

"Damn, where did she get all that money?" Jimmy asks noticing the amount on the check.

"You can read the address just as well as I can, Jimmy!" Evan answers.

William looks at the check stub and says, "No explanation of payment is on the stub of this check."

"What is Fun Coin?" Tom asks.

"I know what it is!" Jimmy answers proudly and pauses.

"Well, are you going to tell us? Or do we have to guess, Jimmy?" Evan asks losing patience.

"Yeah, I'm gonna tell ya. Fun Coin is a video, pool table and pinball machine leasing company. They put machines in pool halls, bars, game rooms, and all!" Jimmy says.

"One of us needs to investigate this check and this company," C.D. says.

"I think it should be Jimmy because he's familiar with the company and where it is," Tom says with confidence in Jimmy. Jimmy smiles. Ambivalence shows across Evan's face.

William speaks, hoping to dispel Evan's doubts. "I think Jimmy is the impeccable choice. He knows more about these places than any of us. He also is the perfect type to enter such an establishment. Any one of us would look conspicuous. His demeanor and attitude could be perfect for getting information from them." C.D. agrees.

Jimmy looks puzzled, not understanding William's words, but thinking William had just complimented him.

Hesitantly, Evan agrees. "Yeah, okay, but no hero stuff, Jimmy. Any signs of trouble and you get out! Do you understand?"

"I got it, cop. I didn't know ya cared so much, cop," Jimmy says smiling sarcastically to taunt Evan. Jimmy happily agrees to visit Fun Coin tomorrow to get possible details on the check. Evan gives the check to C.D. for safekeeping, after giving Jimmy the check number and amount for use in his Fun Coin investigation.

CHAPTER X

The Funeral

1

Kizzy's burial day is cloudy and rainy, but with no thunderstorms. The weather suits this dreaded occasion. Rain reminds William of the big tears Kizzy had cried when she was a child. However, no grand exit exists for her, just as no thunder or lightning this day is present. The five men present will be crying, if not openly, then in their hearts. Mr. Alexander is the only other attendant. At the last minute, Bettey shows at the service with her recorder and note pad, but remains discreetly in the background to respect Evan. She never approaches Evan or the other men. She senses their authentic bereavement.

Pete is queerly absent. Evan figures he is spending his time and energy finding the perp. Evan's parents have sent flowers because they had briefly known Kizzy.

Evan reveals before the service that he has just recently learned that Kizzy had been raped a couple of hours before she died. Fury fills each man, even C.D. who fights this anger deep in his heart. Evan's superiors have given him strict orders that he is not on Kizzy's case officially. The Captain has explained he is too involved personally, and Pete is placed in charge of the case. Evan has promised to share information with him. Unofficially, Pete has agreed to work with Evan without telling the Captain.

Father C.D. performs a brief service. The casket is closed during the service because the men want to remember Kizzy alive. However, each has a formidable time forgetting the horrifying sight of her poor mutilated, bruised body at the morgue.

Father C.D. finds it difficult to pray through the lump in his throat. Tears fill his eyes frequently during the service, forcing many pauses. Each man places a rose next to the casket for Kizzy, except for C.D. who places a petunia. Death has not been kind to Kizzy. All the beauty she had inside has been taken away. Just as a vacant house, she looked empty and lonely when they viewed her body in the morgue.

During the reading, Evan notices an old man, slovenly dressed, loitering around another grave in the cemetery and looking over toward the funeral party. He is far away, so Evan cannot get a clear view of him to get a description. After the last prayer, Evan opens his eyes to see if the old man is still in the distance, but he is gone.

After the service, Mr. Alexander approaches the men. "I forgot to give you something that she left for you. Kizzy enclosed a key in the envelope with her will."

William takes the key in his hand. "What is this key to?" William asks.

"Mr. Newton, I have no idea. She just gave me the envelope." Evan inquisitively takes the gold key from William's hand. No identification numbers are on the key. They have been purposely removed. Each man looks at the key. None can identify it. C.D., who has become the keeper of the evidence, takes the key.

Jimmy leaves early to make his visit to Fun Coin. The other men linger around the grave, as though their staying kept her alive somehow.

After everyone leaves the burial site, the four remaining men agree to meet later in William's hotel room. Jimmy lives in a boarding house near Rice University. Evan's apartment is far out on the northwest side of Houston. William's hotel is centrally located near downtown, near Kizzy's, and the police station. Yes, meeting at this place is logical. Evan has already informed Jimmy before he left. They are going to compile the evidence together, to piece together the tragic life of Kizzy, a task of inheritance.

2

Quickly, Jimmy drives to Fun Coin, finding a large warehouse with a two-story, brick office building in the front of the warehouse. A tall fence with barbed wire encompasses the entire property with an open gate.

"Beware of Dog" signs are along the fence. Jimmy parks his cab in the parking lot front area and sits, tapping his fingers on the steering wheel taking stock of the premises. He notices a black limousine parked discreetly in the parking lot corner. Through the windshield Jimmy can see that the driver is inside, so he does not intend to approach the vehicle. He goes directly inside. A pleasant looking young woman sitting at a front desk asks whether she can be of assistance, smiling flirtatiously at Jimmy.

"Hi there. My name's Jimmy," Jimmy says, smiling and sitting charmingly on her desk. "You see a friend of mine named Keziah Theriot was murdered. Anyway, babe, we got this check for fifteen thousand dollars from here. Can ya tell me what's it for?"

The young lady's attitude changes quickly from friendly to irritable with the mention of Kizzy's name. She asks, "Exactly how are you related to the deceased?"

"Well, we're not related. She was a really good friend of mine. I'm one of the executors of her estate," Jimmy says trying to cajole her cooperation. Jimmy feels important and proud announcing the fact he has such a classy title like "executor."

"First you let me see the legal paperwork declaring you as an executor," she says.

Jimmy decides to use another method. Using his suave, debonair sex appeal, he makes small talk. "Ya know, I think I've seen you somewhere before. I don't think I'd forget a babe like you." His act is working as she smiles at him. "Listen, did ya know Keziah Theriot, or Kizzy as she was called?"

Her attitude changes instantly. She exclaims insistently, "Look, I think you'd better leave! I don't have to answer questions for you."

Jimmy tries smiling and using a gentler method. "I'm sorry if I upset ya, babe. I'm really a nice guy. How about me buying ya a cup of coffee?" Jimmy says smiling. This time it does not work.

She announces, "I want you off my desk, now! If you don't get out of here right now, I'll send for someone to remove you. Do you *understand?"*

Jimmy removes himself from her desk as he looks through the windowed doors directly behind her. Two extremely large men in suits are staring his way. They outnumber Jimmy, and sensing he is out muscled, he politely says, "Okay, babe. I'm sorry. I'm going. Don't get excited." He leaves before trouble starts with the two large men peering at him from behind the doors.

When Jimmy is entering his cab, he notices that the two large men have followed him out to the parking lot. They stand staring at him, daring him to come their way. He flashes one of his haughty smiles and jumps quickly in his cab. He drives straight to William's hotel room to disclose his uncooperative experience at Fun Coin.

CHAPTER XI

The Meeting of the Minds . . . Memories

1

Each man arrives at William's hotel room as promised. The other four men wait patiently for Jimmy to arrive, making small talk to pass the time. Evan is even more on edge than usual.

"Are you all right, my son?" C.D. asks.

"Yes. I'm fine, Father. It's just not knowing the answers is driving me crazy!" Evan answers.

Tom says sympathetically, "Yeah, I guess a man in your line of business is used to being able to find the answers. It must be harder for you than the rest of us."

"Patience, my son, we'll find the answers. I know in my heart we will!" C.D. answers. They wait for Jimmy's arrival, continuing with small talk. Evan is positive that Jimmy will come whether he finds answers or not. Finally, Jimmy enters the hotel room. Evan finishes making small talk with C.D. and Tom, as he tosses his coin from one cupped hand to the other in his usual way. Jimmy is nervous. He stands at first jiggling his leg.

"Why don't you have a seat, Jimmy, so we can get started?" William says, politely noticing Jimmy's arrival. Jimmy sits and nervously bounces his leg. He starts tapping his fingers on the windowsill. To get things started, William says, "I know this is not going to be easy for us. Nonetheless, we agree that what happened to Kizzy was unspeakable. We are going to have to work together to solve this puzzle. Each one of us *must*, let me repeat and stress, *must be honest.* We must tell everything, no matter how trivial it is. Agreed?" Each man nods his head to William's statement. Jimmy is exceedingly nervous today. He taps loudly, irritating the others, especially Evan. Evan looks toward him with a stern look. Jimmy sees, but chooses to ignore Evan's look.

William starts, "Okay, I will go first, because I knew her first in her life."

Jimmy interrupts saying, "Look, let me tell y'all one thing before we get started. I went to Fun Coin. The girl at the front desk wouldn't even admit knowing Kizzy. She wouldn't tell me nothing without papers setting me up as an executor of Kizzy's estate. That little company sure has fancy furnishings, at least in the front office. Everything was first class. Anyway, the interesting thing is that for a small company, there sure was a big, black limo in the parking lot. *And* two big thugs in suits inside the building serving as bouncers!"

" That's very interesting," Evan says to show genuine interest, trying to ignore Jimmy's bouncing leg, which this day irritates him more than usual. "Did you get a license number on that limo, Jimmy?"

Jimmy has thought that he performed his investigation admirably. Still, as always, Evan has found a mistake. Jimmy's confidence is shaken. He shakes his leg furiously and begins to tap his fingers on the windowsill, increasing the annoying sound. Nervously, alternating standing and yelling, Jimmy says, "Nope. Damn, cop, I forgot about shit like that!" Jimmy sits, resuming the drumming of his fingers on the arm of the chair.

"Maybe, that limo is involved somehow with the strange gold pen with the initials, 'T.U.'," says Tom.

Evan, whose fuse is short this day, says, "Will you stop that incessant tapping, Jimmy?"

"What's it to ya, cop! It eases my *freakin'* nerves!" Jimmy yells back.

"What the hell is wrong with you! Are you some kind of *nut case?* I've never seen anybody have so many damn nervous quirks! I'm sick of your shitty habits!" Evan says.

Jimmy leaps from his chair and catches Evan's tossing coin in mid air. "Well, I'm *sick* of you tossing your freakin' money around! What? Is it just to show us ya got freakin' money in your freakin' pocket, you sorry sack of shit?" Jimmy spouts holding the coin tight in his fingers and pushing his hand in Evan's face.

"Why you *little*—" Evan screams as he jumps on top of Jimmy. The two men fall to the floor, wrestling and tumbling about. They bump into a table, knocking a lamp to the floor, breaking it into a million pieces.

"*Stop it!*" William yells. Tom rushes over, grabbing Evan by the collar, yanking him and securely holding him. C.D. and William try their best to restrain Jimmy.

"I can't take that damn ass hole anymore!" Evan yells.

Jimmy starts to yell when C.D. says, "Obviously, you two are going to have to settle this! I have an idea."

"I think we are open to anything, Father," Tom says.

"A place that I know about has a boxing ring. I think you two men should resolve this before we go further with the matter of Kizzy's murder.

Your frustration with each other is becoming distracting for all of us," C.D. says.

"I think that is an excellent idea," William says. "Do you agree to resolve this matter definitively in the boxing ring?"

"Hell, I can *kick* his cop ass anywhere!" Jimmy spouts.

"*Yeah!* Let's go!" Evan says angrily. The five men leave for the amateur boxing arena that C.D. has mentioned. During the ride, they make sure to keep Jimmy and Evan separated.

2

Jimmy and Evan glove up and enter the ring. Jimmy is a good three or four inches taller than Evan. However, the two men are muscular, so the match starts. Jimmy throws the first punch. Evan counters with a blow to Jimmy's chin. The boxing bout goes on and on. Blow after blow, blood drop after blood drop, neither of the men concedes. Obscenities are flying, and eyes start to swell and discolor.

"I hope this stops their bickering," William says.

"So do I," says C.D.

"I think they are just as oil and water. I don't think they're ever going to mix," Tom says.

"Well, they have to get this antagonism out," William says.

"Yeah, maybe it'll vent their energy until we can find out who killed Kizzy," Tom says. Jimmy and Evan fight and fight until neither can stand any longer. They grab onto each other struggling to remain on their feet through their exhaustion.

C.D. steps in the ring. "I'm willing to call it a draw. Do you two men agree?" Jimmy looks at Evan, not willing to concede unless he does.

Breathlessly, Evan says, "Yeah, okay." Jimmy nods his head in agreement. Evan and Jimmy separate. When Evan's guard is down, Jimmy throws a punch to Evan's stomach. Evan bends over moaning in pain.

"*Jimmy!* That was uncalled for!" C.D. yells.

"Yeah, where I come from, ya take a damn freakin' punch whenever ya get the chance. I saw a freakin' chance!" Jimmy says loudly.

Tom steps in the ring. "*Shit!* Look, kid. We're not where you came from! We're all here trying to get along and solve Kizzy's murder! Knock that damn chip off your shoulder and start cooperating, or *I'm going to knock it off for you!* I like you. Don't make me change my damn mind about you!"

Tom yells, shaking his fist in Jimmy's face.

Jimmy looks at Tom's overshadowing size. Jimmy is smart enough to know Tom could kill him with one blow. "Yeah, okay, football. Ya like me, huh?" Jimmy says smiling. C.D. coerces Evan and Jimmy to shake hands and brings out a first-aid kit. With William's help, he applies antiseptic and a band-aid to Evan's lip. Antiseptic and a band-aid are applied to the cut over Jimmy's left eye and an ice pack to each man's swollen black eyes.

The men drive back to William's hotel room. Jimmy is too tired to bounce his leg or tap his fingers. Evan, so distracted by his fatigue and aching body, forgets about tossing his coin.

3

They sit quietly and rest as William says, "Evan, may I see you out in the hall for just a moment?"

"Yeah, sure, William," Evan says. Evan and William exit to the hallway.

"Listen. I need to talk to you about Jimmy. I know you don't like him. Regardless, you two men have to get along," William says.

"You're right. I don't like anything about him. He's always got something moving. If it's not his leg, it's his tapping fingers!" Evan says.

"Those are nervous idiosyncracies, just as your coin tossing," William says.

Evan looks dumbfounded at William's comment. "Well, I've never thought of my coin tossing as a habit, but just something I do that helps me think better," Evan says.

"I think the tapping and shaking of his leg, help Jimmy think," William says. "Think about it. Your coin tossing is just as distracting to the rest of us as Jimmy's habits are to you."

"Well, he's so damn rude, too. I hate punky ass hole guys such as him!" Evan says.

"Just because his life was atypical from ours that doesn't give us the prerogative to berate him, Evan. I agree that he is not a polished sort of person. Yet, I think a story is behind Jimmy of which we aren't aware. Give him time. When he trusts us more, he'll talk to us. Then, we'll discern what made him so callous. Indeed, a portion of this flamboyant man must be good. Kizzy cared about him," William says and returns inside.

William's words make Evan think. He stays in the hall alone thinking. William is right. Kizzy cared about that ass hole punk. One good thing about the guy is that he does not have a criminal record. Evan realizes maybe he is expecting too much from Jimmy. After all, he is no detective. Sure, he has made a few mistakes. He has had a small amount of good input, also. Evan decides to tolerate Jimmy for Kizzy. Maybe William is right and more exists in Jimmy than he shows to people. Evan returns to the hotel room.

William, upon seeing Evan enter, says, "First point of business, please, everyone call me William, not Bill or Will, but William. We're going to get to be close working on this situation which is so profoundly sensitive to all of us. That puts us using first names. Jimmy, I will call the attorney, Mr. Alexander, about obtaining the proper executor papers for us all, just in case anyone else asks for this authoritative paperwork. These papers can be vastly beneficial in obtaining the information we need. We'll get the answers from Fun Coin."

"I don't think those papers are going to make any difference about getting information from those people. I'll feel better if Jimmy doesn't go back. It might be dangerous with those two men present," Evan says with genuine concern. "I think you got some interesting information about Fun Coin already. Good job, Jimmy." Jimmy smiles at Evan's surprising compliment.

William says, "To start with my story. Oh, Father, be sure and take notes on each testimony. The information could be crucial."

"What's this shit? Testimony? Hell, I thought we were just telling a story. Ya make it sound so legal. I don't like legal shit!" Jimmy says in his usual impertinent way to correct William. Then, he turns to Father C.D., asking him to please excuse his language. Father C.D. nods, expecting nothing less from Jimmy than his usual atrocious language and mannerisms. Father C.D. has almost become accustomed to his language and behavior always being followed by an apology.

"I am sorry, Jimmy. Okay. For Jimmy, we will call this information, our 'stories,' not testimonies," William says to make Jimmy feel more at ease. Jimmy nods in approval. Father C.D. pulls out his notebook and tape recorder.

William starts telling his story. He tells everything. When he reveals the information about Kizzy's abortion, he is interrupted.

Tom stands with a bolt, shifting his weight from his injured knee.

"Damn, she was pregnant with my child? I never knew! Why didn't you tell me?"

William replies looking coldly at Tom, "She made me promise. Besides you were too involved with yourself to care."

Wistfully, Tom says sitting down, "I'd have married her. I loved Kizzy. I only wish you would have told me." In sadness, Tom puts his head in his hands. C.D. briefly goes over to comfort him. William considers that maybe he had been wrong in denying Tom this information so many years ago. However, it had been Kizzy's wish. Now that she was gone, Tom should know about the pregnancy. William thoroughly feels relief at revealing this secret. William continues speaking, finishing his chapters in Kizzy's life.

William's abortion tale disgusts Evan. William is an attorney who has taken an oath to uphold the law. However, he was responsible for arranging an illegal abortion. Evan feels no mercy for anyone who breaks the law. Evan holds his thoughts to himself.

Each man takes his turn, listing the details as much as he can without being disrespectful to Kizzy. All in different ways, each man has known and loved her. Each man has known the same Kizzy, and yet, an entirely different woman. Full of emotion, the disposition in the room is somber.

After the testimonies, C.D. closes his notebook, turns off the recorder and says, "Obvious to me, each one of us loved Kizzy in some way. Each of you knew her in a much different light than I. Sometimes, it is as though she were a different person with each of us. I can only conclude that she was a difficult person to know."

"No, Padre, I think she was just a woman. And, we're all men. Sometimes it's like the different sexes make us from different worlds," Jimmy says.

Tom says, "Two things are beyond doubt. We recognized her special beauty, and we each loved her."

William takes a deep breath, turns gazing out the window and says, "Maybe Kizzy was what each of us wanted or needed her to be. Maybe that is why she never stayed with any of us. Not one of us loved her for who she was. Maybe we shortchanged ourselves and her by not learning who she was. I think that is sad for us."

Evan, disagreeing with Jimmy's comment, says, "No, I don't think Kizzy ever really knew herself, who she was. She was just searching trying to find herself. But I guess none of us helped her in any way find out whom she really was. Maybe we were just as lost as she was."

C.D. adds, "Son, we are each looking for our 'true' selves and on a long journey. For most of us, it takes a lifetime. Someone took it upon himself to shorten Kizzy's journey."

"What the hell! Let's find out exactly who Keziah Theriot was," Evan blurts out throwing his arms in the air.

"Yeah, and let's start by finding the low life who killed her!" Jimmy concludes.

Aloud, C.D. starts slowly to go over the notes. They decide upon the important clues, deleting the others. C.D. highlights these in detail in his notes. Then, C.D. starts to review them aloud. "Okay, here is what we have. Kizzy had an abortion at age sixteen. She left home to be a movie star. She arrived in Hollywood and lived at the YWCA for a year. We know she did some babysitting with Evan at this point. When she was about twenty-one years, she meets me, C.D., and works in the soup kitchen. A little after this, she met and started living with Jimmy after failing at a commercial. She was broke financially until this point. Her personality changes here, and she becomes more remote, but she doesn't move out on Jimmy. Then, he sees her in the red dress in front of the restaurant."

"Whoa, hold it right there, Father," Evan interrupts. Evan, standing, continues his responsive interruption. "What was the name of the restaurant, Jimmy, where you saw her in that dress?"

"Geez that was a long time ago," Jimmy responds. Evan rolls his eyes impatiently to Jimmy's response.

"Think, son," C.D. adds.

"This could be crucial, right Evan?" Tom says.

"Uh . . . Picconnes. That's it, Picconnes," Jimmy mentions.

"That swanky Italian place?" Evan asks.

"Yeah, that's it," Jimmy answers. Evan makes a note in his black book.

William speaks up, "You act as though the starting place is there. Is it, Evan?"

"Yeah, Mr. Newton, I mean William, I think it is. Something happened there to change her. We have to find out what. We've no leads from her life in the present. Therefore, we'll start at that point in the past," Evan says as he puts his notebook back in his shirt pocket.

"Continue Father, please," William says, as he motions in the air

"Next we find her in my church in Houston. She looks as if she has been hurt and gives me the expensive earrings. Then she spends that short time with Evan in the hotel room. They live together for a short amount of time. William gets the birthday card from Rio. Evan sees her at an organized crime party while undercover. Six years ago, Tom runs into her in a hotel bar with a strange older man. Well, that's about it!" C.D. says.

Suddenly out of the blue, Jimmy stands quickly and proclaims, "Listen, I gotta go." Before anyone else in the room can say a word, Jimmy bolts out the door in the impulsive way expected of him by the others. Jimmy's action piques Evan's curiosity, so he excuses himself and follows Jimmy.

"Hey, cabby, wait a minute will ya?" Evan yells out to Jimmy as he travels down the hall after him. Jimmy looks back over his shoulder, but does not stop. Evan runs after him, since he notices Jimmy is not stopping. Jimmy enters the elevator, and Evan, quickly putting his hand in the doorway, enters the elevator with him. The elevator starts progressing down.

"You're going to Picconnes aren't you, cabby?" Evan asks.

"Do ya have to call me cabby? My name is Jimmy."

"Look, I kind of think cabby, or maybe *crabby,* fits you!"

Jimmy hates Evan's response, but holds his temper. He, too, remembers the painful punches from Evan in the boxing arena. Jimmy starts jiggling his right leg nervously. "Look. I don't really like cops. I don't need ya to take care of me. I'm a big boy. Give me some space and stay the *hell* out of my way, will ya?"

Jimmy's reply enrages Evan, whose nerves are on edge already because of this situation. Evan grabs Jimmy by his T-shirt neck and shoves him hard against the elevator control buttons, hitting the "stop" button. The elevator jolts to a stop.

"Take your *damn* hands off me, cop!" Jimmy yells as he shoves back against Evan.

At this point, Evan senses Jimmy is not going to back down. As a police officer, Evan knows he is acting inappropriately. Evan also remembers the boxing ring and how Jimmy can take care of himself. He also remembers William's words echoing through his head to give Jimmy a chance.

"Okay, I'm sorry. All this with Kizzy has me a little upset. I don't usually act this way," Evan says as he lets go of Jimmy and straightens Jimmy's T-shirt. "I know that wasn't the way to talk to you about this, cabby. Come on, I like calling you cabby. I know your name is Jimmy. You call me cop."

"Hey, cop! You're not the only one upset by this. Ya act like you're the only one that loved her," Jimmy says, seeming a little calmer.

"Okay, okay, Jimmy. I'm sorry I roughed you up. I was wrong. We have to work together. Come on shake hands, huh?" Evan holds out his hand to Jimmy. Jimmy releases the elevator stop button and it starts downward. The two men are reluctantly shaking hands, when the elevator door opens.

C.D. is standing, waiting for them, a little unhappy that they left without the others. "You two thought you were going on this adventure by yourselves? *Not on your life.* I ran down the stairs. William and Tom were a little slower, but they are on their way. You two *hot shots* are going to wait! Do you hear?" C.D. says impatiently to the two men.

This is the first time that Evan and Jimmy have seen C.D. annoyed or upset in this way.

"Yeah, yeah, Padre, don't get excited. We'll wait, right Jimmy?" Evan says as he gestures to Jimmy.

"Geez, if we all go, we're gonna look like a damn parade on the way to Picconnes," Jimmy blurts.

"Well, if we look like a parade, we'll just *look like one!* We've agreed to work together. That means *together.* Do the two of you understand what together *means?"* C.D. says as he points his finger in their faces. He is still a little wrathful at being left behind.

"Yeah, we do Padre," Evan answers trying to calm C.D.

"Hey, Padre, loosen your collar and chill, will ya?" Jimmy answers with his smart, joking humor. This comment brings a smile to C.D., extinguishing the hot moment for everyone.

Meanwhile, in the stairway, William and Tom slowly come down the stairs together. Tom stops to rub his knee. William stops to gasp for air. While they descend the stairs, step after step, they talk. William says breathlessly, "You have grown that moustache and gained a little weight, but I still recognized you."

"Well, you're a good bit grayer and more wrinkled, but I recognized you," Tom says grimacing from the pain in his knee.

"You know you are going to have to pay for what you did to her someday. Don't you, Tom?"

"Okay. I got her pregnant. But Kizzy had a little bit to do with the pregnancy, too. I didn't do it by myself!" Tom says irritated by William's remark and the pain from his knee.

"No, not just that, Tom," William says stopping on the step briefly. "You left her and broke her heart!"

"Yeah, well, I was young and stupid. We all make mistakes, William. We're not as *perfect* as you are!" Tom says limping down the stairs. "You wronged Kizzy and me by not telling me she was pregnant! Who put you in charge of my life?"

"I did what I thought was best at the time. Just know, somewhere, somehow, you *will* pay!" William says emphatically, knowing he has not forgiven Tom. Tom knows William is still as relentless, judgmental and unforgiving as ever. Things never change.

William and Tom have made it down the stairs and approach the other men. Tom has stopped to rub his bum knee. William has stopped to catch his breath. A breathless William speaks to get things rolling. "Jimmy, you supply the taxi fare to the airport. I'll pay for the airline tickets to Hollywood for us. Okay? We'll go together."

"Hey, football, you okay?" Jimmy asks.

"Yeah, it is just an old football injury," Tom says, rubbing his knee.

"Can I help ya out to the car?" Jimmy asks.

"No. I can manage. Nevertheless, thanks for asking, buddy," Tom answers. Jimmy smiles at Tom's reference to him as his buddy.

4

The five men pile in the taxi. With Jimmy driving, they whiz to Intercontinental Airport hoping to take the first flight out to L.A. By pay phone from the airport, Jimmy signs out with the cab company for a few days. He claims he is ill, and Jimmy is ill. He is ill with an obsession to solve this murder and this mystery and swelling with the excitement of the event.

Problems at the airport occur. All the flights to Los Angeles are booked. They purchase tickets for the first flight departing early in the morning in two days.

5

The men return briefly to William's hotel room. C.D. uses the telephone to check on happenings at the church. William goes down to the lobby to complain about the cleanliness of his room and to report the broken lamp. Evan has left the others to return to the station for a brief time. He has a few notes to finish on another case that have slipped his mind.

Tom and Jimmy sit together.

"So, football, would ya have really kicked my butt at that boxing ring?" Jimmy questions Tom, smiling.

"To get some peace in this investigation, hell yeah!" Tom answers. "It's not something I was looking forward to, but we've got to keep our minds on solving this."

"Did ya really leave Kizzy? Or was that just a line for the others? You can be straight with me."

"Yeah. Of the five of us, I'm the stupidest!" Tom answers.

Jimmy looks puzzled at Tom's answer. "Hell, *she* left all of us. We were the ones left looking stupid, not you!"

"You don't get it do you, Jimmy? Kizzy was the most beautiful woman, inside and out, that I have ever known in my life. Believe me, I have known many women. Not one ever measured up to Kizzy. Because *I was stupid,* I lost her not once, *but twice* in my life. So, you guys aren't stupid, at least not in my book. I am."

"Geez, ya really loved her, huh?"

"Didn't you?" Tom asks. Jimmy looks down pondering Tom's question and a little embarrassed because of his love for Kizzy.

"Hey cabby, man, it's no sign of weakness to love someone and lose them. I think it's weakness when you can't open your eyes enough to recognize what you have, so you throw it away. I was weak and stupid."

Jimmy is serious at this point. "If she were here, Kizzy, what would ya say to her, Tom?"

"Gosh, I would have so much to say," Tom says pausing for a moment between words. "I think I'd say, 'Kizzy, babe, please forgive me. Forgive me for messing up your life and my own. I'd tell her how I ache for the times when we were together. I'd tell her that my life has only been alive the few spans of time when I was with her. I'd tell her that I will love her forever and that nothing in the world will ever change that." Tom pauses. "What would you say to her, Jimmy?"

Jimmy is different at this point. Tom notices a disheartened gentleness about him as he takes a deep breath before answering. "I guess I'd tell her I was sorry for hating her throughout these years. I feel bad that she got killed. Kizzy didn't know how to survive on the streets like me. She was too trusting and too hungry."

"What do you mean, too hungry?"

"She was always hungry for attention, for money, and for fame. That's a weakness on the streets. Ya can't survive. Kizzy had these dreams—" Jimmy says.

However, C.D. who is listening to this private conversation interrupts him. "What is wrong with dreams, Jimmy? We need them to survive the bad times in our lives."

"Dreams don't come true where I come from, Padre. Dreaming only takes your attention away and can get ya killed," Jimmy answers.

Tom says, rubbing his painful knee, "Dreams got me through the pain in my life. So in that way, dreaming was good. I still dream about Kizzy while I'm awake and asleep. But sometimes dreams do cost you. Jimmy is right about that. Everything in life has a price. Nothing comes free. My dream of a successful career cost me her and my knee."

Behind deafening silence is a certain known realization. Each man thinks of Kizzy, of life, of her suffering and of theirs.

The time until the airline flight is to leave allows each man a day of pondering to finish. They each go their separate ways with thoughts of Kizzy, death, and trouble rolling around in their troubled heads like marbles.

CHAPTER XII

Pondering and Picconnes

1

In his room, Jimmy sits on his bed, tapping his fingers on the bedside table. He looks down at his tapping fingers and thinks of Evan, smiling at the thought of how this act irritates Evan so much. His room is not the quietest place in Houston. People have always surrounded Jimmy, so he likes it that way. The sounds of life around you make you less lonely, or so Jimmy tries to convince himself. Yet, loneliness is the one constant in his life. Jimmy, a survivor, is tough, street smart and able to take care of himself. He has learned from the streets to keep emotion buried deep inside or keep it void. Showing sentiment makes a man vulnerable, or so Jimmy believes. He lies back on his bed, listening to the sounds around him and staring at the ceiling, feeling the coolness of the sheets against his bare arms. For the first time in his life, Kizzy had made him care about someone other than himself. He had felt vulnerable and weak with her. He hated that feeling, and yet he longs for that sensation again. Jimmy has to believe that nothing he could have possibly done would have changed what happened to Kizzy. He did not make a mistake in letting her go. She is the one who wanted to leave, not him. He had not thrown her out or left her. He believed she had left him for that guy, William. However, after seeing William, he doubts that theory. William is an old man! Why in the hell does he care about this after all these years? Why does he feel he has to find these answers? Why is he even thinking about this? Maybe he will just wait, let the others solve this mystery and just collect the money Kizzy owed him. He knows the bitch owed him! Then, he will be free! Jimmy walks over to the wall mirror behind the sink. His undershirt is wet with sweat. However, in actuality his room is cool. Jimmy knows that when someone murdered Kizzy, *the murderer* had pushed *him* in a corner. Nobody pushes Jimmy Smithson in a corner! If they do, they better be prepared for the fight of their life! And Jimmy will fight dirty if needed. The murderer had chosen to enter his territory! Kizzy was his, no matter what she thought. In his mind, Jimmy knows he is in this thing until the end. Hell, he has survived a lot worse than this in his life. Jimmy washes, changes his undershirt, puts on a clean T-shirt and prepares to go out for a bite to eat. Hey, a beer with a burger sounds great! He smiles remembering how Kizzy loved burgers with extra onions. Out he goes.

2

Tom spends most of his day at the bars in downtown Houston. When one bar stops serving him, he moves onto another. The more Tom drinks, the more he wants and craves the deadening effect of the alcohol. Only now it takes more alcohol to reach this effect. The alcohol and pills deaden the pain in his knee. However, no matter how much he drinks or how many pills he takes, nothing can deaden the misery deep in his heart. Tom has never felt excruciating heartache such as this. An emptiness seems to ache inside. He cannot have surgery or see a trainer to fix this kind of pain, which hurts thoroughly. At times, he even feels his heart will break into a million pieces.

In one bar, he sees an enticing dark-haired woman sitting at a back table. Her back is to him. His heart skips a beat as he hopes it might be Kizzy, hoping this entire thing is a big mistake. He hopes with all his heart that it is Kizzy. When she turns, though, he sees this is not she. Then, his heart sinks. He knows the alcohol is just giving this false hallucinating hope. He turns and gulps down his drink, burning his throat, making his eyes water. Tom knows he will never see her, hold her, hear her soft voice, or sniff the natural fragrance of her sweet flesh again. Tom wishes he could just have one more chance to tell her how sorry he is about the abortion. He concludes that perhaps the incident with the baby hat was Kizzy's memory of the pregnancy and abortion. If she were here, he would explain to Kizzy that he would have married her. He would have made it right for her. That chance will never come. He will never have the chance to *love her again*! His selfishness and huge ego have destroyed his life, and even hers.

Tom leaves the bar, staggering out to the street. He goes down the sidewalk recklessly, bumping into the few people he passes. What has he done with his life? What a mess he has made of everything. Suddenly, no one else is around him on the sidewalk. He is strangely alone in darkness and gloom. Slow-moving clouds shadow the moon. The street is deserted. Tom hears footsteps approaching him from behind. He tries to turn to see who it is. However, the alcohol slows his reflexes. Without warning, something is placed over his head. He cannot see, or breathe. As someone holds him and carries him, Tom struggles. Thrown in the back of a vehicle, lying on his side, he tries to lift his arms, but cannot. They seem to be tied down or restrained in some way. He turns over on his back. The bag is still over his head. He can only hear several mumbled voices. Who are these people? He tries to yell out, but is unsure if anyone can hear him. He can feel that the vehicle is moving and hears the engine. Tom has no way to trace the time he is traveling. Unable to take a deep breath, it seems like a long time.

At last, the car stops, and he hears doors opening. Roughly, they lift him. Once again, someone is carrying him. Someone throws him down. He lands on his shoulder giving him much pain. Unexpectedly, suddenly he can move his arms. He tries to fight, yelling at the top of his lungs. "*Hey*! What the hell is going on?" he outcries. No one answers. Once more, someone is holding his arms again, but he thinks the rope that was holding him has been removed. Someone removes the bag, but before he can see anything or even focus his eyes to the bright light, a blindfold replaces the bag over his eyes. Sitting up, his arms are tied down again, so he cannot move. His legs are tied down against the legs of a chair. He cannot see. He hears the shuffling of feet. Tom asks again, "What is going on? Who are you people? What do you want with me?" No one answers him. Tom repeats the message angrily at this point, struggling with all his might. "Who in the *hell* are you people? Let me *go!* Do you *hear me? Let me go!* You don't know who you're messing with!"

Someone speaks in a muffled voice trying intentionally to mask the sound of his voice. Tom listens to the voice closely. "Why are youse guys investigating Kizzy's death?"

"Who are you? I can't see you?" Suddenly, Tom feels pain in his left jaw. He knows someone has hit him.

"If you answer my questions, I'll let cha go! *Coppish*?" the voice asks with a strong muffled dialect.

"Yeah, yeah," Tom affirms to appease the man.

"One more time, why are youse guys investigating Kizzy's death?" the man's voice asks, demanding a response.

"We want to find out who killed her. That's all."

"Why? Who is she to youse guys?"

"We were her friends. Friends care about other friends. Someone brutally murdered her. Was it you that killed her?"

"No!" the man answers angrily without hesitating. "I am asking the questions here! Not you!" The man is hostile at this point. "What have youse guys found out so far?"

Tom knows he has to give this guy some kind of answer, but not too much. "Well, she was stabbed to death and dismembered. Her apartment was a mess. Somebody seemed to be looking for something. Uh . . . that's about it."

"That much was in the newspaper. Youse guys ain't found out nothing else?" the man asks still masking his voice.

"Nope. That's about it." Tom can feel pain in his jaw again. He knows someone has just slugged him. This time the slug is so hard that Tom and the chair topple to the floor. Tom feels dizzy. He shakes his head trying to clear the feeling. The floor feels cold and hard against Tom's shoulder. He surmises it must be cement.

"I think you know more, but ain't telling me! I want to know everything! Or I'm gonna let this guy rearrange your face! He's very good at that!" The man laughs.

Tom thinks he must shock these people or they may kill him. He must say the unexpected, so Tom laughs aloud. "Hell, it wouldn't be the first time I had my face rearranged! I'm a former pro-football player." Tom can tell the men have moved away from him. He can hear garbled voices. He is hoping that what he has said will make them abandon the beating. He hears them come closer. Suddenly, someone hits Tom so hard it knocks his chair over, crashing brutally against the hard floor surface. Tom feels dizzy after this blow. He cannot tell where the blow hit or where the pain is. He feels a hasty blow to his stomach and ribs that takes his breath away. He thinks they must have kicked him. He feels them lifting the chair upright with him in it. At this time, he wonders if what he said did any good. Maybe his comment has backfired, and they think he is tough because he is a football player and used to suffering pain. They may be thinking of beating him to death. Tom tries to search his mind for a tidbit of information he can give to this man so that the beatings will stop. Suddenly he blurts out, "Meat cleaver! The killer hacked her up with a meat cleaver! I know that! That wasn't in the newspaper!" A pause happens. Tom senses the man is standing right in front of him. He can smell a strong, distinctive, expensive man's cologne. When the main man doing the questioning is around him, the smell is stronger.

"Yeah, yeah! We ain't gonna get much outta this guy! He's probably been hit in the head too much." The man's comment provokes laughter from several voices. "Take him back where you got 'im, and youse guys get rid of 'im!"

Tom feels panic. What does this man mean when he says, "get rid of 'im?" Tom wonders if they plan to kill him. Tom has never thought of dying. He has never been this close to death before. After untying his legs, they jerk him, and Tom's body almost leaves the floor. He knows these are strong men because he is no lightweight. Again, they drag him out to the car. They do not wait for him to get his balance and walk. They throw him inside. The tightly tied blindfold is still covering his eyes. No longer sniffing the strong cologne, he knows the man doing the questioning is gone. Tom feels the motion of the car but does not know how long they travel.

Finally, Tom feels the car stop, and the doors open. He feels himself being thrown. He lands hard. Tom has a hard time catching his breath. The hard surface has knocked the breath out of him. He cannot see where he is. He hears sound, but far in the distance. Tom yells, "Help! Help! Somebody help me!" At last through maneuvering, he gets to his feet. He walks a short distance and falls, collapsing on a pile of debris. He lies there, not moving, but conscious. After a while of working his hands lose from the rope, he removes the blindfold and tries to focus his eyes. His head, jaws and stomach are hurting, and it hurts to take a breath. Feeling this symptom before, he knows he may have a cracked rib. Blood is on his lip. He licks the salty taste, and it stings. He understands how poor Kizzy must have felt waiting to die. How can he correct the unfortunate way he treated Kizzy? How can he make this right? He raises his head to vomit. His throat burns from the thrust of the alcohol filled vomit. He lays his head back down and moans. Here he lies, in a trash heap in his own vomit. Tom can feel tears running down his cheeks, but he is not crying. He wonders what is the source of these tears. Tom hears footsteps. Oh no! Are they coming back to hurt him more? Someone is approaching.

In the alley, a young teenage girl approaches Tom. "You okay, mister?" she asks. Tom raises his head and looks at her. The vision of her is blurry. He squints his eyes hoping to clear the view, but clears it only slightly. He can see that her hair is light brown.

"You need help, mister?" she asks gently. Here she is, this tiny young lady, asking Tom, a grown man, if he needs help. Tom's vision clears a little. Squinting, he looks at her painstakingly. She is about the same age as Kizzy when Tom had first met her at school. She has the same shoulder-length light brown hair. Darkness fills the alley, but Tom can tell her eyes are blue or perhaps even *green*. Is she *real*, or is she his imagination working overtime? Is this an angel? Is this Kizzy? Tom tries to hold on to consciousness, but he cannot. Tom passes out.

Tom awakes an hour or so later with his head splitting and staggers onto his feet. Not even knowing how long he has been lying in this alley, he knows he cannot stay in this alley forever. He remembers the young girl. In desperation, he looks around the alley, seeking the sight of the young girl. No one is around. Tom cannot erase the sight of the young girl from his mind, standing over him looking down, offering help to him. The more he sees her in his mind's eye, he knows it was Kizzy. In his mind, Tom has to believe that the young girl he saw was Kizzy. The superstitious side of Tom grasps the thought that this is a sign. She had come to help him. Tom knows what he has to do. He has another chance. He has to help Kizzy as much as he can, this one last time. He will stop drinking and help the others solve Kizzy's murder, just for her.

Tom walks back to the hotel, staggering the whole way partly from injury and partly from alcohol. He goes inside. His hands are shaking. With an urgency, he wants another drink and needs another drink, now. He looks at the doorway to the bar as he walks through the lobby. From the need of alcohol, his body hurts. This time, he passes by the bar doorway, only glancing over his shoulder. He goes straight to his room and takes a long, hot shower. His knee is beginning to hurt again so he takes a pain pill with water and goes to bed. As his body shakes profusely, he has trouble getting to sleep. Yet, with great relief, sleep comes, and Tom welcomes it.

3

William finds great solace in his hotel room being empty at last. Wiping things with a towel, William straightens the room. He phones his office in New York and speaks to his partner, explaining the situation with the murder. His partner, also his friend, is understanding, stressing that William should take a sabbatical and resolve everything. His partner mentions to William that the police have phoned him to check William's alibi. William is not surprised when he mentions this information. The understanding from his partner takes a great load off William's mind. William takes responsibility intensely seriously. By resolving this, he can return his thoughts to Houston, Texas, and Kizzy. William retrieves a clean glass and holds it up to the light. Smudged ever so faintly, he washes the glass at the sink, wipes it and fills it with ice and water. While sitting, relaxing and thinking, slowly sipping the water, William starts to review the events that have transpired in his mind since he has arrived. William is a man who, methodically and in great detail, looks at the facts, angles and emotions. He deliberates about the men he has met. These are the same men that Kizzy had loved. William can recognize the attraction to each man after hearing their stories. He sees what she has loved in each man. Evan is strong, lawful and moral. Everything for him is either right or wrong, black or white. Tom, being her first love, would always be special to Kizzy. William does not care for Tom much, but his hatred is lessening. William recognized that even though Tom is older, he is till a fine specimen of manhood—the muscular physique, the fine dimples and large soft brown eyes. Jimmy, a handsome-looking young man, is strong in a tough-mannered way. William realizes Kizzy thinking that Jimmy needed her, allowed him to feel weak. Yet, his street strength was there for her at a crucial time in her life. William is happy Jimmy gave refuge to Kizzy all those years ago. C.D. is perhaps the strongest of the group. His religion seems to answer his questions and perhaps even Kizzy's. Then, William contemplates himself. What had Kizzy needed from him? What had she found in him? William knows he was always a thinker, a solver of problems. He sees himself as highly rational. William sits upon his bed, thinking. He knows the answer. The one thing the men have in common is strength. Each has a different kind of strength, but strength all the same.

William goes over every detail of the case. He hopes they are on the right road to the solution. He has never been an investigator before, but he does recognize a clue when he sees one. As emotionally draining and upsetting as this entire business is to him, William finds it refreshing and intellectually stimulating. His mind is thinking in an entirely new way, a welcome challenge this late in his life. Harshly, William coughs. He hopes physically he will be able to finish this case, such an important case to solve. William realizes he has been thinking of this as "just a case." However, it was not "just a case," but Kizzy's death. William thinks how much he has missed Kizzy throughout the years. He has yearned to see her, to make sure she was well and happy. He will never get that chance. With deep hurt, William knows he will be alone for the rest of his life, an insufferable thought. Maybe the reality of this is as painful as Kizzy's death. Memories of Kizzy and their love are so bittersweet. Life is so dead since she left him. William sighs and feels restless. He leaves his hotel room to go for a walk with a thirst to see people, even strangers. He wants to hear the clamor of people and of life surrounding him! He walks the busy, downtown streets alone, losing himself in the people and noises of life.

4

C.D. has a million things to do this fine day at the church office. Even so, he has difficulty concentrating. He shuffles the papers around without aim, trying to get organized. Physically exhausted, he is unable to sleep at night. He cannot eat. Emotionally, he is drained. He lays his head on his desk, trying to find a tiny bit of contentment for his weary body.

Father Lawrence, the associate priest at the church, comes in the office. "C.D., are you okay?" Father Lawrence asks.

"Yes. I've got to get organized. The church festival is just around the corner. It's our biggest fund raiser," C.D. answers.

"C.D., you're exhausted. I can see that by just looking at you. You can't go on like this! Is there anything I can do to help you with this?"

"Lawrence, you are a good man, a good priest and most of all, my good friend. By just asking, you've helped me. I know I've left so much of the church work for you to do lately. I'm exceedingly sorry about this because it hasn't been fair to you." C.D. looks down with embarrassment.

"Don't feel bad, C.D., you have the need now, not me. Someday, it may be me. I know you will be here for me if I ever need you!" Father Lawrence says. "Not to change the subject, but do the police have any leads?"

"Well, we seem to be working much harder on her case than the police, Lawrence. We're not even professionals except for Evan, who is a police detective, but not on the case officially. We just cared for her, and that is our interest. I've wondered why the police seem to be dragging their feet on Kizzy's case. I think they believe she's just another murdered prostitute. Still, she had value! She was a human being."

"Well, you know they've many murder cases to solve, C.D. You men only have hers to solve. Maybe that's why it's going so slowly for the police."

C.D. is silent for a short time, pondering the thought Lawrence has given him. "Yeah, Lawrence, you're probably right. She was just so special. You didn't know her. She was God's finest creation of womanhood. I'm finding out many things about her, and many are not good. Yet, I know, deep inside, she had a good soul."

"Well, the soul is what the Lord judges. You know, no matter what man says about her, only God will judge her."

C.D. smiles at Lawrence's comment. "Oh, Lawrence, you're right. See, you are a good priest, Father Lawrence." C.D. finds comfort in Lawrence's wise words.

"Coming from you, C.D., I take that as a great compliment. Thank you a lot, Father." Lawrence says patting C.D. on the back, "Put the work away, Father, and leave this office. Go for a walk in the garden or the park. Get some fresh air and sunshine to help with your paleness. Let the Lord unburden you with his beauty of the world."

C.D. smiles at Lawrence, deciding to take his suggestion. C.D. walks to the church garden. Birds fill the large oak trees singing. C.D. runs his hand across the rough bark of one of the trees. The flowers in their glorious bloom bring notice to the weeds growing among Kizzy's flowers, which saddens C.D.. It reminds him that he desperately needs to hire a gardener. He has been so busy since Kizzy's death. C.D. reaches the petunia bed, bends and slowly pulls one of the weeds from the bed. C.D. thinks it is much as the weeds in her life. A small hummingbird flits from flower to flower, seeming to stop, increasingly inserting its bill in a small petunia, draining it of its sweet nectar. The smallest petunia in the bunch reminds C.D. of Kizzy, small and pristine just as when he first met her. Petunias were her favorite. Someone had drained the life from Kizzy, just as the hummingbird is draining the nectar from this tiny flower. C.D. is inclined to boldly scare the tiny bird away from the flower, but he does not. At long last, the bird departs the small flower. C.D. bends down and closely looks at the small petunia, still there, still delicate and beautifully unspoiled. C.D. knows nature will replace the nectar, by God. However, no one will replace the blood that drained from poor Kizzy's mutilated body. This thought brings gloom upon C.D. She is gone, forever. C.D. can wish, can dream, and can pray incessantly, but nothing will bring Kizzy back to this world. C.D. looks at the clouds, billowy, soft, blue and white. He finds contentment in knowing that Kizzy is in a far better place than on this earth. She is an angel in Heaven. God will know her good soul. He will feel her good heart. No one will convince him that Kizzy was bad, not deep inside where it mattered. C.D. knows whoever has killed her must pay. Yes, vengeance is the Lord's, but maybe this group of five men who loved Kizzy in such special ways are on this earth to do God's will. Possibly they will find the killer. They will help the police bring this killer to justice. C.D. will help. He is feeling better, now. Father Lawrence was right. God has touched

C.D.'s heart, giving it relief, wonderful relief. Nonetheless, C.D. knows it will be short lived. In his heart, mind and soul, he knows he will return to this garden again for God's caress and God's renewal of his soul. C.D. puts a small smile upon his lips and walks inside.

He is just in time to offer comfort to a needy parishioner. This is C.D.'s life's work, giving help and support to others, all God's children!

5

Evan arises early. As usual, he goes to the station to finish a large stack of paperwork, awaiting his attention alone. These are the cases that Evan and Pete have solved together before Kizzy's death. Evan methodically punches the keys on the typewriter and computer and signs each report. Evan knows he is good at his job. Difficult to keep his mind on these repetitious reports, he deliberates Kizzy's case. Evan knows he is a good cop. *No, he is a very good cop.* He feels confident as a police detective. He has solved many murder cases using his distinct second sense. Why does he feel so helpless when it comes to Kizzy's case? Maybe he feels this way because he is working without Pete. Evan concludes, without misgivings, that he must work with Pete officially on this case. Just outside the door to the Captain's office, he stands and thinks. He has to convince the Captain and make him understand. This is extremely important! Probably, this is the most important case in Evan's life. Evan walks straight inside the Captain's office without knocking. He starts to beg his case with the Captain. "Look, Cap. You know I'm damn good at my job. Pete and I are a pair. We're as two bookends. The books fall down without the two bookends. Pete's on Kizzy's case, and he needs me. Come on, Cap. Give me a chance. I knew her. I know things about her that Pete could never know or understand. I have an inside track on this case."

"Evan, you know you are too close to this. You can't be impartial. You know I can't let you work on this one."

"I have to!"

"Hell, if you caught the perp, Evan, you'd kill him. Wouldn't you? Admit it Evan!"

"Cap, you don't know—"

Before Evan can finish, the Captain interrupts. "Wouldn't you? *Answer the question, Evan!*"

"Hell, Pete hasn't even found the perp, Cap!"

"Yeah, but when you do, when you come face to face with the guy that killed her, the guy that literally hacked her up, what are you going to do, Evan?"

"I . . . I don't know! *Damn it, I don't know*!"

The Captain, trying to push Evan to the break of his emotional control, points a finger and yells, "You remember how she looked. She was *dismembered! Raped! Tortured!* Envision her pain, her screaming, her crying and begging for the hurt to *stop,* Evan! The perp did whatever he wanted to her before she died! She was *entirely his!*"

Still standing, Evan, moved by the Captain's words, leans against the desk, wincing in heart-rending agony. He cannot take listening to the words pouring from the Captain's mouth. The picture of Kizzy being handled, hurt by that perp runs across his mind's eye like a movie reel. His anger builds. He yells out loudly, "*Yeah!* Yeah! The *son of a b—*" Evan stops before he finishes the words. Then he starts again, "He deserves to—" Again, Evan stops before finishing his sentence, trying desperately to regain his control. He cannot let the Captain know the way he feels inside. He must stop these feelings.

"What, Evan? What does he deserve? *Tell me, Evan*!" the Captain yells.

Exhausted from emotion, Evan yells at the top of his lungs, "To *die!* To die! I want *him* to *die!*" Evan sits in the chair laying his head on top of his folded arms against the desktop coolness.

The Captain hates the necessity of speaking to Evan in this way. However, he has no choice because he cares a lot about Evan. He tries his best to comfort an extremely distraught Evan. The Captain's calm voice pours forth, "Evan, it's okay. You are only human. I'm sorry, but I had to do that. You can't work on this case. You know that—" Before the Captain can finish his statement, Evan runs from the office—from the building to his car.

Evan knows his chance of working on this case is over. He feels powerless. His only chance is to work unofficially through Pete. Evan goes home. He eats a slice of old bologna from the refrigerator and drinks a half cool beer. He calls Pete ,who is not at the station or at home. Evan leaves messages everywhere for Pete. Anxiously, he waits for Pete's return call.

The phone rings. Posthaste, Evan answers expecting it to be Pete, but is disappointed. He hears Bettey saying insistently, "Come on, Evan! I've been patient. I want information on this damn case."

Evan explains, "Look, Bettey. I 'm not on the case, Pete is."

Bettey explains, "I can't get hold of Pete. The jerk won't answer my calls. Alice explained that ya knew the deceased quite well."

"Yeah. I knew her a long time ago but don't want to talk about her death."

"Why not, Evan? I don't—" Before Bettey can finish speaking, Evan hangs up on her. The phone rings again. Evan lets the machine answer, thinking Bettey is calling back. He listens to the machine, screens the call and discovers she is calling. "*Damn it!* Damn it to hell, Evan! I don't deserve to be treated like this!" she says angrily, feeling insulted at first. Then, her voice turns to one of pain. "It really hurts me that you hung up on me. I thought we were friends. I guess I was wrong. I'm the only one who had the friendly feelings in this relationship."

Evan feels guilt ridden about what he did to Bettey, but he cannot talk to her about Kizzy's case yet. Hoping to make amends, he telephones the florist and orders a small flower bouquet to be sent to Bettey at the newspaper. On the card, he apologizes for his behavior, asks for her famous forgiveness and her patience. He signs only "Evan."

Evan analyzes the clues in Pete's reports. He wonders who the owner is of the gold pen with "T.U." engraved on it.

The phone rings again. The machine answers. "Hey Evan. Tom here. I was kidnaped tonight by some men who wanted to know about Kizzy's case. I—"

Before he can finish, Evan answers the phone. "Yeah, I'm here, Tom. Are you hurt? Who were they?"

"Yeah, I'm okay. They just slugged me several times and kicked me in the ribs. I don't know who they were. I was blindfolded or had my head covered with some sort of bag. The guy doing the questioning used extravagant, expensive smelling cologne. He tried to mask his voice, but he had this accent, much like a street kind of accent."

"Did you report this to the station, Tom?"

"Yeah, I reported it. I left the info for your friend, Pete."

"Did you see the vehicle, Tom?"

"No. They came from behind me. The only clues I have are the smell of the man's cologne and his accent, Evan."

"Did you tell them anything?"

"The only thing I told them was that she was dismembered by a meat cleaver. Everything else I told them about the case was in the newspaper. I only told them about the meat cleaver, hoping they would stop beating me. For a while there, I thought they were going to beat me to death, Evan!"

"Good thinking, football. You're sure you're not hurt badly? I'll be happy to come and take you to the hospital." Evan is truly concerned about Tom.

"Yeah, I'm fine. I've had better beatings than this one during playoffs!"

"Well, get some rest."

"Yeah. See you tomorrow, Evan." The phone call concludes. Evan feels they must be getting close to something if people were interested in their investigation, but what? During the wait for Pete's call, Evan realizes that all he has are the other four men. They alone want to help him. Maybe together they could solve this case. He knows they each have a fixation to solve this case for different reasons. Evan sits in his apartment alone the rest of the day. He fills his day for a while with watching a game show, drinking a few beers, eating more old bologna and cheese.

Evan waits the entire day for Pete's call. Late in the night, after he has slightly dozed off, the phone rings. The machine answers. Then, a voice comes through. In the darkness, Evan struggles to find the lamp button, or the answering machine "off" button, or the phone receiver. He is all thumbs. Because he is too clumsy to do these duties, the machine continues to record. "Uh, this is Fred. I got news for ya. My clean ears done heard somethin' good." Fred pauses and laughs as a child. "A couple a men I know thats live sometimes in the alley near Miss Kizzy's saw this lady comin' outta the place wheres ya park the cars the night Miss Kizzy was kilt. They says she got in a real fancy dark blue car with gold lines on the sides like the kind real rich people drives. She wuz a real thin lady and not too tall. She had on dark sunglasses at night. She had this piece of cloth, uhhhh, bandanna, uhhhh no, scarf. Yeah, that's what they calls it, on her head! One of the guys says she is wife of real important man on streets. They says her man is one of those mob kinds of guys. They ain'ts got no watches or clocks, but they says it was right 'fore tha closin' of the restaurant down the street, which I thinks is 'bout eleven o'clock." Fred pauses to cough right in the receiver rudely. "See, I told ya I'd gits somethin'!"

At last, Evan reaches the telephone receiver after turning on the lamp light. Fred has already disconnected. Evan rewinds the recorder and listens to the message carefully. Evan finds Fred's message interesting. He remembers what the reporter from *Scandal* had said about Kizzy. Surely this has been trash! It could not be true, not about Kizzy! The suspect is a thin woman wearing sunglasses at night. She visited Kizzy's building the night she died and is driving an expensive dark blue car with gold stripes. How could a small thin woman have the strength to hack Kizzy? Evan writes the information in detail in his pocket notebook with a note reminding him to give the information to C.D. the next day. Evan knows this information will be difficult to check. People who live on the streets seldom give information to police. Evan makes plans to check this information out as soon as he returns from L.A.

Pete never phones.

6

The next day, the five men arise early and ready themselves for their flight. They meet at the airport. Evan pulls out his cellular phone and calls Pete. Surprising to Evan, Pete answers.

"Haven't you been getting my messages, Pete? Why didn't you call me back?" Evan's voice is filled with impatience.

"Look, I'm sorry, Ev. I've been so busy. What's up?"

"Busy with Kizzy's case?"

"Yeah, mostly. I've been canvassing people in the other buildings trying to find somebody who saw something, Evan. You know that takes time."

"Did you get anything, Pete?"

"Nope."

Evan remembers the message from Fred. He explores telling Pete, but something stops him. "I've been thinking about Kizzy's case, Pete. Another apartment is on the same floor with Kizzy's. Was it robbed?"

"No. I checked on that, Ev."

"If it were a burglary, why didn't they rob the other apartment?"

"Well, the only thing I can figure is maybe they planned to hit the apartments one at a time," Pete says.

"Have you figured out how the burglar entered the apartment building, Pete?"

"No. That one's got me stumped. You got any ideas, Evan?"

"Nope. If it were burglary, why did the perp leave that valuable art work and expensive jewelry? That doesn't make logical sense to me."

"Maybe he was interrupted, panicked and ran, Ev."

Evan feels that Pete is stonewalling. "Did you get the report of Tom's abduction last night, Pete?"

"Yeah. I'll look into it," Pete's voice sounds uninterested.

Evan loses his patience. "Listen, Pete, I'm going to be out of contact for a couple of days."

Pete's voice is suddenly anxious and inconsistent. "What's up? Are you going somewhere? Where, Evan?"

"Well gotta go, Pete. Talk to you in a couple of days." Evan disconnects the telephone before Pete can pursue him with questions any further. Evan turns his cellular phone off. He knows Pete will be trying to phone him. Evan knows why Pete has not received the same tip as he received from Fred. Pete has been questioning everyone around the area. However, street dwellers seldom share information with the police.

He remembers again Fred's message and the trash the *Scandal* newspaper reporter had given to him. He tries to push it from his mind. Could it be true? No, he will not believe it! Evan clears his mind of that thought.

7

While waiting at the airport, Tom's hands are shaking. His battered jaw and lip are sore. He has told the others about his experience the night before. C.D. notices the trembling hands. Tom is wearing dark glasses to hide his bloodshot eyes. C.D. thinks the glasses might be to hide a black eye from the beating, but Tom says they did not hit him in the eyes. Tom excuses himself and goes to the men's room. C.D. follows him, wanting to be sure that he is all right. Tom has removed his glasses and is splashing water on his face at the sink. His eyes are much worse than C.D. has visualized. They are not blackened, but are bloodshot from the alcohol.

"Are you okay, Tom?" C.D. asks concerned.

Tom looks down at his hands, ashamed and trying to hide his bloodshot eyes. "Yes, finally, I think I am okay, Father. That beating and what happened to me last night has changed me."

"Being beaten often changes a person, Tom. That's not abnormal."

"No, not that way, Father. I've had plenty of beatings on the football field but never thought I might die. I know what Kizzy was feeling waiting to die that night she was murdered. It was awful. And something else happened."

"What do you mean?"

"I'm going to stop drinking, Father. I made a promise to myself last night."

"That's wonderful! If there is anything I can do to help you, please let me know."

"Can I ask you a question, Father?"

"Sure, anything, Tom."

"Do you believe in angels or spirits, Father?"

"Well, I believe in life after death. I don't know whether God permits the a soul to return to earth. Angels were mentioned in the Bible. I suppose people have unexplainable evidence of angels these days. Why are you asking me this, Tom?"

"Last night, laying in that alley, beaten, and still drunk, I saw Kizzy. *She* wanted to help *me*."

"Are you sure it was Kizzy, Tom?"

"No, I'm not sure," Tom answers quickly. After pausing with a puzzling look on his face, he responds, "Yeah, it was Kizzy. She was there, and then she was gone. I genuinely believe it was her. It was Kizzy when she was young, when I first knew her years ago. She was tiny, beautiful and with the purity she had in those days. I think she came to help me. She wants to help me change my life. That's why I am not going to drink anymore. Do you think I'm stupid, Father?"

"No. Tom, if you believe it was Kizzy, that's all that matters. Whatever gives you the strength to stop drinking, I applaud wholeheartedly." Tom smiles at C.D. and puts on his dark glasses with his shaking hands. The two men leave the men's room just in time to make the flight. Tom runs limping on his bad knee with C.D. helping him. The two men just barely make the flight. The other men have already boarded after checking the luggage, among them C.D.'s and Tom's.

The flight is short, only a couple of hours, and is filled with discussion of this proposed adventure.

Jimmy says leaning brazenly over C.D. talking to Evan across the aisle, "Ya know it's been a long time since Kizzy and me were at Picconnes."

"Yes, you are right about that," William says agreeing.

"Yeah. I know it's been a long time. However, I got an intuition in my gut about this—a cop's instinct," Evan says.

"Oh, great! All the way to L.A. on a feeling in a cop's gut!" Jimmy says, tapping his fingers against the arm of the seat.

"Look. I can't explain it! I just feel it!" Evan says.

Tom says, "Well, I agree with Evan. Hey, I believe in stuff like that.

He's the cop, not us!" C.D. and William also agree. Jimmy shakes his head disgustedly, realizing they outnumber him. Evan feels confident knowing the accurate history of his long shots over the years.

At the airport, the men pile in a taxi. Jimmy taps his fingers nervously on the front passenger side door, irritating the driver as he barks out instructions on how to drive a cab efficiently. The driver makes facial signs of displeasure.

8

The men arrive at Picconnes Restaurant, an opulent building with expensive furnishings and the finest linen tablecloths and napkins. Although the restaurant is closed at midday, the men talk, or bully, their way inside where the employees are busy with the preparation for the evening meal. William has a photo of Kizzy when she was about eighteen that he shows around. Evan has one he and Kizzy had made in one of those in-store photo machines. He shows it around. C.D. has several photos he took of Kizzy, which he shows. Everyone denies knowing Kizzy. Jimmy and Tom take notice of a young Asian girl in the back of the room, just watching and listening. The five men walk out to the entrance of the restaurant.

"Something squirrely is going on in there," Evan says quietly to the others.

"Yeah, I think they're hiding something," Tom adds.

Jimmy and Tom disappear from the others, walking around the rear of the building to the back entrance. The door slowly opens. The young Asian girl, who was standing in the back of the restaurant inside, walks out carrying a trash can full of garbage. She looks alarmed, as she looks around anxiously and with caution to see if anyone else is in sight. "I know her. I know Kizzy," she whispers purposely to the men. "Please, talk quietly. Once she was very kind to me when owner was cruel. Kizzy save me. I owe her. I cannot believe she is dead," the young girl says with a heavy oriental dialect.

"Do you know anybody with the initials 'T.U.' that was involved with Kizzy?" Tom asks.

The young girl considers briefly. "No. Nobody with those letters in name."

"What can ya tell us about Kizzy?" Jimmy asks quietly, honoring the girl's wishes.

Again, the young girl looks around in fear. She speaks with her voice shaking in almost a whisper. Fear is evident across her face. "Kizzy was with very powerful man, Dominici Giovanni, who was not nice man. He gave her much money and fine clothes. Kizzy was only his girl for a while. Later, she was girl of whoever Giovanni wanted. That all I know. Tell no one I told you this, please," the young girl begs.

"When was the last time you saw her?" Tom asks.

"About one year! Please, tell no one about this," she continues to plead.

"Don't worry. We won't tell anyone," Tom says to the young girl shaking her hand. "Thanks, kid." She smiles briefly and hurries back inside after hastily emptying the trash. She quickly locks the large door behind her. Jimmy and Tom walk around to the front. The owner is out front talking with William, Evan and C.D.

Evan utters impatiently, "Where in the hell did you two disappear?"

"I had to take a leak, cop. Ya know how I *love* to take a piss in alleys," Jimmy affirms nonchalantly, purposely to irritate Evan.

With sarcasm, Evan says, "Why did Tom go along, to hold your hand?"

"No, cop. I had to go, too. Is that okay with you?" Tom replies. Jimmy smiles at Tom's remark to Evan. The owner is paying close attention to the conversation.

"Gee, Jimmy, it's against the law to take a leak in the alley!" Evan responds.

"Hey, can we discuss my bathroom habits another time? Did any of ya find out anything?" Jimmy asks.

C.D. replies as he points at the owner, "No. This man has been most helpful in trying, but he just doesn't know anything about Kizzy. I guess this lead is a dead end." They politely thank the owner and climb back in the cab.

9

Later at the modest L.A. hotel, Jimmy and Tom share their information with the other men.

"Back at the restaurant, when Tom and me went into the alley, we ran into a young slant-eyed girl. She knew Kizzy," Jimmy says, flaunting his knowledge before Evan.

"What did she say?" William asks.

"Well, it seems Kizzy was with this real 'powerful man,' as she put it, named . . . uh, what was the name, Jimmy?" Tom asks.

"Dominici Giovanni," Jimmy answers. C.D. has opened his notebook and is writing down everything.

"Yes. That's his name. Anyway, he gave her money and nice clothes. Then, according to the girl, he put her, our Kizzy, out to prostitute for him," Tom says.

Evan asks, "Did she know anything about the ink pen with the initials?"

"Don't worry, cop. We asked her about the pen. She didn't know nobody with those initials," Jimmy says proudly.

"Anything else?" Evan asks.

"Yes. She was afraid to talk to us," Tom inputs.

"Yeah. Scared to death. She acted like somebody might see her," Jimmy adds. "But dealings with Dominici Giovanni could scare the hell out of anybody."

"Who is this man?" William asks. "His name is familiar to me for some strange reason."

"A crime lord. No nice guy at all," Evan answers.

"Well, if this man is in Los Angeles, maybe we should stay here and investigate," C.D. says.

"That won't be necessary," Evan says. "He's in Houston a lot these days."

"That's where I have heard the name. He was in the crime family from New York, my home state," William says.

"He even has a home in Houston. We don't like his kind in Houston. We inherited him from Dallas. I think before Dallas, he was in New York. We in law enforcement are always trying to find out his business, but to date we have been unsuccessful. He has a rap sheet a mile long. I wonder if he's the one who brought Kizzy to Houston from L.A.?"

"You might be right about that, Evan. You know I met Kizzy in Houston, and believe me she was well dressed," C.D. says, agreeing with Evan's surmise.

With a decision to return to Houston and continue searching, each man wonders how Giovanni fits in with this case. His initials are not "T.U." Evan remembers the time he saw Kizzy undercover at an organized crime party. Maybe Giovanni had brought her to the party, but had not been arrested. Then who is "T.U.?" Well, maybe by questioning Giovanni they will find the identity of "T.U." Maybe Giovanni had Tom kidnaped, but why? What is he afraid that they will find? Evan feels elated with the new information.

The pieces are starting to compute. Or, so he thinks.

CHAPTER XIII

Jacko

1

The men arrive back in Houston early the next day after spending a restless night in hotel rooms in Los Angeles, courtesy of William. The men separate, each going his own way.

Evan visits his apartment briefly. His answering machine light is blinking. He pushes the button, and the voice pours forth, "Damn, Evan, call me! I need info from ya. You know who this is! But, let me refresh your *damn* memory, it's Bettey. Use your finger for something other than picking your nose and scratching your—Shit! Just dial my damn number!" She sounds enraged. Following her message are a couple of hang ups.

Evan's thoughts return in a fleeting moment to Bettey's phone message. He thinks Bettey may not have received his flowers yet. He calls the florist and gives them an ultimatum to deliver today or else lose his future business. Regardless, Evan does not take the time to phone Bettey. Fred's words are echoing through his brain. He cannot wait to hit the streets. Evan leaves the apartment quickly. Maybe he will ride by the alley and just take a look. First, he must contact Jacko. Evan has things about this case to resolve with Jacko.

Jacko, an occasional muscle man for the mob, is Evan's stoolie on the streets. He is an organized crime "freelancer". His full name is Jacko Henry. He always pretends to be witless, big and dumb, but he is as sharp as a tack. Jacko is a large man who likes to dress nicely in expensive suits. Evan searches the streets, knowing Jacko's usual hangouts. He finds him outside a sleazy bar in downtown, and their eyes meet. Jacko, understanding what this means, goes to the nearest pay phone. Evan pulls around the corner and waits in his car, staring at his cellular, waiting for it to ring. He pulls out a coin and tosses it from cupped hand to cupped hand to pass the time and help him think. Jacko does not call. Evan glances at his watch. Ten minutes pass.

Someone occupies the pay phone so Jacko has to wait his turn. At last, the call comes through on Evan's cellular.

"Yeah. Jacko here. What do ya need?"

"Info, Jacko," Evan says cramming his coin in his pocket. "A murder of a beautiful woman named Kizzy, or Keziah Theriot, happened about a week ago. She was supposedly Dominici Giovanni's lady. What do you know?"

"Ooowee! That's high class shit—a stone fox! Yeah, I knew her, but not personally though. A classy ass like hers, men like me don't get to know. She played with the real big boys. She was a beauty all right. If anyone even dared to look at her, man, ya could pay with your life. Used to be Giovanni's all right. He still watched over her a lot. But rumor has it, she had become exclusive stock of Luigi's."

"You're kidding!" Evan says to Jacko, doubting his word. "Luigi? Luigi is married. He's always been faithful to his wife, according to everything I've ever heard. That's about the only decent thing the guy did. You know whose daughter she is! Do you think his wife knew anything about her?"

"Yeah. Hell, her old man is like the king godfather. Look, cop. I heard not even Luigi could resist this piece of ass. Ya know. She had this special way about her! I don't know if his wife knew anything. I kinda doubt his wife knew anything, because if she had known, her old man would have put a hit out on Luigi."

"Do you know what kind of car Luigi's wife drives?"

"Yeah, mostly she is driven around town in one of the limos. Ya know, in their business they need protection. But I think she owns a dark blue, foreign luxury car customized with gold stripes down the sides that she drives occasionally. But I know Luigi doesn't like it when she drives off alone."

"Dark blue, huh, that's very interesting. Do you have information about the deceased being a lesbian?"

Jacko laughs. "Shit! Are ya kiddin'? Damn! She was the most heterosexual broad ever. That stone fox *liked men!*"

"Jacko, do you know anybody on the street with the initials 'T.U.'?" Jacko pauses for a moment exploring Evan's question.

"Did ya say 'T.U.'?" Jacko asks.

"Yes, Jacko. 'T.U.'"

"Nope, cop. Nobody I know has those initials."

"Jacko, do you have any idea who killed her or why?"

"Nope. I don't know nothin' about her hit."

"Why did you say 'hit'?" Evan asks.

"Shit, even I can read the paper, cop. I know it was a murder. I don't think a robber would hack her like that. Damn, I know she's involved with the mob. It doesn't take a genius to figure it out. One and one do equal two!"

"Do you think this 'hit' might be mob business?" Evan asks, knowing Jacko is privilege to a lot of mob business from the street.

At first, Jacko pauses, hesitating to answer. "Look I'm not sure, cop. I don't think it was Giovanni. He was freaked out. I'm almost sure it wasn't Luigi. Rumor has it that he was really torn up over her murder." Jacko stops speaking briefly while several people walk by the pay phone. He continues. "Several people told me he totally lost control and went nuts. Screwy, huh? A tough guy like Luigi with feelings for a hooking piece of ass, even though she was a delicious, high class one."

Evan suddenly becomes enraged at Jacko. "Hey man, don't call her a hooker!"

"Yeah, okay. I'll keep my ears open," Jacko says impatiently, wanting to end this conversation.

"Wait, Jacko. I'm not through with you yet."

Jacko pauses.

Evan continues, "What do you know about a company called Fun Coin?"

"It's a video, pool table—"

Evan interrupts anxiously, "Damn! I know all that shit, Jacko. Tell me something I don't know."

"Shit, it's supposedly a legitimate business. But, between me and you, I think it belongs to the mob. I think they invest dirty money in that clean company. Ya know, a little scrubbing of the money to remove the shitty smell. I don't know who controls it, though. I'll keep my ears open. I gotta go!"

"Hey, ass hole! Next time don't take so *damn* long to call me back! Got it?" Evan yells.

"Look. It's a damn public pay phone here. I can't help it if I have to wait my turn. I don't want ya calling me on my cellular. It might be traced." Jacko yells at Evan, "*Gotta go!*"

Evan hears the click as Jacko quickly, not giving Evan the chance to object, hangs up the phone. Evan yells after him, "I'll be waiting for *more, Jacko*. And soon, too!" The conversation ends. Evan, not sure if Jacko heard his last comment, hangs up spouting an obscenity.

Evan goes to the station to talk further with Pete about what he has learned. Evan, being an honorable man, remembers the men giving their word to share information. While driving, Evan phones C.D. and gives him the information he has gotten.

C.D. passes it along to the others. William is remarkably upset over the information. The thought of Kizzy with mobsters nearly breaks his heart. C.D. comforts him.

2

Evan arrives at the station. Without revealing his source, he tells Pete the information Jacko, his exclusive stoolie, has given him. Pete has always wanted the name of Evan's stoolie. At first, Pete tries to get Jacko's name. Nonetheless, Evan holds fast and will not even share his stoolie with Pete. Pete denies that the story about Giovanni and Luigi being linked with Kizzy can possibly be true.

"Pete, what the hell is wrong with you! Why don't you bring in at least Giovanni, and maybe Luigi, too, for questioning?"

"Evan, look buddy. Just let it go. You know a burglar and rapist killed her. She didn't hear him come in because she was full of sleeping pills."

This is a new clue for Evan. "Sleeping pills? Well . . . no, Pete, damn it. I don't believe it was burglary! You don't either! You're a better cop than that!" Pete stands there shaking his head, disagreeing with Evan, but Evan persists. "No forced entry occurred. That place is like Fort Knox. He didn't rape her, and then wait two hours to kill her!"

"Evan, the M.O. on this killing is not Giovanni's or Luigi's style. You know that! Maybe the guy tortured her for the two hours. You know there were the whip marks."

"Two hours of torture, and only a few visible whip marks? That doesn't hold water, Pete. Okay, I'll agree that it's not usually their style to dismember their hits, but they may know something. Maybe one of them went crazy or something." Evan shakes his finger in Pete's face with insistence. "You bring them in, or I'll go to the Captain with the info! *Got it, Pete?*"

"Okay, Evan, I'll bring them in for questioning. But I really think it's a waste of time."

"When you pick them up, you call me. I plan to be here. Listen. I also have info that a woman was seen leaving Kizzy's garage in an expensive, dark blue car with gold side stripes the night of the murder close to the time of the death."

Pete's expression looks queer. "Where do you get this stupid shit? Hell, Evan, maybe she lives in the damn building."

"Pete, she was wearing sunglasses at night!"

"Maybe she's having an affair with one of the residents and doesn't want to be seen, Evan. Maybe she has a kind of eye condition. I'll check with the residents. I'll see if anyone else saw her. Okay? Evan, you're off the case officially. I can't bring you in on everything. You've got to trust me."

Evan is tired of arguing with Pete and loses control. "Okay, Pete. I'll take care of it myself. *Forget it!*" Evan says throwing his hands in the air in disgust.

"Damn Evan, what are you going to do?"

"Remember. I'm not on this case. See you, buddy!" Evan blurts out as he leaves the station.

3

Evan knows he is on his own. Slowly, he drives by the alley Fred mentioned, but no one is in sight. Curiously, the alley is oddly absent of litter and garbage. Evan finds this unusual. Alleys between buildings containing dumpsters usually have some sort of debris. He has never seen an alley look this neat and clean. Quickly, he drives to William's hotel with a special plan.

Tom is now sharing the room with William. Tom was asked to leave his hotel because he could not pay his bill. At their request, Mr. Alexander is holding the men's inheritance. William phones Jimmy, instructing him to meet the others at the hotel room immediately. C.D. is busy with church business and cannot leave. Evan explains his plan by phone to C.D. He will be their outside contact in case anything goes wrong. The men discuss the plan. They will go to Giovanni's first. Evan will use the proper procedure, flashing his badge to gain entrance, and then begin interrogation. Evan explains that just observing a suspect's motions and expressions during interrogation can tell you a lot. Jimmy and Tom will join him inside. William will stay in the car. If trouble happens, he will call for backup from Pete at the station using Evan's cellular. If they are not back in William's hotel room in three hours, C.D. is to phone the police. Everyone knows their part of the plan because Evan has drilled repeatedly every detail.

4

The men drive to Giovanni's palatial home in an exclusive area of Houston. While parked out front, the gates open, and a large black limo drives out. Evan recognizes the limo as Giovanni's. Evan starts the engine and discreetly starts to follow the limo. The limo drives for about fifteen minutes to another attractive home. The gates open, and the limo enters. Evan makes sure he parks about a half block from the gate entrance.

Jimmy taps his fingers on the door. "Whoa, we're gonna get two for the price of one," Jimmy blurts out, electrified by the espionage.

"What do you mean, Jimmy?" William asks.

"This is Luigi's house," Jimmy boldly proclaims.

Evan asks. "But what I want to know is how in the hell did you know this was Luigi's house, Jimmy?"

Jimmy ignores Evan and shrugs his shoulders. William phones C.D. on the cellular and gives the new location and asks for an extra thirty minutes' time. William retrieves the binoculars he has purchased earlier for use on this case. He plans to watch as much as he can from this parked car. The men leave the car with William inside.

Jimmy is nervous and excited this day. The espionage idea is thrilling. However, the thought of being in front of crime lords opens old childhood fears. He remembers his stepfather and his cruelty. Jimmy shakes the fear back to the deepest recesses of his mind. He pulls the excitement forward and takes a deep breath. Jimmy will not let anyone in this car know he is afraid. He smiles, deliriously.

Even Evan, the professional in the group, is nervous. Not every day do you solicit for entrance to *Hell*, and then interrogate the *devils inside!*

CHAPTER XIV

Interrogation

1

Evan, Jimmy and Tom approach the large iron gate, leaving William to wait in Evan's car. Evan pushes the button to ring for approval for entrance. A voice answers the buzz, asking, "Yeah, who is it?"

"Detective Evan Picard," he answers, identifying himself by displaying his badge to the security camera. Evan is prepared, expecting many varied arguments to entail before gaining entrance to this house. However, surprisingly, the gate opens swiftly. Two armed men, who Jimmy, whispering nicknames "crime soldiers," frisk them for weapons at the gate and escort the three men inside a black sport-utility vehicle. A little discussion happens when Evan will not relinquish his weapon. Someone by an intercom instructs the soldiers to allow them entrance and permit Evan to keep his weapon. One of the men escorting them is a huge young man with a shaved bald head and a scar on his left cheek. The other man is smaller in stature, but muscular and capable of taking care of himself and anyone else. In his one pierced ear, he wears a large blue rosary cross. The car winds around the long cemented driveway to a stupendous rock home with a steep, blue, tile roof that could pass for a hotel. The two crime soldiers escort the three men inside, always keeping their eyes directly on them, watching every move.

Evan whispers to Jimmy, "Keep your damn mouth shut in here, Jimmy. Hell, don't piss these guys off with your shit!"

Jimmy leers at Evan's comment scornfully.

Tom, deciding to play intermediary between the two men, urges, "Please, don't cause any crap. Okay? This is damn serious shit, Jimmy."

Jimmy likes Tom so reluctantly he answers, "Yeah. Okay, football." The three men enter a massive foyer with a huge crystal chandelier hanging from the three-story ceiling. On the expansive staircase stands a woman dressed in a posh floor-length satin robe. She is thin and petite. Her long, frosted hair is swept away from her bony, dignified face and high cheekbones. Her eyes are a light, icy blue, almost ashen. She does not say a word, but glares at the men as they pass her. Evan concludes this must be Lorena Luigi, Antonio's wife. From the description Fred has given them, Lorena Luigi could be the strange lady leaving the parking garage the night Kizzy was murdered.

The crime soldiers escort the men through several rooms after they leave the foyer. The rooms are immense, impressive and icy cold. Jimmy thinks that it must cost a fortune to air condition a huge house like this, especially keeping the temperature this low. Hazy rooms with thick heavy drapes prohibiting the entrance of daylight are filled with a shadowy darkness from the artificial lighting. These rooms stimulate Jimmy's image of the dark closet with only the sliver of dim light entering around the door cracks. He remembers his brutal stepfather. Jimmy shivers maybe from the cold, and maybe from the memory. He pushes the memory away, pausing for a moment in one room for a childlike gesture opening his mouth and pushing his breath out, making smoke. A crime soldier pushes him from behind to hurry him on his way.

"Yeah, yeah!" Jimmy replies, as he starts to move with the others.

The furnishings of every room are luxuriant and affluent. The house reminds Tom of the old castles in Europe that he has visited. Classic, expensive art pieces line the walls in every room.

At last, they reach the intended room. Consistent with the rest of the house, the darkened room has only dim lamplight. The walls are covered with dark paneling. Thick, dark tinted drapes prohibit daylight from entering. A large stone fireplace is in one corner that reaches upward into the darkness of the ceiling. The ceiling is towering, making vision upward impossible because of the dim light and obscurity. A massive, heavy table with large, overstuffed leather chairs around it stands alone. At the head of the table sits an attractive dark-skinned man in his early forties. His dark hair is combed straight back. His dark eyes are serious and piercing. Calm and programmed are his emotions. To his right, sits an older, heavyset man with salt-and-pepper gray hair and receding hairline. The men, dressed in expensive suits with every accessory matching, are perfectly combed and manicured. The aroma of their expensive cologne fills the air in the room. Tom inhales, sucking the cologne aroma inconspicuously into his nostrils, noticing the familiarity. He scans his mind trying to remember where he has smelled this cologne. Well, maybe the aroma is not so familiar. He probably smelled it in a bar somewhere or maybe at Kizzy's.

"Youse gentlemen," the younger man at the head of the table says gesturing, politely, "please sit."

Evan, Jimmy and Tom sit. Jimmy gazes slowly around at the room, impressed by his expensive surroundings. Jimmy thinks of what he could do with money and a house such as this one, and starts to fantasize.

Tom's knee is paining him profusely. He reaches down to rub his knee with his hand. He notices the two soldiers, standing at the door, are watching him closely. They show interest at what he is doing with his hands under the table. Tom pushes back his chair so they can see that he is only rubbing his knee and not reaching for any sort of weapon. He does not want to panic these men. Tom can see the weapons strapped to their sides.

Evan is anxious and wants to get started. He wants to begin the conversation, hoping to manage and monopolize the conversation with his questions. Evan knows keeping domination of an interrogation when talking to powerful men such as these is essential. Keeping control is what Evan has in mind. Evan recognizes the younger man at the head of the table as Antonio Luigi. His inky eyes are eerie. Evan looks Luigi straight in the eyes, and says, "Mr. Luigi, did you know Keziah Theriot, or Kizzy as she was called?"

With great confidence, Luigi answers without showing emotion. "What makes you think I knew this lady?"

Evan has expected the men will try answering questions with questions. This is a common response from mob types. "One of my accurate contacts says you knew her *very* well," Evan says quickly with equal confidence, determined to keep control. "They say she was your 'exclusive stock!"

Luigi answers, motioning with his hands, pretending not to understand Evan's question. "What is this 'exclusive stock'? I never heard such words!"

Tom rolls his eyes knowing this is going to be a long, drawn-out questioning, especially if Evan has to explain every phrase he uses. Tom knows the men are just evading Evan's questions.

Evan, irritated by Luigi's indifferent question, answers him in a harsh, patronizing way. "'Exclusive stock' means she was *yours alone*. You didn't share her. *Do you understand now, Mr. Luigi?"*

"I don't know. That 'exclusive stock' shit sounds like white slavery to me. I ain't connected to no white slavery, cop! Besides I'm a married man! I got a beautiful wife!"

Dominici Giovanni, sitting quietly with his legs crossed and hands folded, decides to enter the conversation. He looks over at Evan with a stern look and comes to his feet abruptly. "Maybe your *accurate* source ain't so *accurate, huh cop*?" The soldiers at the door laugh loudly, finding Giovanni's remark targeting Evan funny.

"Dom, it's okay. Keep calm," Luigi says to Giovanni in a calming controlled voice. Luigi has a contemptuous smile upon his face, thinking he is in control of everything. Evan knows Luigi wants to dictate things.

Tom gawks blatantly, looking closely at Giovanni as he stands with the lamplight spotlighting his face. Tom recognizes this face. This man is older, a little heavier and has more gray hair and a receding hairline, but Tom knows Giovanni is the man he had seen Kizzy with at the hotel bar many years ago. "I know you," Tom says as he stands pointing an accusing finger at Giovanni. Tom is forgetting where he is, at the present time. Evan is surprised to see Tom lose control. He has expected it of Jimmy, but not Tom. Jimmy stops looking around the room as he feels terror pierce through his heart. He wonders wha the hell Tom is doing!

"I saw you with Kizzy about six years ago in a hotel bar downtown. I *kno* you knew her! You might as well admit it!" Tom blurts out loudly at Giovann The two soldiers standing at the doorway come closer in the room. Evan see them move in and senses trouble. Should he reach for his gun?

Giovanni sits and leans over toward Evan. "Who the *hell* is this guy?" Evan pulls Tom to sit. "Cool it, Tom, please." He turns to Giovanni and says "He's with me. He knew the deceased. I think he's just a little shook up. Evan is trying to calm the intensity of the room. "It's okay, Tom. We'll discus it later. Let it go for now." Evan has thought that it would have been Jimm he would have had to calm down, not Tom. Luigi motions to the two soldiers and they return to their post, standing at the door. Luigi is paying clos attention to the information pouring from Tom's mouth throughout thi emotional flood.

Tom sitting, continues with his accusations looking toward Giovanni. "Yo know that I know who you are! Why don't you tell the truth? Or, can peop such as you tell the *truth?* Evan, I know him! I'm telling you that I know him

Evan, trying to appease Tom and gain control of the conversation agai says in a sterner tone of voice, "Okay, Tom. We'll talk about it later. Shut up will you!" He is losing his patience with Tom.

Suddenly, a red-faced Luigi shoves back his chair, looks straight at Tom and yells, "*You,* son of a—"

However, before Luigi can finish his response, Giovanni stands sternly between Luigi and the other three men. He starts speaking in Italian, using a soothing, relaxing toned voice, and gently touching Luigi on the shoulders. Unluckily, his voice and touch do not calm a substantially irritated Luigi. Wide eyed with mortification, he glares at Tom. "*You* are the one she was *with!* I should—" Luigi does not finish his statement. Overcome with distress, Luigi stands. The veins in his neck are protruding.

Evan, knowing Luigi and Giovanni are killers, fears for Tom's life. Evan fears that they will allow none of them to leave this house alive.

Evan is not the only one that becomes nervous. Jimmy is no longer fantasizing. Jimmy, jiggling his leg under the table faster than usual, is smart enough to recognize when an explosive, dangerous situation exists. His heart is pounding in his chest. However, he does not tap his fingers in his usual way, but holds his hands so tightly folded that his knuckles are white. He cannot help Evan with Tom, overwhelmed with his own fear. Luigi's belligerence looks all too familiar. Jimmy remembers the flamed, antagonistic face and yelling voice of his stepfather before they locked him in the small dark closet.

Giovanni grabs Luigi, stopping him as he lunges at Tom. While understanding he is not in control of Luigi, Giovanni continues speaking in Italian. Overcome with despair, Giovanni turns to the soldiers at the door for their assistance. "Rick, help Mr. Luigi out of here," Giovanni says to one of the crime soldiers. He comes over and escorts a raging, suffering Luigi from the room. Luigi is mumbling repetitiously in Italian. His wrath is replaced with agony and mourning as tears stream down his face like a child. He is almost incoherent. Giovanni is trying desperately to calm him, speaking Italian in the same soothing voice. The pitiful sight of Luigi almost brings sympathy from Evan. The soldier escorting Luigi from the room takes over speaking Italian, hoping to disperse the pain and suffering that Luigi is feeling. Giovanni gains a small amount of composure, straightens his jacket and sits in his large chair.

Evan asks, "Mr. Giovanni, can you tell me where you and Mr. Luigi were the night of June sixteenth?"

"Uh—Yeah, we went to the Houston Ballet. Then we went to

Minieri's Restorante. We didn't get home until way after midnight. We didn't leave the restaurant until around eleven fifty-five." Impatiently, Giovanni turns to Evan and says, "I think the time has come for youse guys to leave."

Jimmy stands, appreciating the privilege to leave this danger den, but then sits again after the others do not stand. Evan, still sitting, responds stubbornly, hoping to regain control of the conversation. "I will check that alibi. Before we leave, I must say something important to you."

"Yeah? You check the alibi. You better get this important something out of your mouth really quick, cop!"

Evan knows from Giovanni's voice he is losing his tolerance with their presence. Evan starts speaking quickly before Giovanni says any more. "Something you don't know is that we're *five* men that loved Kizzy. We're not going to stop until we solve her murder. We'll overturn every stone, kick any ass necessary, call in every favor, and pull any stunts we have to, to get this solved. We don't care whose toes we step on, including yours! You're going to have to *kill* us to stop us!" Jimmy swallows hard at Evan's comment. With fear covering his face, Jimmy wonders what the hell is wrong with Evan. He is afraid Giovanni might accept Evan's offer to kill them.

"Hey, that can be arranged, but not here. I don't wanna mess up Luigi's nice house." Giovanni stands and motions toward the door with another invitation for them to leave.

Evan ignores the gesture. Jimmy feels panicky and even nauseous.

"I'm not finished yet!" Evan adds in a determined way.

Giovanni leans against the table, gets close to Evan's face and exclaims, "You better hurry the *hell up!* I'm gettin' bored by youse guys and all this shit!" Then, Giovanni slowly sits in his chair.

At this point Evan is desperate. He knows he must use his trump card—all he has now. He knows that even though Giovanni and Luigi are killers, they are strict Catholics. They have great respect and honor for their religion. It is ironic that two killers such as these men can believe in religion so much, but they do. Evan has been holding on to this information. This is Evan's trump card, his only trump card! Evan says, "You could kill me and the other two men sitting here, easy." Jimmy's eyes widen with fear, but he does not say a word.

"Our fourth man, an attorney, you could probably kill easy, too. I imagine you've killed plenty of attorneys." Tom wonders what point Evan is trying to make. His heart is pounding.

"Ah-hah, but our fifth man is a *Catholic priest.* I don't think he's going to be so easy for *you* to kill! Is stopping us with our investigation worth damning your very soul to hell?" Evan watches Giovanni's face for a sign of sentiment or shock. He does not seem surprised that the fifth man is a Catholic priest. Jimmy and Tom smile meekly at Evan's trump card. Jimmy looks a little closer at Giovanni.

Giovanni stands, turning his back on the three men sitting at the table. Evan knows this is a good sign. Giovanni is thinking over the information Evan has just given.

After a brief pause, slowly he turns and faces the men. "You're right. It ain't very easy snuffing out a priest. That is . . . " Giovanni stops his speech and looks down. He sits in the big chair. Evan knows the wheels are turning in Giovanni's devious, but intelligent head. He pauses, looking around the room and at the three men as an element of time passes. Everyone is quiet and still. The friction in the air is overflowing and makes Jimmy want to bolt. He jiggles his leg and clasps his folded hands tight against the white knuckles. However, the three men sit quietly waiting.

A much calmer Tom is not sure how to take this pause. What if the man is thinking about killing them? His knee is still filling him with pain. He could run, but not fast enough to beat a bullet. This painful knee would surely slow him.

Jimmy is still feeling nervous. Not trusting these men, he keeps an eye on the soldier at the door as he tries to get a better look at Giovanni.

Giovanni clears his voice. "You not gonna let this one go are you, cop? You gonna dig and dig 'till you get the answers."

"No, I can't let this go!" Evan answers. "We're dealing with murder!"

"You think one of us killed her, huh?"

"Yes, I do. Killing is the 'specialty of the house'! Right, Giovanni?" Evan says. Evan's reply angers Giovanni. "It's *Mr.* Giovanni to you, cop. You'll show some respect to me in my friend's home. You're not on the streets or in *your* police station. Respect! *Mr.* Giovanni! You got that?"

Sarcastically, and with a sneer on his lips, Evan replies, "Excuse me! *Mr.* Giovanni."

Giovanni smiles and regains some dignity. "Okay, cop, what if I deal?"

"What do you mean, 'deal'? What is to deal on?" Evan asks.

"If I tell you some things, cop, will youse guys keep it under your hat? Will you stop this and not question Mr. Luigi again?"

"If either of you killed Kizzy, *hell no!*" Evan says without giving it a hesitating thought.

"I swear on my mother's grave, neither of us killed Kizzy nor had her killed." Giovanni says seriously looking Evan straight in the eye. "You know I am a good Catholic."

Somehow, Evan is convinced Giovanni is finally telling them the truth. "Okay, we'll agree to keep the information you give us in strictest confidence. I give you my word, Mr. Giovanni."

Giovanni starts after taking a deep breath. "Okay. I am only telling you for Luigi's peace. He can't go through the questions about her. Give me your word, cop, that you won't question him any more."

Evan agrees with a nod. Then Giovanni asks the other two men, Tom and Jimmy, to give their words that they will not make the information he is about to reveal public. He wants to hear it from their lips. They agree. Giovanni insists on handshakes from the men confirming their agreement. They oblige him. Jimmy would agree to anything to get them an exit from this place.

Giovanni starts with his story, intermittently sitting and standing with pocketed hands and gazing out in space throughout his speech. "I met Kizzy at Picconnes Restaurant in the Hollywood area quite a few years ago. I don't remember exactly when."

Jimmy knows why Giovanni looks so familiar. He listens to Giovanni's words.

"She was young—a real looker—but innocent in those days. Of her own free will, she went to work for me. She entertained the gentlemen that I did business with, if you know what I mean. She was very good at her job but different from the other girls. You know. She wasn't some cheap hooker. I don't know what it was she had, but it was special. I began seeing her myself. I didn't plan it, but, as a fool, I fell in love with her. I didn't want anyone else to be with her. Hey, I took care of her, bought her beautiful clothes and all. She liked that kinda shit. She became mine. Well, not long after that, um-mm-maybe a year, Mr. Luigi met her. She was so young, still in her twenties. Boy, was she beautiful. You know, some broads get ugly the older they get. She just got better lookin'. Mr. Luigi couldn't take his eyes off her. He wanted Kizzy. You knows. I have great respect for Mr. Luigi. So, I decided not to stand in the way of their special relationship. I was just a contact between Mr. Luigi and Kizzy. You knows. Mr. Luigi is married and all. It just wasn't proper for a married man like him to have action on the side. So, I took care of the public appearances. Anyway, he *really loved Kizzy!* That's about all there is to tell."

"Did Mrs. Luigi know about Kizzy and her husband having an affair?" Evan asks.

Giovanni answers quickly, but warily. "No."

Evan thinks Giovanni answers a little too quickly. He feels Giovanni is lying to them.

Jimmy, at this point feeling secure, knowing they do not want to kill a Catholic priest, says, "Yeah, yeah. This is a bunch of genuine shit! So, who in the hell killed her?" Before waiting for an answer, Jimmy states, loudly and intrusively, "Maybe Luigi or you did, in a jealous fit of rage, huh? Ya know you two had the hots for her. Or maybe she knew something about your business, huh?" His words that are pouring forth surprising and embarrassing even Jimmy before he can stop them. He does not seem nervous anymore.

Evan, shocked by Jimmy's comment, looks sternly at Jimmy who is not supposed to be asking questions.

Giovanni rises from his chair, comes directly over to Jimmy, points his finger in his face angrily and says, "Look you *damn* little street punk piece of shit. Luigi loved that woman more than life. He'd *never, never kill her*! Since you're thinking it, neither would I! If we *ever* find out who the hell killed her, they're—" Giovanni stops before finishing his statement and straightens his jacket by running his hand along the inside opening.

"They're what, Mr. Giovanni?" Evan asks sensing a weakness in Giovanni. He hopes to gain as much possible information during access to this man.

"I think we're about finished here, cop!"

Evan asks, grasping at his last chance to question this big, powerful, organized crime leader. "Just one more thing, what about the business? Did either of you kill her because she knew something about the business?"

Giovanni returns slowly to his chair, reserved and in control. "We kept Kizzy *out* of the business. She was never even around when we talked business. I already told youse guys neither one of us killed Kizzy. I'm not gonna tell youse guys that again."

"Do either you or Mr. Luigi know anyone with the initials 'T.U.', Mr. Giovanni?" Evan says, using a respectful tone with the hope of squeezing in this one last question.

Giovanni has a puzzled look on his face. "No. I've never heard those initials. But what do these initials mean?" Giovanni asks with interest.

"Oh, it's nothing!" Evan answers.

"Now youse gentlemen have overstayed your welcome. Time for you all to go!" Giovanni stands and motions this last time. Evan knows his time is over.

The two soldiers escort the men to the large iron gate in the sport-utility vehicle. The men walk through the gate and to the car where William is nervously waiting.

Upon entering the car, Tom says, "Man, remind me to thank Father C.D. for being a priest the next time I see him." William looks at Tom with a questioning grimace on his face not understanding Tom's comment. The other two men laugh at Tom's statement. A yellow cab pulls alongside Evan's car. Father C.D. leaves the cab and joins the others in Evan's car. He explains he could not wait any longer, wondering what was happening.

Tom says, "I think one of those two men was the one that kidnaped me. Remember the cologne aroma I told you about, Evan? Well I'm almost sure it was the same cologne those men were wearing, and the way they talked was familiar sounding." While sitting in the car listening to C.D.'s explanation and Tom's information, the men notice a dark blue, foreign luxury car with a woman driving leaving Luigi's driveway. A reflection shining from the side of the vehicle brings their attention to the gold stripe down the side. The men decide to follow the car.

2

The car goes downtown to a large high-rise building. A woman leaves the vehicle wearing dark sunglasses and a scarf.

"Whoa! Same description we got from that nasty bum Fred!" Jimmy says. C.D. scolds Jimmy for his tasteless remark about Fred. The woman enters the building with the men discreetly following her. She does not notice them. She enters the elevator and proceeds without the men. Evan notices the floor numbers as they flash by on the elevator display. The elevator stops on the fifteenth floor. Evan walks over to the building directory. Houston Psychiatric Consultants occupy the entire fifteenth floor.

"Hey, a nut doctor," Jimmy says reading the directory looking over Evan's shoulder with the others.

"Damn, Jimmy," Tom says, scolding Jimmy for his insensitive remark.

"Do we go upstairs to see this lady and the doctor, Evan?" Father C.D. asks.

"No. I do not think we will obtain any information from the psychiatrist because of patient confidentiality. Is this correct, Evan?" William adds.

"Yes. You're right. We'll wait in the car. When she comes down, we'll ask her the questions we need answered," Evan answers.

For about an hour the men wait in the car. Small talk is made between the men. In his usual way, Jimmy sits tapping his fingers on the seat.

"Hey, Jimmy, that tapping reminds me," says Evan lightheartedly. "Thanks for not doing that in Luigi's. I think it would've gotten us shot!" Evan smiles. Tom, C.D. and William laugh at Evan's comment.

"Very funny, cop," Jimmy says with a smile on his face. He looks down at his tapping fingers and consciously stops.

At last, the woman leaves the building and stops briefly to dig through her handbag for her keys. The men approach her.

"Excuse me. Ma'am, could we ask you a few questions about a murder?" Evan asks politely approaching the woman.

"I don't know you people. No. I won't answer questions. Leave me alone or I'll call the police!" she says still nervously digging through the handbag.

Evan pulls out his badge and holds it in clear view of her vision. "Ma'am, I'm Detective Picard. I need to ask you some questions."

She is irritated that Evan has pulled out his badge hoping to get an advantage. Angrily she says, directing her conversation to Evan. "Do you have any idea who I am? Are you *crazy?* People don't ask *me* questions. Not *even cops!*"

Father C.D., who was standing at the back of the group with William, moves forward making his presence visible to the lady. C.D. senses this lady has a troubled soul. His pious senses and the cross hanging around her neck tell him this lady needs his knowledge, not Evan's. "Excuse me. I am Father C.D. Casmiersky." He holds out his hand to the lady. "Would you permit me and my friends to buy you a cup of coffee? We just have a few questions we think you might be able to help us with. These are crucial questions to me. Please, can we buy you just a cup of coffee?"

With just the sight of C.D., her entire attitude changes. The lady, being a good Catholic girl, smiles and says, "Oh, Father, I did not see you back there. I would be honored to have a cup of coffee with you." The men and lady cross the street to a small coffee shop. They choose a table in the back for privacy. They order coffee for everyone. Evan, seeing C.D. has an advantage with this lady, lets him take the lead in the conversation.

"Let me introduce my friends to you, ma'am. I think you've met Detective Picard. This is Mr. Smithson, Mr. Hastings and Mr. Newton."

"Are they all cops except you, Father?" the lady asks.

C.D. reveals, "No ma'am—"

Although before he can go further, Jimmy interrupts. "No way I'm a cop, lady," Jimmy spouts. "I drive a cab."

C.D. says pointing to each man, "Mr. Newton is an attorney in New York. Mr. Hastings is a former football player who sells automobiles in Colorado."

She smiles at each man cordially. "You're a strange group."

"May I ask what your name is, ma'am?" C.D. asks.

"My name is Lorena Luigi."

"Ms. Luigi—"

Lorena smiles at C.D. "Father, I would be honored if you would please call me Lorena." Evan senses this is going well. C.D. is on a first-name basis with her already.

"Thank you, Lorena. We were very good friends with a young lady who was found murdered here in Houston on June the sixteenth. Her name was Keziah Theriot, or Kizzy as she was called. Did you know her?"

"So that's why you are here!" Lorena says. Lorena pauses and looks down stirring the coffee nervously, clanking the spoon against the porcelain of the cup. "I did not know her, Father."

"Did ya know *of* her, then?" Jimmy asks, pushy, an act common to Jimmy. Lorena clanks the spoon in the cup of coffee even more noisily. Evan kicks Jimmy under the table and gives him a dirty look, hoping he will keep his mouth shut and let C.D. resume the questioning.

"Did you know of her, Lorena? You can tell us," C.D. asks politely.

Lorena removes the dark sunglasses and scarf from her head. She looks at C.D. strongly, searching for just an ounce of trust. "Can I trust you, Father?"

"Lady, he's a priest," Jimmy spouts, bouncing his leg under the table.

"Yes, Lorena, you can trust me," C.D. says.

"Okay. Yes, I knew of her," she responds.

"Lorena, we know you were at the apartment house the night of the murder. Why were you there? Can you explain this to us, please?"

Evan watches her response to his question closely. She does not look panicked or afraid. She looks queerly calm, but she does not answer the question right away. Thinking, she starts to clank the spoon noisily in the coffee cup again.

"Lorena, we know about the relationship between your husband and Kizzy. Can you tell us why you visited Kizzy's apartment?" C.D. asks her calmly.

"We mean you no harm, Mrs. Luigi. We're just trying to ascertain the truth," William says, reassuring Lorena.

"Okay, I'll tell you. I didn't kill her. I would have *liked* to have killed her. I hated her. I went there to kill her, but I didn't. I'm a coward! I'm not proud of that fact. My father would kill me if he knew I was a coward. But I am a coward. I couldn't do it! I just couldn't bring myself to kill her." Lorena directs her eyes downward at the coffee cup as though she is ashamed that she is not Kizzy's killer.

"Can you tell us what happened that night?" C.D. asks. "Please child, relieve your mind of the memory."

Lorena holds her scarf in her hands, twisting the cloth tightly around her fingers nervously. "I found out by accident about Kizzy and Tony. I overheard a phone call he made to her a couple of days before she died. Hearing him professing his love to her on the phone made me sick! I wanted to go to my father about it but knew what Papa would do. He would kill Tony. I love Tony, so I approached him about it." Lorena looks sad and disheartened, but she continues. "Tony swore to me that he was only using her to get me a baby. He promised me that it was me that he loved, not her. Stupid me, huh! I believed him. I wanted to believe him. I love Tony very much, maybe too much. But I couldn't wipe the picture of the two of them together from my mind. So that night, I begged off going out with Tony and Dom. I said I had a headache. Tony was so understanding and kind to me. After they left, I stole her address from Tony's address book. I went to the apartment. I just wanted her to leave Tony alone. I swear! But, on the way there, my anger grew. I kept seeing him with her. I kept seeing Tony touching her, kissing her. I wanted to kill her by the time I got to the building. But when I got to the door of the apartment, I broke down." She slurps the hot coffee and pitifully continues. "You see. I'm not strong. I've been seeing this doctor. I didn't go inside. I wanted her dead, but I was a coward. Foolishly, I stood outside her door, shaking. I couldn't even knock on her door!" Lorena takes a tissue from her purse and blots the tears from her eyes. C.D. touches her shoulder gently to console her. She smiles and continues talking. "Dom was upset over her death. But my poor Tony! From his actions, I know he loved that girl. As much as it hurts me, and believe me it does, I have to admit that it wasn't me that he loved. It was her and is her! He hasn't been the same since her death. I wish *I* had been the one who killed her, now that I know how much he loved her! I think he wishes I were dead and she were still alive! I'm such a fool!"

C.D. gently pats Lorena's hand. "God will show mercy on you for keeping his commandment and not killing her, my child. Keeping his commandment is no sign of cowardice or weakness, but a sign of great strength!" C.D. says to soothe her troubled soul and mind.

"Mrs. Luigi, the night you were outside her apartment, did you see or hear anything unusual?" Evan asks gently.

"No, not really, I was terribly distraught. I left in a big hurry. I heard her moving around inside the apartment, but no screams or nothing!" C.D. smiles gently at Lorena.

"About what time was it when you were outside her door, Mrs. Luigi?" Evan respectfully asks Lorena.

"I don't know. I was so upset. I guess it was close to eleven. Maybe, but I'm not sure."

"How did you get in that building through the security?" Tom asks.

"Through the parking garage," Lorena answers.

"How?" William asks. However, Lorena with tears in her eyes is too distraught to answer further.

"Lorena, you're God's child. He'll comfort you through this difficult time. I'll pray for you, and you must pray each night for His strength."

Lorena squeezes C.D.'s hand gently. She looks in his eyes pitifully. "Thank you so much, Father. You have been so kind. I'm glad that I talked to you. I would love to visit your church sometime. I have to go. I have an appointment." Lorena's voice is almost relieved in tone. "I can't talk about this anymore."

"Can't we talk about how you got in the building through that garage?" Jimmy asks.

"No. I said that I have an appointment. I can't do this now!"

"I'd love to have you visit my church, my dear," C.D. says as he gives her a card with the church address.

The group finishes the coffee. Evan pays the check. The men walk Lorena back across the street to her car. She gets inside. The men go back to Evan's car and sit waiting for C.D. C.D. stands outside her car window.

"Father, one last thing! I just remembered something. When I was leaving the parking garage in my car, I saw a man. The gate opened for me to leave and he walked inside. He had on a dark, long coat and dark, long hair pulled back in a ponytail. That's all I saw," Lorena says looking at her watch. "I've really got to go, Father."

"In a ponytail? With a long, dark coat? You've been most helpful. Thank you so much! May God be with you!"

C.D. walks back to Evan's car and tells the men the last clue Lorena gave to him. C.D. writes Lorena's information down in his notebook, thinking that something about this information sounds familiar. Tom, C.D., Jimmy and William are making small talk about the weather and the city of Houston. Evan is strangely quiet, thinking. Without a suspicion, Evan knows for sure that the rumor about Lorena and Kizzy and the lesbian affair is false. He feels relief. Yet, so many questions exist that must be answered!

3

They return to the hotel. After everyone is situated and ready for discussion, they tell William and C.D. the story of their visit to the powerful mobster's house. They explain to C.D. how his occupation as a Catholic priest saved their lives.

C.D. comments with great confidence, "Once again the soldiers of the Lord have gone into the enemy's camp, and returned unscathed." C.D. feels much pride knowing he was with them in spirit and made a big difference.

"Did anything about that black sport-utility vehicle look familiar to you, cabby?" Evan asks, testing Jimmy.

"Yeah, I've seen it somewhere, cop," Jimmy says.

"You didn't notice it had no license plate, but a red bumper sticker?" Evan asks.

"I know where we've seen it. It was the vehicle that followed us that day in the cab when we left the city morgue after viewing Kizzy's body. Remember?" Tom says with certainty.

William says, "Now we know Mr. Luigi and Mr. Giovanni, one or both of them, are interested in where we are going and what we are doing. I wonder why? If they had nothing to do with her death, why would they care what we do?" William has made a good point.

The men continue to discuss the evidence and clues they have gathered to date. C.D. reads the notes from his notebook aloud to the others. "Kizzy was interrupted before her bath, or so we think. Someone murdered her and removed her arms and legs with great detail after death with a meat cleaver, leaving them on the floor beside the bed; everyone agrees a meat cleaver is not a weapon a burglar just happens to be carrying; no murder weapon is found in the apartment, nor is the meat cleaver; also, none of her knives are missing; the killer had removed her body from the bed where she died of one stab wound to the abdomen, by a knife, to the floor before the severing. Her body was full of sleeping pills; she had been beaten, tortured and raped about two hours before death; the killer took the time to clean up in her apartment before leaving; the prints in the apartment were wiped clean, except for a few of Kizzy's, so he must have been there quite some time; no forced entry had been present; an expensive gold ink pen was found with the initials 'T.U.'; the place had a security guard, security card keyed elevator and keyed locked front door; she left an estate of more than two million dollars; she had been first Giovanni's and then Luigi's girl; she had been pregnant probably with Luigi's child, and he may not have known because he did not mention it; but the mobster's grief looked genuine, strangely genuine; one of the two mobsters probably kidnaped Tom for information; Why? Lorena was not the killer, but may have seen the killer entering through the garage; the killer was wearing a dark-colored, long coat with long, dark hair in a ponytail." C.D. closes his notebook with a strange look on his face. He has a strange memory to verify. However, he will say nothing at this point.

Evan says confidently, "I don't think either Luigi or Giovanni had anything to do with her death. I believe Giovanni. I can't believe I'm saying this. I've questioned many professional criminals. I can usually tell when they are lying. This guy wasn't lying! He looked me straight in the eye. That's rare for his kind."

"It may be rare, but I've known a lot of crooks that like to lie," Jimmy says argumentatively.

Evan, who does not like to be contradicted, opens his mouth to speak, but is interrupted by Tom. "I trust Evan's police experience and instinct, but the question keeps repeating itself. Why were they following us that day if they didn't have anything to do with her death?"

"I don't know, but we're going to find out why," Evan answers.

"Did you notice Lorena never answered my question about how she entered through the parking garage?" says William.

"Yeah. You're right. She didn't answer," Tom says.

"The clues are not taking us anywhere. We are overlooking something. Yet, what? Every suspect leads to a dead end. Did one of these people, Lorena or the two mobsters, kill Kizzy?" William says. No one can answer William's question. The men scatter, each going their own way.

4

William and C.D. decide to perform background research work on Kizzy. Research is within their limits of expertise. However, C.D. is preoccupied with something. Together in C.D.'s car, they travel to the courthouse to perform the task. They hope to discover who owned the company that paid Kizzy the large sum of money, Fun Coin. The research takes much longer than they anticipate, seeming to go on and on without end. The men search through the books desperately. Each time, they find an owner, another company leads them back to another company, and so on, and so on . . . .

The courthouse is about to close, and it is very late. The two men are tired. C.D.'s eyes are blurring the print. After researching dummy corporation after dummy corporation, the name at last appears on the page.

"Here! Praise God! Oh! I can't believe this! Look, William!" C.D. yells out.

"I'll be damned!" William says as he looks at the name staring back at him from the page. They know who owns Fun Coin. In amazement, the men stare at the page as the name jumps out at them!

CHAPTER XV

Answers . . . More Questions?

1

The men gather at William's hotel room late in the evening. This time, William and C.D. have news to reveal. Presenting the information they have discovered gives them a feeling of being a member of this important investigative team. The surprising owner of Fun Coin is officially Keziah Elaine Theriot. The men are puzzled. Why did Kizzy hide that she owned the business through the dummy corporations? Why would she go to this much trouble? Why not just enter herself in the file book as the owner? And who was parked in the business parking lot in the large, black limo at Fun Coin? Could it have been Luigi or Giovanni? Evan explains that he has verified the alibis of Luigi and Giovanni. They were at the ballet and the restaurant just as Giovanni had said. Once again, who is the ambiguous "T.U.," and how does this person fit in with the murder? Not one of the men have the answers. They separate, pondering the facts and the new questions.

2

Evan stops at Kizzy's apartment on the way home. He watches to make sure he is not being followed. Today, there is no tail. He questions the security man to learn if there is another entrance to Kizzy's apartment. The security man states that the only entrances are through the front door passing by him and through the parking garage. Evan decides at this point to take a look at the parking garage entrance because Lorena mentioned this is how she had entered. The entrance to the parking garage is entirely hidden by a large, metal security gate that extends to the ceiling. However, to activate the gate to gain entrance, you must say your name and apartment number in a computer box. The tenants have voice prints on file monitored by the computer for comparison. Then, after the voice matches, the security card key must be inserted in the slot as a double security check. The gate opens after the security card key match. Okay, the perp probably came in the gate when Lorena left. However, the security card key must be used again to operate the elevator. Otherwise, the perp could not have gone to the apartment. The stairs do not come all the way down to the parking garage. The stairs stop in the lobby behind the security guard. Evan notices a security camera directly over the computer box at the gate. From the basement parking garage, Evan uses the security man's borrowed card and goes back up the elevator to the lobby to discuss the questions he has been rattling around in his head. He asks the security man why the camera is not operating.

He explains to Evan, "A big, red button is on the lower side of the computer box."

"Yeah, I saw it. A sign says delivery people should push it for service."

"Yes, when they push the button, the security camera activates, so that I can see down at the gate. Otherwise, it stays off, and I activate the cameras here in the lobby. After I okay their entry, I speak to the computer with my voice print, and override the security card key using mine. See I insert it here."

"So you can sit here, and without leaving your desk, override the security card key system with your voice print and your card. Can you let them up the elevator the same way?"

"Yes, Detective, I can."

"But, you let no one up the elevator from the garage the day or night of the murder, no visitor or tenant. Is that right?" Evan asks.

"Yes, no one, Detective."

"Sir, do you know anyone with the initials 'T.U.' that ever visited the victim?"

"The other policeman asked me the same question. No, I don't know anyone with those initials. None of the tenants or anyone that ever visited Kizzy had those initials. She had no visitors, Detective Picard."

"So were there any deliveries the day or evening of Kizzy's death?"

The security man pulls out a large, black book. He opens the pages to the date of Kizzy's death. He generously lets Evan look at the book with him. The security man is efficient and cooperative.

"Nope. I keep a log of deliveries or visitors in this book. Looks as if they delivered only the mail that day, which comes in right here at the front door. See the boxes are right over there. Oh, yeah officer, speaking of mail. I have more mail that arrived yesterday for Ms. Theriot." He opens his desk drawer, retrieves an envelope and hands it to Evan. Evan thanks the man and, feeling heavy exhaustion, leaves for the evening.

3

During his drive, the questions bounce around inside his brain. From Lorena, Jacko and Giovanni, he knows Luigi and Giovanni had relationships with Kizzy. However, the security man said she had no visitors. If they did not enter through the lobby, then they must have entered through the garage. How? How did Lorena get inside the garage and up to Kizzy's? Could the perp be the strange man with the ponytail? If he is the perp, how did he get up the elevator? Could his initials be "T.U.?" Evan arrives at his apartment. He looks down at the seat, almost forgetting the envelope that came in the mail for Kizzy. He carries it inside and opens it. Again, another check, but this time it is from Maracuja Modeling, Incorporated, for fifty thousand dollars. Whew! Modeling pays well! Evan lays the check on his desk and turns in for the night. He lies in the darkness, tossing and turning as he cannot turn the thoughts inside his head off. Ceaselessly, they play with repetition. This case is driving him crazy! He looks at the clock, seeing three o'clock. Quietly in the darkness, he lies thinking.

CHAPTER XVI

The Confession

1

Clues, the story and questions keep running chronically in C.D.'s head. Each time they find an answer, another question arises, or so it seems. Nothing seems to stop it. It is two o'clock in the morning, and the man with the ponytail keeps repeating in his mind. Exhausted, after tossing and turning, he dozes off. He jerks awake at four, sweating profusely from a fitful sleep. Even the palms of his hands, sticky from the sweat, are cold and clammy. After putting on his robe, he runs quickly to his office to his calendar lying on his desk. He looks back to the last date he gave confession to the church members. *THERE!* That day, the next day after Kizzy died. Oh, dear Lord, how can he have forgotten! He had given confession the day of Kizzy's death and the entire next day into the night. He had even told Evan the first night he met him about the confessional duty on the night of the murder. How could he have forgotten this? Maybe he forgot because of the sentimental torment connected with Kizzy's death, or perhaps he forgot because this was not his first murder confession, which made it seem commonplace.

The confession from the strange man has haunted him. He was no regular member, or even anyone C.D. had previously seen. C.D. sits in his chair and remembers the strange incident.

2

C.D. had been in the confessional box on June seventeenth, the evening after Kizzy had been murdered. Late, around nine p.m., he heard someone enter. The voice had a slight accent which had sounded Spanish. The stranger tried to murmur, but it was difficult with the coarseness of his voice.

"Padre, please, I have sinned."

"May the Lord our God be deep within your heart, son. May he guide your lips to confess your sins honestly. When was your last confession?" C.D. asked to comfort the troubled soul before him. "What sin have you committed—a mortal sin?"

The man's hoarse voice continued. "It's been a long time, Padre. I have committed a mortal sin!" Leaving the usual Rite of Penance at confession, he blurted out with his voice quivering, "*Murder*, Padre. I've committed murder just last night. This was difficult for me, Padre."

C.D. responded, trying not to show surprise at the man's words, "Son, taking someone's life is always difficult. Every creature on this earth is our Father's. You must go to the police and confess, my son and do the right thing." C.D. knows he must convince this man to confess to the police and face the proper punishment.

"I can't, Padre."

C.D. pursued him. "You must! This is important."

" Padre, I said that *I can't!*"

"Why not? This is important to your soul."

"I said I can't go to the cops, Padre. I *promised*."

"A promise is not more important than the saving of the soul. You must go to the police."

"Padre, I promised on the Bible. When you swear on the Bible, it's a promise to *God*. Right?"

"Well . . . Well, I guess. You promised on the Bible not to go to the police?"

His quivering hoarse voice said, "Yes, Padre."

"Who made you promise not to go to the police?"

" Padre, does that matter? Isn't a promise a promise?"

"Yes . . . I suppose you are right. Okay, I suppose I understand your situation."

He pleaded, his voice quivering more, "Please, Padre, give me forgiveness—absolution. I'm sorry for killing, Padre. I didn't want to do this. Her *beautiful green eyes* will haunt me forever. She was looking right at me, Padre, but it had to be done! I did it for money. I'm so sorry, truly, Padre, but I did this for her!"

Curious about the man's last comments, C.D. asked, "Have you atoned for your sin in any way?"

"Yes, Padre, in the poor box, I atoned."

"You will say the Act of Contrition. Do you know this?"

"Padre, I do. My mother was a good Catholic. She taught me the act. Padre, she would be ashamed of me."

"You will also stay and pray for the soul of the person you killed for at least thirty minutes. You will say ten Hail Marys. Do you understand?"

"Yes, Padre."

C.D. sat in the box, reading his Bible during the man's prayers. C.D. finished the Rite of the Sacrament of Penance upon the completion of the penance. He believed the stranger was truly penitent and would not commit the sin again. He was just beginning to try to convince the man to reconsider confessing to the police when he heard the door to the confessional close. The strange man had left the box. C.D. looked out and saw the back of the man as he left the church. He was tall and thin, but dressed nicely in a dark colored topcoat. C.D. wondered why he had worn a topcoat in this Houston heat. The man's hair was dark, long, straight and was pulled back in a ponytail. Quickly, the man looked back over his shoulder. C.D. was able to see only his ebony, cold, penetrating eyes. C.D. believed these were truly the eyes of a killer. Later, C.D. had found a fifty thousand dollar cash bundle in the poor box. He believed it was donated by the strange killer for atonement.

The stranger's words had played repetitively in C.D.'s subconscious mind for many days after the event, and then he had thrust them in the back of his mind. What had those words meant? What had he meant, he had "done it for her"?

3

C.D. closes his appointment book and goes back to his bed. In the darkness of the night, he lies there. The sweat beads upon his forehead. His mind races. What can he do? He is a priest. He cannot divulge the information given to him in the confessional. However, what if that man is Kizzy's killer? Lorena's description of the man entering Kizzy's garage is the same. What if he is the person for whom they are searching? Surely many women were killed that night in Houston, such a big city. C.D. knows he is trying to convince himself, and maybe he is not being honest by amplifying the statistics. Whom is he kidding? How many women were murdered that same night with Kizzy's "beautiful green eyes?" Oh, God in heaven, what can he do? C.D. rises from the bed, falls upon his knees and starts to pray. Prayer is the only way to get the answer. He goes back to his bed and dozes into sleep.

4

C.D. wakes the next morning just as baffled and troubled as ever. He knows he needs help with this decision. Because of his developed respect for William, who somehow seems to have the wisdom of life, he calls William at the hotel. William is awake and alone in the hotel room. Tom has gone for a walk to end the waking stiffness from his knee. Without hesitating, C.D. rushes directly to the hotel. The two men greet each other just as old friends. An easy friendship has developed between the two of them.

C.D. says, "If you knew something that *could* be very helpful to Kizzy's case, maybe even the answer to the killer, but it was a violation of client confidentiality, what would you do? Would you tell?"

"Ooo, Father, that is a tough one. I think if the information is only a possibility, it should be kept confidential. However, could you possibly give a hint without violating the confidentiality?"

C.D. starts to ponder the information. He knows he cannot divulge what the confessor said in the confessional. William is a wise man who has given C.D. the answer. God has answered his prayer and sent William, a new friend, into his life. Soon the other men are contacted and brought together once again.

After everyone arrives, C.D. starts his explanation. "On the evening of June seventeenth, the day after Kizzy was killed, a man came in my church. He wore a dark-colored topcoat even though it was midsummer. I believe very strongly that this man may be Kizzy's killer. I can tell you he was tall and slender with long, dark hair pulled back in a ponytail. He also had dark, penetrating, cold eyes. This description is similar to the description given to us by Lorena Luigi, if you all remember. I believe he was from another country, because he spoke English with a Spanish accent. He also had a deep voice. I did not see his face, only briefly his eyes."

Evan notes, "You must have conversed with this man or you would not have known that he spoke with an accent."

"I cannot answer any more questions. Just know what I told you is true and crucial. That is all I can say, Evan. Please, do not question me further."

Evan has to ask. This is too important. "What did he say to you?"

"Please, Evan, I cannot say!"

Jimmy says for the first time agreeing with Evan. "Oh, come on Padre! This could be important!"

Tom says, "Can't you tell us just a little something about what the guy said to you, Father?"

Evan begs, coaxing C.D., "We need more, Father. Please, do it for

Kizzy."

William knows that Evan will not quit, and knowing the story behind C.D.'s story, adds in his defense. "Look, he's told us everything he can. Do not pursue him on this matter. We must respect his duty as a priest."

Evan says, "Gee, that's not a whole lot to go on, Father. A tall guy with an accent, dark hair and dark eyes fits about twenty percent or more of Houston. Houston has a large Hispanic community."

Jimmy says with his dry, insulting humor just to irritate Evan. "Well, at least it cuts out the other eighty percent, huh, cop?" Jimmy does not always show his humor at the most proper time.

"Okay, let's not argue," Tom says. "You two are like two old tom cats after the same female! At least the description is the same as Ms. Luigi's. Let's concentrate on our new lead. Do it for Kizzy, you guys."

"Hey, before we go further, let me give you men something to chew on," Evan says as he pulls the check from his pocket and hands it over to William. "Kizzy got another check for fifty thousand."

William says, "Well, I guess Father C.D. and I will spend another day at the courthouse." The men separate.

5

Tom leaves the hotel, hails a cab, and goes to the cemetery. He tells no one that he is going to Kizzy's grave. Upon arriving, Tom looks down at the headstone. How sad it is that her entire life is summed up on a small piece of rock. Tom has feelings that he cannot hold inside any longer. He is here, hoping to resolve these deep feelings. "Hey, babe. I'm here. I had to come and see you. I wish you had told me about our little baby. I truly believe I would've married you. I loved you even back then when we were kids. But you know, I've been thinking. I was a selfish little punk back then. I probably wouldn't have made you a good husband. I'm sorry, babe. I'm so very sorry!" Tears are filling his eyes, and he sniffs holding them back. "I was rotten to you. You deserved better than I. I'm so sorry you had to go through that abortion. I hope you can forgive me for that someday. I can't stop thinking about it! *Damn*, it is driving me *nuts*!" Tom pauses, trying to regain a little control. He wipes the mucous from his nose on the back of his bare hand. "I still love you, babe. I just had to come and talk to you this one last time. I probably did it for myself. Hell, I guess I'm still selfish. I love you, babe, so damn much that I hurt so bad inside! I don't think that I will ever stop missing you and know I'll never forget you!"

He pauses, wiping the wetness from his nose and moustache with his hand. "I stopped drinking, babe. After I saw you in that alley, I had to. God knows what I'd do to have another chance with you. I don't know where my life is going after this is over. I guess I'll have to figure it out one day at a time. I'll tell you this, whoever killed you is going to pay, babe. I promise!" As he stands over the grave, Tom starts to sob openly so hard that his shoulders jerk.

After his open weeping is spent, he gains composure. Tom looks at the headstone once more, seeing the neatly carved name. Then he looks at the wilted flowers. He sees the bouquet that the men had purchased, Mr. Alexander's flowers, Evan's parent's flowers and then, these two large, expensive looking bouquets. No cards or florist identification stickers are anywhere on the two bouquets. Next, he notices a small, plastic flower and a handpicked small bouquet. The small, fresh wildflower bouquet looks as if someone had picked them from a field. The plastic flower is old and dirty. However, this must be the right grave for these flowers. No other graves are near Kizzy's. Tom is curious, wondering who brought these flowers to Kizzy? The two large, expensive bouquets, the small, handpicked bouquet and the plastic flower were not here during her funeral. Why did these people not come to her funeral? Tom leaves the cemetery and returns by cab back to the hotel.

Something keeps going through Tom's mind as he rides in the cab. His mind goes back to the visit the men made to the apartment. Why did the killer remove Kizzy's dead body from the waterbed to dismember her? The killer must have known it was a waterbed. If the killer tried to hack her with the cleaver on the waterbed, it would puncture the mattress. Besides, how did the killer know it was a waterbed? The killer had to know before he came to her apartment that night. The killer must be someone that had visited Kizzy's apartment before and had seen the bed. These thoughts rush through Tom's mind with a resemblance of a freight train racing over and over the same old tired tracks.

CHAPTER XVII
The Tips

1

In William's hotel room, Tom reports the strange flowers at Kizzy's grave to the gathered group. Evan mentions the two large bouquets are probably from Luigi and Giovanni. However, no one can understand the handpicked, wildflower bouquet or the strange, plastic flower. Could one of these bouquets be from "T.U.," or is the mysterious "T.U." the killer? Next, Tom mentions to the others the questions he has about the waterbed. He then insists that he and Evan return to Kizzy's apartment. William and C.D. leave for the courthouse to research the new, large check. Jimmy claims he has to work. Evan, as always, doubts Jimmy but does not mention this to him because it would cause an argument. Evan and Tom leave together for Kizzy's apartment.

While driving, Evan notices the black sport-utility vehicle discreetly following them again. Evan decides to just allow them to follow to promote worry as to why he and Tom are returning to the apartment. Evan parks his car, watching the sport-utility vehicle park about a block away.

2

Tom and Evan enter the apartment and go directly to the bedroom and the waterbed. The bloody sheets have been removed as evidence. Someone has draped a fresh bedspread over the waterbed mattress. Tom removes the bedspread. He gapes down at the bare light-blue waterbed mattress. You can see down into the water.

Evan says as he sits on the waterbed, "Damn, I don't see anything squirrely about this mattress. It looks normal to me. Hell, maybe the killer just noticed she had a waterbed, and didn't want to make a mess by puncturing it."

Tom says, "A neat killer, huh? I don't know, Evan. I got a feeling about this."

The water sloshes around the mattress walls. Evan looks down at the mattress, joining Tom in the search. While the water sloshes around, for an instant, Evan sees something floating in the mattress.

"Hey, Tom, I just saw something," Evan says pointing at the mattress.

"What?"

Evan answers as he walks over and opens the drapes, allowing sunlight to flood the room, "I don't know. It looked as if it were a little package of some sort."

Tom, staring down, looking at the mattress says, "Yeah, there! I just saw it float by. Maybe it'll tell us who 'T.U.' is!" Tom says with excitement in his voice.

"Evan, how are we going get that out without making a big mess with this water? Hell, we might even flood the whole apartment. I mean this thing has a lot of water in it!"

"I don't know, but we'll figure something out, Tom." The two men slosh the water. They fish, with great patience, through the drain plug with a small piece of wire that Tom found in the kitchen drawer that he has shaped into a hook, without success. The two men are stumped. They have no idea how to retrieve this little package through the small drain opening of the waterbed. Somehow they are going to have to drain the water from the mattress.

3

Meanwhile, on the other side of town, Jimmy speeds down the streets. He meets with several of his local street contacts. He questions everyone about the nice dressing, tall, thin man, perhaps foreign, with long, dark, straight hair in a ponytail and dark penetrating eyes. Leaving no one out, Jimmy questions everyone, strangers, casual acquaintances and friends. Jimmy is desperate.

His desperation pays off! The leads start adding up. One man tells Jimmy the killer is a professional hit man hired by someone in town. Another contact, Cyndi, a hooker that Jimmy knows, tells him the man left town two days after this hit in June on a good-looking, high-dollar hooker. She explains this hooker was top dollar oozing with class. Another man tells Jimmy that the hit man is a pro from South America. Jimmy remembers the birthday card William received from Rio. He wonders how these two tips hook together.

Another contact, an old lady with big ears for details, tells Jimmy the man is back in Houston at this moment, but not on a hit this time. He came back to take care of drug business. After questioning a few other contacts, Jimmy finds out the name of the hotel where the man is registered. Jimmy also finds out the man undoubtedly has mob contacts stemming from South America into the United States. He wonders if somehow Luigi and Giovanni are connected. Jimmy has not trusted Evan's opinion that Giovanni and Luigi are innocent. Jimmy's history with people such as those two spells that you can never trust what they say or do. "Once a thug, always a thug" is Jimmy's motto.

Jimmy adds the pieces of information together. He finds the nice place, a hotel in downtown Houston, where the hit man is registered. After bribing the front desk employee, Jimmy gets the name of the man—Manuel Carrara. Jimmy remembers hearing the name around town at different times over the years. He knows this man is good at his job, and his job is death.

Jimmy continues asking several questions of other street contacts. One contact tells him that the man is leaving town on a midnight flight back to Rio. The information he gets signifies that Carrara is a specialty hit man for Geraldo Saude, a vicious South American mobster according to the contacts. Jimmy thinks that Geraldo Saude does not have the initials "T.U." and neither does the hit man, Manuel Carrara. Jimmy drives to the hotel again, sitting outside and watching. He taps his fingers on the window edge as he watches and thinks. Realizing this man is a pro, and he cannot handle this alone, Jimmy knows he is going to have to act fast, or this man will escape back to Rio. What should he do? He rides to a nearby convenience store, uses the pay phone to call William's hotel room and shares the information he has gotten with William. William agrees to contact Evan, Tom and C.D. They will meet at William's hotel room as soon as possible.

William phones C.D. at the church. He calls Evan on his cellular. They agree to meet. Evan and Tom agree to return later to Kizzy's apartment to retrieve the package from the waterbed. They know the waterbed will still be there tomorrow. This information from Jimmy is much more pressing because this man could leave Houston at any time. Evan notices as they leave Kizzy's apartment building that the black sport-utility vehicle is gone. No one follows them as they go to William's hotel room for the meeting.

4

The men meet at the hotel room. Tom and Evan share the information about the mysterious package floating in the waterbed. They agree to retrieve it later. Jimmy even suggests syphoning the water from the mattress using a water hose stretched to the bathtub. He explains to the others how you have to suck on the end of the hose to get the water to flow from the mattress to the bathtub.

He tries not to show it, but the information cocky Jimmy has gathered about the stranger so quickly from the streets impresses Evan. The men, exhilarated by the fact they may at long last have the killer, derive a plan with Evan in charge. Evan does not favor moving on this plan so late in the day, because it will be dark soon. If they wait, this suspect could escape back to South America. He considers calling Pete. However, for whatever reason, Pete has been dragging his feet on this case.

They drive to Carrara's hotel in Evan's car. They look at the layout of the entire place. The plan they decide upon is similar to the interrogation plan of Luigi and Giovanni. The ten-story hotel faces the street in the southward direction. A front entrance, a small east entrance close to the front corner, and a fire escape on the west side, also close to the front of the building, are the only entrances. C.D. and William are to stay in the car on the east side of the building in a small alley just behind the small east entrance. This east exit has a small door, but anyone leaving must go through the restaurant and kitchen to reach it. They are to watch the exit and call for backup if they need it. They have William's newly purchased binoculars, Evan's cellular phone, and the police radio.

The fire escape on the west side of the building will have Jimmy guarding it. Conveniently, he just happens to have a gun. He says he has it to protect himself as a cab driver from robbery. He will have it with him at the fire escape and assures Evan he knows how to use the gun. He also swears to Evan that he has a permit for the weapon, but just does not happen to have it with him at the moment. Evan and Tom decide that they will go inside through the front entrance to the room. Tom has agreed to stay back, waiting at the elevator entrance. He will keep the elevator door open so that the exit is ready and not accessible for civilians' use. Evan does not want innocent bystanders to be at risk. Their plan is ready. Everyone knows their positions and expected responsibilities. They return to William's hotel to prepare for their adventure. Evan checks Jimmy's gun and his own. Tom considers taking a pain pill for his knee but decides to tough out the pain. He needs a clear head for this adventure. C.D. leads the group in a prayer for success. William rests briefly.

Evan again explores telling Pete of the plan. He calls Pete and questions him about when he is bringing in Luigi and Giovanni. Pete explains he does not have enough evidence to warrant bringing them in for questioning. Next, he questions Pete about leads on the gold pen and the initials "T.U." Again, Pete has nothing. Hot-tempered and unhappy, Evan does not question Pete further, finding Pete uncooperative. Pete is not investigating the few clues he has given to him. Why should he give Pete any more? Besides, the interrogation of Luigi and Giovanni went well using these guys without Pete. Evan decides to keep the details about their plan and the hotel from Pete. He tells Pete only that something is "going down in about an hour downtown." He needs Pete to be ready. Pete tries to question Evan, but he hangs up. Evan instructs C.D. and William not to take incoming calls, just to use the cellular phone to call out if needed.

5

The men leave the hotel with Evan driving. Filled with heightened nervousness, they go to Mr. Carrara's hotel. Evan hates the lateness, and he hates working with untrained people. Nonetheless, he has to admit that they have been helpful in the investigation, each in their own way. They have been more helpful than Pete, a trained police detective.

A black cat crosses the road. Evan has to hit his brakes to keep from hitting the creature.

Tom, sitting forward in his seat yells, "No! Turn around! We can't go this way! It's bad luck!"

The rest of the men find Tom's remark almost humorous. C.D. replies, "An animal, my son, can't bring us any harm." Evan goes down the road not adhering to Tom's foolish warning.

Unlike the others, Jimmy laughs aloud. He is not as civil in considering the feelings of others before he speaks or laughs. "Boy, football! You're losing it!" Jimmy says between eruptions of laughter.

Tom says, sitting back in his seat, "I know something awful is going to happen. Just wait. You should have turned around. I tell you. You messed up, Evan."

Evan says, "We don't have time to turn around, Tom. If we turn around, it'll be pitch dark when we get there. When this goes down, it's going be dark enough. Think of it this way. Getting there in the light and allowing us the time to get in position is good luck!"

"A good point, Evan," William says.

Tom says mumbling and shaking his head in dismay, "You guys don't understand. I know about this stuff. I know."

Suddenly, Jimmy, sitting in the front seat passenger side, looks in the side mirror and says, "Evan, our favorite four-wheel driver is behind us again!"

Tom mutters, "See we got bad luck already."

"Yeah, I see it," Evan responds. "But I can change this bad luck."

"Man, get the hell away from them! Step on it! Go, cop, *Go!*" Jimmy yells out instructing Evan and tapping his fingers against the window edge. Evan increases speed, not having the time to scold Jimmy for having the nerve to give him orders. He turns several times trying to lose the tail, but the tail holds tight.

"You know, I think that's those same men that were in that sport-utility vehicle at Mr. Luigi's house," William says as he looks back through the rear window. Everyone is too busy watching the sport-utility vehicle to acknowledge William's statement in any way. Evan makes two quick turns in a row.

"Hey, they're gone!" Tom yells out.

"Yes! Ya lost 'em, cop! When ya drive like I tell ya, you do okay!" Jimmy yells.

Evan spouts back, "You are so full of yourself, cabby!"

"You are so full of—" Jimmy says, but Tom interrupts.

"Come on, guys! We don't have time for this!" Tom says insistent and nervous.

Evan tells Tom, "See, I told you I'd take care of that bad luck."

C.D. says with skepticism and worry, "Yes, we lost our tail. But we're only a couple of blocks from that hotel. That sport-utility or four-wheel drive vehicle may find us."

"See, more bad luck," Tom inputs.

"Well, we are going to be in that dark alley. I don't think they will see us, Father," William says reassuringly. Everyone feels relief that they have lost the strange, black sport-utility vehicle that persistently tails them so closely.

Worriedly, Evan thinks, yeah, we will park in the dark alley—we will be working in the dark! Evan has a bad feeling about the apprehension of this hit man. He wishes they could wait until the morning and daylight. However, the man is flying out at midnight. They cannot let this man get away! This might be their last chance. He strives to shake this premonition of doom and gloom. Evan voices aloud in rage, fear and frustration. "Why in the hell do those guys in that damn sport-utility vehicle keep following us?"

No one knows the answer. Silence fills the air. . . .

CHAPTER XVIII

The Accidents?

1

The men arrive at the hotel with nerves on edge. Evan looks at the sky and sees the sun going down. Darkness is upon them, inciting mixed feelings of excitement and fear. Each man takes his predetermined position. The outside is dimly lit on the front and pitch black at the side entrances. This bothers Evan. However, the event goes in motion.

Evan and Tom take the elevator to the fifth floor, the floor of the suspect's room. Tom stays at the elevator door. Tom's shaking hand pulls the stop button to keep the door open and ready for an exit. He is dying for a drink to deaden the shooting pain in his knee. Tom has not taken the pain pill. He wants his wits about him to think vividly. This night is too important. He feels needed, and this is a good feeling, a feeling he has missed. At least, he has to do this one thing right in his life. To succeed at this for Kizzy is important to Tom.

Jimmy is ready at his station with his gun drawn. His hands are shaking and so is the gun in his hand. He is not jiggling his leg as usual as his legs are frozen rigid with fear. He starts to think, worrying about the darkness. Briefly, he can barely see the gun in his hand as the clouds part, revealing the moon. Yet, the dark returns after the clouds cover the moon. The blackness envelopes him, much as the darkness of the closet in his childhood. Jimmy hates the dark! His mind fills with fear. Maybe fear from his past is all this is. However, that past fear fills his body, his soul and his mind here and now. He has never killed anyone. He has beaten them, hit them, but never literally taken the life of another human being. What if that killer, Carrara, comes down the fire escape? His heart is racing. What will he be able to do? Will he be able to pull the trigger? Again, briefly in the moonlight, he looks down at the shaking gun in his hand and swallows. He tries to take a deep breath, but only struggles nervously and looks at the darkness around him. Fear overwhelms him, filling his very entity.

C.D. and William sit together in Evan's car at the east side in plain sight of the door. They are ready with the lights off and the key in the ignition. William gasps for air with his emphysema suddenly present. Possibly this shortness of breath is just nerves. Not even realizing what he is doing, he wipes the steering wheel nervously with his handkerchief. Not that the steering wheel is dirty, but William feels the steering wheel is germ laden. William perceives he is too old for this "apprehension of suspects." He is an attorney, not a policeman or even a private investigator. What in the world is he doing waiting in a dark alley with a priest as *his* backup! The cellular phone rings once, but they ignore it as Evan has instructed them. He hears C.D.'s words as he prays aloud first, and then silently. Sensing William's fear and apprehension, C.D. can only hope his prayers also offer some comfort to William.

This is it! Evan draws his gun, approaches the door, knocking once loudly. He announces that he is with law enforcement and just needs to ask Mr. Carrara a few questions. He hears movement inside the hotel room. That is when all hell breaks loose. A shot rings out piercing through the door. The bullet almost hits Evan, as he ducks for cover and returns fire through the door. Evan forcibly kicks in the door to the room. The suspect has already escaped through an open window. Evan looks at the fire escape found just outside the window. Evan knows he should have determined this as a possibility before this happened. With only a flashlight and in the darkness, he looks up and down the fire escape. Evan stands still and quietly listens. He cannot hear footsteps against the metal stairs on the fire escape. He looks back in the window. Next to the bed, on the floor, are the suspect's shoes. Evan realizes why he cannot hear footsteps. Carrara is barefoot. He yells down at Jimmy, in case the suspect is coming down the fire escape. However, a train is going by, so he does not know if Jimmy hears his warning. Evan decides to go down the fire escape, concluding downward is the most logical direction for escape.

2

At the same time, inside waiting in the hall, Tom hears the gunfire, and Evan entering the hotel room. Tom hears Evan yelling down at Jimmy, but he cannot understand the words. He only recognizes the sound of his voice. Tom senses the suspect is no longer in the room. He hears Evan's footsteps through the open hotel room door and open window, going down the fire escape to help Jimmy. Tom sees a sign marked "stairs" going toward the roof just a short way down the hall from the elevator. He is not sure what to do next. Time stands still, as the picture of Kizzy flashes across his mind. Almost seeing her standing in front of him, he can hear her laughter, and the smell of her fills his nostrils. Tom sucks the smell in his nostrils and looks down at his hands. They are no longer shaking. Just the thought of her has steadied his hands and suddenly filled him with courage and knowledge. He knows what has to be done. Without pausing to think further, he decides to take the stairs to cut off the suspect on the roof, just in case he went up the fire escape instead of down. Tom shoves his way through the door marked "stairs." Tom sprints the stairs, forgetting about his old football injured knee. At this moment, the pain is uniquely absent. He enters the roof through an open door. He wonders why this door is already open. Pain and throbbing return to his knee as he enters the roof of the hotel. Tom stops cold in his tracks. The suspect is standing there in the dim moonlight, the light from the stairway and the lights from other buildings. He has on dark slacks and a white undershirt that catches the light illuminating him. He turns, gawks at Tom, looking wild and wretched, as a trapped animal. For the first time in a long time, Tom is not afraid. Tom sees the light reflection from the gun that the desperate suspect has in his hand. Tom knows he is no match against a gun. However, he cannot let this man get away! "Hold it right there!" Tom yells.

The man looks bewildered at Tom's demanding words. "Where's your gun, cop?" the man says in his coarse-voiced strong, Spanish dialect.

"You killed her, didn't you?" No reply comes from the man. "*Damn it*, answer me!" Tom yells.

The man, fitting the suspect's description, does not answer Tom's question. He says emphatically in his accented voice, "I'm leaving this roof. Nobody's going to stop me."

Tom is desperate. He cannot let this man escape. He uses the only means of physical restraint that he knows. Tom lets out an old football attack caterwaul and plunges savagely toward the man to tackle him. Moving quickly, he limps on his knee and grabs the man's hand holding the gun. The two men struggle. The man is strong against Tom and hits Tom, knocking him backwards. The man turns and starts over the roof ledge onto the fire escape. Tom grabs him at the waist and drags him backward onto the roof. With the gun handle, the man hits Tom hard on the head. Briefly, Tom is stunned. The man starts over the roof ledge again.

Yelling "*No!*" as loud as he can, Tom tackles him again. They roll around the roof top together. After kicking Tom backward, the man struggles to his feet and starts again for the ledge. Tom pursues him yelling, "You shouldn't have killed her! You shouldn't have killed her!" As they struggle over the possession of the gun, Tom can feel the strength of this mighty man, the suspect Carrara. Valiantly, Tom struggles with all his might on the ledge. Beneath him, he feels his injured knee collapsing.

3

Meanwhile, Evan nears the bottom of the fire escape. Jimmy hears someone coming. He elevates his shaking gun pointing it into the darkness toward the sound of the footsteps. Jimmy freezes. He cannot move.

"Don't shoot, cabby! It's me!" Via the darkness Evan appears.

Suddenly, from nowhere, a terrible mournful scream breaks the night silence. Through the darkness, a body comes plunging from the roof to fall only a few feet from where Evan and Jimmy are standing.

4

During the same interval of time, down below on the street level, C.D. and William hear the first gunshots. The two men panic. Should they call for backup? Nervously, together, unanimously they decide to call Pete. During C.D.'s conversation with Pete, they hear a loud scream that originates from the other side of the building and then, only silence. Thinking they are safer staying in the car, William quickly starts the engine hoping to move around to the source of the horrible shrill. He turns on the lights and travels up the alley toward the front of the building, passing the east entrance. When they pass the east entrance, a man flies suddenly in front of them from the doorway, as though he were pushed. William slams on his brakes, but too late. He hits the man with the car. C.D., sitting on the passenger side and much nearer to the doorway, sees another man standing in the doorway. He yells, "Look, William, in the doorway!"

"Yes, I see him! I have seen that man somewhere." The door closes. The man is gone. William and C.D. leave the car to inspect the poor man they have hit.

William says, "This man fits the description of the suspect, Carrara."

C.D. says, "Yes, that's the man I saw in church." He knows this man is the same man to whom he gave confession and Penance. Police sirens break the eerie silence of the night air. After feeling for a pulse and deciding that the poor suspect is dead, William walks quickly around the building to find Evan, Tom and Jimmy. C.D. stands over Carrara's body praying.

William is horrified when he arrives upon the scene around the building by the fire escape. Evan is bending over a bloody body on the ground. Jimmy is frozen, in shock standing with his gun clenched in his hand. His knuckles are white from the tightness of his clenched hand. The body is Tom.

Evan feels for a pulse, but none is present. Unable to accept Tom's death, Evan starts CPR. "Don't you die on me! *Damn it, Tom! Stay* with *me!"* Evan yells between breaths, creating a pitiful sight. Tom's tragic death so moves two such strong men, each in a different way.

The police and emergency personnel arrive. Pete is exasperated that Evan allowed this operation to take place using untrained personnel. Pete yells at Evan, "What the *hell* is wrong with you, Evan? I was only a *phone call away*! How could you be so damn *stupid?* You cost this guy his life!" Evan stands there accepting Pete's harsh words, feeling he deserves this and more.

The Captain arrives on the scene hoping to soft pedal the media attention for the police department. "That's it, Evan. I told you *not* to be involved in this case. Look at this mess! I have two dead bodies to explain! What the *hell* is wrong with you! Give me your badge! This will be investigated!" the Captain yells at Evan.

At the location, Tom is declared dead. The suspect, Carrara, is also declared dead. The police search Carrara's room. They find a photograph of Kizzy in his wallet.

Evan says, "Okay, Pete. That should prove to you that Carrara killed Kizzy. That picture ties Carrara and Kizzy together!"

"So? It doesn't prove Carrara killed her, but only that he knew Kizzy," Pete says. This maddens Evan. Alice tries desperately to calm Evan. Filled with anger at Pete, he pulls away from her and goes to sit in his car.

Tom has no next of kin, so C.D. agrees to make arrangements for his burial. Evan is about to leave the scene in a huff of indignation and frustration, when William opens his car door. He stands in the open doorway talking with Evan. "Evan, they're taking Jimmy to the hospital. He's upset by this and will be treated for shock."

"Boy, I really *screwed up* big time, didn't I, William?"

"Evan, you made only one mistake. You allowed four other men who loved Kizzy with their entire hearts to come along on this event. Your heart was in the right place. Don't be so hard on yourself."

"Yeah, but William, a cop can't think with his heart. His head has to be in control at all times. Thinking with your heart kills people!" William pats Evan on the shoulder and leaves the car. He waits around outside talking with Alice.

5

Bettey of the *Houston Register* newspaper is on the scene with the other media. This time Evan cannot get away from her. She opens the passenger's door and places herself in his car abruptly without being invited. "What the hell is going on with you, Evan? Ya don't return my calls. You're totally *inaccessible!* This isn't like ya!" She grabs Evan's shirt at the shoulder, tugging hard.

"Okay, Bettey, I'll talk, but it has to be off the record for now. Promise me."

"Yeah, but I get an exclusive later. Deal?"

Evan agrees because he trusts Bettey. Once she gives her word, she keeps it. Evan feels he is at the end of his rope. He cannot take this anymore. He chooses to confide in Bettey and starts to tell the story to her. She records and takes notes. He tells her the clues, the questions, everything.

Evan's confidence in her touches Bettey because she knows this is not easy for him. She can see the misery in his eyes, never seen before, as he speaks. Bettey puts down her pen, turns off the recorder and looks seriously in Evan's eyes. " Evan, we go way back. I'm your friend. I really care about ya, Evan. Let me help ya. I'm going to do some digging on my own. I don't know what is up with Pete. Pete's been totally uncooperative. I understand now why ya didn't talk to me, but don't understand what burr is up Pete's ass hole! I'll let ya know if anything turns up." She smiles, gives Evan a big hug and leaves the car. Evan appreciates this show of affection.

6

Evan starts the engine. Knowing he will not be able to sleep this night, he tells William he is going back to Kizzy's to retrieve the package from the waterbed mattress. William climbs in the car with Evan. That package had meant a lot to Tom—the one clue he had cued on which was his! Evan has to go tonight, before the station puts the word out to keep him from the apartment because he has lost his badge. William and Evan drive straight to an all-night department store. He purchases a water hose and drives straight to Kizzy's apartment. The two men talk as they drive.

"You know, William, I liked Tom. He was a down to earth kind of a guy. I think every time a black cat crosses the road in front of me, I'll think about him. You don't think there was anything to that black cat crossing causing that to happen, do you?" Evan asks.

"No! It was just coincidence, Evan."

"Yeah, right," Evan agrees. "Well, I still will think of him—you know, when the black cat thing happens. I'll miss the guy."

William says, "Yes, I will, too. Amazingly, I was slowly starting to like him a little, too. I did not want to, but I was. I think the years had matured Tom. I had known Tom, the boy. I didn't like him much."

"Why?"

"He was such an egocentric boy. He was so brutish to Kizzy, Evan. He hurt her so much. I hated him for that."

"Tell me something, William. Did you ever hurt a woman or young girl in your life?"

William thinks back. He thinks of Sylvia, and oh yes, the menagerie of other women he had destroyed in his youth—used and thrown away as if they were garbage. William remembers seeing the genuine sadness in Tom's eyes when he had revealed Kizzy's abortion. After all these years, he knows that Tom had never known about the pregnancy. Oddly, he feels sad for Tom at the moment of that agonizing revelation. Now it is trivial. However, when it happened all those years ago, he had wanted to beat Tom within an inch of his life. The memory of the sadness on Tom's face makes William realize that Tom would have married Kizzy if he had known. William reaches an important realization. "You're right, Evan. We've each used and hurt women. I think I saw myself as a youth in Tom. I guess I hated that part of me! He was brave on the roof."

"Yeah, Carrara shot at me through the door and was still armed. Football could have gotten shot! I don't know what happened, but Tom must have attacked Carrara trying to stop him from escaping. He went on that roof knowing Carrara might be there."

William says as he smiles at Evan, "I guess if Kizzy could forgive him all that hurt he caused her, I sure should."

"You know, William. When you told us about Kizzy's abortion, I thought lowly of you. You're an attorney, but you broke the law arranging that illegal abortion. I was wrong about you. If I had been in the same situation with Kizzy that you were, I would have done the same thing." The two men feel a strange closeness. A friendship has just begun.

7

The men arrive at the apartment. The syphoning is a long process, which takes at least three hours to finish. They lie around the apartment on the couch, pondering over the events of the last several weeks. After a draining night, the death—no, the deaths—the mysteries, they at long last drift off to sleep. Not good sound sleep, but the kind you have and then awake feeling as tired as ever. The morning sun wakes the two men as it peeks through the balcony drapes. At last, the mattress is empty. William retrieves towels to absorb the small amount of water left in the mattress. Evan rips open the mattress using his pocketknife, retrieving the small, sealed plastic bag containing a handwritten letter from Kizzy. Evan unfolds the one sheet of paper and starts to read with William peering politely over his shoulder.

This information is for William, Tom, Evan, Jimmy and C.D., I hope you are the ones reading this. I am not leaving this with my will in case I was wrong about Mr. Alexander, and he can be bought. I know you must have the key. I removed the number so finding what the key fits would be difficult. It's to a bus station locker. The locker number is 424. Inside you will find everything you need. The answers are there. I love you all!

Kiz

Evan says, folding the piece of paper, "Her usual insignia is on here. The key is to a locker in a bus station."

William will gather the men together in his hotel room for the revelation of this evidence. Then, they will go together to the bus station.

Evan will drop William at his hotel.

William says, "Thank you for what you said to me last night about Tom. You resolved an old painful vexation in me."

"Yeah, sure, William." Evan leaves William at the hotel entrance.

8

Evan has to do some thinking. Too many things are happening so quickly. Evan has a favorite spot for thinking. He will return to the hotel in a small amount of time, allowing William the time to reach everyone. Evan drives to the Houston Museum of Science. Since it is early, the museum is not crowded, but remarkably cool and reassuring. He walks around gazing at the exhibits. Knowledge of a lifetime surrounds him, and he feels each thought. Only answers are here, no questions. He almost feels a temporary relief, realizing answers are what he needs. He is so sick of dead-ends and questions. The important question is answered. Carrara killed Kizzy, or so he believes. Yet, who hired him and why? One down, many more questions to go! He is truly afraid that all the answers will not be in the bus station. Where will he go next? He is running out of clues. Questions surround each piece of evidence, and each question just has another question following it. Children come in the museum, and their voices fill the empty silence. He smiles at the pleasantness of hearing life around him. Evan feels renewed and relaxed, at least for the time being. He is ready to face the questions ahead.

CHAPTER XIX

The Pieces

1

Once again, the men gather in William's hotel room. William has picked up Jimmy, whom the hospital has treated for shock. They have released him, and he is much better, but not his old self. William notices a definite change in Jimmy, a calming and quiet. William asks, "You seem different, Jimmy. Is it the accident with Tom that has changed you?"

"Yeah, I guess so. First, the crap with Kizzy happened. The only good thing about this with Kizzy was that I met Tom. He was a nice guy, and I liked him. I think we could've been good friends but guess we'll never get the chance to find out. Ya know a guy like me doesn't have a helluva lot of *good* friends," Jimmy says painfully.

"Well, Jimmy, maybe you'll find a friend in one of the rest of us." Jimmy meekly smiles at William's comment.

Evan is a little late arriving, so the others wait patiently for him, biding their time with brainstorming of the clues to date. Someone had hired that hit man, but who and why? William mentions information he got from Evan. The man worked for South American mobsters according to the police computer. Why in the world would the South American mob want Kizzy dead? Logically Luigi or Giovanni would not order the hit, or so they think. Jimmy mentions that even Evan's stoolie thinks neither Luigi nor Giovanni has planned or been connected with the hit in any way. Evan swears the information from his street stoolie is nearly always correct. Why did Giovanni and Luigi have them followed? What are they afraid will be found? Why had this professional hit man dismembered Kizzy, an action which was not a pro's style? Who raped her two hours or more before she died? Was it the hit man? Why had the waterbed mattress been purposely spared? Why would a professional hit man spare a waterbed mattress from being punctured? How did the professional hit man get past the requirement for the elevator card key? Yes, he could have picked the lock to the apartment. The men agree on that detail. However, the card key, how did he get past that problem? Who was "T.U.?" Why was "T.U.'s" gold pen left in Kizzy's apartment? Why did Kizzy hide Fun Coin through the dummy corporations? This was not Kizzy's style. Everyone had thoughts, but no answers to these questions. What did these pieces that did not compute mean? Eventually, the four men are present in the hotel.

Evan discreetly asks Jimmy, "How are you doing, cabby?"

"Okay, I guess. It was quite an event, ya know," Jimmy answers.

"Yeah. I'll never forget it," Evan affirms. Evan notices Jimmy's mellowed attitude. The two men are finally having a civil conversation.

"Ya know, cop, I couldn't have shot that Carrara dude if he had come down that fire escape. I froze."

"Cabby, don't feel bad. We all screwed up last night. Hell, I was the biggest screw up of all!"

"Ya know. I was actually scared, cop."

"So was I, cabby," Evan says. He truly feels a closeness to Jimmy for the first time since he has met him. Maybe William and Alice were right. Tough guys such as Jimmy do have the same emotions as the rest of us. They just hide them better beneath their lousy attitude. Evan hesitates, wrestling with the emotion he is feeling for Jimmy. "Jimmy, I—uh—I mean I want to—" Evan says striving to tell Jimmy what he is feeling and apologize for being so hard on him.

Jimmy, too, is at a loss for words. "Yeah. I—uh—well."

"Well, cabby, I just want to say that—uh, well you know!"

"Yeah. I know," Jimmy says gently smiling. Evan pats Jimmy on the back. Each man deduces that a birth has just occurred, the birth of a new relationship. Because of each man's eccentric habits, it will not be an easy relationship. Yet, it may just work.

Evan presents the note from Kizzy that was retrieved from the waterbed to the group. He presents it as Tom's clue. William smiles, finding compassion in Evan's act. C.D. gives notice to the men of Tom's funeral, which is scheduled for later in the week. They plan to attend.

2

The men drive together to the bus station. Warily, they watch for anyone that might be following them. No tail follows this time. C.D. retrieves the mysterious key he has been holding for the group. The men find the locker, use the key and find a large stack of old pictures on top of a bundle tied with a small red ribbon. Holding them in his hands, Jimmy inhales the fabric of the ribbon. The ribbon has Kizzy's aroma on it. He realizes Kizzy has tied this ribbon. C.D. takes the stack from Jimmy's hands and unties it. C.D. quickly glances through the pictures. The other men continue to look through the locker, finding a shoe box full of money in large bills. C.D., after his brief picture review, confirms most of the pictures to be old pictures. Pictures of her parents, the five men, and one strange picture of an obscure newborn baby are present. William confirms the old pictures of her parents, but does not recognize the baby picture. Another interesting snapshot contains several authoritative people. C.D., Jimmy and Evan recognize several people in the picture and point them out to William. They include Patricia Conner, the previous mayor of Houston, and Perry Roman, a United States Senator representing Texas. Also shown in the picture is Kizzy, an unknown pretty Spanish girl, two South American men and a young black man. Neither C.D. nor Evan recognizes the other people except for Kizzy. Evan takes the picture to show to Bettey for assistance in additional identification. In the locker is a brown envelope addressed to the five men in Kizzy's handwriting, sealed with her kiss insignia and thick with many pages. The men decide not to review the contents in the locker out in the bus station openness. They know they should review these contents in privacy. The men gather the contents, place them in a bag William has brought from his hotel room, and leave the bus station to finish their private review at William's hotel room. They can hardly wait to read the contents of the thick, brown envelope.

3

The car is quiet during the drive to the hotel. Each man holds hope and prayers that the answers will be inside the envelope. Wonder, depression, anxiety and frustration fill each man with a craziness. Each man reveals that he has not had a good night's sleep since Kizzy's death. Exhausted, physically and mentally and emotionally drained, they admit not one of them has been thinking with clarity.

The car trip to the hotel room seems endless. Each man ponders silently what the answers will mean for him. Each hopes it will mean final peace for Kizzy and peace for them. Her face, the memories of her, still haunt their thoughts, their dreams. They can only hope that in a few more minutes, they will lay all to rest at last. They arrive at the hotel. With eagerness, they open the envelope. Inside, are many handwritten pages in Kizzy's special recognizable handwriting.

CHAPTER XX

The Letter

1

C.D. starts to read the letter aloud as the other men listen anxiously, but attentively.

> *"My very special, precious men,*
> *I have written this letter in the event of my death. This is the only time I know I can get away to put it in my bus station locker for safekeeping. If you're reading this letter, I'm dead. I can only pray to God to please, let it be you five that find this letter, and not Dominici Giovanni, Antonio Luigi or any of the others. I'm not sad. I feel I'm at last winning the race of life and am in control, where I've always wanted to be, but have been unable to get. Please know that death is where I want to be, now. I will try my best to be brave and face my death in an honorable way. I only hope I'm strong enough to do this. I'm tired, so very tired. I'm tired of the pain, tired of being dominated, and tired of waiting for someone else to choose when, where and how I die. Death is what I have chosen. Death is my only way out. No other way exists."*

Father C.D. pauses to clear the lump in his throat and then continues reading.

"I hope this letter will explain to each of you the pain I've given you throughout the years. I had so many dreams. I wanted to be a movie star. I had a dream that one day, when I was famous, I would have you, the people I loved, around me forever. I'm only hoping and praying that the five of you will give me dignity in death and keep the circumstances of my death a secret. Oh, to marry you, Tom, was the first big dream of mine. You were my first love. When I looked at you, I saw no one else in the whole world but you. I would've been such a good wife to you. I would've been happy to stay with you for the rest of my life and raise our children."

"Yes, our beautiful children. I murdered one of our children because I loved you so much. I did not want to stand in the way of your dreams. I knew how important playing football was to you, and you loved football as much as I loved you with all your heart. If I would've told you about the baby, you would have married me. Your parents raised you to do the honorable thing, but I know you would have hated me for destroying your dream. I couldn't do that to you. I never forgot that abortion. Uncle Wills, I know I never spoke of it, but something in me died that day. I lived with the pain and guilt and that little face floating in and out of my dreams every single night of my life. Tom, I know I behaved strangely in the store that day with the baby hat. I was pretending that it was for our baby, our poor little dead baby. Then reality set in, breaking my heart one more time. I hope God will forgive me, so that I may love that little baby in Heaven. Thanks to you, Father C.D., I believe that forgiveness is possible. I'm sorry, Tom, that you will not get the chance to know and love our little dead child. But you will have a chance to love our child. I'll explain later in this letter to you.

I have forgiven Tony, Dominici, P, and even myself, finally."

"This is really awful. I wish Tom were here so he could hear her saying this to him," Jimmy says with much regret.

"Don't worry, Jimmy, she's with him in heaven. He knows!" C.D. says in an encouraging tone of voice. C.D. continues to read.

"Tom, the last time we were together was so wonderful, but I belonged to Tony by then. I was his, but he never owned my heart. Never! It drove him crazy that I did not love him. No way existed for us, Tom, to get away from him, ever. Tom, I can't have the tomorrows with you, but I had the most wonderful yesterdays of my entire life, loving you."

"Jimmy, you were so kind to me. You gave me a home and love. You act tough, but you're a nice man deep inside. Life just hasn't been kind to you.

I know, now, how that can make you do things you would not do otherwise, just to survive."

Jimmy looks serious and almost embarrassed by Kizzy's words. C.D. continues reading aloud.

"I know that I hurt you when I left you. I had no choice. If I had a choice, I would've stayed with you forever. I met Dominici Giovanni just outside Picconnes one night when I went without you, Jimmy. I swear I only wanted to be discovered by a successful producer or director. I thought I would surprise you with fame. Dominici treated me as a lady. We had dinner with a genuine director. This man impressed me. Dominici knew many powerful people. He always promised me movies with influential Hollywood directors. Dominici was very convincing. He bought me beautiful clothes. He made me feel as if I were a queen. Once, an important director agreed to star me in a movie. Little did I know, but Dominici was the co-star of this cheap, X-rated flick. I slept with Dominici in the movie. We had sex, but did not make love. I never made love to anyone but you four men. Having sex with Dominici was not something I wanted to do. They had drugged me with something he put in my food. He blackmailed me with this movie, always threatening to have it released.

Oh, Jimmy, the last night I saw you was so awful. Dominici was furious to meet you in front of Picconnes. He thought of me as his, only. Dominici liked games. That night, he wanted me to be his cheap hooker. He said it was good practice for me, if I wanted to be an actress. He told me I would leave you that night, or he would have you killed. Again, he stressed I should pretend not to love you to sharpen my acting skill. I was good, wasn't I, Jimmy. I had to make believe that I didn't care about you and that I didn't need you. Although deep down in my aching heart, I was dying. I broke your heart that night. To hurt you so much, broke my heart. The next night, I tried to commit suicide with some pills, but he wouldn't even allow me to succeed at that! Dominici had my stomach pumped. Then, he took me home with him from the hospital. That night, after he finished with me, I wished I had died. I was too weak to defend myself. Dom had a skill at sexual torture. He left few marks. He said marks made me less beautiful. He said he hated to punish me, but he had to control me. From that day forward, he had me watched and followed always. This was a living hell for me. I've always loved my freedom. I tried constantly to escape. When I'd escape and get away, perhaps for a walk or to put things in my bus station locker, he would punish me. Giovanni loved punishing me. He was a horribly, sadistic man. I always tried to protect myself from the tortures, but he was always too strong."

Jimmy says aloud with agony in his voice, "Oh *damn it*. She really loved me. She took that pain, just for me." William puts his hand on Jimmy's shoulder to comfort. C.D. again resumes reading the letter.

> *"I met Antonio Luigi through Dominici. Tony wanted me from the first day he saw me. Whatever Antonio Luigi wanted, he got. At first, I was shared with other business contacts. I guess that made me a prossie. Tony only shared me with the most elite. I would refuse sometimes, only to receive Dominici's punishment. I learned quickly if I refused, I'd be restrained or drugged. The men would do whatever they wanted with me anyway. I had no choice. So it became easier not to care. When I was with those men, I would take my mind somewhere far away. It was the only way I could permit such sickening things to happen to me. Tony became obsessed with me. During this time, I met Maia, dear sweet Maia. I met Maia in Rio. She was with a powerful man down there named Geraldo Saude. He, too, was very cruel, just as Dominici. Maybe he was even more depraved than Dominici."*

Jimmy says, "This must be when she sent ya the birthday card, William."
"Yes. I think it must have been," William answers.
C.D. continues the reading.

> *"I was never allowed to have friends—man or woman—by Tony or Dom. They wanted me to themselves. But Maia and I had so much in common. I was so lonely when I met her, and so was she. We met different kinds of people in Rio; Senator Perry Roman, who wasn't a senator yet, Patricia Conner, who was a businesswoman that became the mayor of Houston, Reverend Peter Felps, who was just beginning his religious post, and last, but not least, Carlos de Franco, another dynamic drug dealer in South America. We had many sick sex parties. The things that happened at these parties are too unspeakable to imagine. Once, Maia's cousin took a picture of us. The others were high on drugs and didn't realize someone was taking their picture.*
>
> *Maia made the mistake of blackmailing those important people. She sent me a copy of the picture for my own insurance. They killed Maia."*

"Oh, great! They kill her only friend, and she goes back to being alone," Jimmy says sympathetically.

"Yes, and loneliness was always her greatest fear," William says.

C.D. continues reading aloud.

> *"She was using the blackmail money to support her poor family in Brazil. I took over the blackmail scheme, not for me but for Maia. Each month I receive money from Maracuja Modeling. I cash the check and buy a money order for Maia's family in Brazil. I feel it's the least I could do for her. Maracuja Modeling has many interesting owners; the present Senator Perry Roman, former Mayor Patricia Conner, Geraldo Saude, the Righteous Christian Church, since Reverend Felps died, Carlos de Franco, Dominici Giovanni and Antonio Luigi. This is hidden in a mountain of paperwork and dummy corporations, but you can find it if you look hard enough. They furnish modeling, prostitution in foreign countries, and drug smuggling. They use the models to smuggle drugs in the United States in the makeup. They empty the makeup containers in South America, fill them with cocaine and other powdery drugs, and smuggle it in. Luigi has protected me from de Franco and Saude throughout the years since I started the blackmailing for Maia. I was Luigi's possession only. Tony was very obsessive with me. He was even worse than Dominici. Dom is afraid of Tony, because of his wife's father. Tony would indulge me with gifts, cars, clothes and loads of money. He thought it would make me love him. I never loved him. I always hated him with my whole heart.*
>
> *Whenever I was smart enough to sneak away from the goons that watched me, they caught and punished me. Dom was the issuer of punishment. Tony permitted Dom's punishments to control me. After they punished me, Tony would give me presents. He said I was naughty and had to be punished, but I believe he genuinely felt guilty. Evan, it was during this time that I met you in the hotel room. How wonderful it was to be with someone who was so innocent and gentle. Thank you so much for making me feel alive. I had believed I had died until we were together. I escaped Tony to live with you for that short time and was so happy with you. Still, one day he found me. He threatened to ruin you at the academy by setting you up as corruptible. You have to understand. Tony has powerful contacts everywhere, among them 'P'. I knew he would succeed so I went back with him."*

Evan stands and walks over to the window. He wonders who "P" is to whom she is referring. Evan knows in his heart he could have helped her. Why wouldn't she trust him? Oh, who knows! Maybe she was right. Maybe Giovanni and Luigi were too powerful. Tears fill his eyes. He rubs his nose with his hand. Yet, he would have fought for her, his special

Kizzy. He knows this in his heart.

William asks concerned, "Evan, are you okay?"

"Yeah, I'm fine, but boy, it hurts," Evan affirms teary eyed.

"I know, and only time will heal. We will have to go through this time healing process," William says.

C.D. starts reading the pain-filled letter again.

> *"The times that I spent with you, Father, over the years were so wonderful. You gave me the only hope and strength that kept me going."*

C.D. finds the lump in his throat is too large to continue. His voice is twitching, and his hands are shaking. William takes the letter from his hands and continues reading the letter aloud.

> *"You, alone, gave me the hope that kept me going. Without you, I would have died years ago. Through you, I met Mr. and Mrs. Paoli. I thought they were wonderful people because I met them at your church. I was so wrong. Tom, during the last amount of time that I spent with you, I conceived a child, our child. Tony believes this child is his. I think Tony would've killed my child if she had not been his. He could not bear that another man could have touched me since I belonged to him. I'm burning my diary so he will never know until the time is right. He'd love to get his hands on my diary and that picture of those powerful people. I think he wants the picture to have control over the senator and other important people in it. Please, use this picture to make these monstrous people pay for Maia's death in some way. Maia's only fault was being poor. She used her only asset, her beauty, to get money for her family. It was never just for her, but for her entire family. My diary was the only thing Luigi or Dom could never take away from me, my innermost thoughts and feelings. William, aren't you proud of me? I kept these to myself in my diary just for you. You always taught me how important controlling our own thoughts are. You taught me independence."*

William smiles taking much satisfaction in the message to him. He knows in his own small way, he gave her fortitude and endurance.

Jimmy says, "Well, we know why we didn't find the diary. She burned it!" The reading continues.

> *"William, thank you for making me always feel special from the time I was a young child through becoming a woman. Many of the sweetest days of my*

entire life were the days I spent loving you, William.

Tony has been trying for years to impregnate me with a son, so he and his wife could raise my child as their own. His wife is unable to have a child. Tony believes a child should be of 'your blood' and not adopted. He's obsessed with leaving a male heir for his dynasty of corruption. When I became pregnant with my little girl, Tony praised me by giving me a company called Fun Coin. In reality, he just needed a clean name to use. The company does some legitimate business, but Tony uses it for money laundering most of the time. I get stock checks, but he and Dominici run the company. I'm not even allowed to visit the company. When I gave birth to my little girl, I took her to Mr. and Mrs. Paoli, thinking he would be safe from Tony with them. I was never going to tell Tony her location no matter what he did to me. Tony was unhappy that the baby had been female. He didn't want her. I didn't know that Mr. Paoli owed Tony a great debt. He told Tony that they had my baby. Tony has used Alana to control me for years. So now she stays with the Paolis. They are cold, loveless people. I know why God never gave them children of their own. When I'm cooperative, I get to see my little girl.

Now, I am pregnant with Tony's child. I can't bring myself to kill this baby, even though I hate its father with my entire heart. But it'll kill me if my baby is taken away from me. I can't live without another baby in my arms. I'm hoping somehow the police will blame Tony or Dom for my death. They're not guilty of killing me directly, but they have surely given me the reason to want to die. Tony is to come and visit me tomorrow again. I'll not let him touch me again. I know this will make him very angry. When he touches me, afterward I vomit. He'll tear my home apart looking for the diary and picture, as he always does when I defy him. Tony hates being denied anything, he wants. He never asks me for them until he's angry with me. I think this makes me uncooperative in his mind so letting Dominici punish me is okay. I can't take this anymore. When he touches me, I hate myself because I hate him so much. I know they'll punish me. I plan to fight with all my might for myself and my children. They do not know about this baby.

My life has not turned out the way I wanted. When I was a little girl, I had so many dreams. My life was perfect before my parents died. William, as my uncle, you tried so hard to make me happy. Even so, I realized that no one could make me happy except me. That is why I left you. I wish I would've stayed with you. You were such a kind and gentle man. I loved you so much. Yet my dreams took control of my life and sent me out in the world. I thought if I made my dreams a reality without help, I would be happy. I never was happy except for the brief times spent with you five men. Thank you so much for the days of happiness you've given me. Maybe in death, I will find the lasting happiness I've been searching for my entire life.

I made a friend in Rio. He is a kind man, but he's an assassin for Saude. I've hired him to kill me. He'll enter through the garage using my taped voice to gain entrance. Ironically, Luigi uses the same way to gain entrance to my apartment. He gave me the idea. I've given him my security card key and made him a duplicate key to my apartment. He will leave the security card key behind in my purse after I am dead. He is to kill me, and then make it look brutal. I hope the police will think of this violent death as a passion hit by the mob. I instructed him to save my waterbed, because my note is inside. I trust this man to do this for me. I must be free. I want to love my children. I can't take the pain anymore. It's unbearable.

Please, this is up to the five of you. Each of you has something special to give to my little girl, Alana. William, you will give her wisdom and parental discipline and love. Tom, you, as her father, will teach her about sports and fair play. C.D. you will teach her about faith and hope and God's love. Evan, you will teach her to obey the law. Jimmy, you will teach her about the streets and how to survive. Please help her not to make the same mistakes that I did. She's a lucky little girl to have the five of you. I must ask you to keep the tragic part of my life and my death from her. Please, do this one last thing for me. You men must protect her from this horrible story.

Before my mother died, she taught me a special lesson. God puts women on this earth to protect the ones they love. A woman must do everything in her power to do so. I believe I've protected each of you from pain, suffering and maybe even death from Dom and Tony. You must protect my little Alana from the story of my bizarre life. I'm taking my life in this way, to protect my daughter, Alana, and my unborn child from having a father such as Tony. Enclosed is a document declaring Alana not to be Tony's child and a copy of the hotel receipt where Tom and I conceived her. Tony does not love or want her. Once I'm gone, he'll not want her anymore. He just wants to use her to control me. Please use this document, William, you know how legally to get custody of my little girl for the five of you. Love her, as you have loved me. I can only pray her life will turn out good, unlike mine. Tell her every day how very much I loved her. I'll be watching you from heaven with my two babies in my arms.

Father C.D., I have confessed my sins this day and gotten forgiveness from God. Evan, don't let anger for Dom and Tony destroy you the way it has destroyed me. Please, just let it go. Life is too short to be filled with anger. Please find love, Evan, with someone else. You are such a special man. Father C.D., I'm sorry I made those sexual moves on you. I never meant them. You were just so cute blushed and embarrassed. You are a good man, so deep inside. Thank you for sharing your goodness with me.

Good bye, my precious loves.
God bless you!
Keziah Elaine Theriot"

At last, they have the answers. Silence fills the room.

"Nobody leave. We need to talk," Evan says pausing for a short time so that everyone can regain an amount of dignity and control. William sucks in the air through his emphysema and the tears in his eyes. Jimmy sits unusually quietly, not tapping or jiggling. C.D. finds a sad comfort from Kizzy's letter.

Evan starts to piece together the final days of Kizzy's tragic life. "Okay, let's see what we've got. The day before she died, she went out shopping. But we know that she really went and put this letter in the bus station locker."

Jimmy says, "Yeah, she must've used shopping as her cover."

William says, "She did not leave this letter or the note leading us to it with her will, because she was not sure they could not bribe Mr. Alexander."

Evan continues, "now is when she gave the key that she had made and the card key and tape of her voice to Carrara."

"She must have paid him also," William adds.

"Well, I guess we know how Lorena entered the apartment house. She probably used the credit card key, apartment key and voice print that Luigi, her husband, had," C.D. says.

"Can ya imagine how hard this must've been for Kizzy to do? Man, she *paid* for her own *death*!" Jimmy says. "That girl was much stronger than I thought."

William takes over continuing to piece things together as he paces and wipes his hands, eyes, and nose with his handkerchief. "Okay, that's why when she returns to the apartment, the security man has to use his security card key to operate the elevator. Kizzy goes upstairs and has her own key to open the apartment. Okay, she probably went to sleep that night."

"I hope the Lord gave her peaceful sleep that night," Father C.D. says.

"Okay, Saturday, Luigi and Giovanni show. Who knows, they may have even brought their thugs to watch," Evan says to the others, hating the thought of such an action. He has taken over the review from William who gasps for air.

"Oh, God forbid! Please," C.D. says, giving the sign of the cross.

"Luigi tries to get her to go to bed with him, but she won't. So he rapes her!" Evan has to take a pause here. The thought of Luigi's hands hurting Kizzy makes his skin crawl. While thinking of the rape, William reflects back to the past and the gentleness of Kizzy. He tries to take a breath. He finds his breath labored, maybe by the emphysema or maybe by the agony in his heart. Jimmy is sitting quietly picturing in his mind the events of her last days. C.D. remembers in his mind's eye the gentle way she stroked the petunia petals.

Evan perseveres with the painful last days of Kizzy. "Okay, Luigi is extremely mad at Kizzy at this point. He had to force her to have sex with him, which would work on his masculine ego. You know, he thinks no woman can resist him. Angry at her, he gets on the kick of wanting to see the diary. Kizzy refuses. By this point, she's bruised and in much pain. Luigi calls in Giovanni to try to make her talk. This is probably when they use the whip and torture gadgets. Still, she will not talk. Luigi comes in and after looking at her, he can see that he can't hurt her too much more. Besides, he and Giovanni have already left marks on her flawless skin that can be seen. This transpired during the rape and torture. I'm sure Kizzy put up a fight. So sweet and gentle Giovanni doesn't get to party any more with Kizzy this night. This probably made him mad because that son of a bitch enjoyed hurting her. Luigi is probably mad at her for refusing to give him the diary, so he demands the picture. Kizzy refuses again. I think this is when Luigi, Giovanni and maybe several of their men, take Kizzy's apartment apart looking for the things he wants. Maybe by accident or maybe on purpose, Kizzy's telephone has one of its batteries removed at this point. I think it was on purpose, because the battery wasn't found on the floor in the apartment. This wipes out the memory for redial and everything. Her incoming message tape also is either wiped clean, or it's replaced. I don't know why Luigi or Giovanni did this."

"That sounds logical, Evan," William says in agreement. "I think I know the answer to the answering machine riddle. Kizzy says Luigi was controlling. Maybe when he visited her, he would take the incoming message tape, replace it with a new one, and take it home to play. That way he would know who had been in contact with her."

"I think you're right, William. Good thought! Okay, after they leave, Kizzy probably fixes herself a sandwich. The officers mentioned a half-eaten one in the report near the overturned trash can."

"I don't know, Evan. After just being raped and beaten, Kizzy probably went and lay in her bed to sob a while. Supposedly, it must have been during this time that Lorena came to see her. She heard Kizzy moving around inside the apartment," William introduces this thought in the conversation.

Evan says disagreeing with William, "No, I don't think Lorena came yet. Still, Kizzy must do several things before Carrara entered."

William continues piecing together the details. "Then, I think Kizzy would have taken a bath, trying to wash away Luigi's filth from her body. The letter said how much she hated him." William mentions this, because of his long-term relationship with Kizzy. He knows the way she thinks and her reactions to different situations.

Jimmy speaks with sadness in his voice, "Poor Kizzy, laying in that bed crying, in pain. Then, scrubbing herself in that tub, trying to remove the foul filth of Luigi from her sore and pain-filled body. Boy, I'd like to *kill* that—" Jimmy stops before continuing, seeing Father C.D.'s eyes upon him.

Evan says, after taking a deep breath, "Okay, guys, let's not dwell here. We don't even know for sure she took the bath. It's too painful to dwell on this. Next, she gains composure and fixes herself a sandwich. She eats only half the sandwich."

C.D. inputs, "She probably couldn't eat the complete sandwich because of the pain from her lip."

Evan agrees, "Yeah, you're probably right about that. He cut her lip bad. The coroner said it should have had stitches. I think it's during this time that Lorena probably comes to the apartment, but she doesn't knock. She probably hears Kizzy inside making the sandwich and trying to eat it. Lorena leaves. This is when the killer, Carrara, enters as Lorena is leaving the apartment garage. I don't know what Kizzy does during this time. With her apartment in shambles, maybe she reads or watches television. Maybe she just sits, and thinks, and cries. I don't think we'll ever know exactly what she did. We know she made no phone calls."

C.D. says, "Okay, she's waiting for Carrara to come and kill her. I can't imagine what that was like for her."

William feels this is his area of knowledge. He knew Kizzy the longest, and perhaps the best of the men. "Knowing Kizzy the way I did, it was not easy for her. Kizzy was an extremely strong-willed woman. However, she was not brave. During her childhood, loneliness petrified her. After her parents died, she would have damnable nightmares about being left alone.

I think the reason she took those pills was her fear. I think she lay alone in that bedroom thinking that death was what she wanted." For a moment William pauses to clear the lump in his throat.

Jimmy says, "I remember those bad dreams. She had them several times when she was with me. I understand why she was afraid I'd leave her. But she was so wrong. I'd have *never* left."

"Yeah, I remember the bad dreams, too," Evan says understanding Kizzy's fear.

William continues, "I believe in her heart, she thought death was her only escape from Giovanni and Luigi. With her entire heart, this is what she wants. However, the battle between the fear in her head of dying alone and the decision of her heart must have been fierce. She took the pills to combat the fear. I think she planned the pleasing, hot bath to relax and get through this horrible ordeal. I don't know if she ever took the bath. She left the candle burning, not common to Kizzy. Nonetheless, this night, I'm sure she was not thinking. Maybe the pills had muddled her mind just enough to forget to extinguish the candle. Whether the pills and bath worked, we'll never know."

"Alcohol was there, too. The coroner found a small amount of alcohol in her body. An empty wine glass was found in the bedroom on a bedside table with Kizzy's prints on it. She probably even washed the pills down with the alcohol." Evan knows the time for revelation is now, but he has been dreading it, putting it off. With a quivering voice he says, "I don't think the pills, or the bath, or even the alcohol did the job. Pete put in his report that Kizzy had her eyes open in a desperate stare during the moment of death. He said she was trying to hold on to the last sight of life."

Evan's statement incites the men, creating a pause, a long pause. Air in the room is intense. Each man has to resolve himself to this fact, obscure to anyone except the police and Evan until now.

Evan has not seen a reason to tell the other men until now. Saying the words aloud created a vivid picture in Evan's mind. He could see the desperate look on Kizzy's face. Slowly, he gains his composure and continues with Kizzy's last night. "Okay, she waits. Meanwhile, Carrara arrives at the parking garage gate. He's planning to use the audio tape and Kizzy's security card key to gain entrance. However, he sees Lorena leaving and uses the chance to enter as she departs. This was an outlandishly stupid move on his part, because he was a pro. I'm guessing he's probably on foot because Lorena says he entered on foot. He probably parked his car down the block. This is the reason the security man never saw him enter. He did not buzz for entrance so the camera was not activated. He uses Kizzy's card key to use the elevator. When he arrives at the apartment, he uses the key Kizzy had made to enter. He puts the key in his pocket and disposes of it later, probably with the knife and cleaver. He goes over where she has neatly laid her purse on the table after Luigi and Giovanni left. He opens it and places Kizzy's security card key back inside. You can go down the elevator and get out of the garage without security devices. I guess Kizzy may have heard him coming. She didn't fight though, and she didn't scream. The neighbors heard nothing. Conveniently, the place is sound-proof, you know, to maintain privacy. Her bedroom was the farthest room away from the other penthouse apartment. But you know, the neighbors never reported noises from her apartment. You know she had to make noise when Giovanni tortured her."

Jimmy says, "She was probably too weak from those pills the night of her death to scream or fight. Maybe they gagged her when they tortured her."

Evan continues. "But she knows what is happening. While wearing gloves, he stabs her, draining the life from her. She falls on her back on the bed. I'm sure he was the last thing she ever saw. He waits until she is dead, probably only a few minutes. He drags her dead body off the bed, as instructed by Kizzy. He knows he's not supposed to puncture the mattress. The meat cleaver comes out, and he continues with the gruesome duty. Afterwards, he cleans and wipes prints he may have left. He isn't sure where he may have left prints, because he is upset. After all, he just killed someone about whom he cared. We know he cared enough about her to carry her picture in his wallet. So, this murder was not an easy one for this guy. He probably wiped prints from everywhere. In wiping his prints, he also removes Kizzy's, Luigi's, Giovanni's and their soldiers that might have been in the apartment. That's why only a few of Kizzy's prints were found. This guy is a pro. He leaves the way he enters, quietly in the middle of the night."

William adds, "The apartment is in disarray from Luigi and Giovanni's search which makes it appear as if a burglary has ensued. However, valuable items are left behind because it was no burglary. With a disarrayed look, it mimics a murder of passion."

"What a sad story," C.D. says.

"So who in the hell is the guy, 'T.U.', that left the pen behind?" Jimmy asks.

Evan answers, "I don't know. I'd like the answer to that one myself, cabby. Kizzy didn't give us any clues in her letter."

"Who kidnaped Tom for sure, cop?" Jimmy asks.

Evan responds, "I think it was either Giovanni or Luigi. I don't think we'll ever know which one. I think they wanted to know just how much we had found out about their operation and involvement with Kizzy. They were trying to cover their illegal drug smuggling and money laundering. They were afraid our Kizzy investigation would reveal their dirty business. That picture with the important people and Kizzy's diary also were floating around in that apartment, or so they thought. They wanted the diary and picture before we got them."

"You know this is supposition. We will never know what happened in Kizzy's apartment because she and Carrara are deceased," William says. He notices the frown on Jimmy's face as though he has not understood William's statement. So William clarifies, "Supposition means guess, Jimmy."

"Yeah, yeah . . . I knew that," Jimmy says, not wanting anyone to know he did not understand the word.

"Supposition or not, it's what the evidence points to," Evan says.

"I think we know everything Kizzy wanted us to know," William says philosophically.

C.D. says, "I think we should discuss what we are feeling in our hearts." However, none of the other men respond, so C.D. continues. "William, I don't think you have to be strong for the rest of us. You've had your emotions locked inside since this thing began. Everyone has lost control at one time or another except you!" Receiving no reply from William, C.D. turns to Evan. "Evan, please remember you are a man first and a cop second. Allow yourself to feel heartache and emotion like a man."

Evan responds saying, "I think we should stick to the facts, not sentiments. Emotions get a person confused. Facts, or knowledge, are the only thing nobody can steal from you!"

"Facts are only opinions, Evan. They are someone's interpretation of what they saw, heard or experienced," William responds. "Not even facts are genuine sometimes."

"I don't believe in this psychological *bull!* Going over all that shit can drive ya *nuts*!" Jimmy says loudly. "Sorry, Padre!"

Silence fills the air. Not one of the men can speak any more words. Evan gathers the picture to take with him. Each man leaves quietly.

2

Jimmy starts driving in his cab, faster and faster with the windows down. The hot Houston air blows against his face. He tries desperately not to face what he is feeling. Kizzy's face flashes through his mind recurrently. The words of the letter play in his brain like an old forty-five ,slowly through each groove. He can feel no peace so he pulls over. Sitting on the outskirts of Houston, his face wet with tears, he realizes he cannot escape himself. He knows the only woman he had ever loved truly loved him in return. She loved him so much, she was willing to give him up to save him. That was true love! No one had ever loved Jimmy in that way in his entire life. He will never forget Kizzy. He will always hold her in his heart. She was more than his lover. She was his friend. Kizzy was his best friend. Jimmy weeps loudly alone in his cab while the rest of the cars pass him. At last, the tears stop. Sadness is present, but he feels relief.

3

Evan leaves his car parked and starts walking. The sun is hot. He walks through the people crowded on the sidewalks and stops at a phone booth. Placing a handkerchief over the mouthpiece of the telephone receiver to disguise his voice, he phones the police department. Evan plans to speak promptly before they can get a location on the call by tap. He knows the rules. Alice answers the call. He tells his story. "I've got information for you involving illegal drug trafficking in the United States. The Maracuja Modeling Company is bringing in the drugs from foreign countries in makeup containers. They empty the containers in the foreign countries and refill them with narcotics. Large amounts are smuggled in using this method. Contacts in South America are Geraldo Saude and Carlos de Franco. Contacts in the United States are Dominici Giovanni and Antonio Luigi. With a little bit of research you'll find that they, and several other interesting people, own the agency. You need to move fast on this. The story will be out in the newspaper by day after tomorrow." Evan quickly hangs up the telephone before Alice can say a word. Evan feels good about starting the wheels of justice in motion. He proceeds with his walk, walking faster and faster. He notices the homeless people crowded on the sidewalks and thinks of poor Fred, the bum. Kizzy had been nice to him by giving him hope. Evan wonders whether he will ever feel good again. He feels numbness throughout his body. The one woman in the world he would have protected with his life suffered horribly to *protect him! How could he live with this?* With a lot left to resolve, Evan does not know where to start. How will he? How can he understand this? He has to let her go. However, in his heart and in his mind he is holding on so tightly. When she had left him all those years ago, he had wanted to find her and beg her on his knees to come home with him. He whispers aloud while walking, "I loved you so much Kizzy. I couldn't help myself. God, I couldn't even help you!" He has to find peace. Tired and needing rest and food, he will go home.

On his way home, Evan stops for a bite of his favorite food, coffee and delicious jelly-filled donuts. The radio is playing. Evan sits at the bar waiting for his order. Evan asks Larry to raise the volume on the radio as he hears the news starting. "On the international news, a brutal murder in Rio de Janeiro, Brazil, has occurred. Several men identified as organized crime members in South America were gunned down early this morning. Two of the men, Geraldo Saude and Carlos de Franco, are well known in South America for their leadership in organized crime. Several other men were murdered with them that have not been identified yet. The police have no leads and assume this is a professional killing by another organized crime group."

Evan's mind stops. He knows or suspects who did the killing. He guesses either Giovanni or Luigi ordered this hit. They think because Carrara killed Kizzy, the mob in South America ordered it because Kizzy was blackmailing them. Evan smiles, taking a level of satisfaction in the death of two more evil, murdering, drug-running mobsters. He finishes his food, strolls to his car and drives home. Maybe he will be able to rest.

4

William finds himself in the empty hotel room with the letter folded on the dresser. William thinks back to the birthday card he received from Rio. She had still cared for William. However, she had been sad. He now knew what the inscription meant. She was referring to herself as the flower.

Even though she was involved with these heinous people, she still was feeling a smidgen of beauty within herself. Relief finds William now that he knows what she had meant by the card. William knows his life has been dead since she had left him. Loneliness was all he ever felt. He pushes back his love for her deep inside. He knows it will be there forever. William still has a lot to do for Kizzy. He is not finished. Not yet! He will get custody of her child. He will call Mr. Alexander for assistance because he is not licensed in Texas to practice law. Then reality hits him! Kizzy has left him with another child to raise. He is so old and so tired. He does not know if he has the strength to go through the parties, colds, nightmares, proms and boyfriends again. William is tired of the complications and hardness of life. He coughs harshly into his handkerchief. He will worry about that later. As he dials Mr. Alexander, he puts the cogs in motion. He must do this last thing for Kizzy.

5

Father C.D. cannot wait to return to his church. Maybe he needs to feel something strong, supportive, good around him. Possibly he needs to kneel at the altar and pray. C.D. had thought it would be the garden he returned to for consolation. However, not this time . . . . Only the altar would take away this pain. C.D. kneels at the altar, closes his eyes tightly and prays for Kizzy's soul. He knows that praying for others had always brought him a great sense of peace. He prays for Kizzy's poor little child, Alana, and for poor Tom's soul. He prays for the suffering of the other three men. He opens his eyes when he finishes, and he starts to rise. C.D. looks upward at the statue of Jesus Christ stretched before him, feeling as though the eyes of the statue are looking straight into his eyes. Filled with tenderness and quivering, he falls down upon his knees. He can feel the love of Jesus run through his very being. His soul absorbs the feeling, and his folded hands start to shake. Once again, he bows his head, feeling it a sacrilege to gaze into the Christ's eyes. His heart is open and receptive. This time, and for the first time in his entire life, he prays for himself. He prays for the Lord's endearment and the healing of his own heart. He had always misunderstood Kizzy. Sexuality had been a part of her being, and she had meant it innocently. Her sexuality had been a gift to her, much as faith had been his gift. Sexuality had only been one of the enchanting things about her. Many more beautiful things about her existed. Her heart had been kind. She had helped the people in the soup kitchen and the old man in the park. At her insistence, he had sold her jewelry to help feed the poor at one time. She had fed the hungry animals of the streets. She had helped poor Fred by giving him hope. Kizzy had given Tom hope after her death which gave him the needed strength to stop drinking. C.D. knows that he had done his duty with Kizzy. He had provided strength for her, the strength of faith. He had not failed her. He had not failed God, ever, but had fulfilled the duty the Lord gave to him with Kizzy. No longer feeling guilt inside, C.D. at long last forgives himself. This is what Jesus has wanted from him. For the first time in his life, he is feeling the greatest peace. C.D. knows seeing the statue of Jesus Christ and feeling his wonderful love has been a special miracle. A peaceful smile covers his lips.

CHAPTER XXI

The "P" Connection

1

The next morning, the start of a new day, William is thinking but not dwelling on the past depressing events. He is unable to change the deaths of Tom and Kizzy. William knows he has a lot to finish for Kizzy and the child. Suddenly, he feels refreshed. His emphysema is less present today. Possibly it is just having a productive task and the ability to accomplish it, or maybe he is finally adjusting to this abominable Houston humid heat. William knows that of the four men left, he is the only one with the skill to complete this duty for Kizzy. The operation is in progress. William has given the proper paperwork to Mr. Alexander for the review of the court. He knows he cannot handle this case because he is not licensed in Texas, but only in New York.

William retrieves the newspaper. Details in a front page article identify two murdered crime lords in South America as Geraldo Saude and Carlos de Franco. He believes Luigi or Giovanni probably sent the assassin. Oh, well, maybe they will annihilate each other and leave a better world for us! William's mind returns to a more pressing problem needing resolution. William saw Evan's eyes as he left after reading Kizzy's letter. Evan is the only one of the four men with much left to resolve within himself. In Evan's eyes no peace is present. Trouble is still brewing behind those youthful, luminous blue eyes. William telephones Evan, but no one is home. He does not leave a message. When he opens his hotel room door to go for ice, there in the doorway stands Evan. Evan has learned through the events of this case and the wisdom and strength of his new found friend, William. Unlike C.D., William does not seem to be bogged down with the morality of religion. William never lost control through any of the problems with the case, unlike Evan, Tom or Jimmy. He expected control from the priest, but William is only a man. He has gained a great respect for William. He is nothing like Jimmy. However, Evan likes the new changes happening in Jimmy. Evan's face is drawn and saddened. William forgets the ice and invites Evan inside. The two men sit in two chairs by the window around the small round table. The sunlight hits on Evan's troubled brow.

William knows Evan wants and needs to talk. However, William knows it will be he that will open this conversation. "What can I do to help you with the problem lurking behind those eyes, son?"

"I don't know. I thought if I had the answers, I would feel resolved and at peace, but I don't. I still feel as though I failed her. I should have been her protector. I even took an oath to 'protect and serve.' My stupid decision cost poor Tom his life. Tom was a good guy. What kind of cop am I? Damn! Maybe I shouldn't even be a cop! What kind of man am I? I seem to be making one mistake after another. I just want this to be over. I'm so tired, Mr. Newton."

William sees the heavy tiredness of suffering. "Please, call me William. I feel we know each other well enough to be on a first name basis after everything that we have been through together." Evan nods his head in agreement.

"Evan, first, you did not fail Kizzy. You are a cop, but you are not *God.* Luigi and Giovanni have operated outside arms reach of the law for years. You, as a cop, know that better than anyone. What makes you think you could have changed that fact? After all, you were a young man, not even a cop yet, when you and Kizzy were together. Don't be so hard on yourself. Kizzy made many decisions. Maybe they were not all right. Still, if we had been in her shoes, maybe we, too, would have made the same decisions. I don't judge her. You should not either. I also have reminisced and searched my own morals. I allowed her to leave. Maybe I conveyed a myriad of erroneous feelings which urged her to leave. Perchance when our relationship transformed from uncle and niece to lovers, it destroyed her. However, I can't go back and change things. I never ever would have hurt Kizzy. If I had forced her to return home to me, she might still be alive. Perhaps she would have only left me again. So many *'ifs'* and *'mights'* exist. We don't know what might have happened if any one of us had responded in a different way or made a different decision. We were each human, I included. Maybe we made mistakes; maybe we didn't. We loved her. That's the one thing we must each remember. We loved her!" William pauses for a moment looking for a facial response from Evan to his words.

He sees one. Evan seems to understand what he is saying. His face changes as though William's words lessen the misery. Evan relaxes his brow. William knows he is making sense to Evan.

"Evan, about Tom's death, you are not to blame. Tom wanted to go there. He insisted. He, too, needed to right a great wrong he did to Kizzy. C.D. told me Tom believed he had seen Kizzy as an angel. This had changed him. He needed to do something for her. This was *his* choice. Tom's death was an accident, unlike the death of that other guy. Therefore, ease up on yourself and—"

Before William can finish, Evan looks deep in William's eyes and interrupts. "What do you mean Tom's death was an accident unlike the other guy?"

William responds, "Tom fell off the roof during the altercation with the hit man, Carrara. Maybe the guy pushed him, or maybe Tom just lost his balance and fell."

"No, William, not *Tom!* What did you mean about Carrara's death *not* being an accident? I thought you accidently hit him with the car when he ran out in front of you!"

"No, Evan, that's not how it happened. Carrara had another man standing behind him in the doorway. C.D. and I saw the man in the doorway put his hand and arm against Carrara, pushing him out in front of the car."

"How in the world did you see this? It was pitch black dark!"

"Yes, it was dark, Evan. However, after engaging the headlights, C.D. and I saw it. The headlights offered some light. Some light also came from the doorway opening which wasn't closed. The man that pushed him was the shorter of the two men who escorted you, Tom and Jimmy inside of Mr. Luigi's house. I saw him when I was waiting in the car."

"That's great! We'll get Luigi after all! We can nail him for the murder of the hit man. *Yes!*" Evan jumps from the chair and says with a positive hand and arm gesture. Evan paces excitedly thinking aloud, "Uh . . . Rick, that was the guy's name. I'm so glad you remembered this and told me, William!"

"Remembered it? What do you mean, Evan?"

"Well, now I can call Pete, and the police will be able to nail Luigi and Giovanni! Nail those two *low lifes* to the *wall!*"

"Evan, I've already told this to your friend, Pete, at the police station."

"You what?" Facts William has just revealed dismay Evan.

"Yes, I told Pete. Father C.D. also gave him the man's description. I identified him as the man at Mr. Luigi's. Yes, Father C.D. and I told him the night of the dire accident with Tom. He said he would take care of everything. I thought that he had resolved the entire matter, Evan. I wondered why I hadn't seen anything in the newspaper about it."

Evan asks loudly still shocked. "You told Pete the night of the accident?"

"Yes, Evan, I did, there on the scene before we left."

Suddenly, Evan looks noticeably troubled again as his brow tenses and tightens into a frown. William can almost see the wheels turning in his brain. "Look, William, I've got to go take care of something urgent!" Evan says. Evan runs from the room and the hotel in great haste. William stands in the doorway with a puzzled look on his face.

2

Evan drives as fast as he can to the station. He even places his light on top using the siren the entire way. So many things are going through his head as he travels. Why has Pete never brought Luigi and Giovanni to the station for questioning? Why has he ignored the obvious evidence against this being a burglary? Gee, Kizzy was planning to take a bath. What the hell is going on! He has known Pete since before he graduated from the academy. They have been partners and friends. Pete has eaten dinner at the same table with Kizzy at Evan's apartment. He cannot believe Pete is connected with a cover up! However, the questions are there, staring Evan boldly in the face! Evan wants answers, and he wants them right now! Upon arriving at the station, Evan finds Pete away from the station. Evan waits around, impatiently pacing. Alice offers him a cup of coffee, suggesting decaffeinated because he is so irritated.

"Ya know, Evan, Pete has really been acting dang weird on this case," Alice says. "Do ya know what's going on with him?"

"What do you mean, Alice?" Evan asks.

"Well, I've been following this case closely. I am anxious for the experience, and because Pete was without your assistance on this one, I've been following the case. Pete won't take assistance at all from anyone on Kizzy's case. It's weird. He tries to hide the reports. I think this was a cold-blooded murder according to all the evidence. I mean a burglar wouldn't ransack an apartment and leave the purse and keys neatly on the table. A burglar wouldn't leave behind valuable art and jewelry. Yet, Pete insists on listing it as a burglary."

Her comment on the purse and keys shocks Evan. He has not seen anything about the keys and purse in Pete's reports. Evan remembers that evidence being in C.D.'s notes. They had noticed the neatness of the purse in Kizzy's apartment the night they visited the scene. If Alice noticed it and brought it to Pete's attention, why was it not in the reports?

Alice and Evan start to compare notes. Evan questions Alice about the details of finding the DOA.

She thoroughly reviews everything in detail with Evan. "Ya know something else weird is the long phone call Pete made from the crime scene, Evan."

"What is so squirrely about a long phone call, Alice? Maybe he called the coroner."

"No, Ev. *I* called the coroner. He says he called you. The weird thing is he made it from the pay phone booth on the corner. He had his cellular with him."

"Wait a minute. Why would he go to a phone booth to make a cellular phone call? He could have made that from his car, if he needed privacy. You said it was an extended phone call. About how long was this call, Alice?"

"Well, probably about five to six minutes."

"Alice, Pete only spoke to me for about a minute on the phone that night. Is it possible he made a call on the pay phone?"

"Yeah, I guess, very possible. He had the time. But why would he make a phone call on a pay phone when he had a cellular phone to use free, Evan?"

"Alice, that's a very good question. Clearly, Pete made a phone call that he did not want listed on the cellular phone bill for the police department."

Alice's blue eyes open widely in disbelief that her friend, Pete, could do such a thing. "Whom could he call that he does not want the department to know about, Evan? Pete's a damn good cop. What is going on?"

"I don't know Alice, but I plan to find out."

"Ev, I could get the phone company record of calls from that pay phone number the night of the murder. I know the approximate time and location of the phone booth."

"That's a good idea, Alice. Do you know whether Pete has anything on the gold pen with the 'T.U.' initials engraved?"

"No, I know he doesn't. But he's been obsessed with trying to figure out who the pen belongs to, Evan."

"Yeah, I just *bet* he has been obsessed! Listen. You go talk to the Captain. Tell him what is going down here. I'm going to question Pete when he comes in myself. *I want some damn answers!*"

The door to the office opens. They did not hear Pete coming, but they stop their conversation. Pete enters the room in a jovial frame of mind, happy to see Evan. "Hey, Evan, good to see you here! Sorry, this trouble has been happening to you, old buddy. Are you doing okay?"

"Yeah, Pete, I'm fine, but how are things with you? Squirrely shit is going on around here, Pete. I have some questions for you. Alice, will you excuse us. I'd like some privacy." Alice takes her cue to vacate the room, off to do the tasks Evan has given her.

"Hey, look, if it's about Kizzy's death, I'm just about ready to wrap that case up and put it away!"

"Put it away, Pete? Do you think Kizzy would want you to put it away without solving this?" Evan does not give Pete a chance to answer. "Remember when you ate dinner at the apartment with us, Pete? Remember when she surprised you at our apartment with a birthday cake? Kizzy liked you, genuinely liked you." Evan points his finger directly at Pete. "Now you want to put it away! No damn it, Pete, you want to put *her away! How in the hell can you do this?"*

Pete looks down and rubs his hand across his bald head, pushing his few hairs back away from his forehead. Evan is right. Pete liked Kizzy a lot. He is feeling bad at this point. He is not sure just what he should say to Evan. The air fills with a hush. Pete retrieves the calmness from deep in his soul, turns and says to break the intensity of the moment, "Look it was a burglary. The water in the bathtub confirms that the perp caught her off guard. That's all there is to this whole thing."

"Okay, *water* in the bathtub. Let's approach that. Do you think a *hired* killer couldn't interrupt an enjoyable, hot bubble bath? Gee, Pete, don't play *stupid* with me!" Pete looks down with verification of Evan's point.

"What is going on, Pete? Why did you leave the information off the report about the neatness of Kizzy's purse and the keys in an apartment where everything else is out of place?"

"I guess I just forgot to write that information down, Ev. You know I was a little *upset* by this, too. Kizzy was someone *I* knew, *too!"*

"Okay, that's not usually like you, but I'll give you that one. But what about those crazy suspects you brought in for questioning? Those were the most unlikely looking perps I've ever seen, Pete!"

Pete's stomach churns. "I thought I explained that to you. Evan, I brought that guy in because he was picked up in the same area, robbing buildings. *Gee,* I made a damn mistake, Evan!"

"Did you ever find out who kidnaped poor Tom, Pete?"

Pete looks nervously embarrassed. "Uh . . . no, I really don't think *that* had anything to do with Kizzy's murder!"

"Nothing to do with her murder! *Damn,* Pete! That's what those guys questioned Tom about, Kizzy's murder! They wanted to know what *we* knew. Tom thought it was either Giovanni or Luigi. He recognized their cologne."

"You can't convict a man on his cologne, Evan," Pete says patronizingly. Pete, desperate to change the subject off the kidnaping of Tom, asks, "What other questions about the case are you referring to, Evan?" Pete changes his attitude to friendly and professional on the surface. However, deep inside his heart pounds and his stomach churns.

"Questions, okay, Pete, because you cannot dispel the bath idea or solve Tom's kidnaping, let's get to the rest of my questions. First—why weren't Luigi or Giovanni ever brought in for questioning? Gee, Pete, they are organized crime and *prime suspects* in this murder investigation!"

"Well, I didn't have evidence tying them to the case, Evan."

"I told you about the info from my stoolie. If this had been any other case, you would have had them in here in a New York minute! Come on, Pete, give me the honest reason."

Pete, at a loss for words, starts grasping at straws hoping to alleviate Evan's doubts about him. He knows his greatest weapon of empathy is their longstanding friendship and his excellent police reputation. "I don't know what to say to you, Evan. You seem so angry. Come on. We're buddies. You know me, Evan. Man, we've known each other forever. You're like a son to me. Where's this coming from?" Pete smiles at Evan and touches his shoulder with his cold clammy hand.

"Yeah, I know you, Pete. That's exactly why you've *thrown* me off the track. You are the *last* person in the *entire world* I would ever have thought would—" Evan shakes his head repugnantly. Evan will not lose Pete, so he continues pursuing Pete as a hound after a rabbit. Pete is now a suspect, and the worst kind of a suspect, a cop on the take! "Let's get back to my questions, Pete. Second—why does a good investigator such as you list a murder closed as a *burglary?* Not even Alice thinks it was a burglary!"

Pete laughs, trying to dispel the tenseness of the moment. "*Alice*? Is *that* what this is about? Evan, she's new at this! She sees things that just aren't there. She's *inexperienced.* You *can't* be listening to *her!*"

"Yeah, she's inexperienced. But, damn Pete, she's not stupid. Neither am *I!* Third question—how do you explain Luigi and Giovanni not being surprised when I showed to question them? *You* are the only one that might have had the idea I was going to their place. Did you warn them I was coming, Pete? They had been following me. I saw their goons, but not that day. I paid *very* close attention. They were *nowhere* in sight! Someone had to have tipped them off that I might be coming. I think that 'someone' was *you*!"

Pete turns away from Evan with sweat pouring from his face. He takes out his handkerchief and starts to wipe. Evan notices Pete sweating. While he hates to face it, he knows he is right to hit Pete face to face with these accusations.

"I don't know, Evan," Pete mumbles.

"What is the matter, Pete? Am I hitting home with many of these questions? You seem to be *sweating.*" At this point Evan is not ready to surrender this battle. "Pete, please, fourth question—I think this is probably the most *important* one of all! Why haven't you proceeded with questioning Luigi's goon, Rick, who was identified by two reliable witnesses as killing the hit man, Carrara? Rick pushed Carrara out in the alley!"

"I've been too busy on Kizzy's case to follow anything else, Evan." Pete says desperately scrambling for answers. Pete is nauseous and pale.

"Damn, Pete, the two cases are *tied* together. You found the picture of Kizzy in his room."

"A picture just proves he knew her. Not that he killed her, Evan. We didn't find the murder weapon in his room!"

"Pete, the man's a *pro!* You know that, and I know that! You don't think he'd be *stupid* enough to keep the murder weapon as a souvenir? Do you?" Evan asks sarcastically, patronizing Pete with his question. "You knew that Luigi and Giovanni were going to kidnap Tom. I wasn't cooperating with you and giving you all the information about what we were finding out! So Luigi and Giovanni decided to find out on their own. They kidnaped Tom, and you—you covered it up, Pete!" Pete does not respond to Evan's accusation. He has turned away from Evan, overcome by weakness from anxiety.

Evan pushes him harder and harder. "Last, Pete—who did you call from the pay phone and speak with for at least four to five minutes the night we found Kizzy DOA? Don't you *dare* say it was me! I *know* how long we spoke. Alice looked at her watch when you made the call. She's getting the telephone records from the phone company for outgoing calls from that pay phone that night. I bet it will be either Luigi's or Giovanni's number. Would you like to *bet, Pete*? She is talking to the Captain now about all this. The question I want answered most of all is why? Why, Pete, did a wonderful cop such as you go dirty?" Evan walks around in front of Pete, forcing him to face him.

Pete drops his head in extreme embarrassment. He cannot look Evan in the eye. "I don't guess it's going to do any good to deny all this. Is it, Ev? You know, without a doubt, they'll kill me, don't you?"

"Pete, you should have thought about that a long time ago before you became involved with shit such as that. It's too late for denials. Maybe you'll get lucky. If you turn state's evidence, they might even put you in the witnesses' protection program. You know the phone call will be concrete proof. The other circumstantial evidence will just add to the case against you."

Pete is almost pleading, hoping somehow to spur any amount of understanding and compassion from Evan. "Yeah, you're right, Evan. I'm too tired to hide this anymore. I'm too old to hide it. I should have never gotten started with Giovanni. I was a damn fool. But I never killed anybody, Evan. I swear. I just did coverups and leaked information. Neither he nor Luigi killed Kizzy. I swear. But he wanted it covered up. They wanted to keep contact between Luigi and Kizzy quiet. Luigi didn't want to lose his wife. That's all there was to it. A scandal might have cost him her. You know her father is one of the oldest godfathers in organized crime. He has strong contacts even to this day. Luigi fears the old man. Luigi does not want to make an enemy of him." Evan does not look moved by Pete's words, only disgusted.

"Evan, please, that's all it was about. I knew Kizzy was in town. But, I swear I didn't know where she lived. I only saw her when I had meetings with Luigi and Giovanni. I hardly ever got the chance to talk to her." Pete drops his head in shame and says, "I'm sorry, Evan."

"You know Pete, Luigi's wife knew about the affair before the murder. You did this for nothing."

"Well she didn't know in the beginning. He wanted her protected. I think Luigi and Giovanni were afraid Kizzy's murder investigation might lead the cops to other investigations, Ev. You know, shit they don't need the cops digging into!"

"I have to know. Was it for the money, Pete?"

"Yeah, money, excitement—hell I don't know why, Evan."

"You knew all along what Luigi and Giovanni were doing to Kizzy, didn't you Pete? You knew about the torture?"

"Yeah, I did. I saw marks on her sometime. I just ignored it. But nobody *made* her get hooked up with them, Evan. She did that on her own. I even talked to her once in the beginning, trying to warn her to get out. Nevertheless, she said it was too late. She was too far in to get out. She was greedy, Evan. I know you don't want to hear it, but she wanted the money."

Angrily, Evan grabs Pete and draws his fist back to hit him. Pete looks at Evan, but does not defend himself—not any more. He knows he deserves what Evan does to him. He has surrendered. Pete can see the fury in Evan's eyes is really disappointment and pain. "I ought to pound your skull in, you *dirty* son of a—" Evan lowers his hand in disgust. "You're not worth it, Pete. You didn't even try to help her! You make me *sick*."

"Evan, I couldn't go against Luigi and Giovanni. They would have killed me. You know that! Besides, I don't think she wanted to be saved."

"Yeah, right, Pete, you keep believing that! Maybe it'll make you sleep better at night!" Evan shakes his head in repulsion. Upon seeing this, Pete puts his face in his hands and starts to cry. Pete has hurt Evan considerably, and he knows it. Pete loves Evan as the son he never had. He has destroyed that love forever. Evan stares for a few moments at Pete, but he cannot feel pity for Pete.

Alice and the Captain walk inside the room. From the look on Alice's face, Evan knows the phone company confirmed the number to one of the mobsters. Evan knows this situation is out of his hands. He will submit a written statement a little later. The entire mess makes him sick. He does not want to hear any more. He leaves the station and goes home.

3

Evan knows the answers. The "P" that Kizzy had forgiven in her letter was Pete. However, he cannot forgive Pete. He knows he has lost not only the only woman he will ever love, but his best friend and mentor.

Evan takes the picture from his pocket and cuts the right side off, eliminating Kizzy from the picture entirely. From his apartment, Evan phones Bettey. Nobody can tell a story like Bettey. She always prints a truthful, accurate story. Bettey comes straight over, eager to hear Evan's story. Evan shows Bettey the picture. Deliriously, she recognizes the people in the picture. "Whoa, cowboy! Do you know who these people are?" Bettey flashes her bright white smile.

"Yeah, most of them."

Bettey looks at the picture in detail. With carefulness, she speaks about the people depicted, explaining details about each. "Let's see. Here's a very young Patricia Conner; gee, she wasn't even very pretty when she was young. Ummmm, she is the former mayor of Houston, now free lance consultant in economics to the United States government. Hell, Evan, there is even some talk of her being appointed to the White House. Ya know she had such a lily white image! This is *luscious!* This is like spicy hot barbecue to my shit-kickin' Texas pallet. *Hot damn*, will I blow that for her!"

"Gee, I knew she was the former mayor, but I didn't know all the other shit about her, Bettey!"

"You should read my paper more, Evan. Let's see next to her it looks like Geraldo Saude, ooo, a nice guy. This jerk has underworld drug ties, everything. Wow, a gorgeous lady stands next to him."

"Bettey, her name is Maia. She's dead. That's all I know about her. Listen, if you find out her last name or anything about her family, I want to know."

"Okay, no problem. I'll research it. Wow! Here we have Senator Perry Roman. Ya know, Ev, there is talk he's being considered to run on the next presidential ticket in the V.P. spot. Boy, have I got a surprise for that *sucker*! This'll really knock the screws outta his boat! Oh, and see these two?"

"Yeah, that's Luigi and Giovanni."

"Oh, that's right, Ev. They're recent local shit. Dirty and bloody!"

"Who's that one, Bett, is his name de Franco?"

"Yep, Carlos de Franco, youthful in this picture, and deadly in South America."

"This one I don't recognize," Bettey says as she points to the young African American man in the picture.

"His name is Reverend Peter Felps. He's dead, but his church has been receiving 'donations' from Maracuja Modeling for years! I don't know whether they knew it was dirty money, but surely they must have suspected something!"

"Maracuja Modeling? What is that, Ev?"

Evan continues to tell Bettey about Maracuja Modeling and the famous owners depicted in the photo, except for Maia. Evan knows Bettey will do the proper research to expose proper documentation of the owners from the records. She writes as fast as she can possibly push the pencil. Tape swirls in the recorder. Then, Evan tells Bettey about Pete. At first, she is shocked, but she believes Evan. She tells Evan about Pete's recent strange behavior. She also mentions the phone call made on the cellular phone from the phone booth. She cannot wait to leave for the police station and uses Evan's phone to have her photographer meet her.

Before she leaves, Bettey looks at the picture and says, "I know ya cut somebody from this picture. I assume it was the deceased, but I'll never tell, Evan. I swear." She smiles and gives Evan a big hug. For the first time, Evan looks at Bettey. Indeed, she is a considerably attractive lady. Her large brown eyes look golden in the light of the room. She is a warm and gentle lady, but she has this delightful tough streetwise facade. Bettey is a lady with quite a mouth. She can spout tough obscenities with the best of men. He gently pushes a piece of hair from her forehead. She smiles. Bettey has an irresistible smile. Her teeth are radiantly white contrasting her sensational, smooth, olive skin. Straightaway, Bettey embarks for the station, but not before Evan makes a date with her for dinner the next night. She accepts eagerly. Strangely, he has never before noticed Bettey's beauty. Maybe Kizzy had filled his heart and eyes so fully that he could see no other woman. Evan had purposely left out the part about Kizzy hiring her own murderer. The hit man could never talk. Everyone would just assume the mob killed her. Better left that way forever, Evan sighs, knowing this ordeal is now over. After Bettey leaves, he sleeps like an innocent baby throughout the night.

4

The next morning Evan does not rise until eleven o'clock. The details are plastered across the front page. Kizzy's death is listed in the Houston paper as an unsolved murder. Pete has been relieved of duty pending his investigation by Internal Affairs and the District Attorney's office. However, the confession of Rick Coulton has dually nailed Luigi and Giovanni for the murder of the hit man, Carrara. Rick had killed Manuel Carrara acting on the orders from Giovanni and Luigi. The District Attorney's office is pressing charges against all concerned. Evan smiles.

In another article, the picture and the gory details of Maracuja Modeling and the once famous, now infamous, owners are denoted. Bettey has done her homework. She is one smart lady. Evan is happy. The picture is depicted so that he cannot tell Kizzy ever stood on the right side. Evan lays the newspaper down and thinks, oh well, Kizzy, Luigi and Giovanni were not nailed for *your* death, but they were nailed anyway. Kiz, the others in the picture may not get prosecuted for murder, but scandal is going to mess them up for a long, long time. He smiles. Evan thinks that this would have made Kizzy happy. Justice has been served. The man who killed Kizzy is dead. The killers of the killer of Kizzy, Giovanni and Luigi, will probably go to jail for murder. Saude and de Franco, the South American mobsters, were dead, and a cop on the take will be nailed to the wall.

Alice has phoned giving Evan information about Pete. Charges of bribery, acceptance of a gift by a public servant, tampering with or the fabrication of evidence, and tampering with government records are pending against Pete with a sentence of two to thirty years in the pen and a hefty fine of fourteen thousand dollars. Alice has said Pete wants to make a deal to testify against Luigi and Giovanni for immunity and a new life in the witnesses' protection program.

Evan sees the light on his answering machine flashing. The Captain's message explains that Internal Affairs has decided to discipline Evan with two months off duty. Time off is without pay for the bad decision he made involving amateurs in the apprehension of a suspect. They understood Evan's hesitancy to share information with Pete, the investigating officer, especially since he has proven involvement with organized crime. Evan feels relief. Heck, he can use the two months off to look for a new place for them to live. He has to move. Well, a lot is left to do. He needs time to rejuvenate after Kizzy's case. They do not know it, but they just did Evan a favor. He smiles.

5

Evan dresses and goes to William's hotel room to meet with the other men, his new found family. Leftover bacon and eggs are sitting on a room service breakfast tray. Evan gets a piece of bacon. For the first time in a long time, he is genuinely hungry. William frowns at first, offended by such an unsanitary act as eating after him. Their eyes meet, and William smiles at seeing Evan's appetite has returned. William winks at Evan.

They discuss the incident about Giovanni, Luigi, Pete and the picture. They have the answers. William shares some wonderful news. Mr. Alexander presented the papers Kizzy left in family court for review. William proclaims the decision aloud. "The judge has ruled full custody to Evan Picard, C.D. Casmiersky, William Newton and Jimmy Smithson of the child, Alana Elaine Theriot." Elated, the men show exuberant gladness.

The men have to resolve the great question. Can they and will they keep Kizzy's secret?

Evan asks, "Can we keep Kizzy's secret? Is it the ethical thing to do?"

William adds with his wisdom, "I think we need to deliberate that in great detail because the decision is an important resolution."

"How can we not keep it? Ya know she trusted us to keep the secret of who killed her," Jimmy adds adamantly. "She said that in the letter."

William informs, stating the facts in his legal way, "By keeping her secret, we are breaking the law. Kizzy hired her own hit man to kill her. The insurance may determine the death is a suicide, and we will not be able to collect on the million-dollar policy. If we do keep the secret and collect, we are committing insurance fraud."

"Yeah, you're right, William. You and I've taken an oath to uphold and defend the law with our lives," Evan utters with much ambivalence in his voice.

"Father C.D., you're exceedingly quiet about this decision," William says.

"Yes, I suppose I am. I've been listening to all of you talk about the law and oaths. However, no one has mentioned promises. In the beginning of this, we promised each other to make the person who killed Kizzy pay. I think that person has already paid. That person was Kizzy. She paid with her life, and through her entire life. She was tortured, mutilated, controlled, and she lost the people she loved the most! If we make this public, yes, we will lose the million-dollar policy. However, we don't need the money. The loss of the money is not important, as I see it." C.D. pauses momentarily, looking for a response to what he is saying. None of the other men speak.

"Okay, what about little Alana? We're now her parents. Parents make an unwritten promise to protect and love their children. How loving and protecting are we if we destroy the memory that little girl has of her mother? You know the story will make the news media. We'll be able to protect her for now. But when will another child at school question her about her mother's death? For what good will we be revealing this information? Because the *law* says, we should! The law is to serve and protect. We cannot serve and protect Kizzy anymore, but we can serve and protect little Alana. Therefore, I think we should keep the information of who hired Carrara, forever. I think that's the important thing. That's all I have to say!"

"Wow! Padre, when you speak, you speak loud and say a lot!" Jimmy says, meaning the comment as a compliment.

Quickly and definitively William says, "Thanks, Father. You've helped me to make up my mind. I'll promise to carry the secret of Kizzy's death to my grave. I think we should donate the million dollars from the insurance to the church. Maybe, something can be built in memory of Kizzy."

"Yeah, you're right, Father. After hearing your words, I don't feel I'm breaking any oaths. You made it clear to me. I'll promise to keep the secret forever. I like William's idea about the donation," Evan adds as though a load has been lifted from his shoulders.

"You, Jimmy, will you promise?" C.D. asks.

Jimmy wastes no time responding with a smile on his face. "Hell, I was for the promise of keeping all that sh—crap about her death a secret all along. Man, I've got no oaths to worry about. I think Kizzy is what we all loved first in our lives anyway. Hey, it's just an idea, but I think a home for runaways built and owned by the church would be perfect. They could name it 'Kizzy Hall.' Man, I promise to keep it a secret, no hassle!" Jimmy holds out his hand to the other men. With smiles covering their faces, the men shake hands.

Father C.D. says, "Listen, Jimmy, just one more thing."

"Yeah, what, Padre?"

"You're going to have to watch your language around little Alana. A little girl is not used to those obscene words. As a 'Dad' you have to control yourself," C.D. says.

"Yeah, okay, Padre, you're right. But y'all are gonna have to help me. I sometimes can't think of the right words," Jimmy says.

Evan says, "Don't sweat it, cabby. We'll help you!"

The men discuss the items needing resolution before taking custody of the child, Alana. No one says it aloud, but each vents doubts of the ability to love this child within their minds. She is a stranger, and they are strangers to her. Her mother and father are dead. They have buried Tom in a grave next to Kizzy. William had known all of Tom's family in New York were deceased. This poor child has no living next of kin to take care of her. Strangers who did not even know her parents would be raising her. The four men cannot permit this to happen. Kizzy had left the proper paperwork to give them custody of her child. This is her last wish. The men part.

6

Evan goes home and retires early. He has a wonderful dream about Kizzy which engulfs him, taking him to a place he has not been to previously. She is sitting in a euphoric place with two angelic babies on her lap. She is rocking them, holding them close and singing a lullaby. A young and handsome Tom is standing behind her. He is looking down at his little family in the chair. Tom and Kizzy look so happy from the smiles on their faces. Evan awakes slowly and gently after the dream. This dream he will never forget. He knew Kizzy and Tom were at last at peace. They were truly happy. For the first time in a long time Evan smiles and cries tears of pure joy!

7

The resolution to the plans for the child unfolds day after day. A large trust fund is arranged for Alana. Appraisers value the trust at a little more than twelve million dollars. They sell Kizzy's penthouse apartment after removing a few personal items of Kizzy's for Alana. They make a sizeable profit thanks to William's shrewdness. They use a portion of the money to purchase a three-bedroom condominium where William, C.D. and Alana will live together, in a lovely Houston neighborhood across from a park, which seems perfect. C.D. says this will be the ideal place to raise a child because she will need room to play. Evan and Jimmy each purchase condominiums on each side of the one where C.D., William and Alana will live. This will insure their privacy because they are still single, and yet conveniently make them available for Alana's care. William, filled with belief that the time for retirement has come, sells his law partnership in New York to his partner. He sells his home, making a substantial profit. He makes one last trip to New York to get his automobile and personal items. While he is there, he packs a box from Kizzy's old room of mementos for Alana. Someday, William will tell her stories about each of Kizzy's items. However, he keeps the cabin in upstate New York where Kizzy and he were in love. William's realization is that no one will ever replace his once-in-a-lifetime love with Kizzy. Because Kizzy had owned it legally, he and Jimmy take control of the operation of Fun Coin. They disagree abundantly over different business matters but seem always to work out the decisions together. William only tries to intrude when Jimmy makes an impulsive business decision. Jimmy is excellent at the marketing of Fun Coin. Father C.D. requests a permanent position in the parish in Houston, declaring sudden parenthood as the reason. The church approves his appointment. A wonderful thing has happened. Father C.D. calls it one of God's miracles. Because of Kizzy, Fred, the old man that had followed them, has stopped drinking. Quite unexpectedly, he had arrived at the church. Father C.D. has hired him as the gardener, tending the same flowers Kizzy had loved. The petunias received special care from Fred. He named the bed where the flowers grew "Kizzy's Little Garden." Fred purchased a shiny little brass plate with the words inscribed and placed it in the bed of petunias. One day, Fred mentions to Father C.D. that he wishes that when Kizzy died he had had these beautiful flowers to take to her, instead of the old plastic one he found in an alley. C.D. assures him that the thought of giving the flower, not the kind of flower, is what matters. After all, his plastic flower has outlived the live flowers that were placed at her grave. Fred finds comfort from C.D.'s words.

The building of "Kizzy Hall", a lovely new structure for young runaways like Kizzy, has begun. Maybe this will save some young women from going through the same distressing pain Kizzy had endured. William and C.D. are the administrators of this project.

The men never find the answer to who put the lovely wildflower bouquet on Kizzy's grave. Still, every month, a fresh bouquet of wildflowers is placed on Kizzy's grave. Possibly, it will always be a mystery. Jimmy even staked out the cemetery one day trying to catch the mysterious person. However, Jimmy fell asleep. Therefore, it remains a perplexity.

Unsolved to this day, the clandestine gold ink pen with the initials "T.U." found in Kizzy's apartment, remains in the evidence file, marked "Homicide: Theriot, Keziah Elaine." At one point, C.D. questioned Fred about the initials, but he was no help in the solution. C.D. also phoned the Paolis questioning them, again with no resolution to the pen mystery.

Evan has gone back to work and is happy with his brand-new partner, Alice. She passed the test and is now a detective. Jimmy had met Alice at the new apartment when she came to get Evan for duty. Some rare chemical reaction occurred between them. They are dating each other regularly. Who would have ever thought straight-laced police detective Alice would find tough, streetwise Jimmy attractive? Alice and Bettey have helped with the decorating of Alana's new room in the condominium with C.D. and William. The four men had been at a loss for clues to handle that task.

The day is nearing, the special day when the four men will meet their new daughter, Alana. Each man does his own shopping, purchasing her a special "get acquainted" gift. Bettey goes with Evan to shop for his gift. William has suggested the gift, but Bettey helps with the selection. Evan has confided the story of his love for Kizzy to her. Bettey was extremely understanding. Bettey and Evan have developed close emotional bonds.

Jimmy has chosen his gift alone. Everyone wishes that Alice would have gone along to help him. They worry what Jimmy could have purchased for a little girl. However, Jimmy keeps his gift a secret from the others.

The new Dads are ready for Alana. However, is she ready for them?

The important day at last arrives . . . .

CHAPTER XXII

The End . . .

1

The four men are highly nervous the day they are to meet Alana. Bettey phones Evan early to wish him good luck. Evan has purchased several bubble gum cigars with bands stating, "It's a girl" for the proud fathers. He hands one proudly to each new father. They get a chuckle from the gesture, which breaks the tension for a brief time. However, the doubts and tension return quickly, muddling their minds. During the car ride to the outskirts of Houston, where the Paolis live with Alana, they sit quietly. Thoughts wander rampantly through their minds. What if she is a spoiled, ugly little child? What if she is big like Tom, her biological father, and awkward for a girl? She might even have Tom's big broad shoulders.

William can be silent no longer. "You know Kizzy named her Alana after her father, Alan. We only called him Al for short." Everyone hears him, but no one responds to his statement.

Evan is driving. Briefly, he looks down at the rag doll he purchased for a gift with its large, embroidered green eyes and red yarn hair sitting on the car seat. He had no idea what kind of gift to get for a little girl since he has no sisters or even female cousins. William had made the suggestion of the rag doll because Kizzy had one that she was crazy about as a child. Bettey had gone shopping with Evan. She remembered the physical and emotional description of Kizzy that Evan had given to her. She has chosen just the right one. The large green eyes seem to stare at Evan, stirring a mood of discomfort.. He turns the doll over, laying it face down on the seat. Evan feels insecure this day. What is he doing taking on the responsibility of a child to raise? He is a cop. Cops usually make lousy fathers, or so they say. What kind of life will this be for a kid? He was an only child and knows nothing about caring for a child! He takes notice of his hands on the steering wheel. They are shaking. His knuckles are clinching the steering wheel so tightly that they are colorless. He feels the blood pulsing through the arteries in his neck. At meeting this little girl, he is feeling more fear than he ever has while apprehending a suspect. The fear is hard to push away.

Jimmy shakes the box of hard candy mints he has in his hand, noisily. William gives him a look of annoyance. Jimmy looks down at his box, tapping his fingers nervously on the box. Evan looks over at Jimmy. Taking Evan's look as a hint that the sound irritates him, Jimmy stops the tapping. Jimmy had remembered that Kizzy loved these kind of mints. At several Hollywood fine restaurants, she and Jimmy used to steal the "after dinner mints" when the cashiers were not looking. Jimmy smiles at his remembrance. He loves his new job at Fun Coin, which is surely different from driving that cab. He has a fancy little office, and people even call him "sir." He swells with pride, feeling more important and happier than he has ever been. Dread suddenly fills his heart. What if this father shit messes that up? He does not know anything about being a father and surely never had one. Except for the way he used to knock him across the room, he had no memory of his biological dad. All his stepfathers hated him. They did everything they could to make him unhappy until he left home.

Jimmy's mind wanders back to the candy. He looks down at the box and runs his thumb across. What if this kid does not even like candy? Just because she is Kizzy's kid does not mean she loves the same kind of candy. Suddenly, Jimmy remembers something he has seen on television. Damn, candy rots your teeth. Why did he not think of that before he bought this damn candy? Now they will have to take her to the dentist. Jimmy pictures a little girl crying in pain with a toothache. What kind of stupid present is this for a little girl? What a wonderful kind of dad he is going to make! At their first meeting, he gives her candy to rot her teeth! He rattles the candy disgustingly in the box and looks over at the other men's gifts. The others bought gifts she could keep forever. After she eats the candy, the box will be thrown away. *Stupid Jimmy* buys teeth-rotting candy! All she will have to keep after his gift is a toothache!

William rubs the fur on the white teddy bear. William has shopped long and hard to find this bear. Just as Kizzy's, he wanted it to be just right. He remembers the night Kizzy came bouncing inside after going to the fair with Tom. Tom had won the white furry bear with the green ribbon around its neck for her. She prized that bear so much. Poor Tom could not be here. William thought this would be the perfect gift for Tom's daughter—a gift he would have given to her if he could have been here. Someday, William will tell her the story of her parents, their beautiful love and the white bear with the green ribbon. His legs are aching badly today. William wonders when this aching will stop! Gee, it must be arthritis. Old people get arthritis. He wonders what is going to break down on his elderly dilapidated body next. What is he doing taking on the care of a six-year-old girl? He remembers how much energy Kizzy had at six years old. William was younger then, and keeping up with her was laborious! At this time, he is an old man. He has just assumed the role of helping Jimmy with the operations of Fun Coin, a new career. Now he will be a father? He must be crazy! William rubs the bear and shakes his head, doubting the parent idea.

C.D. holds the little bouquet in his hand. Petunias are perfect for a little girl. Kizzy loved petunias. He will show Alana how to press them and keep them forever. Oh, me! C.D. realizes he knows so little about raising a little girl. This is a serious job he is assuming. He always counsels others about parenting. Now, his turn has come. What if he cannot fulfill this duty? He cannot let this poor child down. She is depending on them. C.D. glances at the others and concludes, at least we are in this together. We four men are all she has. At least we are better than strangers. He tries to resolve himself to this fact. While traveling, silently he prays. Everything will be fine.

2

The car arrives in front of the house, a pleasant home, but modest. C.D. rings the doorbell because he knows the Paolis. Mr. Paoli coldly answers the door and bids the men to enter. The men sit in the living room, waiting nervously. The house is neat and clean, but Kizzy is right. It lacks warmth and love. Mrs. Paoli enters the room, explains Alana is almost ready and will be in shortly. She explains that Alana does not know that Kizzy is dead. She thinks that going to live with these men is just something her mother wants her to do.

In a few moments, the child comes bouncing around the corner from the hall. Each man holds his gift tightly in his hand. Here they stand, four grown men, petrified with fear. Alana's hair is light brown, and it curls on the ends. She has beautiful, full pink lips, deep dimples and Kizzy's enchanting, emerald green eyes. Each man gasps as the resemblance to Kizzy is astonishing. Her words and voice are distinctive and familiar. "Hi, I'm Alana. No, don't tell me. Let me guess." She points to each man as she speaks in an enjoyable Texas drawl typical to the South, "You're Daddy Wills, you're Daddy Jimmy, you're Daddy Evan and you're Father C.D. I'm so good at games. Uh-oh, one's missing. Let's see, where's Daddy Tom?" Each man waits for the other to answer, searching their minds for the proper words. Before anyone can answer her question or acknowledge her accuracy at guessing their names, she starts again with her little arms waving in the air ecstatically. "Okay what did ya bring me?" Her eyes key on the bear William is holding. "Oh, a bear! I love it. It's really soft and cuddly." She snuggles the bear to her face, scrunching her nose just like Kizzy. She amazes William.

"What else did you bring? Spoil me, please! A rag doll! My mom used to have one. She told me all about it." Alana hugs the rag doll briefly, then gently places it beside her bear. Even the phrases she uses, such as "spoil me" rings familiarly through William's ears. Her words sound just as Kizzy's.

Alana smiles. Her dimples brighten her beautiful face. She is the exact image of her mother in every way. Just as exquisite as her mother, she holds out her arms to C.D. for his flowers. "Oh, beautiful flowers! My mom used to bring me this kind of flower when she came to visit. I even know their name. They're petunias." She gently runs her forefinger across the petal of the petunia. C.D. has seen Kizzy do this same thing many times in the church garden all those years ago. Alana gently places the small bouquet in the lap of her rag doll instructing the doll to hold them tightly.

Jimmy has put his gift of candy behind his back, feeling insecure and unsure that the candy is the proper gift. With her hands outstretched, Alana walks toward him with a big smile across her lips. "Okay you, give it up!" she giggles as she approaches Jimmy, peeking coyly around his back. The men stand with their mouths open in amazement. Her giggle is Kizzy's special giggle which dazes Jimmy stopping him paralyzed. Alana goes behind his back, taking the candy from Jimmy's hands. "Ya can't keep these from me, Daddy Jimmy! Ummmm, candy mints! My favorite!" She quickly opens the box, unwraps a mint and places it in her mouth. The depth of her dimples increases as she sucks on the mint.

She looks at each man as she speaks. Her green eyes are big, widened with excitement and her lips are pouting just as her mother's. "If you're all good daddies, I'll share a mint with ya!" Then, she giggles aloud.

When she heads for the front door, she has a mint in her mouth perched between her outer teeth and her jaw. With the candy box is in her little hand, she orders, looking over her shoulder fancifully, "Okay you

Dads, y'all please, grab a box or a toy. We've got to get home. I've got a lot to do. I have to fix up my new room and my new toys. Don't dawdle!" Again, she giggles as she heads out the front door to the car.

"Wow, she's not shy, is she?" Jimmy says, smiling as he retrieves one of the cardboard boxes with her belongings stacked inside. He also grabs a small suitcase in the other hand.

Evan says laughingly, "What do you expect? She's Kizzy's girl all right!"

Jimmy heads to the car, saying loudly with a big smile on his lips as he walks, "Don't dawdle, Dads. Alana is in a hurry!"

William and Evan follow suit, gathering toys, boxes, suitcases and heading out to the car. C.D. pauses for a short time. He notices Mrs. Paoli is looking down. C.D. senses the sadness she is feeling. "Mrs. Paoli, our address and phone number are on this piece of paper. Please, feel free to come and visit Alana. We want you to see her." He pats her hand as he passes the piece of paper to her. Mrs. Paoli thanks him with tears in her eyes. C.D. feels she loves the child in her own way. Maybe not enough for Alana's needs, but love nonetheless. If Alana is anything like Kizzy, and it looks as if she genuinely is, she will need an abundance of love and attention. Kizzy has been wrong. The Paolis are not loveless people.

The four men go to load the car. Alana loads herself in the back seat, sitting between William and C.D. They start to drive. Alana talks and talks and laughs. Her mind runs in fast motion. She surely has Kizzy's zest for life. Her hands fly with gestures as she speaks. She knows so much about each one of them, including their little habits. She speaks each word with enthusiasm and gusto as though she has always known them. Everything they pass along the roadside, she questions. She wants to know why birds like to sit on telephone wires. She wants to know why the wires do not shock the birds and animals as they sit or run along them. She wants to know if it is going to rain tomorrow. She wants to know which one of the men owns this car. Since it is fall, she wants to know when it will be turning cooler. She wants to know if she will be going to a brand-new school. When she asks this, the men look at each other with panic. They have forgotten all about school. They know school has already started. C.D. makes a note in his pocket notebook. As expected, the thought of a pleasing Catholic school enters his mind. William writes a reminder note in his new pocket diary, knowing just how a child can tax one's schedule. William deems a good private school might be in order. Jimmy's thoughts are the respectable public school located about two blocks from their new home.

He remembers the fun he had as a child at public school the short time he attended. Evan has no idea where to begin to enroll a child in school. She wants to know whether the men have bad dreams and awaken crying. She wants to know if they like to shop. Shopping for new school clothes for her would be delightful. Just in case any of them are interested, she wants a new pair of black shoes for church, and thinks a new church dress might be good also. She asks C.D. if she can go to his church. As he preaches the sermons, she thinks watching him will be fun. Seemingly, her mother has spoken to her about his sermons. She states she has never been to a church previously. Again, Father C.D. makes a note that she will need baptism. She wants to know if she can have a pet. She pleads that the Paolis never let her have a pet, and she genuinely wants a pet badly. She would like a kitten or puppy or fish or, maybe, all of them. She explains she heard on a television show that pets are good for children and old people. Before the men can answer her questions fully, she moves onto another. Then, she speaks lovingly of her mother, Kizzy.

William notices that Alana acts as though she knows what has happened to Kizzy. She speaks about her mother in the past tense. William has to know. He gathers enough nerve and quizzes her. “Alana, you don't act surprised about coming to live with us. Did you know we would be coming for you?”

Alana's attitude changes. At first, she clinches her top lip between her lower teeth. Her little face has lost its glow. Somberly, Alana looks down at her tiny hands. She rubs her left hand with her right forefinger slowly, pausing to explore the question in detail. She speaks, but the tone of her voice changes to a lower, serious pitch. The bright smile vacates her little face and a frown replaces it forcing her little eyebrows downward. While she speaks slowly, she continues to look down at her little hands. This slow, calculating speech reminds the men of her father, Tom. “Daddy Wills, I knew y'all were coming for me. My mom told me one day not long ago, that this day would come soon. That was the last day I saw my Mommy. Mommy cried when she told me this. I think Mommy must have been sick or somethin’, but she didn’t look sick. When I asked Mommy, she just gave me one of her great big hugs. Ya know I loved my mommy a whole, whole lots! Mommy told me she was gonna go live in a beautiful place called Heaven with my Grandpa Al, and Grandma Keziah. I'm not sure, but I think ya have to be dead to go to Heaven. Don't ya?” Before the men can answer her, she continues. “Mommy, who told me I would be fine with y’all, said y’all would give me a lot of love. Ya know little girls need a lot of love." She smiles coyly. "She also said she would be my guardian angel forever! Boy, I'm lucky, huh?"

Evan asks, "What do you mean?"

"I don't know anyone who has their own guardian angel and five dads!" Alana giggles. The men leave it at that. They know that later they will have to explain to Alana that she has two guardian angels in Heaven, Kizzy and Tom. Maybe they will even explain someday that Tom was her biological father, but not today. This little girl has enough change to cope with for one day. With all of them present, they will tell her and help her understand and cope with the news.

When William looks at her, he feels somehow that Kizzy is living over again. He notices the air conditioning blowing wisps of hair across her face. She wrinkles her nose and wipes it away, just as Kizzy did. He notices how the hairs from her bangs catch in her long eyelashes, just as Kizzy's did. This time they will not make the same mistakes. William has forgotten about his old age, emphysema and arthritis. The pain is gone. Alana's youthful energy overflows to the people around her. William feels younger, newer.

The doubts the men were feeling earlier, seem to be fading away between the laughter and joyous voices.

Jimmy, sitting in the front seat, turns on the radio to an "oldie station." They sing along with Alana's insistence and direction. Jimmy no longer feels insecure. Everything is easy with Alana. Just as Kizzy, Alana has a way of making Jimmy feel important. That feeling is just what he needs and what he has needed his entire life. At last, he has found it.

Evan is not afraid anymore. He knows to feel love and vulnerability is all right. Evan looks in the rearview mirror at Alana. Evan thinks that perhaps he will take her to the station to meet the officers. He will show her the handcuffs and let her sit at his desk in his big chair. Evan, overcome by the pride he feels for his new, exuberant daughter, finds her as intoxicating and magical as her mother. He thinks back, reminiscing the dream of Kizzy and Tom, knowing in his heart they are looking down right at this moment on this car. He knows they are happy that their little girl is with people who will love her with all their hearts. Evan surveys each man's face—Jimmy's beside him and C.D.'s and William's in the rearview mirror. Yes, smiles are all around! They love this little girl already.

C.D. feels only that she is his special gift from God. She *is* his child. He feels this in his heart and in his soul. She is the only child God will ever give him. With God's guidance, he will try his best to be the best parent he can. God has blessed him. The entire world feels so right. C.D. looks around at the other men. Much happiness and peace are present in this car. Each man has found a brand-new reason to live and to love. This luminous, rollicking, beautiful child is God's way of righting the hellish thing that has happened to Kizzy. Kizzy was right. Alana is her "most prized possession." Now, Alana is their most prized possession. Alana is the rainbow after the storm of Kizzy's tragic life. She is their second chance to get it right!

Each man deliberates privately, knowing of the laborious days ahead with so many different personalities, lifestyles and opinions. There will be laughter and tears. They will yell, fight, disagree, and do it all in the name of love. This wonderful, miraculous love they feel deep inside for this precious little girl cannot be equaled. This love will mend the rifts and carry them along the tide of life. They are a family. This is not the traditional family, but a family all the same. What makes a family? *Love* makes a family, and from the feeling floating amid the interior of this car, plenty of love will be present to go around for them all. Through Alana, this beautiful, special little child, Kizzy has joined them together forever. God has truly guided Kizzy. Truly, God has guided each of them to joining their lives with this beautiful little girl's life! They will watch her grow in wonder. She, alone, takes away the aches from the emptiness within their hearts. The laughter and smiles fill the car. Everything feels so very right. Love is here to stay! Forever . . .

Finally, the *END has come . . .*

. . . or just the *BEGINNING!*

SUDDENLY, a sudden flash of sunlight blinds Evan, while driving. The shiny, gold ink pen hanging from the rearview mirror is bouncing and spinning from the automobile motion, creating the reflecting flash of the sun. Abruptly, the pen stops moving. The mysterious initials *"T.U."* stare *STRIKINGLY INTO HIS EYES!* Evan stares across at Jimmy. The sight shocks Jimmy.

Each man wonders, *who put the gold pen here*?

~~~~~~~~~~~~~~~~~~~~~~~~~~~~~~~~~~~~~~

FINAL THOUGHT FROM THE AUTHOR

Life is a gift. The people and events that pass through our lives may seem at the time of occurrence to be disastrous. However, a rose must have a thorn. Each storm is followed by a rainbow. A crop must wither and die to fertilize the ground for new crops. Look deeply inside for the lesson and the good. Use each minute of your life. Life is only an adventure where we are given the chance to learn and grow and love!

~~~~~~~~~~~~~~~~~~~~~~~~~~~~~~~~~~~~~~

. . . Lord Jesus Christ, which is our hope;
1 Timothy 1:1

RESEARCH ACKNOWLEDGMENTS:

Although this book is a work of fiction, research was performed to establish the possibility of subject matter. For further information on subjects in this book, I suggest you read the following books or magazines.

Brantl, George. Catholicism. New York: George Braziller, Incorporated, 1962.

"The New Mafia Order." Mother Jones Bustin' Rush May/June 1995: 45

Stuber, Stanley I. Primer on Roman Catholicism for Protestants. New York: Association Press, 1965

The Holy Bible. King James Version. Thomas Nelson Publishers, 1990

Prologue of An Upcoming Book from Gale Laure:

PROLOGUE OF

Alana–Evolution of a Woman

This is the sequel to *Evolution of a Sad Woman, The Story of Kizzy*. We were left with Alana, the daughter of the deceased Kizzy and Tom, being raised by William, an attorney, Jimmy, a cab driver turned video company manager, Evan, a police detective, and Father C.D., a Catholic priest. The years have passed with the growth and maturing of their beautiful daughter, Alana. The murder of Kizzy was resolved according to William, Evan, C.D. and Jimmy. However, the mysterious gold pen with the initials "*T.U.*" broaches a new world of information and mystery. Do the ongoing serial murders in Houston have anything to do with Kizzy's murder?

Alana is fifteen years old. She is a young woman with millions of questions about the death of her mother and immeasurable persistence. Kizzy's death has been closed as an unsolved case. Alana, who has all of Kizzy's inquisitiveness and beauty, digs right in the middle of the case. Alana's boyfriend, Ty, is pulled into the mystery with her. Her stirrings threaten her life and the peaceful household of William, Evan, C.D. and Jimmy.

Will they definitely find the entire truth, or do they already know the truth unknowingly? Will they save their beautiful daughter, Alana, or lose her as they lost her beautiful mother, Kizzy? Will their lives be *rocked forever?*

ABOUT THE AUTHOR:

Gale Laure, a native Texan, enjoys her life as a writer. She loves input from her readers.

Laure, a full-time author, gains her experience for writing from her past careers. Laure has business experience as an owner of a business service, a consulting business owner, and travel agency business owner. Laure has employment experience in the medical field as an office manager, a short stint as a legal assistant and paralegal and administrative assistant in an insurance office and work in a CPA office. Laure, enjoys her life as a mystery-romance story writer.

Gale Laure finds inspiration from her readers, friends and family. She was born along the coast of Texas in the Golden Triangle. She spent her young adult years in Tyler, Mt. Enterprise and Houston, Texas. Laure has resided in a small suburb town in the Houston area for more than 20 years. She resides with her husband and near her immediate family.

As mysterious as her novel (Laure writes under a pseudonym), she is very adamant about maintaining her privacy and the privacy of her family. With an attitude that "you can do anything you set your mind to," Laure travels forward in life fulfilling all her dreams. Her hobbies include genealogical research, movies, creating stories for the children around her and attending her church and singing in the choir.

Inspiring a fan club from among readers, Ms. Laure is hard at work on the sequel, *Alana—Evolution of a Woman,* and her first historical, sci-fi novel, *The Bunkhouse.*

To find out more about her upcoming books visit www.a-bookstore.com and www.galelaure.com.

Gale Laure's books are available online and in bookstores everywhere. Visit her official website www.galelaure.com.

Soli Deo Gloria

ISBN 142512730-4
9 781425 127305